Her Deadly Mischief

Her Deadly Mischief

A Tito Amato Mystery

Beverle Graves Myers

Poisoned Pen Press

Copyright © 2009, 2010, 2012 by Beverle Graves Myers

Trade Paperback Editions 2010, 2012

10 9 8 7 6 5 4 3 2

Library of Congress Catalog Card Number: 2009924176

ISBN: 9781464200373   Trade Paperback

Poisoned Pen Press
6962 E. First Ave., Ste. 103
Scottsdale, AZ 85251
www.poisonedpenpress.com
info@poisonedpenpress.com

Printed in the United States of America

For my mother,
Beverly McDonald Graves

Earlier Events in the Life and Career of Tito Amato, virtuoso

1713   Tito born to Isidore Amato, organ master at the Ospedale dei Mendicanti, and his wife, Theresa.

1723   Undergoes surgery. Begins vocal studies at the Conservatorio San Remo in Naples.

1731   Tito returns to Venice to take up his public career. Operatic debut disrupted by murder of prima donna Adelina Belluna. Tito's sister Grisella disappears.

1732   Named primo uomo (first man) at the Teatro San Marco, Venice's state opera house.

1734   Tito solves the mystery of a scene painter's murder and meets Liya Del'Vecchio. Marriage of Tito's sister Annetta to Augustus Rumbolt.

1736   Tito spends a disastrous season in London.

1738   Tito's brother Alessandro takes up residence in Constantinople and marries Zuhal Muhammad.

1740   Tito travels to Rome and walks into a murder at the villa of prominent churchman, Cardinal Lorenzo Fabiani. Unauthorized marriage to Liya Del'Vecchio. Later in the year, Tito confronts a midnight killer while rehearsing a new opera on an isolated estate.

1741   Tito buys a new house on the Rio della Misericordia in Venice's Cannaregio district.

Chapter One

Did I lay eyes on the lovely Zulietta before she died? Try as I might, I'm unable to remember...

It was opening night at the Teatro San Marco, with all the attendant bustle and confusion on both sides of the crimson curtain. Though the performance had barely begun, I'd already torn the tunic of my soldier's costume on a nail protruding from a piece of scenery and had my toes mashed by a nervous white stallion awaiting his appearance near the end of Act One.

Several of my fellow singers were as jumpy as the horse, but they needn't have been. In all my years on the stage, I'd seldom performed such a jewel of an opera. In *Armida*, Maestro Torani had crafted a spectacle certain to make even the most jaded Venetian sit up and take notice. Besides its delightful score, *Armida* served up a fiery chariot belching white-hot sparks and an enchanted palace hung with rotating globes that mimicked an array of silver stars. Our wily maestro had even persuaded the Senate to cough up sufficient funds to uniform the orchestra in scarlet and gold to match the interior of the vast theater.

The singing wasn't half bad, either. Thanks to me and my talented colleagues.

I was playing Rinaldo, a knight of the Crusades and hero of the piece. My longtime rival, castrato Emilio Strada, was playing the Crusader captain and would sing an aria while mounted on the white stallion. Better him than me. The rest of the cast were also singers I had worked with before. All made pleasanter colleagues to sing alongside than the arrogant Emilio, who had recently seen fit to inflate his stage name to Emiliano.

While awaiting my entrance cue, I took stock of the house by means of a peephole concealed by a curtain flap. Every taper in the auditorium's massive ceiling chandelier was aflame, as well as those in the smaller chandelier above the stage apron. Surrounding the tiers of boxes, mirrors amplified the light from triple-sconces so that the auditorium was filled with thousands of bright pinpoints. I favored my throbbing foot as I squinted through the smoke-hazed light that fell on patrician and commoner alike.

On the other side of the orchestra, a noisy crowd had gathered on the floor of the auditorium—what we called the pit. Wooden benches sagged beneath high-spirited students who might well have sacrificed their dinner money to see the opera. They rubbed elbows and traded insults with clerks who had flung their arms around black-eyed women in tattered finery. Then there were the gondoliers, the music-loving boatmen who were already stamping their feet and hooting for their favorite singers.

I chuckled. Maestro Torani had arranged a surprise that would soon shut them up. I glanced up into the maze of catwalks and ropes and flying scenery above the stage. Any minute now. Yes!

A stagehand detonated a vivid green lightning flash, and through the clearing smoke a mechanical cloud shuddered down-ward. The machine bore our prima donna, Vittoria Busanti, costumed in a mantua gown of glittering gold with a matching petticoat. I applied an eye to the peephole and watched hundreds of jaws go slack with surprise and delight.

Vittoria was past her first youth, but she had kept her figure and was a fine little actress. Stopping mere inches from the foot-lights, she struck a dramatic pose before nodding her readiness to the conductor at the harpsichord. He replied with a stirring chord. As Vittoria launched into the sorceress Armida's menacing aria, her full breasts rose and fell and her panniered skirts swayed with the suggestion of generously rounded hips. My colleague was certainly on voice tonight. Trill followed trill, up and down the scales, sending her admirers into paroxysms of delight. In a perfect melding of song and motion, Vittoria's sultry femininity spilled over the rim of the stage like summer waves lapping at the sands of the Lido. Every man in the pit would have gladly dived in. Even those who couldn't swim.

Satisfied that the rabble was suitably impressed with our opera, I lifted my gaze to the boxes that curved around the auditorium. The first tier, elevated only a few feet off the floor, held courtesans and other persons of dubious repute. Pointedly ignoring Vittoria's performance, the brightly dressed ladies of pleasure were bantering with young bucks promenading the perimeter of the pit. The higher tiers were occupied by noble families and wealthy merchants who rented boxes by the season, year after year. They were passed down from father to son, these miniature drawing rooms that served as nightly rendezvous for much of the populace.

It was the third week of Carnevale, so masking was in order. Venice had acquired her unsavory reputation partially based on this extended opportunity for disguise, but most mask wearers were not fleeing creditors or hiding out from foreign authorities. They simply enjoyed the frivolity of going incognito. Women from lowest to highest station favored the *moretta*, an unadorned oval of black velvet that lent an air of mystery to their pale, painted faces and didn't compete with complicated hair arrangements.

The men's masks were more varied. I saw several naval officers sporting flat pig snouts; the pointed beak of the plague doctor and the chronically happy Arlecchino were also popular that season. For complete anonymity, many men settled on a traditional *bauta* that combined a white mask of leather or papier-mâché and veiled tricorne.

If I had observed the tragic Zulietta that night, she would have been sitting among the upper tiers, hobnobbing with the ladies and gentlemen dressed in silk and lace. But just then I took no note of anyone in particular. I was searching for my family's box.

It was mere curiosity. A failing of mine, I admit. My sister Annetta and her husband, Englishman Augustus Rumbolt, weren't in attendance. Gussie had turned in his key to the box office before leaving Venice last month. For any other opening, they would have been in their regular place, loyally cheering each one of my arias.

Gussie and I had been fast friends ever since he landed in Venice to sample life as an artist. I was pleased when a bequest from one of his doting aunts liberated him from the ancestral duties he found so onerous, and absolutely delighted when he and my sister announced their intent to wed. Now Gussie had taken Annetta and their three children to visit England for the first time since he had made our island his permanent home— *sheer rebellious folly* his mother had accused in one of her infrequent letters. I'd often wondered how they were all getting on. Did England seem like a foreign country to my brother-in-law who had become thoroughly steeped in Venetian ways? Was the frosty Lady Rumbolt welcoming Annetta or making her feel like an uncouth barbarian? And to assuage my curiosity, who was occupying their usual box on this special evening?

There, just as Vittoria hit her top note, I spotted Gussie's box to the right and one tier up from the Doge's more ornate accommodation. The figures framed by the looped-back curtains applauded furiously. They were strangers to me: two unmasked men in full, starch-white bob wigs flanking a masked woman. Colored jewels glittered on the woman's bosom and her fan fluttered in excitement. Behind the three at the railing, anonymous maskers occupied extra chairs brought in for the night. Impossible to say who they might be. The party could have been anything from an ambassador's retinue to young men on their Grand Tour sharing a courtesan for the night. They could even have been spies from a rival opera house.

I felt a presence at my shoulder an instant before a phlegmy voice whispered, "So far, so good. Don't you think?"

I turned to find Maestro Torani rubbing his hands with cautious delight. The old man was short and wiry, more stooped of late and no longer able to take his rightful place at the harpsichord because of the rheumatism that crabbed his fingers. In honor of *Armida*, he had donned a gold-embroidered jacket and purchased a perfumed peruke with three rows of tight curls. His fashionable new headgear was not on his balding head, however, but in his hand. Our maestro could never keep a wig on for more than ten minutes straight.

Torani and I had worked together for so long I could almost read his mind. He was relieved that Vittoria had climbed out of the cloud machine without tripping on her train as she had in dress rehearsal and delighted at the audience's response to her first aria. But he was still nervous. The natural state of a musical director on opening night, I supposed.

I encouraged him with an emphatic nod. "Everyone loves it. Tomorrow the *Gazzetta Veneta* will be singing our praises."

"They've sent a man?"

"I spotted him first thing."

"Where?" Torani pushed me aside to peer through the small square in the canvas.

"Second tier, center of the fifth box from the left."

"I see…but that man is masked. How can you know who he is?"

"I've noticed him before. His mask can't disguise the way he leans forward and cranes his neck like a stork. And take a look at his right hand. I'd wager he's the only member of the audience holding a quill."

The director drew breath with a hiss. "He's writing his piece even now?"

"Why not?" I shrugged. "If I had his job, I'd carry a small lap desk and get my work done on the go."

"Well, the size of the house should impress him, even if nothing else does. The box office just sent round a note. We're packed to the gills. Every free box has been let. Even the fifth tier."

I leaned over to take one last squint. Torani was correct. Tucked under the coved ceiling painted with cavorting cherubs, the fifth-tier pigeon lofts usually contained only a few middling tradesmen or other penny-pinchers. No one would pay top price for a view of the stage blocked by the massive chandelier. But tonight even this tier was fully occupied. Apparently, everyone in Venice who mattered was depending on *Armida* to make this an evening to talk about for some time to come.

I sighed, suddenly remembering that Liya, the person who mattered most to me, wasn't out there with the rest.

Torani was as sensitive to my moods as I was to his. He let the canvas flap drop over the peephole and turned to me with an inquisitive frown. "Not worrying over the little boy are you?"

I shook my head. He was speaking of Titolino, my adopted son. Over the past several days, the boy had developed a fever and a wheeze in his chest. "No, he seems to be on the mend, but Liya stayed behind. Just to be certain."

"Did you have the doctor in?"

"You know my wife," I replied with a smile. "She'd as soon call for a doctor as one of the quacks who hawk their foul elixirs on the Rialto. Liya's been bathing Titolino with cool cloths and coating his little ribs with a poultice of her own concoction."

"Clever with herbs, your Liya. I thought your inflamed tonsils might scuttle last spring's season, but she managed to cure them overnight."

"Indeed. She's quite adept." My bland tone covered several years' worth of scintillating memories. Liya's herbal skills covered much more territory than simple healing. Torani had no idea.

The director fell silent, his attention diverted by stagehands wheeling in an apparatus that would cause a fountain to spout water in the courtyard of the enchanted palace. "Look lively," he uttered before he dove back into the shadowy wings to see to some mechanical detail of pumps and tubing. "You're on next."

I made my way to a painted flat at deep stage right and readied myself for my entrance. Hidden by batten and canvas, I carefully directed my helmet plumes away from the lamps that ran up the inside lip of the flat. They say misfortune comes in threes. I'd already been stepped on by a horse and torn my costume; I didn't want my third mishap to be flaming headgear.

Almost time. Cheers and applause filled the theater as Vittoria finished her aria. She ended on a sustained high E that threw the audience into a frenzy. From my protected position, I watched as the soprano gathered bouquets tossed from the pit and the boxes that bordered the stage. She acknowledged the adulation with artfully blown kisses and low, sustained curtseys that puddled her shining skirts into pools of liquid gold.

I felt lightheaded, and as often happens before my first entrance, all my senses condensed into sharp focus. My nose was suddenly full of paint and dust and horse dung, undercut by the tangy smell of the rosin box used by the ballet girls. My ears picked up the rustle of Vittoria's skirts as she made her sweeping exit, then heard the whispered oath of her dresser as she pricked her finger in her haste to relieve her mistress of her roses. The brass fanfare from the orchestra sounded overwhelmingly sharp and shrill. My lips felt numb. My foot hurt. My heart hammered against my ribs. *Dio mio*, I was suffocating. How would I ever sing a note?

All was forgotten the moment I stepped onto the wide stage. As I paraded forward, more cheering and applause buoyed me with palpable force. I was no longer the castrato soprano Tito Amato, but Rinaldo the princely Crusader, scourge of the Saracen horde. My pasteboard sword had turned to steel, and the costumer's fabric armor would be capable of repelling the thrust of the sharpest lance.

Why had I doubted my voice for even a heartbeat? A crystal stream of melody poured from my lips, the notes swelling and diminishing with practiced ease. From a celebrated castrato, the audience expected vocal pyrotechnics.

I didn't disappoint.

Plumbing my capacious lungs, I treated the audience to a feast of sweet sound. So forceful was my delivery, so rapid my divisions, so smooth my glissandos, the orchestra was challenged to keep pace. What a noble hero, this Rinaldo. How spirited! How brave!

Even as I played my role to perfection, I studied this closer view of the house over the shimmering light from the footlamps.

The gondoliers were entranced. Excellent. The crucial opinion of these boatmen would pronounce *Armida* a success or failure. If they liked what they heard, they would be warbling the airs down the canals the next morning. By afternoon, the entertainers on the makeshift stages of the Piazza would take up the tunes, and within hours, all Venice would be whistling and humming the latest sensation.

The box holders were similarly agog. Everyone in the great scarlet and gold horseshoe had come to their feet. As I continued to sing, I saw men weeping and women swooning. Many were already tossing bouquets and folded slips of paper that contained impassioned sonnets. Here and there, a bold woman hung over the box rails waving her handkerchief, desperate to gain my notice and elicit some sign that I would welcome a dressing-room assignation.

I was in my element, doing what Fate had prepared me for. A man could hardly ask for better. Every eye and spyglass in the place was glued to my person, every ear attuned to my song.

Except…Could it be? One box had its scarlet curtains completely drawn.

There, in the fourth tier. As glaring as a missing tooth in a great lady's smile. Someone had shut me out. Someone was ignoring me.

Later, after *Armida* had played for several nights, I would expect some curtains to be at least partially drawn. With the arias already becoming familiar, the primped and pomaded nobility would train their opera glasses on each other, this social scrutiny being part and parcel of their nightly entertainment. They would flit from box to box to pay calls, play cards, or enjoy a warm supper wheeled from home by running footmen. And down in the pit, while we players poured out our vital force in song, the gondoliers would turn their backs to gaze on the antics of their betters.

But hold up—this was opening night. What could be so pressing that someone drew the curtains on a bravura aria by

Venice's reigning castrato? Unbridled lust? Intrigue fit to bring down the Republic?

Rubbish! Let love and politics take their course in their own good time. It was music that should reign over all tonight. My music.

I aimed my voice at the thin shaft of light that split the scarlet panels. Gilding the bones of Maestro Torani's lovely melody, I sailed up a flight of semitone octaves and held the last note with all the exquisite power and strength I possessed. That pure, crystal sound sailed aloft, straight as an arrow, driven by the sheer force of my will.

Ah, it was working. I'd gained their attention.

A woman's white arm parted the curtains; a sleeve of peacock blue ended in lace ruffles at her elbow. But something was wrong. The arm thrashed and flailed as if its owner were drowning, and once she had bunched the curtain fabric in her fist, she pulled so hard that the taffeta panel ripped from the rings that supported it.

To my horror, I realized the woman was struggling with a tall man in a full *bauta*. His hat brim shadowed the lower half of his face not covered by the mask, and a thick veil fell down his back, obscuring his wig and blending with his black cloak.

The woman tore at his mask, but the curtain panel that had wound itself around her arm hampered her reach. A froth of white petticoat popped into view. She was kicking, kneeing, aiming for her assailant's groin. But he didn't hesitate. Sweeping his cloak back like the flapping of a raven's wings, he thrust one arm forward to connect with her midsection.

Only years of disciplined training kept me singing until the end of the phrase. By then, the woman had collapsed over the railing and was tumbling head over heels in a whirl of brilliant blue skirts, ruffled petticoats, and scarlet curtain. She hit the floor of the pit with a sickening thud.

For a fraction of a second, the great theater was frozen in silence, then screams and shouts reverberated from the walls and ceiling, rattling the crystals hanging from the grand chandelier.

At the periphery of my vision, I saw orchestra musicians waving their instruments in perplexity, and in the pit, chaos, people running this way and that. Throughout all, my central focus remained locked on that fourth-tier box.

The tall man had taken several steps back. His cloaked silhouette made a dark pyramid against the scarlet wallcovering of the box. Near the top of the pyramid, his mask stood out as a chalk-white diamond.

The smoky light must have been playing tricks on my eyes, for the man's malevolent stare glittered as if we faced each other across a table instead of the breadth of the theater.

My face felt hot. His burning gaze was searing my cheeks! Then he lurched clumsily from sight, stumbling as if he had been hurt in the struggle.

Dimly I realized that the stage curtain was rolling down, separating our make-believe world from the shattering violence and tumult of the real one. I jumped back just in time to avoid being caught in its heavy folds.

Chapter Two

"Zulietta Giardino."

Messer Grande, as the chief of Venice's constabulary was titled, made this pronouncement over the woman's lifeless body, then lifted a corner of his mouth. Smile or smirk? I couldn't be sure, but I noticed that a regretful sigh followed.

"I don't place the name, Excellency," Torani remarked, "but she does look vaguely familiar." The maestro was twisting his new wig like a washerwoman wringing out a handful of rags. He'd been dealt a double blow: the cancellation of his triumphant opening night as it had barely begun and a grisly death that could well keep superstitious Venetians away from future performances.

"Not her real name, of course," said Messer Grande. "These courtesans always rechristen themselves. No pious Maria or Anna or Elisabetta for them. It might remind the men of their sisters back home."

"Ah, a courtesan. What was she doing on the fourth tier, I wonder." Torani cast a questioning scowl toward the box where Messer Grande's men were upending chairs and poking at walls and draperies.

"That is what I mean to find out," the chief constable replied smoothly. "Have you sent for the box office manager?"

Torani nodded glumly.

We made a solemn little group around the body which still lay where it had landed. Messer Grande had been watching the opera from a second-tier box. I'd noticed him particularly, because he'd been sitting alone with his curtains a quarter drawn, wrapped in his red *veste patrizia*, a voluminous robe that covered his dress suit and proclaimed his official status. He had taken charge immediately. First, he rushed to Doge Grimani's box and saw that our ruler and his party of Senators and advisors were escorted from the theater without incident. Only then did he gather his constables to clear curiosity seekers away from the body.

The musicians and singers had been quickly questioned and most sent home. As the Teatro San Marco's director, Torani naturally remained. I was detained because I had been gazing directly into the box at the relevant moment.

Once the audience realized the opera wasn't going to resume, the fashionable box holders trickled away to be borne to their next entertainment by a fleet of gondolas moored at the water landing. The ordinary folk who relied on shoe leather thronged through the entrance that led to the *campo*. Most probably believed the fall had been a tragic accident and nothing more, though anyone on the nearby benches would have seen the very clear and unmistakable evidence of murder.

A dagger's black hilt protruded from the exact center of the woman's peacock blue bodice; blood soaked the fabric in an uneven circle and reprised the scarlet of the taffeta panel still clutched in one hand.

As Messer Grande slowly circled the scene, his pace measured and hands clasped behind his back, I steeled myself to take a closer look. The woman lay on her back with arms outflung and thick, darkly waving hair running riot over the filthy floor. In the latest fashion, only a few front curls had been powdered. At least someone had closed her eyes. Like Torani, I also thought she looked familiar, as if we had passed at many a banquet, ball, and pageant, but had never really spoken. She was a dark sylph: no more than twenty-five, slender, with the dusky complexion of the south, or perhaps more foreign parts, and hair the color of ripe olives. A black moleskin patch had been applied near the corner of one eye, and a simple blue ribbon edged in point lace adorned her throat.

Even in death, this Zulietta Giardino possessed enough glamour to be included in the category of women who could pick and choose their protectors, far above the less-favored women of the town who made themselves available to any man who would meet their price. Somehow I knew that when she moved, she prowled like a cat, supple muscles under taut skin, always on balance, never a hint of uncertainty or awkwardness. But Zulietta wouldn't be prowling anymore. She was a broken thing now.

Messer Grande halted and grunted an order to a hovering constable. His man bent to tug the dagger from its gruesome sheath. I swallowed bile as steel grated on bone and the constable retrieved a blade coated with dark blood. Maestro Torani clapped his wig on his head and squeezed his eyes shut.

After rummaging under his red robe of office, the chief constable drew forth a generously sized handkerchief and took the weapon. Another minion quickly fetched a three-armed candlestick and let its rays fall on the dagger that befouled the white linen like an odious cross.

"This doesn't have much to tell," Messer Grande said after a moment. "Steel blade, hardwood handle, bronze quillions. No identifying marks. Hundreds of men in Venice must own one similar."

He raised his gaze and looked me squarely in the eye. "That makes what you saw even more important, Signor Amato. Let's hear your story again, and this time, don't leave out even the smallest detail."

I shuffled my feet uneasily. I wanted to help; I truly did. But I couldn't provide nearly as much information as Messer Grande seemed to think I possessed. I did catch a glimpse of Zulietta Giardino's attacker, but for God's sake, the upper part of his face had been masked. How much help could a description of his chin be?

"You were the only soul in this theater who had that all-important glimpse," Messer Grande reminded me after I'd said my piece once again. "All the other performers had left the stage for your solo, and like the rest of the onlookers, I was totally caught up in it. I don't know when I've heard better singing."

"You're too kind." I inclined my head, foolishly pleased. How pathetically insecure we performers are. I should have been ashamed, seeking praise for a song when a fellow human's ultimate mortality lay at my feet.

"No, no. I assure you I was enjoying myself immensely." Messer Grande lifted the corner of his mouth again. Definitely a smile this time.

He continued, "But tell me this. Could the man have been drunk? You said he seemed unsteady."

"He staggered only after the woman...Zulietta...had gone over the railing. Before that he seemed totally in charge of his faculties."

"Strong? Vigorous?"

"Yes, Excellency."

"A young man, then."

"Certainly not teetering on the edge of senility."

"Could she have managed to wound him?"

I shrugged. "Perhaps with a well-placed knee. Or her fingernails. I saw her grabbing at his mask."

Messer Grande knelt by the body. His wide sleeves swept the floor as he gave Zulietta's fingernails a quick inspection. "She didn't draw blood." He rose, shaking his head. "Her attacker's *bauta*, was there anything distinctive about it?"

I thought for a moment. "No. The mask was perfectly ordinary—unadorned white with a molded nose and holes for the eyes." I shuddered a bit, recalling the killer's malevolent gaze.

"His hat? Perhaps it was decorated with a feather or an edging of lace."

"I didn't see any."

Messer Grande rubbed his brow with thumb and forefinger. Below his hand, his jaw muscles bulged. When he dropped his hand, his expression was grim but composed. "Think, man. A murderer is running loose in the city. Can you come up with nothing that would help us identify him?"

"Like his dagger, everything else about him could apply to a hundred others."

Only the arrival of the box office manager kept Messer Grande from pressing me further.

Angelo Corsi would have quite obviously preferred to have gone home with everyone else. As he wended his way through the auditorium, stepping around benches that had been scattered or overturned in the melee, he pulled nervously at the cuffs of his cheap broadcloth coat and darted longing glances toward the exits.

To my surprise, Messer Grande attempted to put him at his ease. "Ah, here's a good fellow," he said as he clapped him familiarly on the back. "I'm certain you'll be able to shed some light."

Corsi gulped, caught at the start of a formal bow. Settling for a bob of his head, he said, "I will strive to be of service, Excellency."

"Good man, good man. My first question is simplicity itself. Who rents the box this poor woman fell from?"

"Signor Cesare Pino, Excellency."

"Pino? From the glassworks on Murano?"

"*Sì*, that's the one."

"Have you seen Signor Pino tonight?"

Corsi bit his protruding lower lip. "I didn't notice. We were run off our feet. With the opening, so many were buying tickets for the night…"

Messer Grande nodded sympathetically. Torani heaved a sigh, no doubt contemplating how many of those buyers would be clamoring for a refund.

"But…" Corsi continued slowly, "Signor Cesare Pino is rarely in attendance. I can't recall seeing him for a year or more. It is his son, Signor Alessio, who usually occupies the box."

"With other family members?"

"Not so much. Signor Alessio seems to have many friends."

Messer Grande nodded, fingering his chin and staring into the middle distance. I had the impression of a mind arranged in neatly docketed cabinets that contained details on all of Venice's leading citizens. At last he spoke, more to himself than to any of us: "Alessio Pino, the young Glass Prince. Yes, Cesare's son has attracted quite a retinue of bright young sparks."

I had heard of Alessio Pino. Most Venetians had. The young man came from a family of glass masters, a profession held in the highest esteem. Almost from the time my city had sprung to life on the lagoon salt marshes, Venice was known for the delicate miracles that flowed from the glassblower's pipe. As the guardians of that profession's ancient secrets, glass masters were as close to royalty as any artisan could ever be. They were one of the few groups allowed to marry into the nobility of the Golden Book. And according to gossip, there were two other qualities that led Messer Grande to describe Alessio as a prince: his striking good looks and his lofty character.

"Signor Amato?" Messer Grande gripped my shoulder with a vise-like hand. "Are you absolutely sure there was no one besides Zulietta and her killer in the box?"

I closed my eyes and pictured the scene. The wall lamps had been lit, lending a soft glow to the box's interior. Another seated or standing figure would have been immediately obvious. My eyelids lifted, and I regarded Messer Grande steadily. "Not unless someone was crawling around on the floor."

Messer Grande harrumphed and turned his attention back to Angelo Corsi. "Am I right in assuming the key to the box had been let out to Cesare Pino?"

Corsi nodded. "For the first time that I remember, I didn't have one key on the board in the office. Every box was engaged, either for the season or the night."

"You keep no duplicate keys?" Messer Grande slanted a critical eyebrow.

Corsi began to look as nervous as he had at the outset of Messer Grande's questions. Torani spared him further explanation. "It's standard practice in all the theaters," the maestro told the chief constable. "You rent a box, so you must know how it works. The box holder receives the key when he pays. For the duration of his lease, whether it comprises a week or a year, the upkeep of the box is now his responsibility. His servants clean and appoint it as their master sees fit."

Messer Grande nodded. "The opera box becomes a home away from home."

"Precisely," Torani replied.

"So, since my men had to kick the corridor door off its hinges to search the box, it seems likely that a member of the Pino family opened the door to admit Zulietta Giardino and then relocked it on his way out."

"Alessio might have given the key to Zulietta," I quickly put in.

With a wink, Messer Grande again knelt. As casually as if he were rummaging through a knapsack, he slid his hand through a slit in her panniered skirt and probed the right-hand member of the pair of capacious pockets that hung from every woman's waistband. He withdrew the pocket's scant contents and subjected each item to brief scrutiny before laying it on the floor: a tortoise-shell comb, a few coins, a small bottle of scent, and a square of embroidered cambric. The left pocket produced a folded fan and a small key. Still kneeling, Messer Grande surveyed this miscellany for a long moment; then he swept up the handkerchief, fan, and key as if he were palming the winnings from a game of dice.

"Is this the box key?" He tossed the bit of metal to Corsi.

The box office manager grabbed the key out of the air and turned it this way and that, only a few inches from his eyes. "Yes. This is a Teatro San Marco key. The Lion of Venice is impressed on the shaft. And D-17. That's the number of the Pino box."

"So…this was not the key that locked the door," Messer Grande replied thoughtfully. "The killer must have possessed another to lock the door as he exited."

The chief constable regained the key and slipped it in his waistcoat pocket. Then he unfurled the handkerchief. With a well-manicured fingertip, he traced the letter stitched into one corner. We could all see the dark, curlicued "A" that stood out plainly against the white cambric. There was no need for comment. "A" for Alessio; what could be more obvious? The cloth followed the key into the depths of his robe.

Then Messer Grande unfolded the fan, snapping it open as an angry woman might. He studied the painted scene for a long moment, then chuckled and handed the delicate item to Maestro Torani, saying, "Exactly what you might expect a whore to carry."

The director appraised the fan, raised his eyebrows, but didn't speak. As he passed it to me, I saw that the vellum was painted with a harem scene depicting generously proportioned odalisques disrobing themselves for a swim in a pool. I closed the fan and handed it back to the chief constable.

Messer Grande must have accomplished all the investigating he wished for the moment. After dispatching one of his men to fetch the charnel-house wagon, he gave Torani leave to have the grand chandelier lowered and the candles extinguished. When that operation was well under way, he dismissed the remaining theater staff with the caution that we might still be needed on the morrow.

Corsi bolted from the auditorium like a rabbit pursued by hounds. Torani tarried to discuss when performances might be allowed to resume.

I was delighted to see my manservant, Benito, materialize out of the darkening shadows with my cloak and other outdoor attire. It had been a harrowing evening, and I was more than ready to set off for home. I hoped that Titolino's cough had abated and Liya was snuggled in our warm bed where I would soon join her.

As I readied myself for the chilly autumn night, I couldn't resist dallying a bit to give Messer Grande a stealthy inspection. The current chief constable had been appointed last spring. Unlike his weasel of a predecessor with whom I had sparred on several occasions, this Messer Grande seemed positively benign.

I put his age at five-and-forty: his gray hair dressed in tight waves swept back from a lengthening forehead, and a spider's web of wrinkles surrounded his eyes. He'd once been a handsome man, spare and tallish, and was impressive still. I'd noted that this man who carried the august title of Messer Grande smiled a great deal more than either clerks or government officials were wont to do. In fact, it was his disposition that warmed me to him. So far, he had addressed everyone in a completely natural manner far removed from the studied arrogance of his predecessor.

Settling my hands in my muff of soft miniver, I idly wondered if he practiced Freemasonry. Among their oath-bound secrets of Hiram and Boaz, the brethren were said to preach the equality of men and other revolutionary principles.

Benito and I had passed through the swinging doors to the foyer when a burst of noise echoed off the pink marble walls and columns. Gasps, exclamations, and shrieks emanated from a stairway that led to the upper levels. Messer Grande and Maestro Torani came running, followed by several constables. Another pair of their fellow officers stumbled down the stairs into the foyer. One carried a struggling child slung over his shoulder like a sack of rice; the boy's feet in tiny buckled shoes pummeled his chest. His captor had to fight to retain his grasp. The other constable sprinted toward us and came to rest before his chief.

"Excellency," he said between panting breaths. "We found this…this person shut up in a cloakroom in the fourth-tier corridor."

"Ow!" His partner stopped short and clapped one wrist to his mouth. "I'll be damned," came his muffled cry, "the little monster's drawn blood."

A gruff voice answered in a shout, "Put me down, I say. Unhand me this minute or I'll take an even bigger chunk out of you. I'm quite capable of walking on my own."

The constable roughly lowered his burden to the terrazzo floor.

Benito clucked his tongue disapprovingly, thinking the officer had manhandled a boy barely out of the nursery. My hearing and vision were sharper.

This was not a child, but a small misshapen man who looked every bit as disgusted as he sounded. As he gazed up at his captor with hands on hips, the biggest thing about him seemed to be his head. Beneath his tangled bagwig, his forehead bulged like the egg of some giant bird, and his lantern jaw held a set of teeth that looked like he could eat nails for breakfast. With short arms and legs that joined his torso at an odd angle, he could have been a troll straight out of the stories my childhood nurse used to frighten me with.

"Shut up in a cloakroom, you say?" Messer Grande's eyes glittered with intense interest.

"Hung from a peg and bellowing like a bull calf. Still, we almost didn't hear him because the door was shut and somebody had thrown a thick cloak over him."

Behind his hand, Messer Grande issued a series of terse instructions. His man removed his uniform jacket and went back into the auditorium. Through the glass oval of the door, I saw him move through the dimness to cover Zulietta's corpse with his jacket.

Messer Grande approached the constable who was wrapping a cloth around his bleeding wrist and the dwarf who was still remonstrating with him.

"Something's happened here and I must find my mistress. She'll be worried sick wondering what's become of me." The little man whirled as he sensed Messer Grande loom up behind him. Completely undaunted by the chief's official robes, he asked, "Is this big oaf yours? Because if he is, I want to lodge a complaint."

Messer Grande was unruffled; I thought I even glimpsed a fleeting grin stretching his lips. Looking the little man up and down, he asked, "Your name, Signore?"

Before he answered, the angry newcomer straightened his blue waistcoat and jacket, smoothed his pleated neckcloth, and proudly stretched to his full, but minuscule, height. Fascinated, I couldn't resist drawing near the curious scene. Neither could Maestro Torani. Benito hung back, curling his middle fingers into his palm and aiming the others in an age-old gesture meant to ward off the evil eye.

"My name is Giacomo Michele Gaetano Brosco," the dwarf said brusquely. "But if you are asking what I am called, it is Pamarino."

"Who is this mistress you speak of?"

"Zulietta Giardino."

"I see." Messer Grande cocked his head thoughtfully. "And how do you serve Signorina Giardino?"

"I have the honor of arranging any service she requires. I am her constant companion."

"You supervise her household?"

"To be sure." Pamarino inclined his head regally.

"Escort her through the city?"

"Wherever she goes, I am at her side. My lady has so many admirers I am often called upon to fend off annoyance."

"Are you now?" Messer Grande narrowed his eyes skeptically.

"I carry an iron-knobbed walking stick for the purpose," Pamarino continued in a dry tone.

"I see. You're quite the *cavaliere servente*, then. I suppose you call her gondola when required?"

"Of course."

"And carry her calling cards?"

"Yes."

"And extra handkerchiefs?"

"One must be prepared."

"And pimp for her?"

The dwarf drew his chin back and his hands balled into fists. If he'd been conversing with any other man, I wouldn't have been surprised to see him erupt into a rage of flying feet and fists. Instead, he merely replied icily, "You are misinformed, Excellency. My mistress is no pavement tart. Since half of Venice is madly in love with her, I must constantly chase callers from the door. The messages I refuse in just one week could paper the walls of this theater."

Messer Grande nodded, sighed, then said in a more kindly tone, "I'm afraid I have bad news for you."

"What?" Pamarino's eyes, small and the ochre color of mud, popped wide open. "Has something happened to my mistress?"

"This way, if you please." Flanked by constables lighting the way, Messer Grande conducted Pamarino through the dark auditorium. As soon as the dwarf caught sight of the body beneath the brass-buttoned jacket, he vaulted an overturned bench to reach it.

He must have recognized the vivid blue of her skirts for he uttered a guttural cry as he dropped to the floor on hands and knees. In the twinkling of an eye, he had pulled the covering from Zulietta's still form.

Even knowing exactly what lay beneath the jacket, I still felt a jolt when I again saw the beautiful death-struck face, the pallid whiteness of neck and shoulders. How much more shocked her faithful servant must have been. Pamarino rocked on his knees, cried hot tears. He shook and slavered.

Above him, Messer Grande explained that Zulietta had been stabbed, then fallen or been pushed over the box railing. I wasn't certain the little man heard until Messer Grande himself guided the dwarf away. Drooping forward over a bench with his face pressed into a bent arm, Pamarino continued to sob as the chief constable repeated his tale.

Torani, Benito, and I traded uncomfortable looks as the dwarf gradually collected himself.

When Pamarino came to his feet, he had just one thing to say. "Pino. Alessio Pino. He did this. He killed her."

"Were you in the box?" Messer Grande asked quickly. "Was Alessio Pino there?"

"My mistress was supposed to meet Alessio in his box half an hour before curtain time, but we were late. Since this was an important night, she had dressed with great care and changed her mind about her gown several times. All the way to the theater, she'd muttered and grumbled, fearing that Alessio would be angry. But when we arrived, we found the box locked and empty. Alessio was late, too."

Messer Grande narrowed his eyes. "How did you get in?"

"Alessio had given my mistress his key. Apparently, he had an errand to perform before the opera began and suspected he might be delayed."

Ah, I thought, that accounted for the key in Zulietta's pocket.

"What was this errand?" Messer Grande asked.

Pamarino shook his head. "My mistress seemed to know, but the details weren't explained to me. In all her fretting, she mentioned a tavern. Something to do with the sea—I can't recall the exact name."

Torani and I were standing shoulder to shoulder. I cupped my hand and whispered, "Do you think he means the Pearl of the Waves, just across the square?"

"He must," my old maestro replied. "There's no other tavern nearby with a name that would fit."

"What happened then?" asked Messer Grande.

"We waited. My mistress ordered that the curtains remain closed, and we sat in silence while the orchestra played the overture. I was getting bored, so I put my eye to the slit and watched the woman in the golden gown. As she droned on and on, my mistress became more upset. She paced the box, talking to herself. 'What is keeping him,' she kept saying, 'Alessio will ruin everything.' Next came a flourish of trumpets and the castrato— that one there—paraded out like he owned the stage."

The little man drew breath as if to shout, but only a moan escaped his lips. "My mistress could stand no more. 'Pamarino,' she said, 'Alessio must have concluded his meeting and returned to the theater by now. Someone has detained him. One of his friends is bending his ear over some nonsense. Search the lobby and the corridors and fetch him to me at once.'"

"You left the box?" Messer Grande prompted.

Pamarino twisted his thick neck like a man in physical pain. "If only I had stayed put…if only I had disobeyed her command just that once. But I didn't. I opened the door and started toward the stairs. I made it only as far as the public cloakroom."

"What happened?"

Pamarino stared at Messer Grande. Everyone else stared at the dwarf. The constables' few candles cast long wavering shadows that stretched behind Pamarino toward the darkened stage. The grief he wore like a suit of armor, his form so outlandish—both made the dwarf seem very alone though almost a dozen men surrounded him.

"I was grabbed from behind. Someone wrestled me into the cloakroom and knocked me out with a sharp blow." Pamarino patted the brown wig covering his crown. "When I came to myself, I was dangling in the dark, barely able to breathe." With a lurch, he hopped off the bench and squinted toward the fourth tier.

"It must have been Alessio," he continued in a savage whisper.

"Did you recognize him?"

"How could I? He came at me from behind."

"Was there anyone else in the corridor?"

"With him singing?" Pamarino jabbed a finger toward me. "Of course not. They were all drooling over the box railings. But you must believe me…" Desperation was evident in the little man's tone. "It had to be Alessio Pino. He got me out of the way so there would be no one to protect my mistress. Then he returned to the box and set on her with a vengeance."

Messer Grande spread his hands. "But why? Why would a young man of Alessio Pino's standing brawl with his mistress like the lowest pimp and his tattery whore? At the opera, for God's sake! And ending in murder!"

Pamarino's gaze never wavered. He kept his eyes trained on the gaping maw of the dark box. "It was that damned wager," he said. "I knew it would lead to nothing but misery."

Chapter Three

"It was to be my mistress' greatest triumph," Pamarino said, staring moodily into the glass of brandy Torani had fetched from his personal stock in his office.

The wagon from the charnel house had come and gone. The dwarf and Messer Grande sat on benches facing each other. The rest of us stood, clustered within the ring of yellow candlelight that created a glowing cave within the vast, black, now chilly theater. From the shadows came the rustlings of rats.

"She made the wager with one of her rivals," the dwarf continued. "Perhaps you've heard of La Samsona, the painted giantess."

We all nodded. La Samsona had taken an unconventional route to her present career. She had once been famous as a festival strongwoman. This seasoned courtesan stood a head taller than most men and possessed a statuesque form that she clothed in the latest French fashion and further gilded with a fortune in pearls and diamonds. It was a son of a former Doge who had furnished her ticket off the carnival platform. When he was done with her, she'd proved that the power of her wits matched the strength of her muscles. With great animation and gaiety, she embarked on a series of advantageous liaisons that made her one of the most talked about women in Venice.

"La Samsona pretended to be my mistress' bosom friend," said Pamarino, "but she didn't fool me. I could see through her charming smiles, straight into her canker of a heart. She was jealous of my mistress and coveted any man who courted her favor. Not too long ago, La Samsona accompanied us on a stroll in the Erberia when His Excellency, Signor—"

A cunning look glinted in the dwarf's eyes. "The name itself is of no importance. Let me tell it this way—my mistress was admiring a pineapple, wondering if such an exotic delicacy could possibly be worth the price, when a gentleman gallantly purchased it and had his footman carry it to our lodgings on a silk pillow. Later, my mistress sent me around with a very pretty note of thanks even as she instructed me to refuse any requests the gentleman might feel a fruit from a tropical isle might entitle him to. To make a long story short, he did as he was wont, I did as I'd been ordered, and who do you suppose squired La Samsona to the next masquerade ball?"

Pamarino rocked slightly forward and back as he answered his own question. "The gentleman of the pineapple, of course, though La Samsona had shown no partiality toward him before. When she saw he fancied my mistress, she set out to captivate him. She succeeded for a few short weeks, but his ardor cooled rather quickly. I understand she at least managed to induce him to settle her milliner's bill. It must have run a hundred—"

Messer Grande cut him off with an impatient gesture. "Enough of pineapples and the price of hats. Get to the nature of this wager between Zulietta and La Samsona."

"Begging your pardon, Excellency, I'll go straight to the point. The wager was based on this simple happenstance—both ladies had set their sights firmly on Alessio Pino." Pamarino turned his head and spat, then rubbed a stubby hand across his mouth as if he could wipe the hated name from his lips. "Why don't women see that only treachery can lay behind an exterior as handsome as his?"

Beside me, Maestro Torani shook his head. "They see but cannot help themselves," he whispered. "Poor creatures—the stories I could tell."

I made a mental note to worm some of these stories out of Torani as Pamarino went on.

"My mistress and La Samsona constantly sang Alessio's praises—a profile like Adonis, the grace of a dancing master, the shoulders of a galley slave. It was enough to make you heave up your dinner. Many mornings they met for breakfast, and over their coffee and buttered toasts, they would argue about which of them might capture his heart. La Samsona was convinced her outsized beauty would carry the day, but my mistress believed that Alessio appreciated finer things and would find La Samsona raucous and vulgar."

Messer Grande leaned forward on his bench. "Zulietta and La Samsona set themselves quite a challenge. I know Alessio Pino's reputation. He's famous for his austere principles, his moral rectitude. He puts in long hours at the family glassworks, rarely gambles, and though a string of women pant at his heels, he has always steered clear of romantic entanglements and kept his name as pure as new-fallen snow."

"Perhaps that is part of his allure," Torani observed. "The more inaccessible the fruit, the sweeter its nectar."

Messer Grande shook his head like a dog emerging from a stream. "Please, we're not going to discuss pineapples again, are we?" His gaze focused on the grieving dwarf. "Was that the premise of the wager, which woman would be the first to capture Alessio's affection?"

"As far as it went," Pamarino replied after another swallow of brandy, "but they agreed that there must be some proof. After all, who can say what really happens behind closed doors? It was decided that only a public display of his patronage would do. I thought it was all nonsense, but I grew so tired of hearing them propose one intrigue after another—"

The dwarf's words seemed to catch in his throat, and his face contorted in a grimace of misery that made him look more like a gnome than ever.

"God help me," he cried in a gravelly voice. "I was the one who suggested the opera box. My tongue had barely given voice to the thought when they both hailed it as genius. After arguing over a flurry of details, my mistress and La Samsona settled on a firm agreement. They even called a notary to set it down in writing. The first to join Alessio at the rail of his box at the Teatro San Marco—not merely set foot in the box or join his party for an aria or two, mind you—but the first to sit beside him in a clear demonstration that he was enjoying her favors would win the wager."

"When did the women strike this bargain?"

He thought a moment. "Just when the wealthy folk were returning from their summer estates. Late August or early September, I suppose."

"Roughly two months then."

The dwarf nodded.

After a pensive silence on all sides, Messer Grande observed, "A wager involves a stake. What was the loser to forfeit?"

"Diamonds," Pamarino replied solemnly. "The winner would lay claim to anything and everything she fancied from the other's jewel box."

Torani spoke up again: "Surely the lucky woman would also be acknowledged as the reigning queen of all the courtesans in Venice."

The dwarf shrugged. "Glory is all very well, but it can't be sold to put meat on the table. It was diamonds that drove this wager."

"If I might be excused for interrupting…" I was surprised to hear Benito's wavering treble speak up. My manservant took a step forward, cocked his head like a puzzled canary, and didn't continue until Messer Grande nodded his permission.

"Hasn't Alessio Pino made an open virtue of restraint because of his lengthy betrothal to Maria Albergati?" Benito asked. "They say that Cesare Pino and Signor Albergati wrangled over the match for months. Everyone is speculating why Signor Albergati finally agreed for his noble line to be mixed with that of a common glassmaker. Now that young Maria has come out of the convent and a wedding date is set, her father visibly writhes at the mere mention of the engagement. It is to gain some measure of his respect that Alessio Pino behaves as a model of decorum in all his dealings and appearances in society."

Benito's lengthy comment drew a grinning nod from Messer Grande, a hollow laugh from Pamarino, and a questioning look from me.

Ignoring the others, Benito sent me a knowing smile.

In truth, I would never disparage his grasp of the facts: my manservant must be the deepest well of gossip in Venice. I was merely astonished that he bothered to beg leave before he spoke.

People often ask why I tolerate Benito. For one thing, he is a castrato like myself, trained in a Naples conservatory just as I was. Though the stage didn't suit him, he understands me and the needs of my voice in a way that whole men cannot. And then, I must admit that his irreverence often pleases me. Where good manners and fear of giving offense often render me mute, Benito plunges ahead. Besides, no one, not even Liya, prepares my morning chocolate or calms my stage jitters quite like Benito.

Messer Grande turned to Maestro Torani. "Signor Albergati keeps a box at this theater, does he not?"

"Yes. His grandfather was one of the original subscribers."

"I didn't see him here tonight as I looked around the auditorium."

"You wouldn't have, Excellency, his box is directly above yours. I recall that it was full, like most of the others. Family, I suppose. I noticed several young people, including one awkward young miss that could be Maria."

Messer Grande rubbed his chin. "I wonder if Zulietta realized that Alessio's intended bride might well be watching the culmination of her mischievous wager."

Pamarino set his glass down so hard I feared the stem would break. With a wiggle of his legs, which didn't quite reach the floor, he jumped to his feet and planted himself in front of Messer Grande. Since the chief constable was still seated, the dwarf addressed him face-to-face. "My mistress was well aware of the situation. It made her victory all the sweeter. Not only had she beaten La Samsona, but also Alessio's high and mighty ideals. It took her several months, but little by little she broke him down. She made him burn with passion for her and only her. He forgot the promises to his father, the melding of the two families. How completely that panting dolt threw his reputation aside and became her slave."

"And once Zulietta had collected her victory spoils, what then?" Messer Grande asked with cool composure. "How did she expect her lover to react when he learned he'd been the butt of a wager?"

The dwarf's proud smile fell flat. "That's it, don't you see. Someone must have told him about the wager—perhaps that accounts for his secret meeting. Alessio would have been enraged to learn the truth. I can see him now, returning to the theater, furious, determined on revenge. When he saw me leave the box, he got me out of the way and went back to kill my mistress."

Messer Grande nodded slowly. He rose, snapped his fingers, and whispered a string of orders to a waiting constable. To us he announced in the tones of a Great Council orator, "Everything you heard here is to be kept quiet until I have a man in custody. Understood?"

Solemn nods made the rounds. Unless Alessio Pino had boarded a boat for the mainland, the young glass prince would be in custody by tomorrow morning.

Benito and I followed Torani from the theater at a little after two. The maestro's usual gondolier was waiting on the steps at the water gate, shoulders wrapped in a blanket and tricorne tipped over his face. My boatman had not been so loyal. Though Benito swore he had told Luigi I would soon be coming, my man and his gondola had departed in search of a wench or a warm bed, or both. I would deal with him later.

"You two come with me," Torani offered. "I'll see you home."

I shook my head. The old man was leaning on his stick and his bald head bobbed over the collars of his greatcoat like a cork floating on gentle waves. He looked so tired, a puff of wind could topple him into the canal. "Thank you, Maestro, but you live the opposite way. The night is cool, but fine. We don't mind walking."

"Goodnight, then."

After watching Torani's gondola slide down the misty canal, Benito and I turned in the direction of the Cannaregio. While a boat could take you anywhere in Venice, so could a maze of *calli* and bridges. We proceeded single file through one of the narrow passages that radiated from the theater. With my foot hobbling me but little, we navigated crooked alleys that almost seemed to double back on themselves and dipped through covered *sortoportegi* where velvety darkness was broken only by vigil candles twinkling in wall shrines. I hoped we might meet a Friulian with a lantern who could light us on our way, but all the lamp carriers for hire were doubtless waiting under the arcades of the Piazza where they could have their pick of patrons.

Benito and I had one bad moment when we topped the peak of a narrow bridge to meet a pair of drunken sailors, Greek by the sound of their accents. As we turned sideways to squeeze past, I smelled tobacco, old sweat, and unnamable spices clinging to their heavy jackets and ragged beards. One was tall with a collection of gold rings pulling his earlobes low; the other had a flat nose and a white scar that crossed one cheek from ear to nose. They asked the way to a tavern I had never heard of. It was innocent enough, but I sensed the prospect of violence. The taller one was hiding something that bulged under his jacket, and he held his shoulder in a tense ball as if he meant to brandish a dagger or bludgeon.

He wasn't the only one with a weapon. Smiling and describing nearby taverns as if I were mightily pleased to direct good fellows to food and drink, I carefully removed my right hand from the warm fur of my muff and curled it around the hilt of the dagger in my waistcoat. Many years ago, my sailor brother, Alessandro, had furnished me with the weapon and instruction in its use. When the inevitable demand came, I was ready.

With a wordless growl, the tall one raised a short, stout rod above his head. The other pushed his ugly face into mine. "Your purse and your watch," he ordered on a puff of foul breath. "Make it quick. We've a powerful thirst."

The bridge railing pressed at my back. Using its support, I whipped out my dagger, canted back, and sliced my blade across the ruffian's unscarred cheek. He clapped his hand to his face with a squeal of pain. Scarlet oozed between his fingers.

At the same time, Benito uttered an impossibly high, unearthly shriek that froze the tall sailor's bludgeon in mid-swing. Benito followed his yell with a springing jump that drew his legs up into a diamond and caused the sailor's eyes to pop as if Hell had coughed up one of Satan's imps. My manservant didn't waste his opportunity. He slapped the rod from the fellow's hand. It spun through the air and hit the water with a splash.

Pulling hard on Benito's sleeve, I pushed away from the railing and started down the arch of the bridge at a run. We leapt the last few steps and dove into an alley that was little more than a slit between high walls. The would-be robbers bellowed and gave chase, but I knew Venice better than they did. With my manservant on my heels, I turned right, left, and then right again. I kept to the dark places, ignoring wider passages that beckoned with lit lamps and unbarred doorways. By the time we reached the irregular expanse of the Campo Santi Apostoli, we had lost our pursuers.

Benito fell in beside me, cheeks pink and chest heaving. I was breathing hard, as well, and my heart was hammering against my ribs. Limping a bit, I found my handkerchief and wiped damp sweat from my face and the back of my neck. For a few minutes, we trudged along in silence, our ragged breaths sounding harsh in the cool air.

Finally Benito said, "That was a smart move, Master. Those Greeks thought we were easy prey."

"I could say the same of you. You must have brought that scream up from your toes."

He chuckled, nodding. "And you gave that little one a scar to match the one he already has."

That I had, but I wasn't proud of it. Alessandro was the Amato brother who relished a good fight; I would rather outwit my opponent than draw blood.

"Let's speak of something else," I said as we started up the Fondamenta della Misericordia that flanked one of the Cannaregio's major waterways.

My neighborhood was quiet and tranquil. The distant carnival revels centered on the Piazza San Marco at the opposite end of the island. Here, ashen light from a plump three-quarter moon fell on modest houses whose inhabitants had been in bed for hours. Most of them, anyway. From a high window, the strains of a woman singing a lullaby made a duet with a child's keening whine. As we walked on, a lonely, almost magical gloom enveloped us, and I felt reassured despite the violence that had invaded my life twice that night.

Benito cleared his throat. "What do you want to talk about, Master?"

"Before the Greeks stopped us, I was stewing over something I noticed back at the theater."

"Something of consequence?"

"I don't know. Right now, it's merely curious."

"What is?"

"I've been asking myself…if Zulietta Giardino had a jewel box overflowing with diamonds, why was her most obvious adornment a simple blue ribbon tied round her throat?"

"She wore no jewels?"

"I'm quite sure she wore no rings, bracelets, or pins. Her hair had come down, so I couldn't see if there were bobs in her ears or not."

"Perhaps Zulietta left her fingers and arms bare so she could bedeck herself with La Samsona's rings and bracelets."

"I can't imagine that she would march over to La Samsona's box and demand her jewels on the spot."

"I suppose that would depend on how greedy she was."

I sent Benito an oblique glance. Even in the low moonlight, I saw his eyes gleaming. My manservant was as intrigued by tonight's strange tragedy as I was.

"What can you tell me about Zulietta Giardino?"

"Hmm…" Benito drew out this thoughtful hum as our steps resounded in a comfortable cadence. Finally he said, "Have you never noticed the woman? She has a maid as black as any Ethiopian. You often see them on the Piazza. The maid holds a sunshade over her mistress while that little troll struts in front with his chest puffed out, looking for all the world like a mechanical soldier doll."

"I thought I might have seen Zulietta before. She seemed so very familiar, but I can't actually recall where. I know I've never seen Pamarino. I would remember him."

It wasn't so odd that the unlikely trio had escaped my notice. In any other city, they would draw all eyes, but not in Venice. With the decline of her maritime fortunes, entertainment had become my city's lifeblood. Pleasure was the law of the land and masquerade an article of faith. During the six months that separated one Carnevale from the next, there was a never-ending succession of special occasions. In May came the festival of the Sensa, when the Doge recreated Venice's marriage to the sea with a magnificent regatta, and in July throngs of merrymakers crossed to the Giudecca to celebrate the festival of the Redentore. There was never a day when Venice didn't honor some saint or anniversary or welcome some prince or ambassador. Amidst the constant celebration and crush of foreigners who came to take part, why should I have noticed one comely courtesan and her small retinue?

"*Allora*," Benito began. "I can tell you three things that Pamarino didn't mention."

"Yes?"

"Until several years ago, Zulietta was kept by Signor Malpiero. That old reprobate settled a dowry on her in his will, expecting that she would employ it to attract a not overly fastidious husband. Instead, at his death, she used his money to purchase luxurious lodgings and set herself up as a courtesan in grand style. Her apartments are in the San Marco district, near the church of San Fantin." He paused to wave a hand back the way we'd come.

"All right, that's one. Go on."

"Zulietta managed her business affairs herself and kept them as organized as the most exacting clerk of the Procuratie. She had arrangements with several men of consequence. Signor Monday and Wednesday covered her expenses at the mercer and dressmaker's as well as supplying her gondolier, Signor Tuesday and Thursday each had his own set of responsibilities, and so on."

"Now you're beginning to astonish me. How do you happen to know the details of Zulietta's housekeeping? That's going some, even for you."

He shrugged modestly. "The hairdresser that attended her is a special friend of mine…was a friend, I should say."

Benito delivered this bit of news with a cocked eyebrow that spoke volumes. It was his nature to have a fleeting liaison with any broad-shouldered man who found his delicate charms to his liking. I would as soon try to change him as I would the courses of the stars in the sky.

My manservant continued with a sigh, "A few weeks before we parted, my friend told me that Zulietta had paid him off. She could no longer afford him or the towers of ringlets and feathers and other bits that went into his modish coiffures."

"What happened to Signor Monday and Tuesday and so on?"

"Apparently, the lady was concentrating all her efforts on Alessio Pino."

"I see. And what is the third thing?"

Benito paused in his tracks and focused his gaze farther down the canal, on a lopsided cluster of buildings that rose several stories above the rest. His soprano took on a deeper note. "Like Signora Liya, Zulietta Giardino came from the ghetto."

"What? She was a Jew?"

"A Jew no longer, but born one."

My gaze followed Benito's toward the dark, lofty structures that comprised the ghetto of Venice. Because the Jews were not allowed to build outwards, they expanded their allotted space by building up, higgledy-piggledy, until there wasn't a straight roofline in the place. Ringed by canals, its perimeter walls gated and barred, the ghetto housed several thousand Hebrews in unwholesome, not to say squalid, conditions. Somewhere behind those walls lived my wife's estranged relatives.

"Do you know Zulietta's family name?" I asked.

Benito scowled in thought. "No. Might it be important?"

A sinking feeling at the pit of my stomach told me it might be, but I put it aside. We had reached the small *campo* that held my house.

On nights when Liya did not accompany me to the theater, she would often wait up, eager to hear my impressions of the evening's performance. I would recount my highs and lows as I prepared for bed, and she would listen from our four-poster, muslin nightdress swathed in a bright Indian shawl that Alessandro had given her on the occasion of our handfasting. Tonight, in my weariness, I was hoping that Liya had already fallen asleep. Instead of launching into a gruesome account of Zulietta's murder, I wanted to explain on the morrow when the sun would be streaming through the bedroom windows. When rolls and warm chocolate would be within easy reach on the table before the fireplace. Perhaps then I could begin to forget the terrible feeling of helplessness as I'd watched Zulietta struggle, then tumble to her death.

My hopes were dashed when Liya opened the door in a state of high excitement. My wife's face was pale, her lips drained of their natural red. She clutched her paislied shawl over hunched shoulders and held a candlestick aloft. In its feeble rays, her long hair, let down for the night, rippled like liquid jet. Her eyes were wide with panic or fright.

"Liya, my love! Is Titolino worse?"

"No. The boy is well. He's sleeping." She shoved the candle at Benito and threw herself into my arms. "I was afraid something had happened to you."

"I'm perfectly fine," I answered, my throat thick with emotion as Liya pressed her body against mine. Her warmth and vitality made the memory of Zulietta's corpse all the more stark. "Why would you think otherwise?"

"My cards." She pulled away, shoulders relaxing and cheeks softening, but my wife was still not her confident, resolute self. "I've been laying the cards ever since I got Titolino settled in. Every spread showed someone falling from a great height. I convinced myself that one of those platforms that carry you into the cotton wool clouds gave way. If not you, who was hurt? Vittoria? Emilio?"

Out of the corner of my eye, I caught a peculiar expression sliding over Benito's face, a grimace halfway between suspicion and disgust. I had become accustomed to Liya's uncanny abilities, but her cards and her scrying pot still filled my superstitious manservant with alarm. As Liya continued to press me for answers, Benito pulled my cloak off with more force than was strictly necessary and took charge of my other outdoor things.

"Do you have any further requirements, Master?" he asked in a tight little voice.

"No, you may retire."

Benito touched the glowing candle to an unlit wick, and retreated down the long, dark hall until his light winked out as he turned a corner. I sighed. I could never hope to find a more loyal manservant, but I had to admit that Benito hadn't taken to the changes in my household as well as I'd hoped.

"Tito," Liya continued, stroking my face. "Why won't you tell me what happened?"

I took her hand and brushed her fingers against my lips, then told her about the tragedy that had interrupted the opera.

"Oh, Tito, the poor woman! Who was she?"

I turned my wife toward the stairs. "Didn't your cards tell you her name?" I half-teased, trying to lighten the moody atmosphere.

"You know the limits of their revelations." She gave my shoulder a playful slap. Good. *This* was my Liya, not the frightened wraith who had met me at the door.

As we slowly climbed to the second floor and trod the corridor to our bedroom at the back of the house, I elaborated on the evening's events, holding nothing back except the sailors who'd been looking for a fight. If Liya had been meant to know about the attack, I reasoned, her cards would have told her. I ended by asking if my wife had ever met Zulietta Giardino.

"No...Why would you think I knew her? Women of the town rarely cross my path."

"Of course not, it's just that she was raised in the ghetto and appeared to be about your age..." I rubbed my eyes, suddenly reminded how very tired I was. After a mammoth yawn, I murmured, "I suppose she would have been called something else then."

"Certainly." Liya nodded, her face wiped clean of all emotion. "Zuliettas don't exist in the ghetto."

Chapter Four

We entered our chamber to find a suspicious lump under the bedcovers. I pointed toward it while placing my other forefinger on Liya's lips. "My dear," I said in a hearty tone. "If that boy isn't over his cough soon, we must have Dr. Gozzi bring in his leeches."

Liya answered in kind. "You're absolutely right. I think we should request the doctor's special leeches. The giant beasts he keeps in tubs in the back room."

We crept toward the bed. "Oh, yes. Giant leeches will be just the thing—"

A sharp squeal emitted from the piled bedclothes, and a black, curly head shot up. "But I am well. I haven't coughed once tonight." Titolino stuck out his jaw and crossed his arms in a model of defiance. Only his dark-moon eyes gave his anxiety away.

His mother ruffled his silken curls. "But you won't stay well if you're up at all hours, running barefoot on cold floors."

The boy popped to his knees, bouncing gently on the feather-filled mattress. "What hour is it, Mama? Is it past midnight?"

I took out my watch and clicked it open. "Way past midnight. So far past, it will soon be morning."

"I've never been up past midnight!" Titolino grinned, wriggling out of his cocoon of bedsheets. The pipestem legs that emerged from his nightshirt seemed to go on forever. The boy must have grown overnight. Standing on the bed, he towered over his mother.

Liya wrapped her arms around his waist. "Well, I hope you enjoyed it, because you're going right back to your bed."

"No, no. Let me stay up just a little longer." As he pushed his mother's arms away, his voice rose to a squeak. He shook his head vigorously. "I'll be good—"

Then a telltale cough escaped his lips, and he knew he was beaten. He made his hands into fists and pounded his chest as if to punish that mutinous member.

Liya resumed her grasp, but Titolino extended his arms toward me. "If I have to go, let Papa take me."

I ducked my head, momentarily overcome with sudden emotion. Titolino had only recently begun calling me Papa, and that simple word still sounded more beautiful to my ears than any aria I had ever heard. It had been two years since Liya and I had stood before the wise woman in a garden perfumed with flowers and pomegranate trees. The old woman had pressed our forearms together and wound them with a silver cord. Thus, Liya and I were "twined as the vine as long as love should last." I intended it to last forever and considered the ceremony as binding as if the pope himself had solemnized our union. In taking Liya as my wife, I had also taken Titolino as my son, well knowing that his father had been one of the most godforsaken rogues my sleuthing had ever unearthed.

They say, "Blood will out," but I refused to believe that this innocent child's fate would be determined by a father who had died before his son took his first breath. Titolino struck me as an exceedingly clever child, and I had pledged myself to set his feet on a path that Liya and I would both be proud of.

I shouldered in to carry him away, and he scrambled into my arms, climbing my height like a tree. We left the bedchamber singing snatches of a nonsense song. Over many nights of play, we had adapted an old folk song about a toad and a firefly and made it our own. Titolino sang King Toad in a deep croak, I the mischievous firefly in a parody of my crystal clear soprano.

When I returned, Liya was dabbing her face clean at the washstand. The bedcovers had been pulled back, and the logs in the narrow fireplace hissed and cracked as they settled into glowing embers. I crossed to the table by the dying fire and pulled off my shirt.

Liya's *tarocchi* quartered the mahogany tabletop: a Greek cross of bright, fanciful pasteboards. The cards depicted peasants and kings, monks and nuns, and other figures in the standard suits of coins, cups, batons, and swords. In most people's hands, these cards represented an evening's game, a harmless pursuit to fill the time between supper and bed. But Liya used them to delve into the future. I had once described her *tarocchi* as an unbound picture book, and she'd told me I wasn't far wrong.

I couldn't pretend to understand her cards' hidden secrets, but I didn't doubt their existence. The proof lay before me. At one corner was a white horse with a front foot raised. I shook my head, wondering how the cards could possibly know that a horse would provide part of my evening's excitement. And it wasn't hard to see where Liya had formed the notion about the fall at the theater.

In the very center of the cross, a position to which all the other *tarocchi* pointed, was a card depicting a tower on a rocky crag. The sky behind was a deep, inky black rent by streaks of yellow lightning. One bolt had blown the top from the stone tower; blocks and debris rained down among gobbets of fire. A man and woman flew through the air, their mouths forming silent screams and their fine clothing billowing from the wind created by their fall. I grimaced when I noticed that the female of the pair wore a gown of peacock blue.

"What are you doing, Tito?" Liya called from the basin, drying her face with a thick towel.

"Just thinking, my love."

"Thinking what?"

"That perhaps tomorrow you might visit the ghetto and see what you can find out about Zulietta Giardino."

"Why, Tito?" Her voice was husky with an emotion I couldn't identify. Though my back was turned, I sensed her approach. I shivered as she trailed her cool fingers along my bare shoulders.

"You know I'm not welcome there, and what does it matter, anyway? This Zulietta has nothing to do with us. Messer Grande should be the one to ask questions."

I turned to face her, the card of the lightning-struck tower concealed in my palm. "You know that Messer Grande will be as welcome in the ghetto as a stray cat at the fish market. How much do you think he will really be able to discover?"

My request did not provoke the flash of anger I feared. Liya's expression reflected the poignant resignation it often did when her childhood home was mentioned. In addition, I was glad to see the tiniest glimmer of curiosity.

"But, Tito," she replied, shaking her head until the dark tendrils of hair danced like undulating snakes. "Why do you ask me this?"

I raised my hand. "This card found its way into your design as surely as Zulietta's death found its way into my aria."

Liya sent me a dubious glance from under charcoal lashes. "Surely it's mere happenstance that the woman was killed while you were singing."

"Haven't you always instructed me that there are no true coincidences?"

She shrugged, but I saw that she regarded the card with a new intensity.

"Well?" I asked. "What do you say?"

She tossed her head and threw her towel at the washstand. "I say there will be plenty of time to think about it tomorrow."

Once we had slipped beneath the bedclothes, I drew her to me and we snuggled close. I lay on my back with my arm beneath her warm curves, and Liya notched her cheek in the hollow between my shoulder and chest, tickling my chin with her jasmine-scented mane.

"Tito," she murmured, "do you think Fortunata would turn me away if I visited Papa's shop?"

I stroked Liya's smooth skin. "I can't imagine she would. You were always her favorite sister, weren't you?"

"Yes," she breathed, so soft I could barely hear.

"And unlike the others, Fortunata has written several times since you've been back in Venice."

"Warning me that Mama and Papa aren't ready to see me."

"That was months ago. I would expect your father to have mellowed by now. Pincas was never a man to hold a grudge."

After a moment, Liya nodded and snuggled closer. Sleep claimed us almost immediately.

The next morning, after a breakfast that involved more conversation than sustenance, we both set off before ten o'clock. I watched Liya start down the pavement to the nearby ghetto, head held high, dark hair covered by her finest *zendale* worked in cream-colored silk. Though her neat boots covered the stones in resolute strides, I had noted the quiver of her cheek as she bade me good-by. I sent up a small prayer to the Blessed Mother. Surely Our Lady could spare a moment to look in on the ghetto, heathen as it was.

Luigi, my gondolier, had his boat waiting at the quay just a stone's throw from my house. The man was suitably apologetic about deserting me the night before, so I allowed him to set off for the theater after only a token remonstrance. As he rowed, I buried my chin in the collar of my cloak that Benito had reinforced with a woolen muffler. It was a raw morning on the canals. The sun was playing hide-and-seek with the clouds, and the clouds were winning.

At the theater, I found Maestro Torani adamant that *Armida* continue as scheduled. His wrinkled face held a somber expression, and wisps of steel-gray hair wreathed his shiny scalp. As the singers gathered, our director paced the stage in aimless circles with head hung low and hands clasped behind his back. Every few moments, he stopped to give the scarred boards a pensive stare. I thought he was giving a wonderful impression of a dog who'd forgotten where he'd hidden his bone.

Our prima donna arrived in a whirl of silk skirts, ermine-lined cloak, and penetrating French scent. As her maid collected her things, Vittoria protested that reopening the theater the night after the grisly tragedy seemed disrespectful, if not outright impious.

Emilio, who rarely had a good word for anyone or anything, spread his arms and addressed the empty catwalks above the stage. "Since when is a common whore worthy of respect?"

Ignoring the castrato's remark, Torani rounded on Vittoria with a scowl. "This new opera has been commissioned by the bigwigs on the subscribers' board." He swept an arm toward the orderly ranks of boxes where those very bigwigs would sit whenever our company got back to business. "If they find a dark theater where they expect grand spectacle, they'll decamp to the San Moise or the San Benedetto. Or find some other distraction altogether."

Or find a reason to change the theater management, I thought sourly. The hands that fed us were attached to notoriously fickle patrons.

Vittoria licked her full lips. She patted upswept curls that were already perfection. She knew, as we all did, that the San Benedetto had recently acquired a young female soprano who was attracting a great deal of attention. Our lovely but aging star sent Torani a sweet smile. "You know best, Maestro. I'll be happy to sing tonight if you wish it."

I thought there might be more to Maestro Torani's decision. As I'd disembarked at the water gate, I'd recognized a familiar figure striding over the bridge that led away from the theater. "Has Signor Lazarini been bending your ear?"

Before Torani could answer, Emilio shot back, "And what if he has? Lazarini's men have to eat. If there's no performance, they won't be paid."

I nodded, noting Torani's abashed countenance. Lazarini was a powerful man in theater circles; he managed claques for Emilio Strada and many other popular singers. Where I trusted the audience to reward my performance as they saw fit, some of my colleagues took out insurance in the form of professional applauders. The going rate for clapping alone was ten *soldi* a man, while a *zecchino* purchased enthusiastic cheering and cries of "bravo." Booing and fisticuffs directed at a rival singer's partisans could earn much more. Though I detested Lazarini and his crew, I could understand why Emilio would make such arrangements. He was several years older than myself, and though his handsome face still turned heads, his castrato's physique was slowly turning to fat. I had it on good authority from Benito that Emilio's manservant laced him into a corset before every performance. More crucially, his silvery soprano had not worn well.

Vittoria was not feeling as charitable as Torani. Shouting over our maestro's protests, she upbraided Emilio with the zeal of the sorceress she portrayed in the opera. The castrato responded like the feckless fool he was, and on they went. The other singers, as well as a few stagehands, drifted onstage to view what promised to be a rousing good fight. I confess I was disappointed when Benito appeared at my elbow to deliver the message that Madame Dumas required my presence in her workroom.

"Tell me what happens," I whispered, then made my way through the wings and backstage corridors to Madame Dumas' domain.

The company's chief costumer, a dignified, gray-haired Frenchwoman, insisted on the title of Madame despite her many years in Venice. Her habitual frown and slate-hard blue eyes terrified most of the company, but her severe demeanor didn't put me off. Madame Dumas and I had been through several adventures together; I knew that inside she was as sweet and soft as a cream puff, especially where I was concerned. She met me at the door of her workroom, scissors dangling from a belt at her waist and needles trailing different colors of thread tucked in the bodice of her faded black gown.

I deposited a peck on her wrinkled cheek. "My angel, you've rescued me from the middle of a vicious squabble. Emilio and Vittoria will start drawing blood any moment now."

After I'd explained, the seamstress gave a very Gallic snort. "Just let it come out that our righteous prima donna employs her own claque—then we'll see some real fireworks."

My jaw dropped. "Vittoria has a claque? She's warmly received, to be sure, but I thought that was because the gondoliers love her."

Madame Dumas chuckled as she guided me toward the mammoth table tumbled with a wealth of luxurious fabrics and trims. In a corner, a pair of young seamstresses were working around a mannequin that wore one of Vittoria's costumes. They looked up as if to join our conversation; Madame put them in their place with a fierce look. Then she retrieved my torn tunic and draped it over my shoulders.

"Vittoria's cabal is supposed to be a secret," she mused as her quick hands fluttered over my chest, tucking here and folding there. "Her supporters specialize in making their praise appear absolutely natural."

I shook my head. "And that doe-eyed soprano has always sworn she would never stoop so low." What other secrets went on in this opera house under my very nose?

"Hold your arms straight," Madame Dumas ordered out of one corner of her mouth. She'd stowed her pins on the opposite side. "I need to fit this to you."

"Did I do that much damage?"

"The tear was easily repaired, but the waist needs taking in. It sags where it should fit like a glove. Doesn't your woman ever feed you?"

As instructed, I made my torso into a living statue. Fortunately, my lips were allowed to move. "Have you ever seen anything to rival last night's tragedy?"

She shrugged as she pinned. "I'm not surprised. These girls of today do not know how to conduct their affairs. In Paris, when I was a young woman, arrangements were made properly. Attorneys made certain the gentleman's funds were secure and drew up a settlement while his breeches were still buttoned. Imagine staking your future on a wager over a jewel box. It was bound to end in trouble of some kind."

"You know about the wager? That business was supposed to be kept quiet."

Madame licked her finger and rolled the end of a thread into a knot. "When did Venice ever keep anyone's secrets? Talk of the whores' deadly contest has been sweeping the city faster than a sirocco wind. A man on my *campo* has already set up his own wager—" She paused to whip in a few stitches.

Tightening my skin away from her needle, I asked, "What sort of wager?"

"On who will be hung for the murder, of course. Odds are running in favor of the young man, but I laid down a *zecchino* on La Samsona. And I wasn't the only one." She straightened and looked me in the eye. Then a smile that was surely meant to wheedle sprang to her lips; unfortunately, several discolored teeth spoiled the effect. "They say you saw the masked killer, Signor Amato. You're a clever one. Tell me now, could I be right? I could certainly use the winnings."

I blinked, and thought for a moment.

"It's possible, I suppose. La Samsona is a tall woman, but the figure I saw was broad, bulky—"

"And so is she," the costumer broke in excitedly. "Her years of lifting iron bars have given her the shoulders of a prize fighter. Many times I've watched her swan from the lobby to her box, and I've seen her in the refreshment room, too. Her dressmaker must be a treasure—she knows how to draw the eye away from those horrible shoulders. But La Samsona is still an Amazon. And a more grasping, ambitious whore never lived, I hear."

"I suppose you believe La Samsona heard that Zulietta was within minutes of winning the wager."

Nodding, she folded my tunic over her thin, tightly sleeved arm. "Heard about it and decided murder was better than losing her diamonds. Think on it, *mon cher*. How easy it would be for that great giant to throw on a man's cloak and *bauta*, leave her box, and commit the deed. She could have smuggled in her disguise for the very purpose."

I took Madame Dumas' free hand in mine. With a quick squeeze, I said, "I wish you luck in your neighbor's lottery, old friend, but I must tell you that Messer Grande favors Alessio

Pino for the culprit. I wouldn't be surprised if he already has him in custody."

"We'll soon see." And with a bob of the tightly wound bun atop her head, she added, "Wouldn't care to bet on it, would you?"

I returned to the stage to find Emilio and Vittoria licking their wounds at opposite ends of the boards. Torani and the accompanist were downstage, digging through a pile of scores. The other singers of the company kept up hearty conversation and forced cheerful smiles as if they had not just witnessed two of their colleagues filleting each other with words as sharp as carving knives.

"Here, I have it." Torani waved a sheaf of music. After sending the accompanist to the harpsichord, our maestro directed Emilio to rehearse a passage that had been sounding more like musical gargling than sweet song. "The rest of you are at liberty for half an hour," Torani threw over his shoulder as Emilio squeaked out a few exploratory notes.

Still displaying anger-bright cheeks, Vittoria blew past me and shoved a prop boy into the nearest flat. I heard her heels tap-tap-tap all the way up the stairs to her dressing room. The others headed to the crooked little room beneath the stairs where we often whiled away our time between rehearsal and performance. Wine would flow from the bottle that always stood on the high windowsill; gossip would flow still faster.

My simmering curiosity led me elsewhere.

I passed through the stage door and availed myself of the stair-case used by footmen delivering dinners and performing various errands. On the fourth level, a swinging door provided entrance to a cloakroom that presented the usual welter of abandoned cloaks and coats, hats with smashed crowns, and other orphaned bits of clothing. A long black cloak with braided frogging made a lumpy pyramid in the middle of the space. I bent to retrieve it. Shaking out its heavy folds, I saw it was fashioned for a man of prodigious size. Had this garment swaddled the unconscious dwarf? If so, it was a miracle Pamarino hadn't suffocated.

I hung the cloak on an empty hook and stepped back. Cocking my head, I tried to imagine the murderous figure I'd observed hoisting Pamarino's dead weight onto the hook and tucking the thick fabric around his slack body. Then I put myself in the dwarf's place. How frightening to be manhandled like a rag doll, to awaken in darkness, helpless, barely able to catch a breath of air.

I was deep in contemplation when a hand on my shoulder made me jerk around with a gasp.

"*Scusi*, Signor Amato," said a workman clasping a push broom, a lanky old fellow with untidy white hair that flopped over shaggy eyebrows. "Is there something I can do for you?"

"No, *grazie*. I merely wanted to see where Messer Grande's men found that poor little man."

The workman folded his hands and balanced his chin on the broom handle. "That ugly little imp? He was hanging right there. A pitiful sight as I ever did see." The man indicated a hook on the back wall.

"You were here? I thought Messer Grande had sent the theater staff home."

"Not me." He made a fist and thumped his chest. "First to arrive, last to leave, that's me. I clean my way out the door after everyone else has left their dirty footprints."

Of course. How easy it was to forget the people that worked in obscurity to make our daily lives go more smoothly.

"What's your name?" I asked.

After a flicker of surprise, he said, "I'm called Biagio. Biagio Zipoli."

"Well, Biagio, can you tell me how the constables happened to find the dwarf?"

He stood a little taller. "I led them to him. I was sweeping the corridor when I heard a noise coming from in here. I almost passed right by. Thought it might be a footman amusing himself with someone's maid. You can't imagine what people get up to around here."

Given the backstage antics I'd witnessed, I could well imagine, but I merely nodded, encouraging him to continue.

"At first, it was just knocking and thumping, but when I heard screams, I pushed the door open. Saw something thrashing under that cloak there. Nearly pissed my breeches when I uncovered the little demon. He begged me to help him down, but I didn't dare touch him."

"Why not? He's only a small man. His name is Pamarino."

Biagio shook his head solemnly. "The good Lord made men, but he never made anything like that. That imp is Old Scratch's work." To reinforce his point, Biagio made the sign of the cross, then kissed his fingers.

It was no use trying to change Biagio's mind. I couldn't explain why Pamarino was made as he was, but I was certain Satan had no more to do with him than the runt in a litter of puppies. I gestured toward the brass hooks. "How was he hung up?"

Biagio let the broom handle fall against his shoulder. He pressed his wrists together, then shot his arms above his head. "He was tied like so. Dangling, hollering with all his might, beating his boot heels against the wall. You can still see the marks."

Indeed, black half moons dotted the pale plaster. "You called for the law?"

"*Si*, Signore. They cut him down."

"What was he restrained with?"

My informant scratched his head and poked his broom at the detritus that had collected in the corners of the cloakroom. A wicker hamper had overturned to spill its contents of muffs and scarves. "Some sort of cords. Not too heavy. But I don't see them here. I think the constables took them away."

Good for them, I thought. Another sign that this new Messer Grande had a head for investigation.

Biagio was still wielding his broom. "Hello, what's this?" He bent to retrieve two pieces of polished wood that had been stacked against the molding where wall met floor. Long, thin, and rounded at one tip, they looked as if they belonged backstage. Levers or some other component of the elaborate scene machines, no doubt. Biagio evidently agreed. He gathered them up and announced his intention to carry them down to the wings.

I laid a hand on his arm. "One more question."

"*Sì?*"

"Around the time the woman fell from the box, did you see anyone who didn't belong here? Anything at all suspicious?"

The workman surprised me with a hearty chuckle. Pressing a finger against the side of his nose, he gave me a conspiratorial wink. "I know what you're doing. You're trying to find out who killed her."

Was I so transparent? I'd hoped he would think I was merely asking a few idle questions—a more interesting way of passing time than gossiping with the rest of the cast. I shrugged. "Well, then?"

"I'll tell you what I told Messer Grande's men, but I wager you'll make more of it."

"Yes?"

"Some time before the singing began, I spied a man going up and down the corridor, asking after Alessio Pino's box."

"A tall man in a *bauta?*"

"No." Biagio gave me a bewildered look. "Who would notice a man in a *bauta?* Half the gentlemen on this level were wearing one. No, this man didn't have a mask of any sort. Though his suit was silk, he moved like a rough cob. A sailor, I'll be bound."

"A sailor?" I demanded sharply, then modulated my tone. "What made you think he was a sailor?"

My informant shrugged. "They just have a look about them, you know. When a fellow spends his days on a rolling deck with salt spray in his face, it marks him."

Try as I might, I could wring no further details from Biagio. He headed off downstairs carrying his broom and sticks of wood, and I strolled in the opposite direction, not thinking of what I'd just learned, but wondering how Liya was getting along in the ghetto. Of late, I'd noticed increasing signs that my wife was having second thoughts about severing ties with her family. If Zulietta Giardino's murder could provide an excuse for Liya to approach her sister or her father, at least one small, extraordinary blessing would come out of the tragedy.

Rounding the bend in the corridor, I came upon box D-17. The door's thin wood had been reduced to splinters by the constables' boots. It sagged inward from one hinge, affording me a narrow entrance. I passed through the miniature vestibule and stepped down into the Pino family's private box.

Unfortunately, its scarlet interior had little to reveal. Messer Grande's men had removed every stick of furniture and anything else that might have provided a clue to Zulietta's killer. Only the draperies and silk-covered walls remained. As I moved to the front of the box, an odd sensation rippled along my backbone.

Dark smears cut across the grain of the wooden box railing, three narrow smudges just where Zulietta would have struggled to gain a last handhold. I scraped at one with a fingernail. Blood almost certainly. Had her killer pried her bloody fingers from the railing? I felt my heart pounding in my ears. How I would love to expose such a brute. I could cheerfully deliver him to the hangman myself.

My vengeful thoughts were interrupted by a trilling run of notes from Emilio. I glanced toward the stage. This was a vantage point I rarely occupied. How near the painted ceiling I hovered, and how small and far away Emilio and Maestro Torani looked as they moved about. Is that how I had seemed to the murderer after he'd completed his awful work? A doll-like figure, wide-eyed and horrified, pinned by his malevolent gaze?

Moving several steps to one side, I focused my gaze directly below, at the exact spot where Zulietta had crashed to the floor. A gentleman in a dark suit stood there, head bowed, walking stick firmly planted, the brim of his tricorne hiding his features.

Ordinarily, the lobby doors would be locked at this hour, but a persistent curiosity seeker must have bribed his way in. Just as I opened my mouth to call out, the man tilted his head and swept off his hat.

I waved a greeting, not certain whether I should be pleased or dismayed.

Though Messer Grande's smile was benign, he beckoned with two fingers as stiff as a tuning fork. I was wanted.

Chapter Five

A sign creaked as it swung in the breeze: the Lion of San Marco, the symbol of the Venetian Republic, flaked by time and weather. Messer Grande had conducted me to a guardhouse on the San Polo side of the Rialto Bridge where a number of government buildings were clustered. He paused under the sign, one booted foot on the steps that led to a turreted, squat pile of brown-gray stones that housed pickpockets, sandbaggers, sneak thieves, and all manner of miscreants awaiting their turn before the bench.

"Leave the talking to me," he said. "Just keep your eyes open. If you can identify Alessio Pino as the man in the box, so be it. If you're not sure, don't think exaggerating the resemblance will make you a hero."

Indignation kindled at the pit of my stomach. "A hero is something I play on the stage. I have no need for such sentiments in real life."

"Very well…" Messer Grande replied in a silky tone. Somehow I formed the impression that he was both pleased and surprised. With a nod, he went on, "Yes. Good. Perhaps you'll be of more assistance than I dared hope."

"I will if I can." Somewhat mollified, I asked, "Did you arrest Alessio on Murano?"

Messer Grande snorted. "We crossed to the Pino factory the minute we left the theater. Most people run home when trouble is brewing, but not Alessio. Obvious why—his father is a terror.

We found the old man tending the night fires himself. He was aghast when I told him about the murder. Even so, he refused to leave his kiln—the melting pots had reached some crucial stage that apparently requires a master's hand. He ordered a servant to lead us on a search of the glassworks and the house that sits behind it. I had him unlock all the storerooms and cupboards large enough for a man to hide in, but we came up empty-handed. Cesare's parting words were 'run that mewling pup of mine to ground and haul him before the Avogaria—just don't bring him back here or I might have to wring his neck myself.'"

"Cesare must think Alessio is guilty, then."

"Guilty of betraying his father's carefully laid marriage plans—certainly. But guilty of murder? I can't say." Messer Grande paused to stroke his chin thoughtfully. "I've seen a lot in my time, but I've rarely come across such a formidable father…"

I looked down at the stone stairs, focusing on the dip worn away by years of passing feet. I'd also been encumbered with a formidable father. Raising my gaze, I asked, "Where was Alessio hiding?"

Messer Grande replied as he ushered me into the guardhouse. "At a house near the theater. We found him by questioning his friends—one was not as firm a friend as Alessio must have thought."

At the foyer desk, a uniformed sergeant was reading the *Gazzetta Veneta* with his feet propped up. After one glance at the senior constable, he scrambled to attention amidst a flurry of dust and official reports. Ignoring the man's stiff salute, Messer Grande turned into a grim corridor. He continued his tale: "Alessio's so-called friend had hidden him in the attics of his family home. This daring young sprig didn't mind pulling the wool over his old father's eyes, but when he saw that this was more than a trifling escapade—and that he'd be courting prison if he continued to lie to me—it didn't take long for him to cough Alessio up like a gristly morsel of pork."

"Did Alessio come quietly?"

Messer Grande lodged his tricorne under his arm and rubbed the back of his neck. "He didn't struggle, if that's what you mean, but when I confronted him with the particulars of Zulietta's murder, he wept and swooned like a woman. My men had to carry him to the boat."

We had walked the length of the dismal corridor and entered a small room. A warden considerably more alert than the desk sergeant awaited us with a bunch of keys. He sprang to open a door with a square grating, and we were admitted to yet another corridor lined with cells of the most wretched type. Most were empty, though I saw a few huddled shapes and easily perceived the stench of human sweat and filth. At least a modicum of fresh air and light was admitted through a few barred dormer windows. We stopped before the last cell but one.

Despite the rumpled clothing, the torn stockings, the dirty face, Alessio Pino was a handsome boy. I could describe him in no other terms, though he was only several years younger than I was. Messer Grande had stated his age as six and twenty.

I observed Alessio closely as he rose from the bare planks where he had been stretching out with his folded arms serving as a pillow. He was slender, with melting brown eyes, and a high forehead that perfectly balanced his squared-off, lightly beard-stubbled chin. His silver-threaded, blue brocade jacket was cut in the latest fashion, with absurdly padded shoulders and a trim waist. He smoothed the jacket's wrinkles, straightened his powdered wig with a firm tweak, and plodded over to the iron bars with weary grace.

Messer Grande bade him good afternoon in a cool voice.

Alessio returned his greeting with a perfunctory bow. As his gaze slid to me, he straightened in astonishment. "What on earth are you doing here? Am I to have a serenade in this anteroom to Hell?"

I'd been recognized, of course. Alessio must have seen me at the opera many times. Before my lips could part to reply, Messer Grande cut in, "My companion is none of your concern, Signor Pino. I came to see if you're ready to tell me where you were before you arrived at the Teatro San Marco last night. No more stalling, if you please."

"But I've already told you—my boatman failed to show at the appointed hour. When I went in search of the fellow, I found him staggering away from a tavern, much the worse for drink. He wasn't capable of rowing the length of the Canale Serenella, much less navigating the waves of the lagoon. I was forced to row myself across to Venice."

"Your father states that you left the house a good two hours before the curtain rose on the opera. The trip from the Pino factory should take a quarter of that."

"But you're not accounting for the time I spent tromping around our corner of Murano. And I wasn't rowing a gondola—I couldn't manage that. I had to unhitch the cockle boat from a shallop that we use to transport sand and other materials. The tide was high and the wind contrary—it took me nearly three quarters of an hour to make the crossing."

Messer Grande regarded him skeptically. Alessio's story did seem weak. Rowing a tiny boat alone, in dress clothes? Could the glassworks supply no other man to convey the owner's son over to Venice?

"I don't know why you don't believe me." Alessio grasped the iron bars so tightly his hands shook. His expression wrinkled into a mask of aggrieved innocence. "If someone from the glassworks has not retrieved the boat, you'll find it at a quay just west of the Piazzetta. It's marked with our family name."

"I'll send a man to look for it, Signore, but tell me this—before you went to meet Zulietta Giardino at the theater, you stopped by a nearby tavern. Who did you see and for what purpose?"

Alessio dropped his hands. They looked very awkward, hanging about his flanks, twisting back and forth. "I don't know what you're talking about. Once I'd secured the boat, I went straight to the theater."

A strained silence followed. I was itching to ask a few questions of my own, but Messer Grande had ordered me to be silent, and I didn't fancy risking his wrath.

Eventually, Messer Grande addressed his prisoner in a tone of sorry reproof. "I've already made inquiries at the Pearl of the Waves."

"Yes?" The question was a whisper.

"You were spotted the minute you stepped over the threshold."

Alessio clutched the bars again. A look of fear passed over his features, but he quickly collected himself. He cleared his throat. "You're right, and I beg your pardon, Excellency. I mustn't lie. It will just cause more trouble, won't it?"

"You may be sure of it. What was your business at the Pearl of the Waves?"

"I was supposed to meet someone, but I was late. The man had already left."

"Who is this man?"

"I…I can't tell you."

"Your tongue seems to be working perfectly to me."

"All right. I refuse to tell you."

Messer Grande slapped his tricorne on his breeches. "This isn't sport!" he cried. "Answer me, man! Who were you meeting before the opera?"

Pale, serious, countenance as cold as the surrounding stones, Alessio shook his head. "It's a matter of honor, involving innocent men. You must take my word that the business had nothing to do with Zulietta's death."

Messer Grande drew himself up. His nostrils flared to twice their size. I shuddered for Alessio's sake. Was the boy brave or foolish or merely stubborn?

"An innocent man has nothing to hide," Messer Grande said. "If you won't answer my simple question, I'm forced to believe that you murdered the courtesan Zulietta Giardino."

Alessio went very still. He replied in exquisitely pronounced words, "I loved Zulietta. I would never hurt one hair on her head."

"Perhaps you did love her…until you discovered that she'd made a cynical, corrupt bargain for your heart."

"The wager? Is that what you mean?" Alessio ran a hand over his jaw. He looked to me as if I could offer help. Finding none, he turned back to his interrogator with a challenge writ large on his face. "I wouldn't have killed Zulietta over that wager."

Messer Grande grunted his disbelief. "Are you made of granite, then? Your lady deceived you shamefully. If her plan had come to fruition, you would have been the butt of ridicule for years to come. Women have been murdered for far less. Just last month, a husband strangled his wife for trying to convince him that his cat-meat stew was really chicken. The magistrate went easy on him—only ten years in the galleys. Perhaps the court would find you worthy of equal leniency…" The chief constable lowered his voice. "If you start telling me the truth."

"I am telling the truth. Some of your questions I'm not at liberty to answer, but what I can tell will be the full truth. The women's wager had no power to wound me. I could have put an end to it whenever I chose, but Zulietta was keen to proceed. She wanted to get one up on La Samsona—payment for past misdeeds, apparently. We laughed about the wager and about her rival's obnoxious efforts to seduce me. Then we went on to discuss more serious things."

"That's not how I heard it," Messer Grande retorted.

Alessio's eyes flashed. "If you heard it from Pamarino, you can be sure it's a lie."

Messer Grande raised his brows in silent question.

"He's a preposterous little man," Alessio continued, "who makes himself difficult in a hundred ways. He took an extreme dislike to me on our first meeting. I don't understand why Zulietta kept him around. She was too kind."

"By his own words, he served as *cavaliere servente* and major-domo rolled into one."

"Pamarino exaggerates his own importance, Excellency. And since I stand behind these bars, I can only assume the pitiful creature has also exaggerated a few things about me."

"You are here because you hid from the law. Why would an innocent man do that?"

Alessio shook his head as if that vigorous motion could dispel a horrifying memory. "I beseech you, put yourself in my place. I was coming up the steps to the opera house when a crowd burst through the doors cawing and chattering like magpies— a woman had jumped from a box and broken her neck—no, someone pushed her—no, a terrible accident. I plunged on, intent on finding Zulietta. But then I spotted an acquaintance who told me Zulietta lay dead—and all of Venice saw her fall from my box." He beat his palm with his fist. "God forgive me, all I could think about was…my father."

I spoke for the first time, words flying unchecked from my tongue. "You ran away because you were afraid of your father?"

As Messer Grande shot me a withering glance, Alessio raised his chin and puffed out his chest. The lace on his shirt front was limp and disheveled, and one jacket pocket had been partially torn away. Even so, he rivaled the noblest prince I had ever played on the stage. He said, "I may be a coward where my father is concerned, but I loved Zulietta. And she returned my love. I had already dissolved the engagement my father arranged and meant to make Zulietta my wife. I was ready to give up everything for her, and yet you have the effrontery to blame me for her murder. It's…intolerable."

Alessio couldn't sustain the pose. I don't know whether grief or guilt or simple fatigue brought him down, but he crumpled before our eyes. We left him huddled on the floor of his cell, sobbing softly, head in his hands.

I followed Messer Grande out of the guardhouse, and we walked side by side in silence for several minutes. He led us through the markets, skirting the Pescheria, where noisy gulls contested for fishmongers' scraps, then straight through the fruit and vegetable stalls, where he stopped here and there to pinch an apple or a winter melon. He finally came to a halt on the crest of the Rialto Bridge and motioned for me to join him as he shouldered in among the gawking foreigners along the parapet.

It took very little to amuse our visitors. The endless serenades of the gondoliers were a source of wonder, as well as our watery landscape. Men and women alike loved leaning over the wide, flat balustrade of the bridge, following the progress of heavily laden barges, pointing and exclaiming as if they had never seen a boat in their lives. When a barge bumped a gondola and a wild outburst of invective ensued, I heard one ruddy Englishman exclaim, "By Jove," and suddenly I was missing Gussie with every fiber of my being.

"Well?" Messer Grande jerked me back to the business at hand. "Is Alessio the man you saw struggling with Zulietta?"

I pondered for a moment. "I can't say. Truly. Alessio is the proper height, but he's very slender."

"His shoulders add some width."

I nodded. "They do. Working the kiln must be good for the muscles. The man in the box had wide shoulders."

"So…you're saying Alessio might be the man?"

"Might be—yes, that's the best I can do."

Messer Grande turned to frown at the gaily sparkling waters of the canal with outright antagonism. In a moment, he jerked round again.

"What about his chin?"

"Alessio's chin?"

"Yes, you said the murderer's mask left the lower part of his face bare. Did it resemble Alessio's?"

I took time to think but had to shake my head. "One man's chin is very like another."

"Of course. It was a faint hope." He again turned his gaze to the water and mused in a milder tone of voice. "This case makes me think of an old fairy tale."

"Which one?"

"The Beauty and the Beast."

"Oh, yes. A beast captures a beautiful maiden and her love restores him to his true self—a handsome prince." I shook my head. "But the story doesn't fit. The only beast in this matter is Pamarino, and handsome he'll never be."

"That's true." Messer Grande turned and propped an elbow on the smooth marble railing. The crowd of foreigners was drifting away. "But," he continued, fastening on me with eyes of deepest brown, "I'd bet my last *soldo* that our little beast was hopelessly in love with Zulietta."

"Pamarino?" I stared back incredulously.

"That misshapen body holds a heart as tender as any other man's, does it not?" My companion's voice again turned silky, a tone I was beginning to realize served him for both suspicion and reproof.

I was instantly ashamed. Who was I to disapprove of a dwarf's longings? For every bouquet tossed at the opera house, I received as many gawking stares or whispered crudities on the streets. My tall height, longer than average limbs, and beardless face marked me as a castrato for anyone who cared to observe these peculiarities, and many a half-wit felt compelled to make a remark about me or the women who found me attractive. For consolation, I had my work and Liya, the love of my life. With his more obvious disfigurement, how much worse must it be for Pamarino?

I asked, "Do you think that's why Zulietta's dwarf is throwing blame on Alessio? Sheer jealousy?"

"It makes sense, doesn't it?"

"Only if Zulietta had truly fallen in love with Alessio as he claims." I shut my mouth and let the sun warm my cheeks. I was surprised that Messer Grande was discussing the crime in such an open manner, but he regarded me with a frank, friendly expression, so I continued cautiously, "Do you believe Alessio's story?"

"What story? So far, that young man has told me very little and absolutely refuses to account for his movements last night."

We both wrinkled our noses as a fisherman climbed the bridge steps with a shallow basket on his head. He was hawking sole and mackerel, but he'd left it too late. His wares were beginning to smell.

Messer Grande removed his snuffbox from his waistcoat and took a delicate pinch. After his sneeze, he said, "I don't like it when cases are this complicated. Usually when a whore is murdered I have only two men to consider—her pimp or the last man who warmed her bed. This affair of the wager is a tricky business—if only you had gotten a better look at the fellow that stabbed Zulietta." He proffered the snuffbox, but I shook my head. Tobacco wrecks havoc on the vocal cords.

"Have you spoken to Signor Albergati? He could at least confirm whether Alessio had called off the marriage."

"Indeed," he replied dryly. "If Signor Albergati would condescend to receive me."

"He won't see you?"

"I was turned away from his door like a humble turnip seller."

"Surely you can insist. You are…Messer Grande."

A grimace twisted his pleasant face. "The citizens of our Republic take my measure with different rods. I hold authority that can frighten a porter or a poor ship caulker out of his wits, but let me present my card at one of the palaces that line this waterway and I hear, 'Perhaps his Excellency will receive you tomorrow.'"

I nodded. In the old days, there had been no official peace keepers. The great families provided for their own security with squads of liveried bravos while the common folk settled their differences as best they could. I wasn't surprised that Messer Grande often ran up against the lingering traces of that lawless era. But there was something else. "It could be that Signor Albergati's reluctance stems from the fact that he and his sons also had a motive to dispense with Zulietta."

"Yes, that has occurred to me. Once those curtains parted, the spectators would have talked of nothing but Alessio flaunting his new mistress." He gave a hollow laugh. "Even your fine talents might have failed to recapture their attention."

"The Albergatis' humiliation would have known no bounds."

My companion nodded his agreement. "All true, but the old father is infirm and hobbled by a chronic case of gout. If any of them is our murderer, it would have been one of Maria's brothers or a loyal bravo from the household. I would bet on the brothers—the one named Umberto is known as a hothead. I've taken steps to obtain a magistrate's writ to force Signor Albergati's hand, but it will be several days before my request is acted on."

"Well, while you're waiting, I did learn one thing that might be of help." I went on to recount the tale of old Biagio's sailor.

"I see," Messer Grande said slowly, studying me with an expression that landed somewhere between amusement and curiosity. "So, you've been asking questions on your own. I suppose that means you're every bit the sleuth they say you are."

"'They say?' Who are *they*?"

He gave me a broad grin. "I think I'll let you find out for yourself."

I felt my own lips twitch in return. Several clever replies popped into my head, but instead I merely asked, "Have you investigated this sailor?"

"Yes, a man of his description inquired about Alessio Pino at the Pearl of the Waves. He waited nearly half an hour, then left the tavern."

"Alessio was late because of the drunken gondolier."

"It would seem so."

"The sailor must have gone to seek Alessio at the opera house then."

"Very likely, but that avenue of inquiry is also at a standstill. All we know is that he appeared to be a seafaring man…" Messer Grande frowned as he swept his arm in a wide arc that took in a flotilla of boats on the canal and a host of foreigners crossing the bridge, all of whom had arrived aboard ship.

I sighed in frustration. "This entire situation is fraught with such difficulties. The murderer wore an ordinary disguise, wielded a common dagger. I suppose the bonds that restrained the dwarf were fashioned of cord you could find just about anywhere."

My companion nodded, and I continued. "What luck this killer has enjoyed. Besides all that, he somehow escaped the notice of everyone in the opera house except me."

"At least I have you," Messer Grande murmured with that amused, appraising look in his eyes.

"Yes, but I bring precious little to your investigation. How do you proceed on such scanty proofs?"

Messer Grande didn't seem near as dissatisfied as I. He smiled broadly. "I have my ways. Continue to assist me and you may learn some of them."

⟨⟩⟨⟩⟨⟩

Later that evening, I stretched out on the comfortable sofa in my dressing room at the Teatro San Marco and closed my eyes. Benito was moving through his customary preparations: hanging my costumes in proper order, mixing cold-creams and powders, laying out puffs, fine-pointed brushes, and crimson paste for my lips. Next door, Vittoria's agile gullet was moving through scales, and somewhere below, a violin sounded a mournful tune. Immersed in this familiar routine, I felt truly at peace for the first time since Zulietta's murder had thrown the theater into chaos.

I had taken leave from Messer Grande with difficulty. He insisted that we cross to Murano immediately. The dogged chief constable harbored grave suspicions concerning Alessio but would not turn his case over to the Avogaria for trial until he had exhausted all possible avenues of investigation. Something about the formidable Cesare Pino must have aroused Messer Grande's suspicions, because he wanted my assessment on the glassmaker's resemblance to the murderous masked figure. I had escaped a windy trip across the lagoon only by pleading that I must coddle my throat for the night's performance and giving my word that I would accompany him to Murano early tomorrow. He promised to call at my house with a boat.

My blessed calm was short-lived. A knock sounded on my door, and before Benito could cross the room to open it, Liya swept in, looking all the world like Titolino when he was trying—very hard—not to tell a secret. My head left the pillow. My feet hit the floor. As my wife enfolded me in a prolonged embrace, I could feel her heart hammering out a staccato beat.

Pushing me away to arm's length, Liya stammered, "I can't stay...I must get home...but I wanted to tell you...I saw Papa."

"And?" When my wife had fled Venice so many years ago, her mother vowed to have no more to do with Liya or the child she carried. Her father was not so hasty to disown his daughter—Pincas stored more loving kindness in his little finger than most people displayed in a lifetime—but Liya's rejection of her heritage and her devotion to Italy's ancient pagan religion tested even Pincas' loyalty.

"Papa was happy...actually happy to see me. He came running out of the back of the shop as soon as he heard my voice." Her eyes glittered with unshed tears. "He embraced me. He wanted to know all about Titolino. And how you are doing, of course."

"He must not be very happy with me." Over Liya's shoulder, I saw Benito nodding as he applied a curling iron to my third-act wig.

"Not very, *mio caro*. Papa admits he would rather see me married to a man from the ghetto, but he's indebted to you for rescuing Fortunata and me from the fire before I left home. He thinks a great deal of you...though he'll never understand why I want to live with an *evirato* who can never become his grandson's legal father."

I nodded as I squeezed Liya's arms. Pincas wasn't the only one. Most of the respectable Cannaregio housewives shunned our unorthodox household. These stern sentinels of virtue had little use for the opera. To them and their hardworking husbands, Liya would always be an apostate Jew with a bastard son and I an odd piece of theatrical riffraff. This was of little importance to me. I spent my days at the opera house, in a close-knit community that often ran counter to the established order. But I worried for Liya and Titolino's sake. The boy would soon be going to school. How would he be treated there?

Despite all that, I felt compelled to state the obvious: "As far as the ghetto and the rest of Venice are concerned, you and I are not married at all. Not a situation to warm a father's heart."

Liya's eyes glittered with more than tears. A peculiar smile played about her lips. "Papa did have something to say about that. I'll spare you the first part, but listen to his last words on the subject…" She paused to press a handkerchief to her lips. I knew this ploy; she was enjoying the advantage of superior knowledge, at least for the moment. Liya continued by repeating her father's words, "'At least you didn't follow the same path as Mina Grazziano.'"

That stumped me. Who was Mina Grazziano?

I tumbled to the answer just as Liya replied, "Silly! Mina is Zulietta. Or was. Her father was Davide Grazziano. He belonged to the same synagogue as my father."

"Belonged? Is he dead, too?"

She nodded. "Signora Grazziano was widowed some time ago, left with five daughters to provide for. Mina was the oldest and the most attractive. Not really pretty. But the girl had a way about her."

"You knew her?"

"In passing. Mina was about Sara's age. They weren't great friends, but still, if your sister knows someone, so do you."

"How did Mina become Zulietta?"

"That must have happened when I was living in Monteborgo." Liya's dark brows drew together. "Papa isn't clear on the details. He just knows that Signor Malpiero caused a scandal by taking Mina away from her family and installing her in his palazzo."

"We must find out more," I said excitedly. At that instant, the approaching performance of *Armida* was the farthest thing from my mind. If the massive ghetto gates hadn't already been locked for an hour or more, I would have set off to find Zulietta's family right then.

"Already arranged," my lovely wife replied as she gathered her *zendale* over her head. "First thing tomorrow, we'll visit the ghetto. Papa has promised to take us to talk with Signora Grazziano. His confraternity from the synagogue has contributed generously to her upkeep, so she will hardly refuse."

I took a loud gulp. "First thing tomorrow? You and I?"

"Why, yes. Papa wants to go after prayers, but before the shop gets busy. Surely Maestro Torani won't have you rehearsing that early."

"No, not Torani. It's Messer Grande that requires my presence." I explained briefly.

"Tito, no. You must come with me—since Papa has been good enough to include you in this favor. We must both visit Mina…er, Zulietta's mother." Liya regarded me intently, clasping the ends of the *zendale* under her chin. There was more here than idle curiosity, more than reuniting with her father. Liya appeared to be as interested in this case as I was. "Besides," she finished, almost accusingly, "you're the one who notices things, who always seems to ask the right questions."

I raised my hands in a placating gesture. "Then calm your worries, *cara*. I'll be at your side."

"But how? You can't cross Messer Grande. If he has ordered—"

I took Liya in my arms and stopped her questions by kissing her mouth. By the time she left, I'd promised that I would hold off Messer Grande and we would pass into the ghetto as soon as the gates opened on the morrow.

Benito joined me as I stood at the door watching my wife hurry down the corridor dodging ballet girls and spear carriers. "Did I miss something, Master?"

"I doubt it," I sighed, bracing my hands against the doorjamb. "You rarely do."

"But I must have"—he draped a towel around my neck and gestured toward my dressing table—"because I don't recall you perfecting the trick of being in two places at once."

Chapter Six

The passage of another hour found me pacing the wings, mentally entering the character of the hot-blooded crusader Rinaldo. Murder or no murder, curtains must rise as scheduled and singers must be costumed and in good voice. For most of the first act, I managed to put thoughts of Zulietta and Alessio and Messer Grande aside. I bathed the house in impassioned song and gave Maestro Torani's opera every credit it deserved. The rest of the cast also did their best, and our maestro drowned his wig in tears of joy when the audience responded with the same explosive frenzy which had greeted the previous night's truncated performance.

It was near the end of the act when my sleuthing nature took hold. Emilio and I shared the stage, which had been designed to represent a sandy cove. Sweets for the eye abounded: most prominently, a dozen ballet girls whose legs were encased in glistening green fish tails. Mermaids, of course, lolling on the sand and combing their unbound locks. Behind them, machinery concealed below stage caused a trio of elongated cylinders to rotate; their blue and silver coverings simulated billows of the sea with astonishing reality. As Emilio warbled through a lengthy recitative and aria describing our journey to find the wise hermit who would provide magical tools to defeat Armida, all I had to do was assume a graceful pose on a sturdy papier-mâché boulder and keep my mouth shut.

Well and good, except that in my case, locked lips give rise to a busy brain. Emilio had completed only a few bars before my gaze strayed beyond the footlights.

At first, only insignificant details met my eye: fluttering fans, a *grappa* seller weaving his way through the pit, twinkling flames reflected by a multitude of opera glasses. Then I took stock more closely, beginning with the upper tiers.

Torani had mentioned that the family of Alessio's intended bride occupied a box directly above Messer Grande's. The chief constable was wearing his bright red robe of office, so despite his beaked mask, I spotted him sitting with several other dignitaries, halfway along the left. I wondered if I should send up a note explaining that urgent business would prevent me from visiting Murano as planned, then thought better of it. Messer Grande would not be put off so easily. I would have to come up with something better, but just now I was anxious to study the Albergati family.

One tier above Messer Grande, a pasty-faced wisp of a girl was tucked between a pair of grim patricians. While Signor and Signora Albergati sat bolt upright, unmasked, barely glancing toward the stage, the girl followed Emilio's performance as if entranced. She swayed to the music and once or twice put a hand on her heart as if truly moved. Behind this mismatched trio, several tall young men shifted about the depths of the box, pouring liquid refreshment and taking snuff. Ah, the brothers. Had one of them been given the charge of dispensing with the meddlesome Zulietta? A priest was hovering, too. I could just make out his black-and-white vestments.

I adjusted my pose on the boulder, mildly surprised. Given the rampant gossip over Zulietta's murder, I would have expected the Albergati family to forego their evening at the opera, or at least close their curtains halfway. Scanning the pit, I saw fingers pointing in their direction, and among their luxuriously seated neighbors, more opera glasses were trained on the Albergati box than on the stage.

Mama and Papa must be made of stern stuff. And Maria? The pale-as-porridge miss grasped the railing as if she meant to vault herself onstage with the object of her adoration. If this was truly Maria, she was either a genius at behaving as if nothing out of the ordinary had occurred, or the arrest of her former fiancé had played little sport with her emotions.

As Emilio moved downstage to deliver what, for him, would be a thrilling finish to his aria, I shot my gaze to the opposite side of the auditorium. On the first tier, La Samsona appeared to be keeping up a lively banter with several dandies on the floor. Her voluptuous bosom was all but exposed as she leaned over to take a small bunch of posies. She made a great show of deciding whether to tuck it behind her ear or down her bodice, and her admirers applauded when the flowers found a home between her breasts.

A mere flick of the eyelids raised my focus to the fourth-tier box where Zulietta had been stabbed. The murder box, as I thought of it now. Someone had replaced the curtain the poor woman had clutched in her fall; the crimson panels were drawn tight.

A mask, I said to myself, the curtains make a crimson mask that conceals the box's secrets as surely as the *bauta* hid the killer's identity. But one thing couldn't be concealed. The murder box was only the fifth along the right-hand side of the horseshoe that made up the auditorium, and La Samsona held court from the third box on the first tier. From her door, it was only steps to the staircase that gave access to the upper tiers. Perhaps Madame Dumas had the right idea. Moving swiftly, the oversized courtesan could have covered the space between those boxes in less than five minutes.

A burst of raucous approval from Emilio's claque put an end to my musings. As I eased off my boulder and strolled upstage to take my place for my next aria—which I intended to put his to some considerable shame—I decided to pay La Samsona a visit.

During the second interval, the mermaids would shed their tails and treat the audience to an extended ballet. The perfect opportunity.

‹›‹›‹›

Maestro Torani considered it bad form for singers to mingle with the audience during the intervals. Still, it was a frequent practice; keeping fame-drunk singers from their admirers was roughly as successful as trapping an eel in a tuna net. Just last season Emilio had left the stage—fully costumed, mind—and popped up in the box of a certain lady where he ostentatiously balanced a hip on the railing and laughed during my finest embellishments. Torani had docked him a week's pay.

I hoped to avoid that fate by donning a disguise of sorts. Once Benito had hastily readied me for the third act, I threw a light cloak over my costume, tied a white satin mask over the upper part of my face, and slipped through the pass door while the maestro was closeted with the box office manager.

Liveried servants whisked up and down the stairway. The curving corridors were a pandemonium of din and feminine conversation. While many of the men remained seated to admire the graceful limbs of the dancers, the women were on the move, shifting from box to box, intent on paying as many social calls as possible. As I threaded my way through panniered skirts of satin and silk, a few ladies recognized me despite my mask and insisted on delivering a compliment on my performance. By thanking them with only a brush of my lips on their hands and moving with determination, I reached La Samsona's box with a good twenty minutes to spare before I had to return backstage.

A willowy footman in snug, cherry-red livery answered my knock. The box was dim, as the curtains were half-drawn and only one of the wall sconces was aflame. At first the footman attempted to dismiss me with a sneer and a firm shake of his proud head. "My mistress is already engaged."

I insisted, making my high, melodic voice carry to the woman who occupied a low armchair angled well back from the rail. A man in a devil's mask sat close at her side. His arm was buried in her skirts up to his elbow. She pushed him away and asked over her shoulder, "Who is it, Lelio?"

I lowered my mask.

"It is S…Signor Tito Amato," the footman stammered, no longer quite so sure of himself.

It took only a moment for La Samsona to dismiss her companion and welcome me to the seat still warm from his backside. In the midst of exchanging the usual courtesies, she ordered, "Lelio, pour Signor Amato a glass of wine. Fetch some *mandorlato*. And," she paused to send me a sidelong, heavy-lidded look, "do close the curtains all the way."

From a small cabinet, the footman produced a silver dish of almond nougat and two glasses of Cyprus wine. As he deposited these on a tripod table before us, La Samsona leaned over to lay a hand on my sleeve. My nose was assaulted by her heavy scent—attar of roses. I ducked my chin. The long fingers that dug into my forearm sported three huge gemstone rings. I wondered if they were real or paste. I was no jeweler, but they looked damned fine to me. I could say the same of the diamond bracelet encircling the wrist that was decidedly thick and sinewy for my taste. But the lady was speaking, and I had better pay attention.

"…so pleased you've given me this opportunity to tell you how much enjoyment your performances have afforded me. Perhaps you'll allow me to repay you in some small way. I am also famous for certain talents."

Momentarily speechless, I felt her hand shift from my sleeve to stroke the silk of my breeches. I captured that hand with my own and locked my gaze on eyes as brilliant as the settings of her rings. They shone from a face defined by high cheekbones, a prominent nose, and a strong rounded chin decorated with a heart-shaped patch. If La Samsona's features had not been as perfectly symmetrical as a classical statue, they would have been overwhelming. As it was, they were simply magnificent, the goddess Athena walking among mortals.

I removed the goddess' roving hand firmly to her lap and said, perhaps a bit too bluntly, "I came to discuss Zulietta Giardino."

La Samsona sank back against her cushion and rearranged the flowers at her bosom. Their gay colors fought with the multihued beads and spangles encrusting the bodice of her lilac gown. She gazed at me with a thoughtful expression. "Oh, dear, have I got it all wrong? Are you like the lead castrato at the San Benedetto? More fond of boys than women?"

I shook my head. "Believe me, dear lady, I'm only here to ask a few questions regarding your friend Zulietta. She was your friend, was she not?"

Was it my imagination that La Samsona stiffened a bit? She covered whatever emotion my statement produced by reaching for her glass and taking a long drink. "You're merely indulging an appetite for scandal? I confess I'm disappointed in you, Signor Amato. I'm also getting tired of answering questions about that silly little wager. It was not nearly so important as people want to make out."

"This isn't an idle visit. I have a pressing interest in Zulietta's murder, and I think you can help me if you will."

She narrowed her eyes and took another generous draft of wine. "Go on."

"Did you realize that Zulietta was on the verge of winning your wager?"

"I judged it couldn't be too long. Zulietta and I met on the field of combat, and the better woman prevailed. I would reproach myself except that the affair took a turn I could hardly have expected."

"What's that?"

"I launched into the contest as an amusement, a mere dalliance. But Zulietta fell in love. She actually lost her heart to Alessio Pino, and that great child gave every sign of being equally besotted."

"Love often flares up quickly and just as quickly fades," I observed.

"Not for that pair. They saw no one but each other and parted with the greatest difficulty. When last we met, Zulietta assured me Alessio was determined to have her as his wife."

"If she meant to marry him, why didn't she call off the wager?"

La Samsona took up her fan, unfurled it, and cooled her cheeks languidly. I couldn't help but notice that this courtesan's fan was painted with a perfectly respectable hunting scene. Or was it? Were the men on horses chasing a stag or an unclad nymph? Difficult to tell in the dimness.

"I don't know, but she didn't. Our pact was signed and sealed and very much in force." The fan halted for the space of a heartbeat. "Perhaps Zulietta wanted to offer my jewels to Alessio as her dowry. Can you imagine? A Hebrew who had been on the town for years and a glassmaker of Alessio's standing, practically royalty in that little world of Murano? Such a match is unheard of, impossible, but my friend—yes, I counted Zulietta as a friend—believed that true love could triumph over all. You'd think she would have learned by now. Poor thing—I would never have begrudged her a few baubles if the affair could bring her happiness."

"That's very generous." I gave her rings a pointed look, then the rope of pearls around her neck. "And hard to believe. The jewels you're wearing tonight must be worth a fortune. I can only imagine what you must have at home."

She snapped the fan shut and drew it through her hand several times. If I chose to consider this gesture a silent message in the fashionable language of the fan, La Samsona was ordering me to withdraw. But I stayed where I was; this woman was not one to hold her tongue and let her fan do the talking. She confirmed my impression by throwing her head back and laughing with a donkey's bray. She continued on a chuckle, "We have only a slight acquaintance, Signor Amato, so I'll forgive you for thinking I'm a fool. The wager specifically entitled Zulietta to the jewels on my person and in the casket in my bedchamber. When I saw how the wind was blowing, I took steps…"

Tossing her fan on the table, La Samsona rose and went to open the door. She summoned the footman who had retreated to the corridor.

"More wine, mistress?"

"No, Lelio." She favored him with a doting smile. "I want you to tell Signor Amato where I sent you Thursday last."

Without missing a beat, he faced me and replied, "The Banco Giro, Signore."

"And what was the burden you carried?" At his hesitation, she encouraged, "It's all right. Just answer the question."

"A lockbox containing your very best jewels."

"Tell him what they did with the box."

"The director of the bank took charge of it himself. He locked it in their vault."

"Thank you, Lelio. You may withdraw."

She swept back and seated herself with a whisper of lilac skirts. Reclaiming her fan, she asked, "Does that satisfy you? Or do you still think I murdered my friend to keep her hands off my remaining trinkets?"

I took a deep breath, thrown off balance by her forthright manner.

La Samsona regarded me severely. Her face was now all angles, her eyes stormy, and she tapped her closed fan against her left ear. I didn't mistake the fan's gesture this time. It meant *I wish to be rid of you.* I was also aware of the ballet music drawing to a close; Maestro Torani would have my head if I wasn't onstage in five minutes.

I stood, made my bow, and murmured apologies for my intrusion. Her frown turned to a smile at the very last moment. She said, "I don't know why you're so interested in Zulietta's death, but you've got on the wrong track. I advise you to take a look at Cesare Pino. To prevent Alessio going astray, his father would have murdered the Doge himself."

"I thought Cesare didn't come to the opera."

"He was here last night."

"You saw him?"

She nodded. "On the main staircase, going up."

"Are you sure?"

"Absolutely. He wore no mask and his face is unmistakable."

I stepped to the front of the box and cracked the curtains. The last ballerina was disappearing into the wings. The orchestra

was silent, but I heard angry shouting and stomping at the back
of the house.

A fight had broken out in the pit! Men raised their fists. Women
stooped over, searching the floor for hard candle stubs or rotten
fruit to use as missiles. What excellent good fortune! If the fight
spread, it might afford me another five or ten minutes.

Returning swiftly to the courtesan's side, I sank back
in my chair and clutched her arm. "What do you mean?
Unmistakable?"

La Samsona yawned, exposing a set of teeth a mule would
have envied. She was toying with me, this infuriating woman.
Life must be just one unceasing game for her.

"Please," I cried, "this is serious. How did you recognize
Cesare Pino and when was this?"

She shook her arm from my grasp and let her hand stray to
pick at the flowers at her bosom, smiling all the while.

I had one more card up my sleeve. "Beautiful *signora*, if you
truly enjoy my singing, let your answer be my reward."

Her smile turned to another braying laugh, and she rolled
her eyes. "Oh, very well. Fair's fair, I suppose. Vittoria Busanti
had just commenced singing when I spotted Cesare. And I
recognized him because anyone would. He had an accident at
his kiln some years ago—it damaged one of his eyes and made
a horrible mess of his forehead." She gave a dramatic shudder.
"Now, aren't you supposed to be somewhere else?"

I certainly was, but I couldn't help wondering what La
Samsona had been doing out of her box when she'd observed
Cesare Pino.

I posed that question aloud. It hung in the air unanswered.

"Lelio," the courtesan drawled as she reached for a morsel
of *mandorlato*. "You'd better see Signor Amato out before he
misses his cue."

〈〉〈〉〈〉

As I pushed through the corridor crowded with servants removing the remains of suppers and latecomers rushing in from rival
theaters, I was so intent on getting backstage for my entrance

that I almost missed Pamarino. If the dwarf had not spoken first, I would have tripped right over him.

"Signor Amato," he cried. "Aren't you on the wrong side of the curtain?"

"For the moment, but…ah…" I stammered to a pause, surprised at the meeting, unsure what to say to the stumpy creature in the blue poplin jacket festooned with silver epaulets and military-style buttons. Benito was right—he did look like one of the wide-mouthed soldier figurines people give to children.

Pamarino relieved me of my discomfort. Tipping his chin back, he said, "I suppose you wonder what I'm doing at the theater tonight."

"Well…yes." I shrugged off my cloak and draped it over my arm, ready to throw it to Benito who would be waiting at the pass door with my helmet. My flimsy mask was already tucked inside my tunic.

"I couldn't stay away. This was the last place I saw my mistress alive…" A spasm of grief passed over his face like a cloud scudding across the full moon.

I began to understand what Messer Grande had known all along. Absurd as it may seem, the dwarf had been in love with Zulietta. He was haunting the corridors, mourning his beautiful mistress.

Pamarino continued. "I last heard her laugh on the stairs over there…last felt her hand on my shoulder in the box above." The corners of his mouth turned down; his brow furrowed.

"What will you do now that she's gone?" The doors that would open for a dwarf must be few, indeed. If Pamarino had some acrobatic skills he might find work as an entertainer. Otherwise, he would be as useless as a castrato with no voice.

His reply was a forlorn whisper. "My mind is in turmoil. I can't even think—"

A blast of trumpets sounded through the open doors of nearby boxes, my signal to run. "I must go," I said, giving him a clumsy pat on his shoulder. "*Addio* and good luck."

I'm ashamed to say that as I sprinted backstage, I spared no further thought for the sad little man. The aria that opened

Act Three was the only thing on my mind as I bumbled into the wings, searching their dim depths for my manservant. But Benito was nowhere to be found. No time to wonder why. I spied my helmet on a handy bench and crammed it on my head. Under Maestro Torani's baleful gaze, I took a deep breath and transformed myself into the hero Rinaldo as I passed from shadow to the glare of the footlights.

It was a technique I should try more often: my hurried entrance left no opportunity for the stage terrors that often sapped my strength and focus. Relieved of all constraint, I sang that aria with a heartrending power that was almost eerie. As I made my exit to cheers and applause, Maestro Torani stopped me by a bank of coiled ropes and sandbags, a scroll of music clutched tightly in his hand. He raised it like a schoolmaster's cane, in mock severity.

"A triumph, Tito! But, by God, don't ever cut it so close again. One more minute and I would have been forced to send the ballet girls back on." He jerked his full-bottomed wig from his head. "Your and Emilio's antics will put me in my grave one of these days."

I hung my head, a rush of shame contending with pride over my performance. The last thing I wanted to do was cause Torani worry or discomfort. He had always been a staunch ally in misadventures both musical and not. And hearing him lump me in with the feckless Emilio—galling!

"I apologize most profusely, Maestro. You may—"

He cut me off by spinning me back toward the stage where flowers were accumulating and applause still reigned. "Save it. Give them the last bit once again and keep your mind on your business. If you ever needed any reminder that music should trump sleuthing, this should be it."

‹›‹›‹›

When I finally reached my dressing room, Benito was ironing pleats into a neckcloth as if nothing had happened.

"Where were you?" I cried, tossing my helmet on the sofa and ripping at the laces and buttons of my costume.

"No need for that." Several buttons bounced off the floor as my manservant sprinted to my side and brushed my hands away. "Madame Dumas will have both our heads if you tear this tunic, too."

If I expected Benito to assume an air of contrition, I was sadly mistaken. Birth or early experiences had stamped his tempo mark as *moderato*; extreme passions were beyond him, and on the rare occasion when he was less than calm and collected, I knew something had to be dreadfully wrong.

While I was steaming, my delicate manservant hummed the melody from my last aria and removed my padded soldier's armor. I began to calm down as he applied deft hands to the tunic and breeches beneath. Then he floated a dressing gown over my bare skin and sat me down at my dressing table. "Close your eyes," he murmured.

I complied and felt the warm weight of my wig rising from my head. Benito released my own hair from its skullcap, and I was soon relaxing under the gentle pull of the brush through my locks.

"Are you ready to hear my story?" he asked.

I cracked one eye open. In the mirror, Benito's reflection was solemn.

"Yes," I whispered.

"Very well. I was waiting at the pass door as you instructed when a woman came through. Not a gentlewoman, but a maid or companion—one tooth in her mouth, as old as God himself, and obviously no idea how to proceed. She was clutching a sealed message."

"A note of assignation, I suppose."

"Such was my deduction. She wandered about tripping over props, nearly getting herself felled by flying scenery, and enduring the curses of stagehands until she could stand it no longer. The poor old thing was actually crying when I reached her. *Where is the castrato? I must see the castrato who sang so well in the last scene,*' she said. 'Not here,' I answered, 'but he is my master. I'll give him that note if you wish.' She shoved it at me and scurried for the pass door like a frightened mouse."

I bent my head to one side as Benito worked at a tangle. "What is so important about this note? We receive those confounded pleas by the boatload."

"See for yourself. It's right there."

I reached for the folded paper resting against a bottle of lavender water. The wax seal had been broken in two. I raised an eyebrow.

Benito responded with a chuckling, sexless laugh. "I took the liberty." He laid the hairbrush down and stepped away to smooth the folds of the costume I would wear in the fourth act.

Shaking my head, I quickly scanned the few lines penned in a slanting schoolbook hand. *My Thrice-Dear Emiliano,* they began, *Just addressing you under such secrecy makes my pen quiver.* The lady went on to praise my rival's singing, express her longing to see him again, and set a time to see him on the morrow. She must be a very young lady indeed, or a wife more carefully watched than most; the best she had to offer was a coffee at a café on a small, out-of-the-way square in the San Barnaba district. The note was signed with a curlicued "M."

"So, you took delivery by mistake." I held the note up between two fingers. "You had better take this along to Emilio or there'll be one very lonely lady at the Café Rosa tomorrow."

"I thought you might want to go in Emilio's place."

"What?"

Benito moved to clasp my shoulders and regard me in the mirror flanked by wavering oil lamps. Bending, he placed his head so close to mine that our cheeks touched. "You missed me when you came backstage because I'd gone to track down the elderly maid. It took me a while, but I finally found her, sitting at the back of a very aristocratic box. Would you like to guess whose?"

"Oh, Benito." I felt the blood course through my veins. "Could it be?"

He grinned. "It certainly could. 'M' is Maria Albergati."

Chapter Seven

The next day dawned sunny and unseasonably warm. Liya and I welcomed it by taking our chocolate and rolls on the little balcony attached to our bedchamber. Bathed in the soft, golden October sunshine, we stretched and rubbed our eyes and lazily came to life.

My activities of the night before had driven Messer Grande's impending visit from my mind. Now I must decide how I was going to row over to Murano, visit the ghetto, and take coffee with Maria on the other side of the Grand Canal within the space of several short hours. I was grumpy as an old bear until Liya coaxed me to talk of Titolino. The boy had recovered from his cough and was begging to see the menagerie of African beasts on display for Carnevale.

"Will you take him?" Liya asked, running her fingers through her sleep-tumbled tresses. "Since Gussie and Annetta left for England, he's missed his playmate Matteo so very much. He would love to have an outing with you."

"I suppose." If my reply was less than enthusiastic, it was only because of my preoccupation, and perhaps because the traditional amusements struck me as frenzied and excessive of late. Casting restraint aside for a fortnight could be delicious fun, but our six-month celebration had changed my city for the worse.

Much of Venice had become dirty and foul-smelling, her beautiful buildings hung with a gaudy riot of banners and notice-boards, her pavements and waterways crowded with merrymakers made bold by the masks that hid their identities. I'd rather spend my leisure time in our quiet Cannaregio with its rows of neat houses, fresh lagoon breeze, and market stalls where familiar dealers sold melons and pumpkins to housewives who had no use for disguise.

I jerked up from my slouch to sit very straight. I was becoming my father, I realized with shame, the fastidious Isidore Amato who I'd often heard rail against the indecencies of the younger generation. The man who could never be bothered to cast aside the worries of his work as the Mendicanti's organ master. Of course Titolino wanted to see the rhinoceros; everything was a wonder to his seven-year-old eyes. I answered in a hearty tone. "Yes, absolutely. I'll take the boy down to the Piazza at the first opportunity."

But my wife had gone on to fret about something else. "I wonder if Mama will come down to the shop," Liya said, tearing off small bits of bread and rolling them between her fingers.

Ah, I expected my wife would bring up our ghetto visit sooner or later. I sank back in my chair. "Do you want her to?" I asked cautiously.

Liya pushed her plate away and turned to stare down at the thread of water that passed alongside our house. A gondola floated lazily by, its sides barely clearing the walls. It carried a corpulent man dressed entirely in black who stroked a small yellow dog on his lap. As if the dog sensed Liya's intense gaze, it bounced up with ruffled fur and barked in furious displeasure. The boatman laid on his oar and bent his knee. Pushing his boot against the adjacent wall, he propelled the vessel forward into shadow.

"No, Mama can stay upstairs for all I care." Liya grimaced. "Yesterday at the shop, Fortunata was as sweet as clover honey, and Papa almost so, but I know Mama's ways. She never forgets or forgives, and I'm certain the years haven't dulled her sharp tongue. I'd just as soon not face her…for now, at least."

"You should have nothing to fear, *carissima*. You're a grown woman with your own household. Her tongue can't wound you unless you allow it."

"Of course, you're right." Smiling now, she reached across the white tablecloth to squeeze my hand. "As you so often are."

"What? Not always?"

She tossed her head, flipped my hand away, and again changed the subject. "The cards were very promising for our expedition."

"What did they say?" I asked, tipping the chocolate pot to refill both our cups.

As Liya's gaze lit on the curl of steam rising from her cup, her eyes took on the dreamy look they displayed when she was staring into her scrying pot. Her voice became husky and deep. "They described a man who hides his upright character behind a disguise…and a woman who does the opposite."

Wonderful. Why did Liya's oracles always have to be so obscure? If only they would hit upon some hard facts for a change. But I knew better to express open criticism. Instead, I merely cradled my warm cup in my hands and said, "I'll be happy to simply learn more about Zulietta. I've always believed that people sow the seeds of their own misfortune. Perhaps something will come to light that will help us find her killer."

Liya sent me a thoughtful nod, then noticed the maid hovering by the door. "What is it, Angelina?" she asked sharply. Liya had hired the girl only last month. Fourteen, shy, and so afraid of giving offense, Angelina was barely able to attend to her duties. She was the exact opposite of Todi, our cook, who bullied everyone from Benito to the kitchen cat.

"*Scusi*, mistress." She twisted her fingers around a corner of her apron. "Visitors at the door."

"Their names?" Liya asked, clearly annoyed at any interruption that would delay our promised errand.

Angelina's thin face scrunched up in distress. "It's Messer Grande. He has two constables with him."

The moment I'd been dreading had arrived. And me with not the flimsiest idea of what I was going to do.

"Tito—" Liya began ominously.

I hurried downstairs with my dressing gown flapping around my calves. Mindful of the aristocratic doors that had been slammed in Messer Grande's face, I invited him and his officers into the salon. When he refused to enter the house, citing the pressure of fleeting time, I was forced to explain my predicament on the pavement. I'd barely begun when a window grated open somewhere to my left. Ah, the wife of the silk merchant next door. Though she always turned her head away if she chanced to pass Liya or me on the street, the woman took an active interest in our affairs. Surprisingly, my conversation with the chief constable proceeded with ease. Signora Zeno wouldn't be able to spread the gossip that I'd been carted off to the guardhouse this time.

"I understand," Messer Grande told me after a throaty chuckle. "My wife often assigns me errands of great importance, as well. I find it saves time in the end to simply comply with her wishes and get them over with. Actually, this development may work to our advantage."

Our advantage? Somehow I had become an undeputized assistant to the chief of Venice's constabulary. Not a post I had ever envisioned holding.

Messer Grande paused as he took in my expression. He gestured in the direction of the ghetto with an ingratiating smile. "I've already paid an official visit to the widow Grazziano. As you can imagine, the good woman gave me short shrift. Her daughter's behavior has been a great embarrassment that she would rather not discuss, especially with an outsider. But…" Here he crossed his arms, hoisted his eyebrows up his high forehead, and regarded me as he had the juicy melons at the market. "You have a connection, my dear fellow, the perfect entrée to the widow's apartment. As she's over the first shock, the moment may be favorable to elicit her confidences. Let me see, is that your gondolier?" He gestured toward Luigi, who was dawdling on the quay across the tiny *campo*.

I nodded wordlessly. Within minutes I had been issued new marching orders: wrest all the information I could from Signora Grazziano, then have Luigi row me over to Murano where Messer Grande and I would have that delayed interview with Cesare Pino. Somehow I would also have to make time to meet Maria.

Was I the only one who remembered I had a four-act opera to sing that evening?

The stout wooden gates of the ghetto were flanked by Christian guards whose pay, Liya had once told me, fell on the shoulders of the Hebrew community. As we stepped through those open portals, we entered a city within a city.

This area, which had once played host to an iron foundry, was riddled with narrow passages overshadowed by tall buildings with scaling plaster and broken window shutters. The few open squares could barely contain the activity that swirled within. Every necessity of life had its own shop: bread, greens, fruit, wine, meat, and cheese. With space at a premium, much of life was lived outdoors. A profusion of accents and alien tongues met my ears as women bargained over goods spilling from doorways and men conducted learned discussions in tight, intense circles.

Since the ghetto's inhabitants had landed there from all four corners of the globe, I wasn't surprised to pass several proud descendants of Spanish Jewry speaking Castilian or catch sight of a fellow in caftan and turban following us down the alley. With a flap of his headgear drawn across the lower part of his swarthy face, he looked as if he could have been miraculously transported from the Holy Land. We also rubbed shoulders with plenty of my fellow Christians who had come to the ghetto to either leave an item in pawn, if their purse was empty, or get it out again if they were flush with coin.

With Liya in the lead, we crossed a small *campo* dominated by the plain stone façade of the Spanish synagogue and made several left turns to reach an even narrower passageway where the air was full of goose feathers floating like ragged snowflakes. We were getting close. I recalled that the poultry shop was just a few doors down from Pincas Del'Vecchio's place.

Liya's father was waiting in the doorway. I had last seen him before my ill-fated visit to Rome several years ago, when I was accustomed to dropping in at his shop to see if there was any news from his errant daughter. Once I'd found his wandering Liya and taken her as my wife, I'd been made to feel that I had stolen his greatest treasure and the friendly visits ceased. I was thus relieved when he hailed us with loud exclamations of welcome. No sneaking us past the neighbors. The eldest daughter of the house had returned, and Pincas wanted everyone to share his joy. In the crowded passageway, I saw faces turn toward us, many wearing smiles, some not.

"You look well," he told me after he'd embraced Liya. Then he rose on tiptoe to kiss both my cheeks.

Somewhat surprised, I returned his greeting. "As do you, Signore. Business must be good."

With pride, Pincas nodded toward the jackets and waistcoats hanging from a line tacked to the side of the building. Linen shirts and neckcloths were piled in baskets on either side of the entrance, and through the open doorway, I could see shelves and racks bulging with all manner of finery. As he always had, my jowly, rotund father-in-law wore a coat and wig in the style of the day before yesterday, preferring to save more fashionable wares for his customers. Unfortunately, he was also still using his oily, overly sweet-smelling pomade; it formed a cloying stew with the odor of simmering goose fat wafting from the poulterer's. I slipped my scented handkerchief from an inside pocket and dabbed it to my nose.

Pincas asked if we required any refreshment, gesturing toward a tiny café at the end of the alley. I declined politely, citing our eagerness to interview the widow Grazziano and privately mulling how I could speed my first errand of the morning along. We'd turned to go back the way we'd come when our mission was immediately forestalled by Fortunata darting out of the shop, intent on saying her helloes. The doll-like girl that I remembered had grown into a beautiful young woman. How old was she now? Twelve? Thirteen? With her striking indigo gown and dark hair fastened up with gold pins, she reminded me of Liya when I'd first met her as she peddled masks and headdresses at the Teatro San Marco so many years ago.

As the sisters chattered, Pincas pulled me to one side and leaned a shoulder against the plastered wall across the way. At first I wondered why he had not invited us into the shop, but then I noticed the open window on the floor above and the curtain twitching despite the still, sultry air. Pincas may have stiffened his spine sufficiently to welcome his daughter, but I'd wager he was still very much under the thumb of his ungovernable wife who obviously wanted to observe her daughter and her capon of a husband without being seen. Yes, out of the corner of my eye, I caught the watchful figure garbed in black.

"It was shocking to hear of Mina's death—so violent and in such a public place," Pincas was saying in his slightly guttural accent. "But then, Mina Grazziano never did anything by halves."

"Did you know her well?" I asked, trying to picture the woman I thought of as Zulietta Giardino existing within the stifling confines of the ghetto.

He nodded. "Her father was a friend of long standing. I remember when Mina was born—Davide nearly burst with pride and gratitude. He and Esther had been married for six years and despaired of ever having a child." Pincas gave a short chuckle. "We always joked that when the Lord got around to sending us daughters, he kept his hand on the pump."

"Liya guessed that Mina had five sisters."

"That's right. The youngest two are still at home, one married a man of the ghetto, and the others married a pair of cousins from Livorno." He sighed and massaged the excess flesh above his frayed collar. "I always feared Mina would come to grief. Davide made a terrible mistake, you see."

"Ye-es," I replied in a tone that let him know he had my full attention.

"Perhaps because she was the answer to his prayers, Davide worshiped his little Mina. He put her on a pedestal and expected her mother and sisters to pay her the same homage. She was petted, indulged, given extravagant presents..." He shook his head sadly. "She ruled the household until a sudden attack of apoplexy carried Davide off. Then she had to fall back on those she'd always put in the shade."

"How old was she when he died?"

"Sixteen. As sharp as a needle, handy with ruses, and already pretty enough to turn every man's head."

"Ruses?"

"Let me just say that Mina told the truth only so long as it was convenient. When the truth became tedious, she invented a story that was more to her liking, generally one in which she took center stage."

"No wonder these walls couldn't hold her."

"It was more than sheer willfulness that led her astray." Pincas frowned and pushed off the wall. "But the rest of the tale is best told by Esther. It's time we go to meet her, don't you think?"

After bestowing kisses all around, Fortunata returned to her shop counter. Liya and I followed Pincas out the way we had come. I looked back at Signora Del'Vecchio's observation post just in time to see the corner of the curtain fall back into place. I also noted something else as we passed the poultry shop. Tucked behind three jocular youths who sat plucking feathers from the limp bodies of geese was a dark gentleman in turban and robe. The very same, I was certain, who had dogged our steps from the entrance gates.

"Without a dowry, what sort of respectable marriage could she make?" Signora Grazziano shifted her gaze from Liya to me, then to Pincas.

She looked older than most other women I knew to be in their fifth decade. Where my theatrical colleagues were skilled in creating the illusion of youth, Zulietta's—or Mina's—mother seemed unconcerned. Her wrinkled face was bare of paint or powder, tendrils of silver-streaked hair escaped an untidy bun, and her massive hips filled every inch of the wide armchair.

Pincas was not an easily angered man, so it startled me when he shook a fist and nearly shouted, "The confraternity provided funds for your daughters' dowries in addition to making sure you had this roof over your heads. There was no reason for you to hand Mina over to Signor Malpiero."

A clay pipe with a goose quill mouthpiece lay between the lady's fingers. She took several fierce puffs before answering. The smoke smelled like burning rags. "Two rooms for me and my daughters still at home. And two windows no larger than the bunghole of a wine cask. Is this what you call living?"

I followed her gaze around the tiny sitting room. It was stuffed with broken-down furniture, and in the corner, wet laundry hung from a rack set before a charcoal stove. Items of feminine attire dangled to the floor, and little rivulets of water ran from the tips of gray stockings across the bare, uneven floor. While the window was actually a good deal larger than a bunghole, the place was still dim and stuffy. And overheated. Whatever else the widow skimped on, it wasn't fuel for the stove.

"You could have managed better, Esther." Pincas was still fuming. "Davide would be heartsick to know that Mina turned her back on her people—and under such circumstances."

"Settle down, Pincas," Signora Grazziano said, "you know the price of eggs. When Davide dropped dead at his desk, he left us with only enough to last a month, if that. My husband must have believed he would live forever, or at least long enough to put money aside for the girls. My poor Davide could add three columns of figures in his head and never made a mistake in his ledger, but he seriously underestimated his allotted time on this earth."

Signora Grazziano drew herself up majestically, as if she were the bestower of charity, rather than the recipient. "We welcomed the synagogue's alms then—and still do—but you must admit they've barely been enough to keep a cat alive."

While Pincas harrumphed and continued to decry Mina's fate, it occurred to me that he was being uncharacteristically belligerent because Mina's desertion reminded him of Liya's. Back then, a generous ladle of tact and kindness could have prevented her flight to the mainland, but Pincas had bowed to his wife's unusual and vengeful dictum that Liya must relinquish the child she carried to one of the Christian convents. Of course, my brave, determined wife was having none of that. She found sanctuary in Monteborgo, a remote village tucked among the ridges and valleys of Italy's northern mountains where the inhabitants kept to the old ways and ancient gods.

Not for the first time, I considered how utterly destiny depends upon coincidence. If Liya's mother had not been so implacable, if Pincas had found the will to follow his own lights, Liya would probably still be keeping the counter at the used-clothing shop and Titolino would be growing up as an Elijah or Solomon of the ghetto.

I turned my attention to my wife. Liya's forehead was puckered, leading me to think this conversation was making her uncomfortable, as well. I reached across the narrow space that divided our hard chairs and clasped her hand. Answering with a squeeze, she settled our joined hands within the folds of her skirt.

Signora Grazziano had puffed at her pipe until the smoke wreathed her head in blue clouds. Now she cut Pincas off sharply. "Listen, if your esteemed confraternity had given me enough to get Mina married off properly, you wouldn't be complaining now and I wouldn't be mourning a dutiful daughter. I know of six or seven widows who receive twice what I'm given plus boxes of food on the doorstep every Friday morning. It wouldn't be this way if Davide hadn't been who he was. With only scraps to depend on, I went along with putting Davide's precious treasure where she could do us some good. It was the gold Mina brought in that married off her sisters. Was I not wise, after all?"

Pincas glowered; Signora Grazziano puffed. Both seemed to have forgotten Liya and me entirely. The building tension in the cramped room could have bowed the walls out.

Confused at the turn the conversation had taken, I squeezed Liya's hand and questioned her with a look. She leaned close. "Mina's father was the ghetto's tax assessor," Liya whispered into my ear. "Known to his friends as an honest, upright man, but nevertheless, you can't convince people that the tax assessor puts a fair value on their belongings."

I nodded, understanding. Taxes are always unfair to those who pay them. Though cruel and senseless, the congregation felt it was getting some of its own back on the tax assessor by slighting his widow. Human nature at its ugliest.

But we were drawing no closer to solving the mystery of Zulietta's murder. To break the Jews' impasse, I rose, crossed the small space between us, and went down on one knee before the angry widow. Skipping over superfluous details, I told her how I had witnessed the death of her daughter and that I felt honor bound to assist the authorities in finding the wretch who killed her.

She gazed at me for a moment, then tilted her chin back and blew a long, meditative curl of smoke toward the ceiling. Finally she responded, "They say her latest lover murdered her—a Signor Pino from Murano."

"That is by no means certain. I've met the young man. He professes the tenderest love for Zu—er, Mina and seems genuinely grieved."

The wrinkles deepened around her narrowed eyes. "What do you think, then? Who killed my daughter?"

"I haven't formed an opinion, but know there are others who wished her ill."

"Hmmm." Low and throaty, it was almost a moan. She shifted in her chair. "I can well believe that, but my good *signor*, how can I help you?"

"Please," I replied. "Simply tell me about Mina. About her life here in the ghetto and what you know of her situation in the wider world." Without breaking eye contact, I pushed up from my knee, pulled my chair close, and waited for enlightenment.

As a sterling example of silent support, Liya also rose and went to her father. Massaging his thick shoulders through the wool of his jacket, she stood ready to prevent any interruption he might offer.

Signora Grazziano had dropped pipe ash all over her lap; tiny round holes among the gray smudges gave evidence of past sparks. I was relieved when she set her pipe aside and shook her skirts out. "Mina was spoilt," she said as she settled back. "Davide led her to expect the finer things, and as long as he was alive, she had them. I warned him that such indulgence was bound to cause trouble down the road, but…" she shrugged. "For all that, you couldn't call Mina lazy or spendthrift. While her sisters helped me at home, she insisted on accompanying Davide on his rounds among the ghetto householders, and, if any business errand took him out into the city or down to the Piazza, our young princess was always ready to go. He gave her a leather-bound notebook when she was barely ten and dictated figures as they poked among our neighbors' possessions. By the time Davide died, Mina shared his head for business and knew the worth of a ducat better than most young men hereabouts."

Pincas was nodding. His expression had mellowed. "Mina was Davide's little shadow in truth. When he was felled so suddenly, it was like someone jerked the rug right out from under the girl." He pressed his lips together as Liya dug her slender fingers into his shoulders.

"Exactly so, Pincas," Signora Grazziano went on. "For several months after Davide's burial, our strong-willed Mina showed all the spirit of a boiled cabbage. Then Signor Malpiero came to call." She cocked an eyebrow at me. "Do you know anything of him?"

"Only what everyone knows." Among the patrician class, Malpiero had been the cream of the cream, a descendant of one of the original twelve tribunes who had elected our first Doge back when Venice was little more than a collection of mud flats.

On one hand, Signor Malpiero had been known for his intellectual pursuits. A fair poet, he frequented several literary salons and often penned selections of verse to open a fete or celebrate the election of a Senator or Procurator. In that vein, he also published pamphlets that espoused such revolutionary ideas as publicly funded education for any child willing to take advantage of it. On the other hand, his physical appetites were huge. Before he died several years ago, his reputation as a gourmand and shameless libertine had overshadowed his better qualities. None of his activities had taken him to the opera or involved him in my circle.

The widow continued, "As a Christian nobleman on the ghetto's Board of Overseers, Signor Malpiero often had business with my husband and never made a secret of his attraction to Mina. When he made his belated condolence visit, he brought me an armload of flowers—useless things! Did he think we could eat them?—but to Mina he brought a new hat. With a bright blue feather. Can you imagine a more inappropriate gesture?"

I shook my head. "Was Mina pleased with her hat?"

"Of course, greedy, shameless creature that she was. Though Malpiero must have been past fifty and already in ill health, she became infatuated with him. I suppose in some small way, his attentions made up for the absence of her father. When the old rogue offered to move her into his palazzo and provide dowries for her sisters, she barely hesitated, even after I explained what would be expected of her." Signora Grazziano paused to reach for her pipe but found that it had gone out.

"Rash," Pincas put in. "That's what Mina was. Headstrong and rash."

The widow nodded, still fiddling with her pipe. "So don't blame me, Pincas. I had the rabbi in to talk to her and she made his cheeks burn. 'My person is my own, and I shall do with it what I please,' she told him and flounced out of the room." Signora Grazziano shrugged. "What was left for me to do but make the best of a bad situation?"

"So Mina Grazziano became Zulietta Giardino when she was only sixteen," I observed.

"That's right. She made the conversion your Venice demands of those who leave the ghetto to dwell in the city, and so she needed a Christian name."

I nodded slowly. I'd toured the opera houses of Italy and Germany and even sung at Covent Garden in London. In comparison with other cities I'd visited, Venice treated her Jews well, but they were still regarded as foreigners, and with suspicion on account of opposing our faith, as well as their mysterious network of monetary ties.

Any Jew, male or female, adult or child, who wanted to live outside the walls and canals that ringed the ghetto had to pass through a certain religious house for instruction in Christian teaching and eventual baptism. Many did, if only to better their lot in matters of import or commerce—and a good proportion of those continued to practice their ancestral religion in secret. To join my household after our sojourn in Rome, my own Liya and Titolino had been forced to undergo this charade at the House of Catechumens.

I asked Signora Grazziano, "Was your daughter allowed to come back to visit?"

"Allowed, yes. Malpiero was quite liberal with her. Besides all her finery, he bought her books and taught her how to understand them. It was by her own choice that Mina barely set a foot through the gates these past eight years. She seemed content to go nowhere except in her protector's company, and the company Malpiero kept I don't even want to think about. Mina did do right by us, though. In addition to the dowries, she saw to it that the old reprobate sent a monthly purse by messenger." She nodded toward Pincas and spoke with a touch of relish. "That money went to keeping my two youngest in school—fat lot your precious confraternity cared about that."

Sensing another eruption coming on, I quickly asked, "Was Mina able to continue giving you money after Signor Malpiero died?"

"Yes. She was a good woman of business, you see. Davide could never have imagined the sort of business she would conduct, but he taught her well. Once she was on her own, she sent even larger purses. At first, a maid as black as the ace of spades brought them, then that ridiculous mannekin."

"Pamarino?"

"If that is what the misshapen creature calls himself," she replied. "I certainly wasn't going to strike up a conversation with him. He's like a golem in the old tales—a man that shouldn't even exist. But I mustn't complain. Gold is gold, whoever brings it. Over the past year, by being very careful, I eked out enough to set Aram up in business."

Pincas shook Liya's hands from his shoulders and sat forward. "That's something else I've been meaning to discuss with you, Esther. Aram is trolling in dangerous waters—"

"Wait," I cried, suddenly bewildered. "Who is Aram?"

Chapter Eight

"Aram is a shiftless wastrel who never did an honest day's work in his life." Pincas sprang up and began to pace the narrow floor space that was clear of furniture.

Signora Grazziano shook her head vigorously. "Aram Pardo is the husband of my daughter Reyna, Mina's next youngest sister. He also happens to be the cousin of my aunt's sister-in-law."

As I mentally unraveled those tangled relationships, the widow continued with a proud smile. "Aram does very well selling furniture and household goods from a shop on the main square." She sent a glare to the man pacing the floorboards. "And I'll thank you to speak of him with more respect, Pincas."

My father-in-law halted in his tracks. "If Aram earns my respect, well and good. So far he's done just the opposite. Do you know what he's doing with that shop you bought so dearly?"

The guarded expression on Signora Grazziano's face made me think she knew exactly what Pincas was talking about, but I could hardly wait for him to answer his own question.

"Aram has managed to open the bricked-up windows that overlook the canal at the rear of his building. When they're closed they look right and tight to the passing patrol boats, but when he swings them back, he has an unauthorized market. Goods go back and forth all night long, in between the patrol's rounds. Mind my words, he's going to bring trouble down on all our heads."

Signora Grazziano was beginning to look uncomfortable. She worked her jaw back and forth as Pincas continued.

"The Board of Overseers makes no distinction among us," he said, face red and brow sweating. "We are many nations here, but to them, a Jew is a Jew, and if one Jew transgresses, we are all punished."

"You must speak to him, Papa. You and the other men," Liya said forcefully. Her face was growing pink, too. Since when had Liya cared a fig about the trials and tribulations of the ghetto? Though our new house existed practically in its shadow, weeks had gone by without her so much as mentioning it.

"We have talked to Aram," Pincas went on. "Several times. He always promises to shut up his illegal entryways but then goes on as he pleases. You can tell him this for me, Esther. Aram had better mend his ways, or we will see that he does."

Signora Grazziano nodded with a scowl, but didn't have time to form a reply. The door flew open and a pair of small boys rushed through it on a burst of pumping knees and boisterous laughter. Each claimed a portion of Signora Grazziano's wide lap. Hugs and kisses were bestowed, and suddenly the widow was all smiles.

I got to my feet and joined Liya at Pincas' side. A bone-thin woman followed the boys into the room. With only a sidelong glance and sharp nod to acknowledge our presence, she flopped down at the table with a girl of perhaps three years on her lap. The woman's red slash of a mouth never stopped talking, warning the boys of dire punishments that would follow any misbehavior and throwing questions at the older woman without pause for reply.

The next person through the door was a weasely looking fellow attired in a dark broadcloth jacket and a black tie-wig that wouldn't have looked out of place at the Piazza's most respectable coffeehouse. A jaunty red rosette on his tricorne enlivened his dour ensemble and seemed at odds with the tight, belligerent expression he aimed at Pincas most particularly. Signora Grazziano introduced him as Aram Pardo and the woman as his wife, Reyna. Speak of the devil, they say.

While Pincas offered the newcomers a cool nod, I bowed from the waist, one eye on Liya. Her nod was even frostier than her father's. Aram's suddenly blossoming smile twisted back into a sneer.

I didn't need Liya's cards to divine that Aram was known to my wife and she to him, but I would have to wait until later to learn just how. While the two boys charged around the room picking up small items and tossing them aside, the conversation turned to Aram's recent call on the rabbi.

"Did you manage to persuade him?" Signora Grazziano asked anxiously once Aram was also seated at the table.

The young Jew shook his head, refusing to meet her eyes.

"Oh, I had so hoped…" The widow hung her head, hand to her brow. "Rabbi Uziel seems to set great store by your opinions."

"You do me too much honor, Mother Grazziano. I did argue that Mina had continued to help you while she lived among the Christians, and I explained that she had made a will that splits her estate among all her family members…" He shook his head. "I even went so far as to claim that Mina had never truly relinquished her beliefs and celebrated Shabbat so far as—"

The last drew a derisive snort from Reyna as she contended with her small daughter. The girl wiggled and struggled on her mother's lap, arching her back in search of freedom to run with her brothers.

"Give her here, do," Signora Grazziano said in a subdued voice, holding out her arms.

"You can't handle her. She weighs a ton and she's into everything."

"As I was saying…" Aram frowned, clearly annoyed at being booted from the center of attention. "Mina cannot be buried as a Jew and that is the rabbi's final word on the matter. If her body goes in the ground, the Christians will have to arrange it."

"No more than she deserves. Miss High and Mighty made her choice long ago." Reyna punctuated her remark with a loud slap on the bare skin between her daughter's skirt and the stocking bunched around her ankle.

"Reyna, Reyna." Signora Grazziano heaved herself from her chair to rescue her pipe from her rampaging grandsons. "What a thing to say. And after Mina has made such generous bequests to all of us."

Reyna shrugged her bony shoulders. "It's the least she could do, after the shame she's brought to our name and our family..."

Her rising inflection made me think she might go on, but Aram trapped her gaze with his own dark look and Reyna locked her lips tight together.

The din from the boys and the fretting girl and their grand-mother's ineffectual protests made it impossible to discover much else of consequence. The two middle Grazziano sisters had married cousins from Livorno and hadn't visited Venice for well over a year. The two youngest were still in school and, like most well-brought-up young ladies, Christian or Jew, were kept close to home when not attending classes or marketing under their mother's watchful eye. Liya, Pincas, and I soon took our leave.

Once we reached the crowded pavement, I let Liya and her father stroll ahead while I scanned the recesses and doorways for our turbaned follower. His identity had me completely baffled. What had I done to become the object of veiled scrutiny? I saw several men in eastern robes, but not the man I sought.

Putting that matter aside for the moment, I gave my watch hasty consultation. It was already after ten, the time that Maria had set for her assignation with Emilio. How long would she wait for my arrogant rival? Squeezing between Liya and Pincas, locking elbows with father and daughter, I did my best to hurry them along.

"Where exactly is Aram's shop, Papa?" Liya was asking.

"The northwest corner of the Campo Nuovo. Turn right directly as you step off the north bridge and you'll run right into it."

"I know just the place," Liya replied excitedly. "The rear of the building overlooks the canal just off the Rio di San Girolamo, and across the water is the sheer wall of the convent. No prying eyes. How convenient for Aram."

"He's certainly exploiting it to the utmost," Pincas said in a low voice. "Esther thinks he has the rabbi's ear because of his scholarship and piety, but I've never been impressed with Aram's learning. At prayers, he's as likely to be dozing as paying attention. I hate to say it, but Aram's influence depends more on the fat donations he's been giving to the synagogue."

The pavement had broadened, allowing us to move more quickly. As we would soon reach the gates I posed a question that had occurred to me back at the widow Grazziano's apartment. "Forgive my ignorance, Pincas, but how does trading out the back door benefit Aram? Can't he get the same price for his bits and pieces through the front?"

Pincas emitted a short laugh, rather like a bark. "Though our commerce may look like a topsy-turvy jumble to an outsider, matters of trade are actually highly regulated by the overseers. Since dealing in new commodities is a Christian prerogative, our shops sell only secondhand goods. Every business has a license to provide certain types of goods, to certain people, in certain circumstances. The prevailing fees and regulations would take me an hour to explain."

"No need. I'm beginning to see how Aram orders his affairs." I lapsed into a thoughtful silence. Aram's sharp, hungry expression should have been enough to tell me his interests would be dishonest.

Liya had been thinking, too. She halted, pulling on my arm. "Aram is not the man," she announced, staring at me with a keen, pensive look.

"What man?" Pincas and I asked in unison. We had come to the gates where we'd entered the ghetto earlier that morning. The sun had climbed high enough to clear the tops of the buildings, and the noisome alley seemed even dirtier under its penetrating rays.

"Aram is not the honest man my cards foretold, the one who hides behind a disguise."

At the mention of divination, Pincas dropped Liya's arm and gave a dismissive shake of his head, but she seemed not to notice. Despite my cautioning whistle, she plowed on in a voice loud enough to be heard on the roofs above us. "Aram is hiding something to be sure, though it's not an honest face. But Reyna must be the openly disagreeable woman I saw in the cards. She's clearly jealous of Mina—now that I recall she always was—and she makes no effort to disguise her vicious character. Did you see how she smacked her little girl? And Aram said that Mina had made a will that left money to them all."

I didn't like the triumphant glimmer I saw in Liya's eyes. Sensing my dismay, her voice became even more strident. "Don't you see, Tito? Aram sneaked out of the ghetto through the back of his shop, went to the theater and killed Mina. He and his greedy wife wanted their inheritance. Aram is the murderer."

This struck me as highly unlikely for several reasons. I voiced one: "Liya, how do you suppose Aram would have known that Mina would be at the Teatro San Marco that night? Her appearance in the Pino box was supposed to be a great surprise to everyone except her closest associates."

For a moment, I thought Liya was stumped. She scrunched her forehead and balled her hands into fists as she pulled her cloak up to her throat. Finally, she murmured, "I don't know, but I intend to find out. I'll go back to the cards. And I heard of a new method for consulting the scrying pot—melted candle wax dripped into still water. I must get home right away." After giving Pincas a distracted kiss on the cheek, she hurried through the open gates and out into the Christian world that scorned her pagan beliefs even more than those of the Jews who lived behind these walls.

Pincas and I could only watch her go. While his doughy face drooped with regret, mine, if I could have held a mirror to it, would have reflected worry and concern.

As promised, Luigi was waiting for me as I hurried toward the gondola landing by the Ponte della Guglie. He was slouching against the bridge's spired corner post, whistling a popular tune from last year's Carnevale. His musical efforts didn't interfere with his ogling of the water girls bearing their precious liquid from a well in the nearby square. I admit they made a winsome sight, their hips swaying in easy motion as they balanced copper buckets suspended from wooden yokes. To his credit, Luigi abandoned this pleasant vista and sprinted to the boat the minute he caught sight of me.

"Murano, Signore?" he asked as he handed me in.

"No, Luigi. The Campo San Barnaba."

His jaw dropped. "But Messer Grande—"

"You heard me—San Barnaba—and row like it's the Holy Week regatta and your most hated rival is two boat lengths ahead."

He still looked dubious.

"There's an extra *zecchino* in it for you if you get me there in twenty minutes." That brought the desired result. As I settled in against the leather cushion, Luigi's strong, young arms propelled the boat under the bridge and toward the Grand Canal. There, an endless line of balconied palaces rose from sun-kissed waters, and heavily laden barges seemed to wallow motionless in our wake. If my mind had not already been overloaded, I would have enjoyed the swift, gliding ride immensely. But I couldn't forget Messer Grande awaiting me on Murano, no doubt checking his watch, wondering when I would arrive. To add a few grace notes of unease, another thought occurred to me about the time Luigi swept us under the Rialto Bridge. As Liya had hastened to consult her oracles, I had neglected to find out just how she'd known the oily Aram Pardo in her old ghetto days.

When the gondola made an abrupt right turn into a smaller channel, I forced my thoughts to the matter at hand. Reaching inside my waistcoat, I fingered the thick paper of Maria's note. She was a naïve, convent-educated girl, seventeen at most. How she had fallen in with Emilio I could only imagine. In other circumstances, I would treat her gently, coax information out of her as if I were a kind uncle concerned only for her welfare. But there was no time. I was planning how to wield the note as a weapon, and suddenly, I didn't like myself at all.

Luigi set me down at the canal-side square that plays host to Venice's down-at-the-heels aristocrats. Snuggling the pavement, a barge offered pyramids of vegetables half-wilted by the unseasonable warmth, and across the *campo*, a leaning bell tower threatened to flatten a shabby church. In between, the flagstones were crowded but not jammed. I waved away several professional beggars and a man selling anise water. A barefoot, hooded Franciscan begging for Christ fastened himself to my elbow, and my purse was considerably lighter when I finally found the *calle* that Maria had specified.

At the end of this narrow alley was a café with a front window nearly obscured by bars and steam. The door stood open to admit the warmth of the day. I hesitated on the threshold, allowing my eyes to adjust to the dimness, letting the hum of conversation and clatter of cups and saucers wash over me. Had Maria waited? Or was I too late?

My heart started beating a little faster as I spied a slender, well-dressed woman masked in black velvet. She sat at a table in the corner, fiddling with a small cup; her demeanor made her stand out from the common citizens that filled this none-too-clean establishment. She obviously recognized me, because she removed her mask, sat up very straight, and watched warily as I wove my way through the café. Emilio must possess charms utterly unapparent to me; this poor girl had waited a full hour after the appointed time for their rendezvous.

Maria Albergati wore a black *zendale* that had fallen onto her slender shoulders and stood out against the bright blue of her gown. Her hair was done up in complicated curls too mature for her years, and a few pockmarks that could have been easily concealed by powder and paint marred her cheeks. Her *moretta* lay on the table, forgotten among the china and utensils.

"May I sit, Signorina?" I asked with a small bow.

"Oh, yes, Signor Amato. Please." She pushed her coffee aside and leaned over the stained white tablecloth. "Did Emilio send you? Has something happened? I've been so worried."

Dodging her questions, I asked several of my own. "Surely you're not here all by yourself? Where is your chaperone?"

She ducked her head. "I'm alone for now."

"How is this? A young woman of your age and station roaming San Barnaba without a companion." It wasn't hard to sound severe. In this neighborhood, no halfway pretty woman was safe, especially in these back alleys.

"Giovanetta has a sister who has been ill for weeks and weeks. Mama gives her only two hours on Sunday afternoon to visit, so we made a bargain." She smiled nervously and pitched her voice in a whisper. "I see Emilio while Giovanetta visits her sister who lives nearby. No one is the wiser, no suspicions are raised, and we both spend a few precious hours with the person we love best in the world."

I sighed, uncomprehending. This daughter of nobility had fallen in love with Emilio? The old adage was true: there was simply no accounting for tastes. "Giovanetta must be the woman who carried your note backstage," I observed dryly.

"Yes. She's my old nurse. But I don't understand why you are here. Where is Emilio?"

A waiter appeared at my elbow. I ordered chocolate. And pastries. "You look as if you could use something more than coffee," I told the pale girl across the table.

She didn't answer but darted looks around the café while biting her lip. I regained her attention by tossing her love note on the tablecloth and announcing, "Emilio isn't coming. He never received this."

She made a grab for the folded paper with the broken seal and gave a tiny squeak—a mouse caught in a cat's paws. She would have bolted if I hadn't grabbed both of her hands in mine.

"Smile," I ordered softly. "Smile and nod as if you were having a pleasant conversation with Emilio."

Her dark eyes were wide with panic, but she obeyed. Cocking her head, she bent her thin lips into a smile that would fool anyone who happened to take an interest in our little tableau.

"How did you get my note?" she whispered fiercely.

"Your Giovanetta made a mistake. She delivered it to my manservant who naturally brought it to me. Do you have any idea how displeased your family would be if they knew you were meeting a castrato from the opera?"

"Displeased? That's hardly the word, Signore. My father would have Emilio beaten within an inch of his life, and I wouldn't be allowed to go to the opera for the rest of mine." She tugged her hands free and dug frantically in her small drawstring bag. What was the girl up to?

Ah, she shoved a small handful of *soldi* and two silver ducats across the table. Less than I'd given Luigi for rowing me here in good time.

Jutting out her rather underslung chin, Maria asked hoarsely, "Will this buy your silence, at least for now? I'll soon have more. My name day is coming up."

It was my turn to duck my head in shame. Was the information I might obtain worth scaring the wits out of this artless creature? Despite her womanly dress and coiffure, she was little more than a child. An image of Tamerlano, a cruel tyrant I had once played on stage, flashed into my mind.

Pushing the coins back across the table, I took a more solicitous tone. "Put your money away. I need to talk with you, and this misdirected message simply provided an opportunity."

Her breath caught in her throat. "You're not going to tell Papa about Emilio and me?"

"No, it will be our secret."

"Will you swear?"

I made the sign of the cross. "By the Blessed Mother and her Holy Son, I give my word." Maria visibly relaxed, and I found myself smiling at her upturned countenance without shame. Her affair with my fellow castrato was her business. While Emilio might break her heart, his attentions could never lead to the humiliation of an out-of-wedlock child. If she was determined to have a forbidden lover, she could do much worse.

"What is it you want, then?"

"I've come to ask about your *fiancé*, Alessio Pino, and I don't have much time."

"Ah, yes. Signor Pino is no longer my *fiancé*, but what about him? Giovanetta says that he has been arrested for pushing that woman out of the box. It makes me feel so sad. I can't believe he's guilty, not for a moment."

The waiter returned with a pot of chocolate for me and fresh coffee for Maria. From under heavy-lidded eyes, he gave me a curious assessment as he set a plate of glistening fruit tarts between us and poured steaming liquid into our cups. Finally he shrugged his shoulders, muttered his *prego*, and backed away. The interruption gave me time to study my companion's expression. Candor and muted concern beamed from Maria's large brown eyes. Guile or subterfuge? No.

I blew on my chocolate. "Were you in love with Alessio?"

From the way she touched a golden locket at the small of her throat, visibly swelling with all the excitement of fresh, dewy love, I knew she was going to assure me that she loved Emilio and no one else. After we'd dispensed with that and I'd admired Emilio's miniature portrait concealed behind one of her patron saint, I tried again.

"What did you think of Alessio?" I asked. "Most ladies find him quite handsome, the perfect gentleman as it were."

"Alessio does have a pleasing appearance." She reached for a tart and looked about as old as Titolino as she spoke between greedy bites. "But being engaged was not nearly as exciting as I imagined. Alessio and I were never left alone, you see, not for one minute. I sat next to him at dinners with a great number of other people. And the few times he called, he perched on the sofa as if it were made of nails while he asked me what books I read and if I'd had nice friends at the convent. He never mentioned love and never once told me I was beautiful. If Mother Caterina had not given me the lecture she reserves for boarders who leave San Lorenzo to marry, I would never have believed that I was going to be a bride."

"How can you be sure that Alessio didn't mu...um...cause the woman's death?"

She licked raspberry off her lip with a pink, pointed tongue. "Alessio was just so amiable and obliging. Beyond his good manners, there was a certain...gentleness. I can't imagine him hurting anyone. And," she broke off to flutter her eyelashes sweetly, "you don't have to speak of 'that woman.' I knew who Zulietta Giardino was."

"Did you, now?"

"Mama and Papa discussed her, of course. They thought they were keeping me in the dark, but I have eyes and ears and know how to use them. So does Giovanetta."

"Did your parents break off the engagement once they found out about Zulietta?"

"No," she explained as she reached for a second tart. "I'm sure they didn't. It wasn't what they wanted at all. Mama has a carrying voice, you see. One night they were getting ready for bed and...I just happened to be in the corridor...."

A mental image of Maria in a nightdress with her ear pressed to her parents' door brought a smile to my lips. I drowned it with a sip of chocolate.

"Anyway...I heard Mama tell Papa that if Alessio would just put Zulietta away until after the marriage, everything would be all right. It was Alessio who broke it off."

"Did you overhear that, too?"

She shook her head. "Alessio told me first. He pulled me aside at one of Mama's musical evenings. In an alcove where we couldn't be overheard, he explained it all quite kindly. He loved another. Together, they had important work to do. He was very sorry, and I wasn't to feel the slightest embarrassment, no matter what people might say. The broken engagement really had nothing to do with me. His words were"—she seemed to struggle for an adequate word—"genuine. It was the only real, true conversation Alessio and I ever had."

"When was this?"

"Two weeks and three days ago."

"That's very precise. How can you be so sure?"

"Emilio had been invited to sing for Mama's guests that night—I was so proud of him—he sang like an angel and is such a fine figure of a gentleman even if he is a stage performer. Anyway, Mama was watching Alessio like a hawk, especially after she saw him maneuver me into the alcove. But she saw no need to watch Emilio. So I managed to slip a note between his music sheets. After his songs, I retired to my room with a headache. He followed and I discovered that his hands are as skilled as his voice…" She paused, blushing to the roots of her hair.

I broke in quickly. Some things I didn't wish to hear. "When did Alessio inform your father of his intentions?"

"Not right away. It was a week or so later. Papa was furious. He'd been counting on the match, you see."

"That's something I don't understand. Why was your father marrying you to a husband with a glassmaker's pedigree? Surely the Golden Book holds enough eligible young men to choose from."

She shrugged and said baldly, "Alessio's father has a great deal of money, and Papa speaks of almost nothing but the expenditures demanded by his position on the Council—that and the failing fortunes of our estate on the mainland." She spread her hands. "I suppose we are poor, Signore. Papa actually seems rather desperate—I heard him tell Mama that he wasn't going to let Alessio slip through his fingers."

Of course, money. Doesn't almost everything that drives this old world come down to money in the end? I stared into my cooling chocolate. Signor Albergati must have harbored notions of reversing Alessio's decision to end the engagement. What better way to nudge the boy back into the fold than to remove his current paramour. I pictured the interior of the theater. The Albergati box was on the fourth tier, almost directly across from the Pino box. If Maria's father had been waiting for an opportunity, if he somehow knew that Zulietta was in the curtained box with only a helpless dwarf to protect her…

I looked up. "Maria, I want you to think very carefully. On the night that Signorina Giardino was killed, who was watching the opera from your box?"

She responded without hesitation. "Just as always—Mama, Papa, Umberto, Claudio, and me."

"Umberto and Claudio are your brothers?"

She nodded.

"Servants?"

"We take Giovanetta and several footmen with us."

"All right. Do you remember me singing? Just before Signorina Giardino tumbled out of the box?"

"Oh, yes. I was enjoying your aria very much. You sound so very like Emilio."

I had to take a deep breath before continuing. "Were any of the servants out of the box during my aria?"

"I don't think so."

"What about Umberto or Claudio?"

She opened her mouth to speak, then after a moment of apparent bewilderment, she narrowed her gaze to a glare. A transformation occurred across the shabby table. Maria straightened her back and crossed the ends of her *zendale* over her bosom. Suddenly I could believe her family had been among Venice's elite for a span of eight centuries. Her voice could have frozen cream. "You must forgive me, Signor Amato, but I must ask you to leave. Mother Caterina always told me I talked too much, and I regret that I've proved her right."

In vain, I tried to cajole the friendly, guileless girl I'd been taking chocolate with out of this new, proud creature. It was not to be. Despite her attraction to Emilio, Maria's loyalty to her family was rock solid. The only hint I had to go on was the look of alarm that had passed over her features when I'd asked about her brothers.

Chapter Nine

Luigi delivered me to Murano shortly after midday. The island was a smaller edition of Venice, a compact cluster of airy bell-towers and brick-and-plaster edifices that seemed to float on the surface of the lagoon. It had its own Grand Canal lined with magnificent houses, and on its outskirts, drifts of glossy ivy emblazoned walls that protected courtyards and fruit orchards, as well as the inevitable glass factories. Their smoke-belching kilns contributed to the island's very solid prosperity by producing that most delicate of all luxuries—glass.

Hundreds of years ago, Venice's city fathers had moved the glassmakers from the big island to the smaller one. The official reason was to prevent fire from escaping the furnaces and destroying the city, but the move had the bonus of confining the master glassmakers and their secrets to one easily guarded location. Back then, Venetian artisans were the only Europeans capable of producing a decent mirror. They had also refined techniques of making vividly colored enameled glassware, glass shot with threads of gold, glass made of multicolored strands cut to resemble tiny flowers, and imitation gems that rivaled the brilliance of real stones. To protect this supremely valuable asset, the Senate forbade the masters and their skilled assistants to leave the Republic and made the transmission of trade secrets a treasonable offense.

But when had government edict ever stopped ideas and designs whose time had arrived? The entire civilized world wanted to drink from Venice's elegant goblets and view their images in silvery mirrors of matchless clarity. Inevitably, Venetian techniques migrated to other European glassmaking centers, especially France, our traditional rival in crafting all things beautiful and luxurious. Despite those ravages, Murano's glassmakers still harbored some secrets, and the Doge's *confidenti*, who reported on everything from salacious books to false religions, still kept a sharp eye on their activities. Punishment, or even the threat of it, was a serious matter.

As my gondola sliced through the cloudy green waters of the Canale Serenella, I wondered if Messer Grande would be furious over my delay. To each side, trees hung over the water and lazy ribbons of gray smoke unfurled over clay rooftops. A peaceful scene—but I wasn't anticipating a peaceful interview.

Pushing on his oar, Luigi paused at a smaller canal that branched off to the left. Murano offered no more signs to guide the bewildered visitor than Venice, but I thought this was the way. I nodded to Luigi, and we soon tied up at a stout wooden jetty where several work boats and gondolas were already moored. A pair of stone pylons flanked a dirt path that led to a complex of buildings plastered in soft, peeling shades of blue and ochre. Each pylon carried a blocky *P* that had been worked in tessellated squares of multihued glass. *P* for Pino: we had reached the right place. After ordering Luigi to stay with the boat, I started reluctantly up the path.

Messer Grande was waiting in a gravel courtyard filled with conical piles of sand and wooden barrows holding other raw materials of the glassmaking trade. Supporting his backside against a rick of wood sheltered by a tattered awning, he was taking snuff as leisurely as if he had been sunning himself at a café on the Piazza. Several constables hovered in the background.

"Ah, Signor Amato." Messer Grande hailed me with a smile, but his voice was chilly. "I was wondering where you'd got to. Finished your business in the ghetto, did you?"

"For now."

"Did you find the widow Grazziano talkative?"

"Fairly so. I certainly learned more about Zulietta and her family than I knew before." I spoke carefully, preferring to digest my morning's activities in the ghetto and the San Barnaba café before I shared them with Messer Grande.

The chief constable didn't press me. "We'll save the good widow for later," he said. "I'm anxious to introduce you to Cesare Pino. I have several witnesses who place him at the theater around the time of Zulietta's murder. Cesare doesn't deny he was there. He does, of course, deny stabbing his son's mistress and pushing her over the box railing. You will tell me if he could have been the man."

"But Cesare rarely attends the opera," I answered as Messer Grande steered me across the courtyard toward a low building made top-heavy by a massive stone chimney. The constables trailed in our wake, keeping a respectful distance. I continued, "What brought him to the Teatro San Marco that night?"

"A messenger delivered an anonymous note warning of Alessio's intention to display his paramour before the opening night crowd. Cesare had put months of effort into arranging his son's marriage to Maria Albergati, so he was determined to stop this ridiculous folly. But Alessio had already taken off in the cockle boat—we found that, by the way—just where Alessio said it would be."

"So Cesare set off after his son. Fit to be tied, I'd wager."

"Exactly. He rowed himself over in another work boat and made his way to the theater intent on preventing Alessio and Zulietta from humiliating Maria Albergati and her family."

"By any means possible?"

My companion shrugged within the red robe of office draped over his black suit and severely folded neckcloth. For this visit, Messer Grande was looking every inch the state official. As he paused and directed his penetrating gaze inward, I again had the sensation of a mind that could call up any number of details at will.

"Here's how it is with Cesare Pino," he said. "His roots reach deep into Murano soil. The Pino glassworks was one of the first moved to this island, and it's been churning out masterpieces ever since. While others concentrated on mirrors or chandeliers festooned with flowers and fruit, Cesare's ancestors made goblets and other vessels that graced the banquet tables of Versailles and princely houses throughout Germany and Austria. Cesare has always tended his fires with an almost monastic fervor, even before he was widowed some years ago. His wife died in childbirth, and the infant that would have been Alessio's brother along with her. Cesare never remarried. If anything, his wife's death sharpened his focus and made him more of a recluse. He runs his factory with an iron hand and expects Alessio to bow to his will in all things."

"As it seems Alessio did until Zulietta came along," I observed.

Messer Grande grinned. "She must have been a bewitching thing, don't you think? To have induced the devoted son to rebel in such a public manner?"

"Did you ever see Zulietta? Before she lay dead on the opera house floor, I mean."

"Only from afar. She was not to my taste—I enjoy women with more padding—but she did have a very fetching way about her. And many admirers obviously."

I nodded as another thought occurred to me. "Have you considered that the killer could have been one of them? One of those…admirers. Hot with jealousy or feeling the stab of humiliation over her romance with Alessio?"

"I've had a word with all four men who shared previous arrangements with Zulietta," he explained with a grimace. "Unofficial talks wherever I could corner them—I spoke to one at the Ridotto in between faro turns. Strange what a man will submit to in order not to ruin a night of gambling. But that's neither here nor there—" He waved an airy hand as his attention flitted to a boy bearing a bucket toward a well in the center of the courtyard. Apparently finding this errand of no interest, Messer Grande turned back to me and continued, "They have all transferred their affections elsewhere and harbor nothing but pleasant memories of their dalliance with Zulietta. Apparently, she gave them their congé around the same time—Ascension Day."

I stopped short, my boots scraping on gravel. "But that was six months ago! Pamarino said Zulietta and La Samsona made their wager over Alessio's affections no later than early September."

Messer Grande slanted an eyebrow. "Interesting, is it not? We have a beautiful courtesan without a protector for a space of months. A long time when you consider the expenses of her establishment."

"Perhaps the dwarf was mistaken."

"Not at all. I've had confirmation of the date from La Samsona. The wager was sealed on the first of September. Since the stakes were so high, she marked it down in her little notebook most particularly."

We started to walk again, more slowly. So Messer Grande had interviewed the former strongwoman. I wondered how he had taken to her charms; she was as well padded as any Venetian beauty could hope to be. Shaking the memory of her burly arms and shoulders from my head, I asked, "Did Zulietta's rival tell you she had sent her best jewels to the bank vault?"

He nodded with a chuckle. "La Samsona was leaving nothing to chance, but it's my impression that losing even her second-best baubles would have wounded her. There's nothing that great whore loves better than diamonds..." He cocked his head like a dog hearing a distant whistle. "Unless it's pearls."

Messer Grande seemed to know La Samsona better than one interview would allow. I longed to continue our conversation, but we were nearly at the steps of the factory and a sizeable man had come to fill its doorway. He was outfitted in work clothes, including a leather bib apron that covered him from neck to knees. His rigid stance proclaimed his annoyance at anyone, perhaps most especially the law, meddling in his affairs.

"You again," he observed with a scowl aimed at Messer Grande.

Ignoring the man's lack of social grace, the chief constable answered, "Good afternoon, Signor Pino. I've brought the man I told you about—Tito Amato, the singer from the theater."

Cesare Pino stared at me for a long moment, then drew back just enough to allow us to pass into his workspace, a long room dominated by a hulking furnace in the far corner. I saw why Cesare was immediately recognizable. His right cheek was marked with the shiny, puckered pink of an old burn. The same fire had also damaged his right eye, rendering it lashless and sunken. Above it, his eyebrow had been scorched away. The rest of the glass master's appearance was unremarkable, if severe: white hair cropped so short it resembled an ermine skull cap, high-bridged nose, firm jaw, muscular forearms emerging from rolled-up sleeves.

"Do you still have my boy?" he asked gruffly.

"For now," said Messer Grande. "If Alessio weren't so stubborn about what he did and where he went between leaving here and showing up at the opera house, I might see fit to release him. Someone needs to drum some sense into that young buck's head." He finished with a pointed look at the young buck's father.

"Don't expect me to go running over to Venice. The boy has closed his ears to me these many months. If he respected my counsel, he would never have taken up with that squalid, grasping Jew in the first place. Filthy *puttana*. Zulietta Giardino! Bah!" He spat on the sand-strewn floor as if her very name were poison. "She's roasting in Hell with the rest of her deceitful race, and I can't say I'm sorry."

Stung by the force of his anger, I jumped in without leave or preamble. "Perhaps you're the one who sent her there."

"I might well have done—if I'd ever met her, Signor Capon." He snorted and fixed a scowl on his lips. Whether he disliked eunuchs as much as Jews or was vexed to have missed the opportunity to dispatch his son's mistress, I could not tell.

"You were at the theater the night she was murdered," I observed through gritted teeth.

"So I was, but all I accomplished was pounding on the door to our box."

"It was locked?"

"That's right. I didn't have the key. Alessio carries it. I called his name and banged repeatedly, but whoever was inside wasn't opening up."

"Did you hear any noise from the other side of the door?"

As Cesare shook his head, Messer Grande murmured, "How could he, with all the racket he was making?"

I showed the chief constable my palm, intent on completing my questions. "Was there anyone in the corridor?"

"Not a soul."

"No small man? Or perhaps a man with a weathered complexion, completely unmasked?"

"Are your ears made of flannel? I told you no."

"What did you do then?"

"I hurried away to make the lout who runs the box office find someone to get that door open. By the time I got to the bottom of the grand staircase, the whore had crashed into the pit. But I must say, Excellency," he twisted his thick neck to face Messer Grande, "I'm surprised at you. Since when do you let a twittering nightingale from the opera conduct your investigation?"

A smile flitted across Messer Grande's lips. "Tito is so diligent, I hate to stop him. But you are right. Questions are not the point of this visit."

"You want to see if I'm lying—if your nightingale recognizes me as the man in the box with that jade of a Hebrew."

Messer Grande nodded.

"I suppose he's already taken a look at my son."

Messer Grande nodded again.

"Whatever he must do, then, be quick about it. The *fritta* is almost ready for transfer." Cesare cast his gaze toward the brick kiln that was shaped like an oversized beehive. Its maw glowed yellow-orange; the flames within roared and groaned. Through the bright, wavering haze, I could see pots baking in the searing heat. They must contain the sand and potash and other ingredients that made up the molten glass. My eyeballs burned after peering at them for only a moment, and a rivulet of perspiration ran down my nose.

Messer Grande was sweating, too. He wiped his face with a handkerchief that came away from his cheeks with a brown stain. Odd. I'd barely had time to wonder about that before the chief constable challenged Cesare in a voice that brooked no argument. "We're here on the Doge's business—you'll give us as much time as we need."

The glass master replied without flinching. "I understand that a crime has been committed, but even so, you must respect the needs of a man's business. The *fritta* doesn't wait. When it's ready for the pipe, it's ready."

"Let your other masters tend the glass." Messer Grande gestured toward several middle-aged men who were arranging wicked-looking pincers and grippers on a bench near the furnace.

Cesare stiffened his shoulders and pushed his chin up into a frown. "I'm the only master here, and today I'm blowing aventurine. There's a lot can go wrong with aventurine. It requires my hand."

"Then we had best get to it. Remove that apron, if you please. Tito, do you want Signor Pino to move a certain way or strike a pose?"

I shrugged as the glassmaker untied his apron and jerked it off with a snap. I required nothing special from Cesare Pino. From the moment I had observed him in the doorway, I began measuring his face for the killer's chalk-white mask. A *bauta* fits snugly over forehead, nose, and cheeks, leaving the mouth free for conversing and drinking. In such a disguise the mutilated face of Cesare Pino would look like everyone else's.

Messer Grande questioned me with a cocked eyebrow.

I rubbed my jaw, thinking intently. There was one other thing I'd noticed. Cesare had moved across the floor with a slight limp. Had the accident that burned his face also injured his leg? It didn't matter how he'd come by his walk. It was enough that his gait reprised the clumsy, lurching steps of Zulietta's killer.

Still I hesitated. Cesare Pino was an arrogant, self-righteous man. He was also prone to ire and obviously hated Jews. I would have loved for Messer Grande to clap him in irons on that score alone. But I had to tell the truth as far as memory would allow, and I didn't sense that Cesare's wounded eye possessed the blistering power that had carried all the way across the theater as I locked gazes with the murderer.

"Well, what do you think?" Messer Grande's voice took on an impatient tone.

"I suppose…" I started slowly. "Yes…it's possible…"

The constables by the door jumped to attention. One reached into his jacket where he would keep his truncheon. The glass orkers traded questioning looks, then shuffled closer to their master. Reluctantly, I thought. Cesare Pino flung up an arm to ward them off.

"I didn't kill that woman." Cesare's expression was loathing itself. With his puckered skin bathed in the kiln's orange glow, he could have been a demon coughed up from Satan's own mouth.

"I was going to add that you don't seem quite right," I quickly replied, wiping sweat from my forehead with the back of my hand. "It's only that you're of the same size and carriage as the man in the cloak and *bauta*."

"Well, I never made it from the corridor into the box, and I never wear a mask. Anyone can tell you that." He spread his fingers and flicked them upwards from his chin. "As ugly as it is, this face of mine is honest. God given, you might say, and fairly earned. I see no reason to hide it."

Messer Grande had waved his constables back.

"You're not going to arrest me?" Cesare asked.

"Not today," Messer Grande replied cheerfully.

The glassmakers also shuffled back. Returning to their implements, they sneaked glances at their master as they sharpened pincers and fiddled with paddles that looked like stout versions of those used in a baker's oven. The sudden tension was abating.

Cesare continued, "What about my son? As rash and disobedient as Alessio has been of late, I don't think he killed the woman either. The fool doesn't have it in him—he can't bear to kill anything—even the goose for our Sunday meal." The glass master shook his head. "Alessio needs to get back here. I won't be able to salvage the marriage contract, but the boy can devote himself to the kiln. You may be sure I'll be giving up that box at the opera house where he idles his time away with Jews and who knows what other trash."

Messer Grande replied mildly, "Your son would hardly be the first man, or the last, to make a fool of himself over a woman. That is not a crime, of course, but obstructing an official inquiry is. I'll be holding him until he decides to answer my questions."

Cesare grunted, gestured impatiently, and threw a glance toward his bench and blowpipe. "So—our business is concluded?"

Messer Grande nodded as he gathered the folds of his long red sleeve that had been trailing on the sandy floor. "For now, but I would like very much to see your wares. Do you have a showroom?"

"In the building next door," Cesare replied in a flat tone.

"Perhaps one of your workers could show us?"

The glass master jerked his chin at a small fellow who separated himself from the group near the workbench. Cesare didn't give us another glance. His focus had shifted, and I recognized his expression. It was the same that Maestro Torani exhibited when he was composing a melody in his head. Or Gussie when he was at his easel.

A pang of jealousy coursed through me. I admired artistic creation, whether it resulted in notes that lived for only a moment or a beautiful painting that could last forever. Someday, when life became more settled, I meant to try my hand at writing my own music.

As his men took their ease in the courtyard, Messer Grande and I followed the glassmaker into a larger building. Empty of workmen or clerks, the spacious, high-ceilinged room was piled with crates and barrels labeled for shipment. Along the front wall, boards on trestles were laid with examples of the Pino tableware. The range of colors was dazzling, even in the low light. Goblets, compotes, bottles, trays, even baskets woven of thin glass strands glimmered as if Cesare and his men were wizards capable of entrapping nature's bright hues in wonderfully wrought crystal prisons.

I hovered over the array, tricorne tucked carefully under my arm, especially admiring a set of decanters and glasses the color of the cerulean sky on the clearest summer day imaginable. No, I was wrong. The pieces actually resembled the blue of the lagoon reflecting the sky on such a day. What subtle workmanship!

Then there were graceful oil and vinegar cruets made of the aventurine that Cesare must be blowing even now. Paper-thin, reddish-brown glass shot with flakes of shiny copper and overlaid with findings of beaten gold. They were exquisite things, fit for a Doge's table, not mine. But I could still look. I was amazed that a man with Cesare's belligerent disposition could create such fragile beauty. It was Messer Grande's low voice that tore me away from the treasures. Smarter than I, the chief constable was taking advantage of this few moments of privacy to question Cesare's workman. I drew near.

The glassmaker was short in stature, with angular cheekbones that looked as if they were about to burst through his sooty skin. Two tufts of graying hair made horns on each side of his balding head, and he gazed at Messer Grande with bulbous blue eyes. He was my senior by at least a decade, but he quailed before the Doge's representative like an untried youth. Even though Messer Grande was using his kindest, most reasonable tone, the workman's voice quavered, and if he hadn't been wringing his hands, I'm certain they would have trembled. His name was Zenobio.

"How long have you worked for Cesare Pino?" Messer Grande was asking.

"Almost twenty years, Excellency."

"It takes many years to master the craft, yes?"

"Yes, Excellency."

"Twenty years is quite a span, Zenobio. Surely, you'll soon become a master of the glass yourself."

Zenobio answered with a small shake of his head. He seemed to be making an effort to keep his lips clamped shut.

"No?" Messer Grande questioned. "I don't understand. *Garzone, servente,* then master. Isn't that the way it's supposed to go?"

Zenobio blinked once, twice. He cast a desperate look round. Checking for any stray clerks? Then a torrent of whispered words escaped his lips. "No one will ever be master at this factory unless his name is Pino. I was only advanced to *servente* last year, even though I do the best work of any man here. Signor Cesare was going to name Signor Alessio master of the glass on his marriage celebration. Now even that will be put off."

Something in the longing way Zenobio explained that last bit gave me an idea. "Are the men expecting things to change once Alessio becomes a glass master?"

"In the shadow of his father, Signor Alessio can change nothing. Beyond Signor Cesare's reach—" A sudden smile enlightened Zenobio's face but was quickly doused. The man dipped his chin and raised it to display his previous anxious expression. "Will Signor Alessio be coming back to us soon?"

Messer Grande frowned. "That depends on a number of things. Signor Alessio is involved in a very serious matter."

The glassmaker shook his head, wildly this time. "Signor Alessio didn't kill that woman. It's impossible, everything would be ruined."

"Why impossible, Zenobio?" Messer Grande fired off. "If you know something of your young master's dealings, you must say."

He lifted trembling hands to pull at his tufts of hair. "No, Excellency, no. I know nothing of my master's business. I work the kiln and take care of my family, that's it."

During the ensuing strained silence, I contemplated Zenobio's statement: *everything would be ruined.* I'd heard someone else use that phrase. But who? For a moment, I felt as if a curtain had parted to reveal a glimpse of a secret play, but Messer Grande asked another question and the curtain closed again.

"Tell me about your family." Messer Grande's tone was calm and soothing.

Zenobio gulped and replied, "I have a wife and five children."

"How have you kept them fed on the wages of a *garzone?*"

"Everyone must work. My boy fetches water all day, though he's going on twelve and should be learning to fuel the kiln by his age. He's not even a true *garzone*, just a boy to be ordered to turn his hand to any small chore that needs doing. My wife and daughters work next door where they make cheap glass beads. They thread the beads for shipping. All day—bead after bead, five hundred per strand, strand after strand. My wife's eyes are going. When she can't work the beads…" He finished with an aggrieved shrug.

"You could threaten to leave," Messer Grande said. "Tell Signor Cesare you'll find work with a rival if you're not promoted."

Zenobio didn't bother to respond, merely sent the chief constable a withering look.

"I know how it is," I put in. "Murano is like the theater where I practice my craft. Everyone has his place, and a man knows he'd best stick to it whether he sings, plays the violin, or lights the tapers in the chandelier. If a man makes trouble, word gets around fast. Then he is ruined where all the opera houses in Venice are concerned."

Zenobio nodded sagely.

Messer Grande regarded me intently. "But, Tito, every Italian town has its own opera house, and impresarios are always looking to fill a tour company. It's different with glass—" He turned back to Zenobio. His voice hardened to a cruel, grating baritone. "You can't leave Murano, can you? At least legally. Though we all know foreign agents tempt workers who harbor the secrets of the glass. What do they offer, Zenobio, those men from Bologna or Paris or Bohemia? Immediate promotion to master? Your own kiln? A fine house for your family?"

A watery look came into the workman's round eyes. Their dark centers expanded until he resembled a skinny owl horned with tufts of hair instead of feathers. He stammered, "Please… Excellency…I don't know what you're talking about."

I thought Zenobio might take off at a run, but still Messer Grande kept digging. He gestured to the display tables. "Did you make any of these things?"

Zenobio raised a shaky finger to point toward a squat, black cylinder sitting on end, somewhat removed and very much at odds with the light, graceful tableware. I went to fetch it and found a tube covered in black leather with an eyepiece at one end. The opposite end was surrounded by a separate barrel that bristled with brass pegs that could rotate the outside cylinder around the inner. It reminded me of the glasses some of the audience employed to view the stage at the opera house, only larger. Yet when I raised it to my eye, all was dark.

"You must look toward the light," Zenobio instructed.

I swung around toward the open door filled with the brightness of the mid-afternoon sun. Oh, what a difference! The blackness exploded into a flower colored with liquid light: purple, deep blue, cherry red, golden yellow, all melding one into another. At a twist of the brass pegs, my flower broke apart and a new pattern emerged. With every notch, the intense colors and complex shapes took on new forms, each more beautiful than the last.

Thoroughly enchanted, I lowered the instrument and turned to Zenobio. "What is this thing?"

"I call it a petal-scope," the man answered shyly. "It's not much of anything—just a metal tube with broken glass in a chamber at one end. And some lenses to make the glass look like the petals of a flower opening and closing."

"But it's absolutely wonderful. How did you come up with it?" Observing the little glassmaker with new admiration, I placed the petal-scope in Messer Grande's outstretched hand.

"At the end of the workday, we're allowed to experiment with broken remnants and leftover materials." Zenobio shrugged, but his broadening smile spoke his pride in his creation. "I was tinkering around with an old spyglass, and the petal-scope happened almost by accident. It's not useful—it really doesn't do anything except provide amusement."

Messer Grande had been holding the scope to the light, apparently as entranced as I'd been. Now he laughed as he threw an arm around my shoulders. "Useful isn't everything. My friend here is hardly useful, but I assure you the opera house pays a goodly sum for his services."

He continued as I shook his arm off, "Have you made more of these, Zenobio?"

The glassmaker nodded. "A few."

"Then I would like to purchase this one."

A few coins changed hands, and soon Messer Grande and I were headed back through the gravel courtyard, down the path to the jetty. I found it impossible to keep my mouth shut. "Not useful?" I asked. "After all that was done to make a singer of me?"

"Well, you know what I mean." He had the grace to appear apologetic. "The opera is a grand spectacle, delicious entertainment. I love it—but singing for your supper is hardly in the league of building a boat, or forging a ship's anchor, or even blowing goblets for a rich man's table."

I halted on the path. "Teatro San Marco was built to reflect the glory of the Doge and our Republic. Its operas draw visitors whose gold keeps half of Venice's hostelries and taverns and wine shops open. And what about the thousands of miles I've covered to bring Italy's unrivaled music to every dull-as-ditchwater town north of the Alps?" The ferocity of my response surprised even me. I realized I was grinding my teeth.

Messer Grande's expression changed from abashed to wounded. "Tito—" he began.

But I forged on. "For all that and all the hours I practice to perfect my performance, you dare say I'm not useful? After all I've sacrificed? After my very manhood was sliced away without my knowledge or consent?"

"Oh, Signor Amato." He looked stunned, as if someone had struck him in the head with a mallet. "I spoke without thinking. I could pull my tongue out by the roots."

I stared him in the face, unmollified, rigid with anger.

He stammered on, "Though…though your voice was created under…shameful circumstances…it is truly magnificent. And you are right, you and everyone at the theater bring glory to Venice. Please—" He interrupted himself to seize me in a bearlike embrace. "I will be desolated if you won't accept my apology. Tell me you will."

"Well...yes...I suppose..." I answered through folds of red silk. "If you wish..."

He pulled back and clapped me on both shoulders. A broad smile split his face. "That's the spirit. I would hate to sully our friendship when it is just beginning. I admire you for much more than your singing, you know. Here—" He removed the petal-scope from a jacket pocket. "I bought this for your boy. Let it serve as a token of my goodwill."

"It's for Titolino?"

"He's of an age to use it, is he not?"

"Yes, he will enjoy it. Thank you. But don't you have children of your own?"

Messer Grande shook his head solemnly. "My good wife and I have not been blessed, and aren't likely to be, married these twelve years—" He shrugged as one of his men ran panting down the path. "Yes?"

The constable extended a paper folded into quarters and sealed with a blob of red wax. "Excellency, a message just rowed across from Venice."

Messer Grande slipped his thumb under the seal and snapped the note open. As his gaze flicked back and forth over the lines, his expression made me feel cold and hollow inside. Something had happened.

Indeed. Messer Grande raised his eyes, but I don't think he even saw me as he announced, "I must leave you, now."

"What is it?"

"Alessio Pino has escaped my guardhouse."

Chapter Ten

Several days after my visit to Murano, I awoke earlier than usual to the promise of another beautiful autumn day. The gulls agreed with me. When I opened our balcony doors, the birds' raucous cries were positively joyful. Allowing the mild breeze and diffuse golden light to fill our chamber, I returned to bed and ran my fingers through Liya's lustrous blue-black hair. She barely stirred before dragging a pillow over her head.

Liya had been keeping a series of late nights, but not in my company. I had seen my wife awake only a few times these past days. She had skipped my ongoing performance in *Armida* to closet herself away with her oracles. Removing her *tarocchi* from their ivory casket after Titolino went to bed, she laid down array after array. If not at her cards, she spent hours staring into a soup pot filled with oil and mysterious herbs.

Each morning, she'd left the house early to poke around the ghetto, following up on clues that her planetary spirits—or was that her elemental geniuses?—had communicated to her the night before. She was beginning to worry me. Her rosy cheeks had paled, and she no longer seemed to listen as I recounted the latest theater gossip. I had to remind myself that I had encouraged her to take an interest in the ghetto for a very good reason.

Last night, I had returned from the theater to find Liya in her nightdress, asleep at the table in front of the dying fire, head resting on her curled arm. A ring of candles surrounding her brightly painted cards had dripped wax all over the tabletop.

I blew them out, gathered up her *tarocchi*, and summoned Angelina to help get her into bed, an innocent gesture that precipitated a heated argument.

"You've mixed up my cards," Liya cried once she'd wakened. "I'd just constructed the pyramid of Aradia."

"My love, you're exhausted. Come to bed and let these foolish things be."

"Foolish things? What are you saying?" Anger flashed from her dark eyes.

I should have stopped there, but my brain was also clouded by fatigue. I told Liya she was endowed with too high an intelligence to rely on pieces of pasteboard to guide her life, even if they did sometimes seem to hit the mark. She responded with a sputtering lecture on all her tools of divination and the immortal, feminine forces that lent them power.

I'd soon heard quite enough. "Ridiculous!" I countered. "They're cards, nothing but cards. Not some miraculous oracle."

Acting on the basest of impulses—rage—I seized the pack of *tarocchi* and threw them into the grate where the flimsy pasteboard immediately flared into orange and blue flames. Our words flared just as hotly. By the time we were through, Liya had attacked the Holy Eucharist as nothing but Christian hocus-pocus and Angelina had given her notice. The maid slammed through the front door, and we heard her howling about "the Devil's playthings" all the way down the pavement.

In the morning light, at the threshold of a new day, the argument seemed thoroughly childish. Admittedly, I found my wife's pagan ways strange at times, but I knew her for a loving, good-hearted woman, whatever her beliefs. I respected those beliefs because they were hers, just as she had never disparaged the mysteries of the religion I held dear.

Of her Hebrew girlhood, we'd rarely spoken. When she'd slipped out of Venice, Liya packed up her old ghetto life like out-of-season garments folded into a trunk. Now that Zulietta's murder had led her to open that trunk and air its contents, our carefully maintained equilibrium had been thrown off balance. I couldn't let that continue.

I lifted the pillow from Liya's head and kissed her shoulder, the notch of her throat, between her breasts. She must have bathed before she'd consulted her cards last night; her flesh was still scented with lavender bath oil. Under my touch, her eyelids fluttered and she woke with a moan. She seemed as loathe to let the argument linger as I was. She kicked the bedcovers off and wrapped her legs around me. Then her arms. I reveled in the familiarity of her embrace. Here was one instance where I had to bow to the wise women of Monteborgo who had schooled Liya in the uses of herbs. Thanks to her invigorating balms and lotions, I suffered no lack of desire or potency despite the violence that had been done to my manhood.

Later, as we lay folded together, our warm bodies cooled by the breeze from the open doors, Liya reached for something on the bedside table. Drowsy, eyelids at half-mast, I felt her slip a cord over my head.

"What is this?" I fingered the red flannel bag that had come to rest on my bare chest.

She traced its outline with the feathery touch of her forefinger. "Something I made for you—protection."

In a heartbeat, I came fully awake. "Why do I need protecting?"

Liya stared over my shoulder, as if a deep vista stretched beyond the very solid wall of masonry, a vista only she could see. Finally she blinked and focused on me. "Before my cards burned, they warned of danger."

"Perhaps you're the one in danger."

She shook her head firmly and answered in a hushed tone. "It was you and no mistake. Swords hung over your head."

Despite myself, an icy shiver raised the hairs on my forearms. "How can this protect me? It's only a little bag of red flannel."

"The *how* doesn't matter. It's enough that I made it for you and collected its contents with my own hands. You must promise to wear it always."

"Never take it off? Not even to wash?"

"The time will come when it will be removed, but the moment is not for you to choose." She waited solemnly, clearly expecting a promise.

Why not indulge her? What harm could a bag around my neck cause? "All right, I promise never to remove it—but now you must be as forthcoming in return. Tell me why you have been so consumed with finding Zulietta's killer."

She pulled the light coverlet around us and plumped up our pillows. Then she answered with a sigh, "Zulietta could have been me, Tito. I could have followed in her footsteps exactly."

"I don't know what you mean. You and Zulietta are hardly the same. You were forced out of the ghetto by your mother's insistence that you give Titolino up to the Pieta. Zulietta was still Mina Grazziano when she let old Malpiero tempt her away. She left of her own free will."

"Zulietta and I were both at a crossroads. Stepping this way or that would change our lives forever. And you forget that Mama had several plans. When she first discovered I was going to have Luca's child, she wanted to marry me off to a ghetto boy, the son of a neighbor across the *campo*."

"Yes, I do recall. You said he had a face like a shriveled melon and teased Fortunata behind your back. You refused him and that's when your mother insisted you give the child of a Christian to the Christian orphanage."

She nodded. "I don't think I ever told you his name."

"Is it important?"

"The boy was Aram Pardo."

I pushed up on one hand. "Liya, my love. Why didn't you tell me at once?"

She ran her tongue over her lips, staring at the sunlight creeping across our faded carpet. "I'd rather not think about those days," she finally answered. "They were terrible. Mama and Papa locked me in my room and arranged the match without so much as a word to me. The one time I was allowed out, our parents toasted the engagement with a glass of Cyprus wine while

Aram and I sat on the sofa. Right under their noses, he dug his fingers into my thigh so hard it left bruises. As our mothers talked of dishes and linens and our fathers slapped each other on the back, Aram had his mouth to my ear, whispering all the terrible things he was going to do to me and telling me how much I was going to like it."

Liya wrapped her arms around her knees and folded herself into a little ball. I could barely hear her next words: "I couldn't stand it, Tito. I threw my wine in Aram's face and said I wouldn't marry him if he were the only man in the ghetto. Mama locked me in my room for two more weeks, but I wouldn't relent. By then, my belly was getting bigger and something had to be done. Mama started threatening to give my baby to the Pieta. She thought that would bring me to heel, but I'd remembered the old wise woman who had cured some ailments I'd had as a child. With my sisters' help, I escaped my prison and found a man to row me to her island at the north end of the lagoon. It was she who arranged my journey to Monteborgo." Liya raised her chin. Her eyes were wet with unshed tears. "If she hadn't, I wouldn't have returned to the ghetto. I would have simply lost myself in the city. I would have ended up lower than Zulietta. No luxurious pleasure casino for me. No fourth-tier opera box. No jewels. I would have been one of the slatterns you find waiting for men outside the Arsenale or haunting the docks."

"Liya, Liya." I stroked her hair, then her small white hands, for by this time she was sobbing in earnest. "What can I do?"

She wiped her cheeks with a corner of the sheet. Her voice grew hoarse. "You can help me prove that Aram murdered Zulietta. Then I'll have the pleasure of watching him dance at the end of the hangman's noose, a fate I'm certain he deserves over and over."

"Liya—" I dropped my hands, shocked at the violence of her words, unsure what to say.

"Oh, Tito, you don't know him. It wasn't just Fortunata he teased. There were rumors of much worse. All the children on our square were afraid of Aram, and the dogs ran whenever they caught sight of him. He's cruel and evil. He thinks the world owes him a living, and he'll take that living any way he can get it. When Zulietta made her will, she signed her death warrant."

"But, Liya, there's no way to prove a man guilty of something he didn't do. At least, no way I'd ever stoop to."

"How do you know Aram didn't kill Zulietta? Thanks to the construction he's done at the back of his shop, he can launch a boat and leave the ghetto under cover of darkness. Yesterday, I questioned people who live in the buildings on either side. They've seen Aram and his henchmen avoid the patrol boat a number of times. Throughout the ghetto, he has earned the reputation of a master of all trades except that of an honest man.

"No." She placed her palm over my open mouth. "Let me finish. There's more. I've also been back to see Signora Grazziano. She admitted that Zulietta had announced something momentous would occur on the opera's opening night. She told her mother to expect a windfall that would allow her to move to a larger apartment. If Signora Grazziano knew Zulietta would be attending the opera that night, she could have easily mentioned it to Reyna—who of course would have told Aram."

I took both her hands in mine. They were ice cold. "Here, get into your dressing gown, and I'll close that door. The sun may look like July, but it's still October." I rang for Angelina, actually forgetting for the moment that our maid had fled the house.

It was Benito who answered, white cloth over his arm, bearing a tray complete with chocolate pot and dome-covered dish. He arranged the table with a minimum of fuss and bowed himself out after sending me only a surreptitious wink to serve as a comment on the tumbled bedclothes.

Once we'd both had a few sips of chocolate and Liya was nibbling at a warm roll studded with pistachios, I observed, "You've been very busy these past few days."

"When you devote yourself to some injustice that no one else cares to right, you're like a bloodhound on the scent. I've watched you for years. You stop for nothing. Would you expect less of me?"

I released a sigh of mingled exasperation and admiration. "No, I wouldn't. It's just that several things bear against Aram as the culprit. For one…" I held up a forefinger. "I saw the man, remember. Aram is far too slight and I doubt if he'd have the strength to overpower Zulietta. And two…" I raised another finger. "The murderer had a key—not the official theater key that Alessio had given Zulietta, but his own. How would Reyna or Aram have come by a key?"

"Keys can be copied."

"True, but you must have an original to take to the smithy."

"Zulietta had access to Alessio's key. She may have had a duplicate made for reasons of her own."

"And one of the Jews got hold of that key? Highly unlikely, I think." I reached for a pastry, picked off a few nuts, and crunched them between my front teeth. "Putting the matter of the key aside for now, we must admit that Alessio's escape has convinced a good many people of his guilt."

Liya raised an eyebrow. "There may be some other explanation for his flight. My cards foretold a sea journey…before they were destroyed."

I hung my head and once again apologized for my rash action. "I'll buy you another set of *tarocchi*," I continued. "The best that Venice has to offer."

When I raised my gaze, Liya was regarding me with a shrewd, unflappable expression. She pushed back a strand of hair that had fallen over her cheek, then replied, "As well you should. But your offer flies in the face of our tradition. A wise woman must search out her own tools, and only she can decide which cards are meant for her use."

"Then I suppose you must start searching."

"I will," she answered with a grave smile. "But in the meantime, we have a murder to solve. How did Alessio manage to escape?"

"The bars of Alessio's cell window were tampered with. The window was much too high for him to reach. Someone must have worked on them from outside and thrown a rope through."

"Alessio has some daring friends, then."

"Not as daring as it might appear on first blush. The work was accomplished during the darkest hours of the night, and while the guardhouse's side walls are only a few feet from its neighbors, those buildings contain state offices that would have been empty of prying eyes. Two men could have done it, one from the top of a ladder, the other keeping watch. Once through that window, Alessio could have thrown on cloak and mask and gone…anywhere."

Liya nodded judiciously. "If he's still in Venice, Messer Grande will find him. Your new friend seems quite clever—and persistent."

"I fear the search for Alessio ended before it began. Messer Grande came backstage last night and told me the Council of Ten has ordered him to shift his resources to another matter. There has been a rash of robberies in the San Polo district, and the neighbors are calling for the thieves to be apprehended. The Ten have judged Alessio guilty of Zulietta's murder but believe he's well out of Venetian territory, so…" I spread my hands.

The Republic's overseers were nothing if not practical. Built on commerce, Venice might as well have had a balance sheet for a constitution. There was no sense in wasting resources chasing a murderer who was well away, especially when the victim had been a woman who inhabited the shadowy world of the courtesan. Honest citizens whose household goods were disappearing in the middle of the night would always take precedence.

"Is Messer Grande satisfied that Alessio murdered Zulietta?"

I thought back to the chief constable's ear-burning oaths concerning our Republic's feared ten-man tribunal. Messer Grande was a brave man to criticize. Men of higher influence had been thrown in the Doge's prison for such disrespect. "Satisfied? No, I wouldn't say that. Messer Grande wants to continue the investigation, but—the Ten have spoken."

"And you? Are you satisfied that Alessio killed Zulietta?"

"Not really. There are others who strike me as more likely to have killed Zulietta than Alessio Pino. At first I judged Alessio as too noble to be true, but after hearing reports of his honorable actions, I've come to believe he is who he appears to be—a high-minded young man who truly loved his Zulietta. Why would he kill her? He wasn't bothered by the wager with La Samsona—in fact he seemed to relish it. I suspect his escape had something to do with the mysterious errand he refused to elaborate on."

"Those others you mention—that brings us back to Reyna and Aram."

"Oh, Liya. They would be the last names on my list of possibilities."

"Who heads your list?"

I took a few sips of chocolate, now grown tepid. "If you consider ease of opportunity, there was someone with a powerful motive to kill Zulietta right there on the fourth tier, only steps away from the Pino box."

Liya tilted her head, then made a face. "Of course, Maria Albergati. The spurned *fiancée* stalking her rival. I suppose she would have had access to Alessio's box key. But if Aram is too slight to have bested Zulietta, how could a seventeen-year-old girl have managed it?"

"I'm not speaking of Maria herself—she has two strapping brothers—though if Zulietta had ever set her sights on Emilio Strada, I can imagine the young lady turning as bloodthirsty as a Barbary pirate."

"Emilio? How does that conceited fool come into it?" Liya set her cup down with a rattle. For once I'd managed to surprise her. I explained by recounting my conversation with Maria.

"Appalling," Liya announced, once I'd finished.

"It makes sense, really. Signor Albergati was drooling over all the gold from the Pino—"

"No, no." She waved her roll in the air. "Appalling that Maria would even look at Emilio with you also on the stage."

I shifted in my chair and shook my head. "I thought you were serious about finding Zulietta's killer."

After a fleeting grin, she wiped her face clean of all mirth. "I am serious, Tito. Please go on. Who else is on your list?"

"La Samsona also had a motive for killing Zulietta. She's one lady who has the strength to have done the deed."

"I thought she'd sent her jewels to the Banco Giro for safekeeping."

"Not all of them, and I wonder if her reputation as Venice's reigning courtesan doesn't mean more to her than she is letting on."

"All right. Since we're considering ease of opportunity, do we know where she was when your aria was interrupted?"

"La Samsona admitted she'd left her box."

"And?"

I shrugged. "Her revelations stopped there."

Liya made a disparaging sound deep in her throat. "Not very forthcoming for a whore was she?" She drew her dressing gown tight around her and continued. "I suppose our last suspect is Alessio's father."

I nodded. "Cesare was on the scene and had sufficient cause, more than sufficient when you consider how much he detested Je—" I bit my tongue, realizing what I was about to say.

"Jews? Is that it?" She regarded me keenly. "Alessio's father hated Zulietta not only because she ruined his plans, but because she was born a Hebrew?"

I nodded, ashamed, though I was only repeating another man's sentiments.

"Cesare and half of Venice. I may have left the ghetto behind, but I well understand that many of your fellow countrymen consider it their Christian duty to inflict insults and beatings on any Jew whose business takes him into the city. A Jew can be physician, banker, poet, or merchant, but he's always a Jew first and foremost…" She let her words trail off, shrugging with eloquent bitterness.

Liya didn't need to go on; I understood nearly as well as she did. In tracking down the killer of the roguish scene painter who had fathered Titolino, I learned how easily Jews could become scapegoats, how quick people were to believe any wrongdoing of our Hebrew neighbors. The diabolical violence visited on

Liya's family the night of the ghetto fire that had almost killed her and Fortunata still haunted my nightmares. That's why I'd been hesitant to feed Messer Grande any information that would point an accusing finger at Reyna and Aram. I didn't intend to mention Zulietta's sister and her scoundrel of a husband unless I found proof positive against them.

I sighed. "None of that brings us any closer to solving the murder. I look at it one way and I'm convinced that Maria's family must be behind it. But if I shift my focus, another of our suspects seems just as likely."

"It reminds me of that toy you brought home to Titolino."

"Eh?"

"Oh, you know." She rose and crossed to the mantelpiece. "He was playing with it before bed last night. Here it is—it makes pictures like the colored windows in the Basilica. What do you call it?"

I joined her before the cold fireplace. "The glassmaker called it a petal-scope." I held the tube to my eye, aimed it at a patch of sunlight, and clicked through several different patterns.

"One turn and you have a whole new way of looking at things. Just like Zulietta's murder," Liya said.

I lowered the scope, frowning. My wife had something there. We must let the investigation flower at its own pace, not force the clues to fit a predetermined pattern. "We need more information."

"Easy enough, we've both been questioning the people around Zulietta—her friends, her enemies, her family. Maybe we should focus on Zulietta herself. Who was she really? What did she want out of her wager? Where did she think her romance with Alessio would end?"

"And how do you propose we do that, clever wife?"

Liya threw off her dressing gown as she fairly skipped to the wardrobe. "We visit her lodgings. See if we can find a landlady. Talk to her maid if she's still around—and the funny little man you mentioned. You haven't been to her casino already, have you?"

"No."

"Do you know where she lived?"

"Ah, yes." Thanks to Benito.

"Well, let's get going. You'll have to help me." She tossed corset and stockings at my head, laughing. "Since Angelina's run home to Mama."

Zulietta's lodgings weren't far from the Teatro San Marco. She kept a casino, one of the little pleasure houses that offered a debauchee either or both of Venice's greatest attractions, women and gambling. Most casinos were clustered around the bustling Piazza. It made sense for all of Venice's entertainments, even the menagerie of exotic beasts that Titolino so wanted to visit, to be located where carnival merrymakers could easily find them.

Luigi set us down at the theater quay, and we crossed the square to enter a narrow alley bounded by a lottery office and the Pearl of the Waves. Casting a glance within the tavern's dim recesses, I recalled the sailor who had attempted to meet Alessio there and ended up searching for his box at the opera house.

Nothing further had been heard from this mystery man, and I had to wonder if Alessio had tracked him down and was now aboard ship crossing the sea to…where? Hadn't Liya just mentioned a sea journey foretold by her *tarocchi*? I glanced in her direction, but kept my mouth shut. If Liya procured a new pack of cards and again immersed herself in divination, so be it. But I wasn't going to encourage her.

Several turns brought us to an arched bridge that angled across a foul-smelling thread of water. Once on the other side, we caught the attention of an old fellow who represented a class of beggar unique to Venice. Crab-catchers we call them; as you board a gondola, they keep it from rocking by kneeling on the landing and grasping the boat's side walls. Of course, they expect a liberal bonus for their service. This one clutched my sleeve, dipping his head respectfully and insisting he be allowed to fetch a gondola for Signore's pleasure and convenience. I shrugged him off, amazed that this grandfather with a tangled white beard was still spry enough to ply his trade.

We soon located Zulietta's building on a damp, shadowy cul-de-sac. A tall wrought iron gate afforded a view of a vestibule open to the sky and stone stairs winding to the upper floors. I pulled the bell for the first-floor apartment. We heard a muffled jangle, but no one appeared. At Liya's urging, I pulled harder. Again, nothing.

Just when we had decided that Zulietta's servants must have abandoned the place, an extraordinary woman hurried downstairs clutching a straw broom. Since Venice rests at the crossroads of the eastern Mediterranean, I was accustomed to seeing skin of every hue our good Lord had seen fit to create, but I'd never seen a person as black as Zulietta's maid.

Observing her through the bars of the gate, I was astonished by the shining ebony mounds of her cheeks, as well as her mass of wiry tresses restrained by a brightly flowered kerchief. This exotic creature was neither old, nor girlish. She was a woman in her prime, with bold, handsome features and a well-padded figure only partially covered by her yellow gown and white apron. The delicate, dusky scent of sandalwood emanated from her person. Her eyes were narrowed in suspicion.

"If you please," I said. "We were friends of your mistress." Well, Liya *had* known Zulietta when she was still Mina Grazziano. By extension, I gave myself permission to claim friendship.

The maid took in my beardless chin, my spindle-thin extremities, and then looked my petite wife up and down. Apparently finding no danger in our appearance, she inquired after our business in polite, oddly accented tones. I allowed Liya to negotiate our entrée.

Sary—as she gave her name, be it Christian or surname I couldn't say—wasn't easily convinced. "My mistress never mentioned a Liya Del'Vecchio. Or any Liya at all, for that matter." Shaking her head, she made no move to open the gate.

My wife continued by fretting over all the years she'd let pass without calling on her old friend, whom she referred to as Mina. She also mentioned Reyna and Aram by name.

Sary scrunched an eyebrow. "If you're in tight with those scoundrels—"

"Not at all," Liya replied without hesitation. "That's why we came, my husband and I."

"Husband!" Sary shot me a disparaging look. It was often thus with peasants who never darkened the door of the opera house. Removed from my prodigious singing voice, I suppose I did cut rather an effete figure.

"Yes!" Liya proudly retorted. "My husband, Signor Tito Amato, *primo uomo* at the Teatro San Marco."

Did I see a glimmer of interest in Sary's eyes? Even if the world of opera was foreign to her, she must be calculating that "the first man" must be someone of importance. She put her hand on the bolt that would unlock the gate as Liya continued.

"We went to Reyna to hear something of Mina…er, Zulietta's last days, to beg some trifling memento for sentiment's sake. We were such friends back at school…more like sisters, really…then she left the ghetto…." Liya dabbed at her eyes with a handkerchief. Real tears! My wife had missed her calling. She would have made a talented actress. "But that evil shrew Reyna would grant me nothing. She was always jealous of Zulietta, and of our friendship. She suggested that I come see you."

Sary slid the bolt open. The gate squeaked on its hinges. "Come up," she said, and we followed her wide hips up to the first landing and through a shiny-painted green door.

Zulietta's apartment was elegant, but dark. The small foyer was lit by girandoles flanking a gilt-framed mirror. Even so, I nearly tripped over a battered traveling trunk set near the door. "Are you packed up to leave?"

Sary hesitated for a heartbeat, eyes showing very white against her coal-black skin.

I pointed to the trunk. "You can't stay here for long—now that your mistress is gone."

"That belongs to Pamarino, my mistress' footman."

Footman was he—that position was several rungs lower than the combination of majordomo and *cavaliere servente* the dwarf had claimed. "Oh, yes. I met Pamarino at the theater. Has he already left then?"

"He's gone to stay with his sister." She shrugged, disinterested. "He'll come back for his things once he's found another position."

"Is his sister also a dwarf?"

The maid shook her head. "She's as normal as anyone. Pretty, too, if you can believe it by looking at Pamarino's ugly face."

"A married woman?" I asked.

"Hardly. Estrella is her name and she makes her money on her back. Lives in a brothel over by the Arsenale."

"Where will you go?" That was Liya, warmly concerned.

Instead of answering at once, Sary led us into the sitting room. Several doors leading to other rooms were closed and the window shutters were only half-open, throwing this larger room into murky gloom. Sary rested her broom in a corner and gestured for us to sit on a comfortable-looking sofa which was bracketed by two elbow chairs. She remained standing with hands crossed in front of her starched apron. "The right position will present itself when I'm ready," she finally replied. "Even though my mistress has been laid to rest, I still have a lot of work here. She had a great many possessions which must be boxed up for auction. The magistrate who read her will allowed me a fortnight."

"What was done with her body?" Liya asked. "Her mother told me they had wished to bury her as a Jew."

Sary puffed a snort from her wide nostrils. "My mistress is in the crypt of San Fantin where she belongs. When she was alive, her family never did anything but stretch their hands out for gold. Why should they be allowed to carry her body out to their desolate sandbar?"

Poor Zulietta. Even in death she was caught between warring religions. Many years ago, the Hebrew cemetery had been consigned to the Lido, a barren, windswept island that protected our lagoon from the full force of the sea. From Liya, I understood that Jews must be buried in the dirt if they hoped to achieve life beyond death. Dirt was in short supply on Venice's main island; most Christians were consigned to the crypts of their parish churches or to the convent cemetery on the nearby island of San Michele. If Zulietta's spirit knew or cared where her earthly remains rested, I wondered which burial she would have chosen.

While Liya wrested details of the funeral from Sary, I put morbid thoughts aside and tried to imagine a living, vivacious Zulietta entertaining Signor Monday or Tuesday over an intimate dinner. Instead, I conjured the image of a tranquil woman in a quilted dressing gown reading alone by the light of an oil lamp.

Perhaps it was the books that crammed the shelves. Or the good taste displayed in the well-proportioned furniture, open writing desk, and wall panels painted with convincing *trompe l'oeil* scenes. But this casino didn't strike me as a place meant for lascivious amusement. It seemed more like the comfortable study of a woman of letters. The only thing that marred the pleasant tone was some soiled articles of clothing draped over a chair, destined for the laundry no doubt.

"All this will be sold?" My sweeping gesture took in the entire room.

"All proceeds to be divided among my mistress' mother and sisters." Sary pursed her lips with a kind of helpless intensity.

"What about you and the footman?" Liya asked. "Didn't your mistress provide for you?"

Her lips relaxed in a sad smile. "Don't worry about us, Signora. We've been well taken care of. My mistress left cash bequests with orders to the magistrate to dispense at once."

"I'm curious about your mistress," I said. "What can you tell me about her?" As I took note of a gentleman's jacket of silver-threaded blue brocade that lay on top of the laundry, I used a casual tone that I hoped wouldn't startle this obviously intelligent woman into wondering why a singer from the opera was asking questions more appropriate for Messer Grande.

Sary fidgeted a bit before answering, "She was a kind mistress, Signore. What more could you wish to know?"

"I was onstage when she fell. It was a shocking scene." I shook my head. "I would very much like to see her killer brought to justice. Can you think of anyone who meant her harm?"

It seemed that Sary was avoiding my question. She busied herself with rolling the jacket and other garments into a tight bundle and setting them on a nearby table. As she again reached for her broom, she murmured, "That is not for me to say, Signore."

"What about Alessio Pino?"

She shrugged, sweeping at a nonexistent bit of fluff.

Liya spoke up encouragingly. "My husband has a knack for solving puzzles of all kinds. Even Messer Grande sometimes seeks his counsel."

"Does he, now?" Sary sent me a long look. "Then I wish you luck. No one would like to see my mistress' killer taken more than I would."

I returned her level gaze. "You could help by telling me if you've seen Alessio Pino since he escaped from custody."

She shook her kerchiefed head. "What strange questions you ask. This is the last place Signor Pino would show up." Then she turned her attention to Liya. "You said you wanted a token of my mistress. Perhaps you'd like to look through her desk. She had several very nice pens. I'm sure we can find—"

"That will have to wait." I rose and went to the bundle of clothing Sary had whisked from my sight. After digging through the bundle, I unfurled the blue brocade jacket. "If you've not seen Alessio Pino, then how does his jacket come to be here?"

Liya stared open-mouthed.

Sary took a deep breath, nostrils flared. "Before my mistress died, Signor Alessio was often here. If that is his jacket, he must have mislaid it."

"No, Sary. I visited Alessio after he'd been arrested. He was wearing this very jacket. The pocket is torn, just as I noticed before."

"You're mistaken."

"I'm quite certain." I buried my nose in the expensive fabric, then held it out to the maid. "See for yourself. It still carries the stench of the guardhouse."

Sary raised her broom as if she meant to wield it as a cudgel. Her ebony skin shone, stretched tight over brow and cheekbones. Her lips drew back from her white teeth. "Get out—both of you. You have no business—"

I heard a creak. Felt a draft of air. A door swung open wide.

Alessio Pino stood in the entrance to the bedchamber, shirt unlaced, loose chestnut hair dusting his shoulders.

"It's all right, Sary." His voice was heavy and resigned. "I'll speak with Signor Amato."

Chapter Eleven

"Have you ever heard of a place called South Carolina?" Alessio asked, leaning forward with hands on knees. His face had grown thinner in just a few days, and his brown eyes were sunken and shadowed.

Liya and I both shook our heads. After calming Sary, Alessio had thrown himself into a stuffed armchair and invited us to hear his story. He had insisted that Sary join us, but the maid shook her head vigorously. She retrieved an armless chair from the desk in the window recess and placed it in the archway that led to the foyer. She kept silent guard, neither in our company nor completely removed from it.

"South Carolina is one of the American colonies," Alessio continued in a weary voice, "a remarkable place. The flat country near the coast is covered with rice marshes—they tell me acres and acres grow as far as the eye can see. Farther inland are plains with loose soil that are perfect for the cultivation of indigo. The planters own vast stretches of land and live like kings."

"Ye—es," I responded slowly. I'd heard of these American colonies whose goods and riches were competing with Venice's traditional trade routes. Some said they would eventually make paupers of us all. "What does this…South Carolina have to do with you and Zulietta?"

Alessio gave a frustrated sigh. "Skilled artisans are in short supply throughout the colony. The residents need glass like beggars need shoes. In the principal city of Charles Town, buildings are sprouting like mushrooms, and in the backcountry, the planters are building villas to rival any we have on our mainland estates. Think of all the windows that must be glazed, the many tables and taverns that need drinking vessels. The opportunities for glassmakers are boundless."

"Fine villas?" I asked. "I thought the warlike savages and wild beasts kept settlers from moving inland. And aren't America's towns just wilderness outposts?"

"Oh, Tito," Liya put in. "America is becoming quite civilized. Papa told me of some distant cousins who traveled to a place called Philadelphia to take up the manufacture of silk. They describe it as a land of milk and honey. You just assume any town lacking an opera house must be located in a wilderness."

Well, yes.

"Charles Town does have an opera house," Alessio challenged my unspoken thought. "At least a theater of some kind, because I'm assured the populace enjoys plays and concerts in addition to all manner of recreations. There is society there—and a blossoming economy. So many boats transport country produce to the wharves, their rivers often resemble floating marketplaces, and the deep harbor can accommodate every type of sailing vessel. Ships arrive daily from all points of the globe—especially England and the Sugar Islands."

"It sounds almost like the prosperous Venice of our fathers," I said.

Alessio nodded, then continued wistfully, "With hard work, a glass master could build a fortune in Charles Town."

"You were going to settle there—you and Zulietta," Liya observed softly.

"We were going to make a new life in a land of fresh ideas and promises," Alessio answered in a rasping whisper, "far from the sink of vice that Venice has become, completely beyond the reach of my father's petty tyrannies." The exhausted young man paused to stroke his unshaven chin. He threw a longing glance toward the open door of the bedchamber, and I almost thought he was going to shed tears. But Alessio went on, straightening his shoulders like a soldier setting off on a twenty-mile march.

"Zulietta and I weren't going alone. We were taking several of the men from the factory along with their families—they all have more skill at blowing glass than I do. In the New World, they will be acknowledged glass masters and I'll run the business. Charles Town is the perfect location for a glassworks. It has pure beach sand, sea plants rich with potash, plenty of fuel in the cypress swamps, and most importantly, investors willing to fund construction of the crucible kilns. A pair of agents from Charles Town approached me last winter, and I've been making plans for emigration ever since. The only thing left was to arrange passage for the lot of us."

Now I understood. The meeting Alessio had refused to tell Messer Grande about was with the captain of a ship leaving for America. It had to be conducted in utmost secrecy because of the Council of Ten's proscription against glassmakers quitting the Venetian Republic. Alessio was planning nothing less than the deliverance of his father's put-upon workers. I remembered the anxious inventor of the petal-scope, his fear that his young master's imprisonment would *ruin everything*.

"Is Zenobio one of the men who intended to make the journey?" I asked.

Alessio gazed at me steadily. "Are you making a habit of questioning all my associates?"

"I met Zenobio by chance, when Messer Grande ordered me over to Murano. I was needed to take your father's measure, just as I took yours."

Alessio managed a weak laugh. "So the astute lawman suspects Father of plunging a knife in Zulietta's ribs, eh? He can't know Cesare Pino very well. My father might have wished Zulietta dead in her grave—he'd ordered me to give her up time and again—but he would never have sent her there himself. That would risk his immortal soul. He might end up roasting on Satan's spit alongside one of the Hebrews he hates so much."

"And yet your father was on the scene, actually standing outside the box rattling the door handle while Zulietta fought her attacker." That was Liya.

"He's not your man," Alessio snapped. "Do you not agree, Signor Amato? You are the closest thing to an eyewitness that exists."

"If the observations of a man who stood across the breadth of the theater are of any worth, I do agree with you. The killer's gaze practically leapt out of the holes of his mask. I doubt your father could muster such a powerful stare given the mutilation to his eye. What I find more intriguing is the anonymous message that brought your father to the theater in the first place."

"A message? I've not heard anything about a message." Alessio narrowed his eyes and stared at the slatted pattern of light on the neatly arranged bookshelves.

"I suppose the glassworkers who broke you out of the guard-house weren't aware of it."

"I haven't explained who made my escape possible," he quickly retorted, snapping his focus back to me.

"You didn't have to. Who else would be so desperate to gain your freedom? On the one hand were the *garzoni* and *serventi* under your father's domination, watching as their chance for advancement slipped away. On the other was the ship's captain either foolish enough to risk the Ten's reprisal or willing to avoid the port of Venice until the incident would be long forgotten. You were the only link between the workers and their passage, and you were trapped behind bars. I can imagine their frustration, the many whispered conferences. The weather has been fine, how many days would the captain wait before setting off for America? I'm only surprised your rescuers delayed so long."

Alessio glared, lips pressed firmly together.

"Not going to tell me if I've hit the mark? Point of honor and all that?"

He rubbed the back of his neck, then replied, "I have the right to discuss my own affairs, but I'll not reveal information that could harm good men."

"So be it." Seeing that there would be no changing his mind, I explained about the message that sent his father rowing over to Venice like a madman. "Do you have any idea who was behind it?"

Liya added, "It had to be someone who knew about the culmination of the wager—someone who realized Zulietta would be displayed in your box for all to see."

Alessio chewed his lip, seemingly deep in thought. Liya must have been uncomfortable with the silence for she brought up a new subject. "It's a shame about your father's injury. Around the blazing kilns, I suppose accidents like that happen quite often."

"It wasn't an accident," Alessio tossed back. He cleared his throat several times, and I realized he was struggling to regain command of his voice. At last, he continued, "When my mother died, and the infant along with her, my father was crazed with grief. I was too young to remember, but I've pieced the story together from scraps I picked up from servants' gossip and loose-lipped workmen."

Liya and I inclined forward in unison, Cesare's mysterious message forgotten for the moment.

"My mother's labor was so prolonged, my father dismissed our local doctor and sent over to Venice for a medical man renowned for saving difficult births. This doctor convinced my father that all would be well. Of course, it wasn't. Hours passed, and still the child refused to leave the womb. With my mother near death, the doctor cut her open hoping to at least save the infant. Neither survived. After my father viewed the bloody scene, he ran straight to the factory and threw himself in the kiln. His workers immediately pulled him out, but..." Alessio released a long breath. "You've seen the damage, Signor Amato."

Liya sank back against the sofa cushion. As she murmured condolences, I thought of the learned ghetto physicians who were often called to Christian sickbeds as a last resort. In exception to the prevailing curfew, a physician attending a patient was allowed through the gates at any hour. Even the Doge was rumored to sometimes employ a doctor from the ghetto. I asked bluntly, "The doctor who tended your mother, was he a Jew?"

"Indeed he was," Alessio answered in a hushed tone. "My father's hatred of Jews is deep and intensely personal. When he found out about my love for Zulietta, he was cut to the quick. He made all sorts of threats, but against me, not her. If I persisted in the affair, he would never allow me to run the business—he would cut me off entirely—he would sell the glassworks to a stranger. He actually believed marrying me into the aristocracy would bring me to heel—poor little Maria was to be some sort of prize." Alessio gave his head a vigorous shake. "Father and I were at a complete impasse."

"You and Zulietta must have been seeing each other for some time," I said. "Months before the wager with La Samsona."

Alessio managed a strained smile. For the first time, he addressed the silent woman in the doorway. "How long, Sary? I've missed so much sleep, I don't trust my head for dates, but I know you remember."

The black woman rose and drew near. She stood with one arm folded across her belly and the other hand to her cheek, the pose of a worried woman, no matter what her race. "Seven months, Signor Alessio. My mistress met you at the theater when it reopened after Lent. She brought you home that very night." After a sigh, Sary added, "Nothing has been the same since."

"Of course," Alessio answered. "It was late March. What a lovely spring it was—just Zulietta and I spending long nights here, and when we felt the need of air, taking a boat to a secluded garden on the Giudecca where no questions are ever asked. This casino was our sanctuary. We were in paradise—until my father intruded with his dictums and threats."

"So the wager over the jewels must have been a complete sham," I said. "You and Zulietta were already lovers."

Alessio nodded slowly.

"Was La Samsona in on it?" Liya asked. "Did she know about you two?"

Sary threw back her head and gave a throaty laugh.

"In on it, you ask?" Alessio replied with a hint of a smile. "Quite the opposite. Zulietta hatched the plan when she realized La Samsona had taken a fancy to me.

"What an obnoxious woman! Dripping jewels, reeking with scent, she pursued me at every masquerade, ridotto, or concert I attended. At the opera, she would send her footman around with invitations as endless and regular as the lagoon tides. If she did manage to worm her way into my company, she couldn't keep those huge hands off me. La Samsona assumed I was without female company, you see. Up until then, Zulietta and I had been very discreet in order to keep gossip from reaching my father's ears."

"What was this plan? Were La Samsona's diamonds and pearls meant to fund passage to the New World? What about Zulietta's jewels?"

Alessio gave me a heavy-lidded look, then gestured to Sary. "Fetch your mistress' jewel box, if you please."

The black woman stepped into the bedchamber and returned with a sizeable marquetry casket which she placed on Alessio's lap. When he flipped the lid open, we saw it was empty save for some simple gold bracelets, a long string of pearls, and several pairs of earrings.

"She'd already sold most of her things?" Liya asked.

Alessio nodded. "Little by little she'd sold everything except these pieces her father gave her. Zulietta would never part with these, and La Samsona would have grown suspicious if she hadn't worn any jewelry at all."

"Zulietta didn't hold back," I observed.

"Neither of us did. Once we decided on our course of action, we set about to gather as much gold as possible. Since we could never return to Venice, Zulietta was determined to leave her mother well provided for. Besides the exorbitant payment Captain Vinci demanded, I was going to use the funds from the wager to also leave my father a sum that would compensate him for the loss of my work."

Liya pursed her lips. "What sum could possibly compensate a father for the loss of a son, especially when he's already lost so much?"

"You think me cruel," Alessio replied gravely. "I've tried to get along with my father, I truly have, but even before I met Zulietta, I couldn't countenance the shabby treatment of his workers. There's no pride in loyalty to a tyrant. A complete break was necessary."

Liya opened her mouth and shut it just as quickly. Before she ducked her head, I saw tears glittering in her eyes. I fancied she was thinking of Pincas, her own deserted father, though one as least like a tyrant as possible.

"What are you going to do now?" I asked Alessio. "The Council is convinced you murdered Zulietta. If you remain in Venice, you'll be arrested again, and this time there will be no escape."

He sighed. "I promised the glassworkers I would lead them to a new land, and I intend to keep that promise."

"How?"

"That I don't know, but I've made my promise and I will fulfill it." Alessio set his jaw and his eyes shone with a steady light. Had I ever been that young and unafraid? He went on, "Perhaps I can tap my investors a bit farther. We'll see. But I refuse to leave Venice until I discover who killed my Zulietta. That's why I'm talking to you—you appear to have your own reasons for finding the brute."

I nodded cautiously. "What are you asking me to do?"

"I ask that you keep my presence here a secret..."

"And?"

Alessio stretched his long legs out and folded his hands over his midsection. He regarded me with his chin on his chest. "In the guardhouse, I had a great deal of time to ponder. I came to the conclusion that I was purposefully delayed on the night of the murder. My gondolier has never been drunk a day in his life. I'm certain someone interfered with him. I can't row over to Murano and make inquiries—I'd be spotted immediately—but you can. And now you tell me my father received a note. I don't understand it. No one knew Zulietta would be at the theater that night besides ourselves."

"You may be wrong about that. La Samsona either knew or suspected because she'd consigned her best jewels to the bank for safekeeping."

Alessio shook his head. "That was strictly forbidden in the agreement—the women summoned a notary to formalize terms—Zulietta's copy is somewhere hereabouts."

"In the desk," Sary spoke up.

I grunted a chuckle. "It seems neither party to the contract was being honest, Alessio. And you're wrong about something else, too." I sent the maid a sidelong glance. "Zulietta's servants knew about the culmination of the wager. Pamarino accompanied her to the theater and actually tangled with the killer. Bravely, too. He could have easily suffocated with that thick cloak swaddling him."

Alessio sat up tall. "Yes, of course, the dwarf was loyal to a fault. He worshipped Zulietta and would never have let our secret out—to my father or anyone else. And Sary certainly knew the importance of keeping mum." He questioned the maid with a look.

She nodded gravely, saying, "I don't see how anyone outside of this household would have known my mistress was attending the opera that night."

"And yet someone did, because she was killed," I said.

Liya spoke up. "Perhaps the killer saw Zulietta in the theater foyer or on the grand staircase, then followed her to see which box she entered."

"You're forgetting the key, my love. The duplicate was made beforehand."

"Key?" Alessio questioned me in a weary, puzzled tone.

"Zulietta unlocked your family box with the key you'd given her."

He nodded in agreement.

"Messer Grande discovered that key in her pocket. The killer had a second key which was used to lock the box after Zulietta had fallen into the pit."

"Then that's another thing I don't understand. There has always been only one key to the box." Alessio bowed his head and cradled it with outstretched fingers. He rocked from side to side, giving the impression that his strength was nearly at an end. "What a tangle! You must help unravel it, Signor Amato."

We were all silent for a moment, lost in our own thoughts. A finger of sunlight streaming through the shutters happened to fall on a panel painted with a walled garden. Realistic herb beds surrounded an ornamental pond, and a brick path led to a stone bench. It would be quiet and peaceful there, pleasantly cool. I could almost smell the sweet fragrance. Liya and I should be strolling in such a place without a care in our heads. Instead we were in the company of a guardhouse escapee who was not only suspected of murder, but planning a glassmakers' revolt. I should take my wife's hand and walk right out the door.

I wouldn't, of course. Solving a mystery that no one else cared, or dared, to investigate had always been my forbidden fruit. Messer Grande had been ordered to concentrate on the San Polo robberies. By necessity, Alessio must remain in hiding. If Zulietta's killer was going to be unmasked, it looked like it was up to me.

It was past noon, and Maestro Torani had called a rehearsal for two o'clock. To satisfy the public's insatiable thirst for new spectacle, the next opera must be readied even as we continued to perform the current offering. The quickest route to the Teatro San Marco lay back the way we had come, but Liya clearly didn't want to give me up. As we left Zulietta's building, my wife slipped her arm under mine and suggested a stroll toward the Piazza. I was easily persuaded. There was sufficient time to enjoy her company and also make a timely appearance at the theater.

As we crossed the arched bridge, I noticed the crab-catcher with the unkempt beard leaning on the railing, face turned up to bask in the sun's rays. Something about his stance seemed familiar, but when I stepped closer to get a better look at him, he chose to take that moment to shade his eyes with his hand. A coincidence? I was reminded of the turbaned Jew who had dogged our steps through the ghetto, but this was a different man. Shorter and older. Besides, the crab-catcher hadn't followed us from home. Of that, I was certain.

Ten minutes brought us to the great square that was the focus of carnival gaiety. On three sides, the Piazza was belted with arcades sheltering shops and cafés, and on the fourth, the tessellated arches and golden domes of the Basilica glittered in the midday sun. Though our mood didn't match the inclinations of the maskers who surged to and fro in a noisy, reeling promenade, we settled ourselves at one of the few unoccupied tables under the Procuratie Vecchie and ordered two lemon ices. In between the capering Harlequins and Brighellas, the comical Devils, and anonymous eye masks, we caught snatches of the entertainment proceeding on a nearby trestle stage.

An Irish giant by the name of O'Bryan was amazing the spectators with feats of strength. Nearly eight feet tall and with shoulders as broad as the table where we sat, O'Bryan lifted a blacksmith's anvil over his head as if it were a sack of meal. "Three hundred pounds of iron, good ladies and gentlemen," his manager cried.

"Oh, Tito," said Liya, mightily impressed. "Do you really think it weighs that much?"

"Probably." Though the Piazza was full of tricksters like the thimble-rig man who fleeced the punters with his sleight of hand or the fortune-tellers who traded promises of health and wealth for a few *soldi*, that anvil appeared absolutely authentic. As did the muscles of the bare-chested O'Bryan.

"I wonder how many pounds La Samsona lifted when she entertained the crowd," Liya mused over her ice.

I leaned over the white tablecloth. "You're really asking if she had the strength to push Zulietta over the box railing."

"I suppose I am. Like you said this morning, 'one twist and a new pattern emerges.'" Liya made a tube of her curled hands and moved them to her eye as if she were gazing through the petal-scope. "Before we visited Zulietta's home, I saw her as a gaudy dragonfly—an airy mixture of charm and cunning."

"And now?"

"Now I understand that Zulietta embellished the contents of her head as much as the exterior. She had far more substance than I gave her credit for. How tired she must have grown of all the forced vivacity—the round of balls and other frolics her mode of life entailed."

"By putting the wager into play, she certainly embarked on a path that would take her away from all that. Far away." I shuddered, still not convinced that Alessio's longed-for Charles Town was not peopled by ruffians and savages. "But does your new viewpoint exclude Reyna and Aram as suspects in Zulietta's death?"

"I would never entirely discount that pair of villains, but seeing those few lonely baubles in Zulietta's jewelry box did change my focus. Perhaps the wager is the thread we need to pull to unravel this mystery. You've talked to La Samsona—tell me about her."

Licking the frozen treat off my spoon, I thought back to the scene in the courtesan's box. "La Samsona is a woman of strong appetites. In every respect, she is beyond extravagance. The French have a word for it—*de trop*—too much. The decors on her gown could have supplied four women of good taste, and her scent..." I wrinkled my nose. "A full acre of roses must have been distilled into the perfume she'd dabbed on her person for that one night at the opera."

"Hmm..." Liya stared out toward the square where the Irish giant was lifting a squealing bull calf with its legs tied together. "A lack of refinement, certainly—but that doesn't translate into murder. I'm more interested in her character. How do you think she would have reacted if she learned that Zulietta had concocted the wager to defraud her of her jewels?"

"I wouldn't want to have been there—she would have been livid. At least initially. Her moods seem to change quickly."

"We know she'd taken steps to protect her jewels."

I nodded. "An astute move on her part. That doesn't surprise me—these women who barter their services are negotiating in a man's world. Their wealthy benefactors are accustomed to imposing terms and conditions on every sort of business endeavor and are practiced in protecting their assets. La Samsona is no empty-headed fool. She must have learned something along the way."

"Perhaps ensuring that Zulietta would never get her hands on her diamonds wasn't enough for this lady. Apparently, La Samsona sets great store by her celebrity. Imagine the blow to her pride—hoodwinked by a little Jew who hadn't been circulating in gallant society nearly as long as she had. La Samsona must have bubbled like a stew pot, her anger growing hotter and hotter until the lid blew off."

"An apt metaphor."

Liya pushed her empty ice cup away, narrowing her eyes like a cat that has just spotted a plump, slow-moving mouse. "It would take steady nerves to attack the dwarf in the corridor, drag him into the cloakroom, then return to the box to murder a woman who had once been her friend."

"La Samsona strikes me as having nerves to equal anyone, man or woman. But don't forget about the key. She had less opportunity to make a duplicate key than any of the other people we agree had reason to kill Zulietta."

Liya emitted a frustrated sigh. "That damnable key—always that key—it's a barricade across the only path that can take us where we need to go. Oh, Tito, at this rate, we may never find Zulietta's killer."

"Don't say that," I replied, reaching for my watch. As much as I would have liked to continue our discussion, the angle of the sun hinted it was time to set off. Yes, near two o'clock. I snapped my watch closed and shrugged my shoulders. "I sup-pose I could visit La Samsona's box again tonight, see if she'll answer a few more questions."

Liya sent me a shrewd squint. "Maybe there's a better way to assess her possibilities."

"Let me hear it."

"You mentioned La Samsona's rose-drenched perfume. So did Alessio. She must wear that fragrance all the time."

I nodded. Most women seemed to favor one scent over another. Those with means frequented a perfumer who would distill a fragrance especially for them; their signature scent would also be incorporated into lotions, powders, and bath oils. Given her vast herbal skills, Liya concocted her own scent, but La Samsona would be the type of woman who ran up a large bill at the perfumer's.

"So," Liya continued, "Aram doesn't wear scent—he would scoff at any tradesman who perfumes like a young buck of fash-ion. And I can't imagine Cesare Pino smelling of roses. Maria Albergati's brothers, perhaps."

"What are you saying?"

"I'm saying that, instead of trying to wring more information out of that wily courtesan, you should question the dwarf. The killer swooped him up and wrestled him into the cloakroom. If La Samsona was disguised under the cloak and *bauta*, surely he would recall the heavy scent of roses."

I sat back and gazed at my wife in silent admiration. I had my own reason for wanting to see the dwarf again; she'd given me another. After congratulating her on a capital idea, I couldn't resist a little teasing. "Did you come to this conclusion all by yourself?"

"Of course, it just occurred to me."

"Oh," I replied airily, "I thought one of your otherworldly oracles might have whispered in your ear."

She arched an eyebrow. "I hope you know you'll pay for that remark."

"I'll take my medicine. But later. Just now, Maestro Torani is wondering if his lead singer is going to be late again." I gave her my arm as we left the shelter of the arcade, heading away from the Basilica and the Doge's palace, toward the Teatro San Marco.

The crowd had thickened as we'd lingered over our ices. A delegation of Albanians in white kirtles and red leggings blocked our path. More bodies buffeted us from both sides.

"Tito," Liya squealed, and I caught sight of a hairy arm reaching around my wife's waist to squeeze her bosom. With all my force, I bent the roving arm back at the elbow and was rewarded with a yelp of pain. A man in a pig mask twisted away and was instantly lost to sight.

I put my mouth to Liya's ear. "Hang on tight. I'll get us out of here."

More easily said than accomplished. I pushed and shoved, but the sea of maskers surged as if controlled by one oppositional force. Suddenly, somewhere beyond the Albanians, there was the sound of wood snapping, metal clanging, and the crash of pottery hitting flagstones. A woman wailed to see her booth collapsing around her. As the crowd turned to view this minor spectacle, a path materialized, like the wake formed by a broad-sterned schooner.

I quickly guided us to an open space near the trestle stage. The Irish giant was trading places with an acrobatic troupe which entered to a flute march played by a white-faced Pierrot.

Catching our breath, we paused to watch six well-formed young men perform a rapid series of handstands and somersaults. They had barely begun to form a towering pyramid when a male dwarf clambered onstage, beating a tin drum. Rigged out in a pink ballerina skirt, dark hair caught back with a ribbon bow, he circled the stage making a fearful din. The tallest acrobat ordered him off with a dramatically outflung arm, but the dwarf made a rude gesture, beat his drum all the louder, and gamboled about the boards in a parody of the ballet girls at the opera house. The other acrobats gave chase. The crowd was drifting back. Hilarity ensued.

"Is that Zulietta's little man?" Liya asked.

"Not him, but very like," I answered as we watched the acrobats catch the dwarf and pull his breeches down. The Pierrot reappeared with a wooden paddle. In mimed gestures he asked the crowd: *Should I lay this to him?*

A roar went up, and several shouts. "Away with the gnat—whip him good—redden his behind."

"Come away," I said in Liya's ear, "while we can still move. Any more delay and Maestro Torani will have my head."

My wife nodded, and together we escaped the crush of mindless confusion and frenzied antics that passed for amusement in those days.

Chapter Twelve

Our excursion to the Piazza left me in a foul mood. Liya's subsequent desertion, especially her refusal to tell me where she was going, only increased my vexation. Luigi's gondola had been tethered at the rear of the opera house, at the shallow flight of granite steps which dropped to the water's edge. After finding the boatman asleep in the shadow of a nearby bridge, I instructed him to row Liya back to the Cannaregio. My wife surprised me by refusing his services. Instead, she kissed me on the cheek, reminded me to be careful, and quickly set off on foot in the direction opposite home. I followed her for several paces, inquiring after the nature of her errand, but she merely waved her hand without looking back. What was she up to now?

The weather mirrored my mood. The sun had disappeared behind a thick bank of clouds that was sweeping across the sky from the mainland. The cloud tops were white and fluffy, but their undersides were gray as ash. One patch of azure blue was defending the eastern horizon, but it would soon be swallowed by the lead cloud that had taken the shape of a gaping maw with two sharp fangs.

I trudged up the stairs to the water entrance of the Teatro San Marco, then turned and paused between the pair of massive columns supporting the portico. I lifted my nose and sniffed the air. It told of snow-covered mountain pastures, wild forests, and dampness. We were in for a storm. I could only hope Liya arrived safely home before it blew down upon us.

"You're late, Tito," a woman's merry soprano rang out. Vittoria Busanti ran up the stairs, and stopped with her hand on my shoulder, panting from exertion and laughing at the same time. It was an intimate, indulgent chuckle that somehow made the day seem brighter. Vittoria was strikingly attractive as always, but her appearance was uncharacteristically unkempt. Her auburn hair, obviously arranged in haste, threatened to slip its few pins, and her chemise was showing above the top of her bodice.

"No later than you, *cara*. Torani will have a few choice words for both of us."

She shrugged and sent me a knowing smile that brought all sorts of lascivious afternoon activities to mind. "Why are you standing outside sniffing like a hare?" she asked, still with her soft hand on my shoulder.

"Testing the air. It's something my sailor brother taught me."

"I've never met this brother. A sailor, eh? Is he anywhere near as handsome as you?"

"Alessandro is the handsomer brother by far," I answered, feeling a blush rise to my cheeks. "At least his wife, Zuhal, would tell you so. You're unlikely to meet either since they live in Constantinople."

"Ah, well." She tossed her head. "The air smells the same as the canal to me—like the inside of a refuse barrel. What does your nose make of it?"

"We're going to have buckets of rain, probably by nightfall."

She clapped her hands together. "*Favoloso*! My prayers have been answered—and so quickly."

"You've come from church?" I couldn't keep the skeptical tone from my voice.

"No, silly. I went to Mass this morning. This afternoon, I've been dining with dear Montague. You know how it is with those elderly English lords—one hour at table followed by one between the sheets—if you delay bed until after the opera, they fall asleep on you. I think it's the pounds of roast beef they put away."

I hadn't known, but now I did. Vittoria was nothing if not forthright.

"Why do you want it to rain?" I asked as we passed through double doors into the back foyer.

"The house has been off these past few nights. Since bad weather always brings them out in droves, lighting a candle for rain was the least I could do. I mean, it wouldn't do to pray for snow. That would be silly. We won't have snow until Christmas, if then."

"I see. You're not expecting a miracle, just a little help."

She nodded brightly, and I couldn't help but wonder what it must be like to travel the road of life as Vittoria Busanti. With this popular prima donna, it was all lovely gowns, gratifying applause, rich protectors. Pleasure was easily within her reach, and she grabbed for it daily, heedless of accident, illness, or the possibility of losing her voice. How pleasant and natural that life must be—a veritable Garden of Eden.

I traveled a road fraught with anxiety, never able to forget the unknown misfortunes the morrow might produce. Apparently Zulietta Giardino's path had been more like mine. She had well understood that a courtesan's career was short and had mapped out a plan that would carry her into a happy, secure future. Until the killer with the malevolent gaze put an end to her. A sudden chill ran over me, and I shook my head. Save the detection for later, I told myself. In a moment, you'll have a new opera to learn.

In the auditorium, Vittoria and I found the benches neatly arranged and the main chandelier lowered so that workmen could replace the spent tapers. As we neared the stage, I noted that Maestro Torani's expression was heavy and sour. Emilio was bending his ear about a recent favorable mention in the *Gazzetta Veneta*. Holding the paper at arm's length, the castrato read, "Our delightful Emiliano continues to amaze us with a throat as tuneful as Apollo's lyre..."

Behind Emilio's back, Rosa Tiretta, our conniving little contralto, was mimicking his self-congratulatory monologue for the amusement of the scene shifters and prop boys. Rosa played soubrette roles as if she'd been born to them. She wasn't a beauty, but she had learned to sing while maintaining a pleasant smile, never distorting her face as some were forced to. When Torani saw Vittoria and me mounting the stairs that curved around one side of the orchestra pit, a flash of relief streaked across his countenance. For interrupting Emilio, it seemed our lateness would be forgiven.

"Ah, we're all here. At last. Come along, you two, so we can commence." Torani clapped his hands several times, then twisted his neck from side to side. "If Romeo hasn't wandered off. Where can the boy have got to? He was just here."

"Probably still at dinner," Vittoria murmured. Our young basso, Romeo Battaglia, might have a belly to rival a Spanish friar, but his voice was clear, sweet, and as mellow as mulled wine. With his vast vocal compass and eager manner, Romeo could interpret roles that varied from a lovesick shepherd to an angry Jupiter hurling thunderbolts.

"I'm here, Maestro." Romeo's sleepy head popped up from a first-tier box. Despite his size, he easily vaulted the railing with jacket and wig in hand. "Just catching forty winks."

"Poor little boy…" Vittoria's whisper took on a tinge of spleen, "has to save his strength, you know."

"You're very cross all of a sudden." I sent the soprano a questioning look. Our prima donna generally displayed a sweet disposition, especially after she'd spent a lazy afternoon in a rich man's bed. "Is something wrong?"

"Not yet. Just wait…" A frown from Torani silenced Vittoria's revelation, but as Romeo plodded across the stage she rolled her eyes.

I wasn't mystified for long. Once the entire company had assembled, Maestro Torani announced the title of our next production: *The Labors of Hercules*. With Romeo to take the title role. Somehow Vittoria had known, or at least suspected, but the rest of the company was visibly startled. Emilio's jaw dropped. Mine also. We castrati were the first men of the company, the kings of vocal ornamentation, the heroes of brilliant sentiment, the major reason people flocked to the opera. In casting a basso as *primo uomo*, our maestro was not just breaking tradition; he was shredding it into tiny pieces, throwing it in the fire, and stomping on the ashes.

A basso in the lead—castrati relegated to secondary roles? Unheard of!

I closed my mouth with a hard gulp, barely aware that Vittoria had laid a sympathetic hand on my arm or that Rosa was stifling nervous giggles. Were my cheeks turning red? Did I grow rigid with humiliation? Emilio certainly did. He was still as stone except for opening and closing his mouth like a fish hauled from the water and tossed on the quay. Strangled, wordless outrage belched forth with each parting of his lips. By contrast, Romeo was expressing befuddled exclamations of surprise and gratitude.

Ignoring Romeo, Torani snatched off his tie-wig and beat it against his thigh. He looked from me to Emilio and back again. "Not a word, not one word! I've found the perfect drama, spent four months putting it to music, and by a stroke of happy luck, the company possesses the perfect singer—with the perfect amount of flesh—to take the principal role. If any man disagrees, let him take his objections and yell them down the nearest privy hole."

I nodded slowly, struggling to master my emotions and find the bright side of this unexpected development. The audience might be intrigued by the novelty of a basso as Hercules; anything that would pump up box office receipts would benefit us all.

Also, being assigned a lesser role would allow me more time and energy to search for Zulietta's killer. Perhaps Torani's new opera wouldn't work out badly after all. I gathered myself up with dignity. "Maestro, I'm certain we can all put partisan feelings aside and enter into the spirit of this extraordinary production."

Vittoria seconded my statement, an act all the more admirable because the casting on the distaff side had also been turned upside down. For once, Rosa had been given billing above Vittoria. Perhaps our prima donna had more depth than it often seemed.

Torani sent a small bow toward Vittoria and me, then clapped his hands at a theater lackey who sprinted into the wings. After a moment, the man returned pushing a wheeled cart stacked with musical scores. As Torani began distributing the hand-copied music, he said, "The orchestral players are due any minute. I'll start with Romeo and the rest of you can be studying your parts."

Rosa practically skipped forward to grab her thick score. Romeo followed, still wearing an expression of happy disbelief. Emilio stepped back as the other secondary players crowded around the cart. I wondered if my fellow castrato would cause a scene by refusing his role, but I wouldn't be onstage to find out.

I accepted the score that Maestro Torani handed me along with instructions to report to the costume workshop and was soon barreling along a back corridor with the music for Hyllus, son of Hercules, tucked under my arm.

Like Vittoria, my old friend Madame Dumas didn't seem surprised that the company pecking order had been turned topsy-turvy. Perhaps her clue had been the fur skins ordered to swathe Hercules' torso; they were considerably in excess of the yardage that either Emilio or I would have required. Many hands prepared an opera: copyists, scene painters, machinists, costumers, and more. Torani must have threatened all those who knew about the casting with dire punishment if they opened their mouths.

An apologetic Madame Dumas tut-tutted over my demotion. Shaking her silver-crowned head, she assured me that Maestro Torani must be a fool to cast "that great ox with the foghorn voice" over her favorite castrato.

"Don't worry, Signor Amato." The seamstress stroked a bolt of rich brown velvet leaning against the worktable. "I'll cut your cape from this fabric—there's none finer in the entire city. Line it with turquoise silk from Lyon, I will. And your waistcoat, it will be embroidered with so many gold threads it will shine in pitch darkness. Romeo may have more notes to sing, but you will be the chief ornament of *Hercules*."

I took her blue-veined hand and gave it a grateful kiss. "I can only hope the fickle public will be as loathe to forget me as you are."

"They'll never forget you—don't trouble your head for one minute." She moved to grasp the bolt of velvet and tried to muscle it onto the worktable. A pair of assistant seamstresses came running to help, but she waved them back. "I'm the only one who will touch the cloth for Signor Amato's costume. Every stitch will be mine and mine alone."

"There's no reason why the wearer of the costume can't touch it, is there?" Madame Dumas was a sterling needlewoman, but her pipestem arms weren't up to the task of readying the fabric for the cutting shears that hung from her waist. I lifted the heavy bolt onto the smooth pine tabletop. It unrolled in a stream of rich chocolate highlighted with caramel where the velvet nap caught the light. When the tail end had slipped from the bolt, I planted the wooden pole on the floor as if I held the lance of a knight errant.

"Beautiful, isn't it?" Madame was bursting with pride, no doubt envisioning the eventual garment.

"Lovely," I agreed. "I'll have to be in my best voice to do your work justice."

In response, the old seamstress cast her eyes down and blushed like a girl of sixteen. Not for the first time, I imagined the charm and *esprit* Madame Dumas must have displayed as a young Parisienne of the last century.

"This is a useful item," I said, admiring the slender pole of polished wood that had held the fabric. It sported a small lever about two thirds along its length to keep the velvet from dragging on the floor and getting dirty. A leather strap affixed with a nail could be fastened around the roll to keep the fabric tightly wound. "I don't think I've seen anything like this in your workroom before."

She winked. "I found it gathering dust backstage—it and its mate. They're probably meant for one of the cloud machines, but they fit my purpose so well, I carried them back here. You won't tell on me, will you?"

"Your secret is safe with me, Madame. Now…" I threw my arms out to both sides and stood straight and tall. "Don't you have some measurements to take?"

Cackling a laugh, she fiddled with the instruments on her belt, and soon her tape was making its customary perambulations around my person. I took the opportunity to give some thought to the remainder of the afternoon. Maestro Torani wouldn't be rehearsing my new part until tomorrow morning. Once Madame was done with me, I would be at my leisure until I must dress for that night's performance of *Armida*. Should I have Luigi row me over to Murano so I could run down Alessio's drunken gondolier? Or should I try to locate Pamarino?

The weather made my mind up for me. When I opened the stage door, all was gray: the damp-slick stones of the alleyway, the leaden sky, the scudding clouds. The looming storm had swallowed the sun.

I turned and ran up to my dressing room, taking the stairs two at a time. Benito had not yet arrived, but he always kept an extra pair of boots, as well as a waxed cloak and beaver hat stashed in the wardrobe. I donned these, thought about a muff he'd also tucked on a shelf, but left it behind. Then I set off for Zulietta's casino. Having Luigi row me over to Murano with a blow coming would be foolhardy, but if Sary could tell me where to find Pamarino, my next several hours would not be wasted.

"I'm sleeping in a cupboard under the stairs—right next to the pissoir." Pamarino curled his thick lips in a frown. He wore his blue jacket with the silver epaulets and buttons, but the metal showed signs of tarnish and his thick brown wig was in dire need of a hairdresser's services. As before, his droll appearance was at odds with his well-spoken conversation.

"Not a pleasant situation," I replied over the hum of voices in the rough café Sary had directed me to. The place had a slanted ceiling and the sour smell of spilled wine and unwashed working men.

"No." The tone of that simple word implied that the proprietor of the brothel that housed his sister had greatly underestimated Pamarino's importance and would suffer for his impertinence in the future. Very proud, this little man, this toy soldier. And yet, under the bluster, I thought I could detect a faint note of resignation.

"Why aren't you staying at your mistress' casino?"

Pamarino shrugged glumly.

"Sary told me it will be several weeks before the household goods go to auction and the place is shut up for good."

"I'm better off where I am," he snapped, but his lips began to quiver and his eyes became glossy.

I understood. The same aching grief that had sent him roaming the theater corridors must have been overwhelming in the close confines of the casino. At every creak of the stairs, his heart must have made a sudden leap, hoping against hope that his beloved mistress would somehow appear. Her possessions scattered throughout the apartment—a favorite book on a tabletop, a lone glove forgotten behind a sofa cushion—all must have been torture.

I'd found Pamarino's café on a narrow canal tucked between the waterfront and the Arsenale, Venice's great shipyard. Every forlorn man who lacks a kitchen, or a woman to tend one, frequents some local café that becomes his sitting room as much as his source of meals. Two *soldi* tendered for a tiny cup of black coffee secures a table and as many gazettes as a man could read in an hour or an afternoon. I had already supplied Pamarino with more than coffee. He was spooning his way through a large bowl of polenta and crisp minnows. To show his thanks, he was putting up with my questions.

"Can your sister not arrange better accommodations for you?"

"The scoundrel who employs Estrella says the cupboard is sufficient, and my sister is not in a position to argue. Whores of her variety are thick on the ground—she could be replaced in a heartbeat. No, she only gabbled some nonsense about the cupboard being a perfect fit as she made me a bed of musty blankets that would insult a stray dog."

I nodded slowly and took a sip of cheap, sour wine. One look at the food-stained tabletop had put me off the idea of sharing Pamarino's meal, and I had carefully wiped my tin cup before allowing the waiter to slop his inferior vintage into it. With a burning throat, I asked, "Are you searching for work?"

He nodded. "I offered myself at Estrella's place. While the men are waiting their turns, I thought I could act the fool for their amusement. You might be surprised to learn I can make people laugh. In between turning handsprings, I recite bawdy poems—throw out a few vulgar witticisms."

"Do you, now?"

"Oh, yes. Over the years, I must have collected thousands." His tone was solemn as an owl, until he dropped his spoon, shook his shoulders, and threw his head back. When he brought it forward, his face was split by an idiotic grin. He could have been the twin of the dwarf Liya and I had watched on the Piazza. In a crude singsong voice, he uttered:

> *There was a young lad from Trevise,*
> *Who would come whenever he'd sneeze.*
> *To the druggist he went, laying down his last cent,*
> *Said, "a barrel of snuff if you please."*

I chuckled with what I hoped was a look of commendation on my face. "The proprietor refused to hire you? I can scarcely believe it."

"Turned me down flat as a pancake. It was only through Estrella's pleading that I came by a temporary bed in that establishment. Her employer fears the bad luck I might bring, you see." Pamarino took up his spoon and slurped a generous mouthful of stew. He continued in a tone curiously devoid of emotion. "There are many who believe that my mother must have lain with a goblin or forest *folletto*. How else to explain the birth of a monster such as I? My ties to the goblin world lump me in with thieves and knaves and other evil folk. Why…I might even possess the secrets of the evil eye or the art of poisoning. I'm obviously a dangerous man." He waggled a finger. "You had better be careful around me, Signor Amato."

"I'll take my chances," I replied with a smile. "I'm well acquainted with the ridiculous assumptions people make based on appearance alone."

His glance flicked over me. "Yes, you would be."

"But I don't understand why you are depending on your sister's charity. I thought your mistress left you well provided for." I continued in response to his lifted eyebrow. "Sary told me about the bequests you both received."

Pamarino's demeanor changed again. He pulled his chin and sent me a concentrated glare. If that wasn't the evil eye, it could pass for a good likeness. "I wonder why my situation should concern you in the slightest."

"Indulge me," I answered in a neutral tone.

We locked gazes for a moment. Outside, the storm had blown in, and the rain that beaded along the overhanging portico fell to the pavement in a steady patter. Pamarino sighed. "I put my mistress' money aside should times grow even worse. In my experience, misfortune is always followed by more of the same…'

"Now I ask that you indulge me—why do you remain so interested in my mistress' death? You claimed no acquaintance with her. If you had, I would have been aware of it."

"You're right. I had no acquaintance with Zulietta Giardino in life. Our bond was forged at the instant of her death. As you know, fate contrived that I be the only witness to her murder."

The dwarf's tone grew warmer. "Yes, that was odd, considering how many hundreds of people filled the theater. Given this…this bond you feel, it must drive you wild that her killer escaped before he could be hung."

"Alessio Pino?"

He inclined his head.

"I'm not at all certain that Alessio is the killer."

He snorted. "Of course he is. I knew it from the beginning—you were there at the theater when I explained it all to Messer Grande. Unfortunately, no one ever listens to me." He spread a scowl around the café, as if the bearded dockworkers who made up its patrons were all conspiring to ignore him.

"I was listening to you. You had a lot to say about Alessio that night, but you left out one important part of your mistress' story."

"Eh?"

"The wager was not sheer mischief as you described. It was a deliberately mismatched contest, and the foregone victory would play a crucial role in your mistress' future. She and Alessio planned to use the bounty from La Samsona's jewel box to travel to America." This point had been bothering me ever since Liya and I had visited Zulietta's casino. Pamarino must have been included in the plan. He was too instrumental in Zulietta's household for her to have kept it from him.

"Oh, that...Sary must have been very talkative." He sent me a sheepish grin. "You must understand that I was only trying to keep my mistress' secret. Perhaps it didn't matter once she was taken from us, but she had been most particular that no one find out about the glassmakers' planned decampment, so I repeated the wager story as the world was supposed to view it."

"And how was Alessio supposed to view it?"

"I can't speak for him—a wolf in a lamb's skin—that's what Alessio Pino is. Counterfeit through and through. Fooled my mistress, but he didn't fool me."

"But does it strike you as credible that Alessio would become enraged over a wager he helped organize? That was the theory you offered Messer Grande, wasn't it?"

The dwarf squirmed in his seat. "It was the first thing that popped in my head. In truth, I don't know what happened to make Alessio furious with my mistress, but something obviously did. I believed she was keen on making a new life in Charles Town, but perhaps she was having second thoughts…" He trailed off, shaking his head in bewilderment.

I sighed, thinking back to the little trunk I'd seen standing by the door of the casino. "Were you and Sary also planning to voyage to America?"

He rolled his eyes. "What would I do in such a savage country? It's all right for Sary, I suppose. She was born on some wild island across the ocean, so traveling to the Americas would be like a homecoming for her. But, merciful heaven, I have no wish to live so removed from civilization."

"Your mistress must have been disappointed at the prospect of losing such a loyal servant."

"It's true," he answered sadly. "I served her well over the years, and she begged me to stay on. But crossing the ocean—that I couldn't do. If only she had lived! My mistress had promised to see me settled in a secure position, you see. She would have, too, with all her influential connections. Damn Alessio Pino! He destroyed my entire life—past, present, and future."

"Imagine for a moment that Alessio didn't kill your mistress."

The dwarf's brow furrowed, and a suspicious look came into his mud-colored eyes.

"Call it an intellectual exercise—it's my nature to solve puzzles—I simply can't help it."

"I thought it was your nature to make music."

I shrugged. "My career suits me, but it was not my choice. If I hadn't been delivered to the surgeon as a boy of ten, who knows what I might have become? Perhaps I would have dedicated myself to justice and reached the rank of Messer Grande." I finished with an awkward laugh, heartily surprised at the words that had slipped from my lips.

"I see." Pamarino gave me an appraising look. "All right, if Alessio didn't murder my mistress, who did?"

"That's the final question I'm trying to answer, but I must start at the beginning. There are many questions to be asked along the path that leads to truth."

"I have a feeling that you're going to pose one to me."

I nodded. "Consider this—I suspect that the murder was meant to be accomplished behind closed curtains. The killer hadn't counted on your mistress struggling so hard or pulling the curtain panel down. The masked figure I saw must have intended to get you out of the way, overpower your mistress without anyone the wiser, and leave her body to be found by the next person to enter the box—who should have been Alessio Pino—"

His lips flew open to speak, but I stopped him with a raised palm. "I want you to think back to the corridor outside the box at the opera house—back to the moment you were attacked."

"All right," he replied in a rumbling whisper. "What about it?"

"When the killer swept you up and stashed you in the cloakroom, did you smell anything?"

"Are you serious?"

"Very."

He shook his head. "I'm not sure what you mean."

I wiggled my nose with thumb and forefinger. "Scent. Fragrance. Anything remarkable."

Pamarino rested his chin on his hands and gazed into the air as if engaging in silent debate. Finally he said, "I was too absorbed with trying to escape to notice much at all. Why on earth do you ask?"

I almost told him. The explanation of La Samsona's attar of roses was right on the tip of my tongue when something in his manner made me hesitate. Instead, I merely shrugged, saying, "No matter. It was a shot in the dark. Tell me, what are you going to do now?"

He pushed his empty bowl away and removed a silver toothpick from a leather case lodged in his waistcoat. "If no one wants to hear my dirty epigrams, I suppose I'll go back to acrobatics."

"Ah, where did you learn your craft?"

Twiddling his pick between his fingers, he sat forward and lowered his voice as if imparting a great secret. "I was born in Puglia to normal-sized parents who worked the land. Peasants. Poor, simple peasants with no way to care for me. Besides my size, my chest was a constant problem. I was always wheezing and coming down with fevers, especially at haying time. My older sister Estrella was the one who looked after me, carrying me on her hip as she went about her chores. Eventually I grew to be such a burden that my parents sold me to a traveling show. My chest liked my new life, though the rest of me didn't."

He paused to pick at his teeth. I remained silent, genuinely curious. He went on, "At first, I was exhibited for my oddity. I had only to sit on a stool under a canopy and look at the people looking at me. I soon grew bored with the daily parade of oafs and lumpkins and experimented with some little tricks—walking on my hands, balancing on my upside-down stool, that sort of thing. The father of a family of acrobats noticed my stunts and took me on to train with the rest of his brood. Eventually, I became a performer instead of a sorry object of scrutiny." He said this last with a proud smile, which quickly turned to a worried frown as he massaged the notch between neck and left shoulder. "I'm not as young as I was. I'll have to ignore a few aches and pains to return to the craft I know best."

Nodding, I reached for my tricorne and cloak. The rain had ushered in an early dusk, and the interior of the café was dim. Waiters were circulating with twists of paper, lighting candles stuck in emptied wine bottles. "I wish you luck, my friend. I'm sure you will find several acrobatic troupes in town for Carnevale." I stood to go, but the little man shot a hand across the table and grasped my forearm.

"Do you claim special acquaintance with any of them? Anyone you could recommend me to?" A desperate light glinted from his eyes.

Our roles had been reversed: now the dwarf wanted something from me. I shook my head regretfully. If I had known an impresario who specialized in carnival entertainers, I would have readily introduced him. But, alas, all my contacts were confined to the musical world. Truly the little man was dogged by misfortune at every turn.

Chapter Thirteen

Venetian rain comes in all degrees of intensity: mists that coat every marble surface in glistening enchantment; brief showers that freshen cisterns along with grimy beggars and perpetual bench warmers; sudden downpours that send men, dogs, and pigeons scurrying for cover. And then there are the incessant, bone-chilling rains that blow in from the north and stall for days as they hammer our clustered rooftops, swell canals, and make silvery lakes of our squares and Piazza. As I left the wretched café, a cold, blowing rain pelted my cheeks and the wind whipped my cloak out behind me. We were in for a northern marauder of several days duration.

As might be expected from a man who lived the bulk of his life out-of-doors, Luigi had recognized the signs before I had. He had attached a *felze* to provide shelter for the gondola seat, procured some flannel blankets, and donned his oilskin jacket and wide-brimmed hat. Still, by the time we reached the theater landing, I was sneezing into my damp handkerchief and Luigi's canvas trousers were soaked. His hands, poor man, must have been freezing.

I asked if he wanted to watch the opera; he shook his head apologetically. No matter, *Armida* was nearing the end of its run and even the most enthusiastic music lovers were anticipating the next production. I suggested that Luigi find a warm tavern and gave him enough coins to provide a seat by the fire and a tankard of mulled wine. "But not so much drink that you forget to return," I cautioned. "I want to get home in good time tonight."

He touched his fingers to his brim and poled into the canal's central channel. Under the driving rain, the water bubbled and steamed like a soup cauldron on the boil.

Thoroughly miserable, worried about my throat and my wandering wife in equal measure, I mounted the streaming stairs and entered the theater. When I reached my dressing room, I discovered that Benito had already arrived and turned my quarters into a warm haven. The portable stove that he used to heat his curling tongs was going full blast, and a pot of throat reviving tea huddled within a quilted hood. Everyday miracles.

Before my manservant could begin fussing, I tossed my dripping cloak and hat on a peg and asked, "Did Liya return before you left home?"

He handed me a cup of tea. "Just before the rain began in earnest, she blew in on a gust of wind—with an armload of packages."

"Packages? I didn't know she intended to shop."

"She had sweets for Titolino, which he tore into immediately, and several tightly wrapped parcels that she insisted on conveying to your chamber unopened."

I could picture the scene: Benito offering most politely and industriously to unwrap her burdens, perhaps even attempting to pull them from her grasp; Liya flinching away, protesting that she had no need of his help.

"In a good mood was she?"

He shrugged. "As much as ever."

Not caring for his tone, I buried my nose in my cup and tried to ready my throat for the coming performance. The tea was redolent of ginger, Spanish licorice, and other ingredients known only to Benito. My wife wasn't the only healer in my household. While Liya had been schooled by the wise women of Monteborgo, Benito had acquired the knack of coddling tetchy windpipes from his years backstage. Perhaps that was part of the problem, I thought, as I took a long soothing swallow: an herbal rivalry. Unfortunately, it would take a much wiser man than I to bring my wife and manservant to a friendly truce.

Eventually, the muscles of my throat began to relax and my nasal passages opened to allow the maximal passage of air. I vocalized a run of notes in the middle range, then jumped up an octave. Yes, I would make it through four acts of *Armida* whether anyone braved the rain to attend the opera or not. My dressing gown was warming by the stove. Anxious to trade it for my damp garments, I let Benito relieve me of boots, stockings, breeches, and underclothes. He was untying my shirt, when he abruptly dropped the laces and stared in horror.

"What is that hideous thing?" he asked in tones more appropriate to question the appearance of an iceberg in the middle of the lagoon.

"What? This?" I touched the flannel bag Liya had hung around my neck. Was it only this morning? It seemed like days ago.

Benito jumped back. He brandished the hand gesture peasants all over Italy use to ward off evil.

"This is nothing." I held the bag as far away from my chest as the cord would allow. "Just some tidbits Liya insists I keep about me."

"It's the devil's work! Witchery!"

"Benito!"

"My grandmother warned me about witches' bags. There's blood and bone and all manner of foul things in there." He shuffled farther away.

"Don't be silly. I've examined its contents. This little bag is filled with ordinary items—a sliver of crystal, a dried flower, a lock of hair. Nothing to fear whatsoever."

He shook his head stubbornly.

I sighed as I released my hold on the amulet. The soft brush of flannel on my skin felt like a renewal of Liya's insistent cautions. For some reason she believed I was courting danger. Though I saw no possible way this bag or her muttered spells could provide protection, I would keep it around my neck as I'd promised. For her sake.

I pulled my shirt over my head and slipped into my dressing gown without Benito's assistance. Knotting the silky tie, I addressed him in a firm tone, "What I choose to wear around my neck is not your business. Neither is my wife's devotion to the Old Religion. If you wish to remain in my employ, you will have to accustom yourself to her ways."

Benito's black eyes widened in surprise. I had never spoken to him in that manner, never thrown down such an ultimatum, even when he had taken liberties that would cause most masters to boot him out the kitchen door posthaste. I realized I was holding my breath. How could I get along without Benito? He had been my loyal companion and fussy mother hen through all but a few months of my stage career.

But a man's wife should come before even the most devoted servant. Shouldn't she?

Benito lowered his eyes. He turned toward my dressing table. Like an organ master testing his ivory keys, Benito touched his delicate fingers to cream pots, jars, and cotton pads. "Yes, Master," he murmured. "I understand. Are you ready for your paint, now?"

I sighed, deeply relieved I wouldn't have to face my manservant's desertion that night. I took my seat before the mirror. The oil lamps gave my solemn reflection a bilious glow. Like a coward, I closed my eyes as Benito brushed my hair and gathered it under the skullcap that would form a base for my wig. I kept them shut as he applied a warm towel to my face and followed it with smoothing cream, but I couldn't remain in my self-made cave. My lids flew open as the sponge loaded with greasepaint stroked my cheeks.

With his tongue at the corner of his mouth, forehead creased, Benito was concentrating on blending the rose-tinted alabaster just so. I stopped him by clasping his wrist. "I couldn't stand to lose either of you," I whispered.

"I know." He smiled, crinkling his eyes in his slanted, bright-eyed canary stare. "You mustn't worry. I'm not going anywhere, and I'm absolutely sure Signora Liya isn't."

〈〉〈〉

I descended the stairs from the dressing room level beautifully turned out in my soldier's tunic, frost-white wig, and plumed helmet. I only wished that my nerves were as steady as my appearance. Why was my stomach fluttering like a novice singer? I would be singing an opera I knew like the back of my hand to a house that would be half-full at best.

The call boy had only just bellowed the ten-minute warning, so I wasn't surprised that the entire cast wasn't down. I spied Romeo sitting deep in the wings amidst barrels of pasteboard swords and spears. Avoiding the white stallion that was doing his best to bite the groom who held his reins, I went over to congratulate Romeo on bagging the plum of Hercules. The basso thanked me modestly, and we talked of company business as the scene-shifters tugged at ropes and scurried up and down ladders. On the other side of the curtain, the orchestra was tuning their instruments and playing snatches of Vittoria's opening aria. Her clear soprano echoed their efforts as she navigated the stairs sideways, hampered by her wide skirts. The other singers gradually followed, and the dim, scene-crowded wings were soon filled with vocalizing, criticizing, and the usual complaints of stuffy head or mucus on the chest.

And then, suddenly, the congenial chatter faded.

I couldn't see the back corridor from where Romeo and I sat, but my colleagues' excited looks indicated that someone or something very surprising was arriving.

Romeo and I jumped up. Without direction from anyone, the performers and stagehands who had scattered over the worn backstage floorboards like pearls from a broken strand now arranged themselves in a neat half circle. Their focus was the long corridor that held workshops and practice rooms. I edged in beside Vittoria.

Maestro Torani advanced in limping strides. Behind him stalked a resplendent creature, a castrato obviously. He was very young and had not yet learned to move his long limbs with grace and elegance, but his wide dark eyes, high cheekbones, and firm jawline made up for any awkwardness. As he reached the wings, he favored us with a smile that beamed with the light of a hundred wax tapers. The audience would be enchanted. He would obviously be performing; he was wearing Emilio's first-act costume.

Torani surveyed us with a cool eye. "Good people, this is Domenico Scalzi—he goes by the stage name of Majorano. He is going to sing Emilio's role and I expect—"

"Where *is* Emilio?" Vittoria broke in.

Our maestro threw up his hands. "Who knows? The traitor threw his new part in my face and walked out earlier this afternoon. For all I care, the great Emiliano and his 'Apollo's lyre of a throat' could have fallen headfirst into the canal. It was a precious piece of luck that Majorano was in town and at liberty."

"But," the prima donna wailed at the top of her lungs, "this is a catastrophe. We've had no rehearsal together. This new man hasn't even had time to learn where he stands onstage."

"Now, now," Torani began, radiating a stalwart calm, "if you'll just—"

But Majorano darted around Torani and took charge. The young castrato grasped Vittoria's hand in both of his. He brought it to his lips. "Signora, calm yourself. I've had the pleasure of watching *Armida* several times since I arrived, and Maestro Torani has been drilling me for hours. Thank the good Lord, I learn quickly. With the generous consideration you and the rest of this excellent company will extend, I am certain everything will go smoothly."

He followed his words with what I was already thinking of as *The Smile.* Vittoria responded with a glowing smile of her own.

The performance proceeded better than might be expected. For the subdued, rain-chilled audience, this handsome boy served as a spring tonic. The meat of an opera lay in the individual arias crafted to exhibit each singer's art and virtuosity, and Majorano had those qualities in plenty. He attacked allegro passages with fire and rendered the legato with fine sentiment and judicious embellishments.

Emilio's claque, unexpectedly robbed of their object of purchased admiration, hardly knew what to do. During the first act, they offered Majorano scattered, tepid applause. During the interval, their leader, Lazarini, must have struck a new deal. Throughout the remainder of the evening, the tempestuous Majorano was greeted with cheers worthy of an established star.

During my silent moments of Act Two, I couldn't help sneaking a few peeks toward the Albergati box. I expected to see Maria brokenhearted over Emilio's absence, or perhaps stiff with anger if she had heard about the demotion that precipitated his walkout. But no. I saw no tears or sign of upset. Each time Majorano flashed *The Smile*, Maria melted like a wax taper left out in the summer sun. By Act Three, she would be his slave.

Madame Dumas was mistaken about the audience not forgetting me. As I had long suspected, all that mattered in the opera house was a passing good voice, a handsome face, and above all, novelty.

⟨⟩⟨⟩⟨⟩

Several hours later, the Crusaders with their pasteboard lances had overrun Jerusalem and the sorceress Armida had been forcibly converted to the Christian faith. The good people of Venice drifted away to their next pleasurable pursuit, and I was bathing my face at the washbowl in my dressing room. A knock sounded at the door. Benito sprang to answer it. Whispers were exchanged. Footsteps crossed the floor. With my face in a towel, I heard Messer Grande's deep tones.

"I sent your man downstairs for a while. I hope I've not overstepped my bounds."

"Not at all." I tossed the towel away and slipped into my dressing gown. "But if you have something momentous to impart, I assure you that Benito can be as discreet as I."

"Not terribly momentous, but I wager you'll be interested all the same." His eyes crinkled with good cheer. "There'll be no more robberies in the San Polo district. We have the gang of thieves and their chief in custody."

"Congratulations."

"Don't you want to know the ringleader's name?"

"By all means, but I don't expect I'll recognize it." I inclined my head with a smile. "Very few thieves run in my circle."

"Does the name Aram Pardo ring any bells for you?"

My knees went mushy and I sank to the sofa. "Aram is married to Zulietta Giardino's sister."

Messer Grande nodded, adjusting the folds of his voluminous red robe. He gestured to the small bench in front of my dressing table, the only other seat in the room. "May I?"

"Of course. Please—But you must tell me—how did you catch Aram?"

"It turned out to be a simple investigation. The ghetto connection was obvious days ago—some of the householders had recognized their goods in others' homes—all obtained from one particular shop on the Campo Nuovo."

"Aram's?"

"Yes. Pardo protested that he'd acquired his stock in good faith. With the innocent look of a babe, he asked how he could possibly be expected to know where a painting or sofa or piece of silver had been before it turned up at his shop. Everyone, according to him, brings their items in with the same poor-mouthed stories—'This has been in my family for generations, Signore, but I must have money.'"

"You could have arrested Aram on the spot—for reselling stolen goods."

Messer Grande flushed a little. "I could have—but I don't wish to make a mockery of the law. If Aram came up before the Avogaria for such a petty crime, he would pay a fine and go his thieving way, laughing behind his hand. Within a fortnight he would be executing the same robberies in another district served by decrepit Watchmen—the city is full of them. No—" Messer Grande paused and let a smile quiver at the corner of his lip. "I put some of my new ideas in play."

"Yes?" I leaned forward, hands on knees.

"It's generally simple luck that brings a man before the Avogaria. The rogues do their worst while in perfect view of the constables, and are thus apprehended. If not, they rob or injure a victim who has the means to file charges with a magistrate and see the prosecution through." He nodded sagely. "A crime committed in secret is generally a crime that goes unpunished."

"That's the way of it," I agreed.

"But not the way it should be."

"Of course not, Excellency."

He sent me a crooked smile. "If I'm going to tell you some of my secrets, we should use each other's given names, don't you think?"

"Then I am Tito."

"And I am Andrea."

I shifted my position on the sofa, dimly aware of the other performers shutting doors and calling their good-byes. "You're making me very curious...Andrea."

"I'll enlighten you at once. You see, I've paid close attention to the habits of the men locked up in my guardhouse. If allowed, they constantly talk among themselves, bragging of their crimes and seeking to impress their fellows with their daring."

"You employ confidential informers, I take it."

"Not at all." He laughed with infectious gusto. "Professional spies only fill your ears with what they think you want to hear. I get the truth by listening to the inmates myself."

"Surely they fall silent as soon as *you* walk into the cell corridor. They're rogues, not fools."

He shrugged. "Well, sometimes both. But you're on the right track."

"So..."

"So, I become one of them."

"How?"

"I have myself put in a cell."

I regarded him for a long moment, disbelief writ large on my face. "You are instantly recognizable. Even if you donned the canvas slops and woolen shirt of the meanest workingman, your face would still stand out."

"Really? Are you so sure?" He half-turned to examine the cosmetics spread across my dressing table. Picking out the gray pencil Benito employed to transform me into a seasoned general or aged king, he said, "Your man has a dab hand with this. But I wonder, has he ever tried painting wrinkles with a bent hairpin that's been darkened in candle smoke? The effect is more subtle and quite natural in appearance."

Suddenly I understood. Messer Grande—it would take some time before I could think of him as Andrea—was an expert at disguise. I recalled the dark smudge on his handkerchief that had puzzled me at the Pino glassworks. He must have been following Liya and me through the ghetto the day we called on Zulietta's mother. I thought he had allowed me to wiggle out of our planned trip to Murano much too quickly.

Several emotions ran through my head—wariness, admiration, a sinking sensation at being so easily fooled. "You were the brown-skinned Jew in the eastern robes," I said accusingly, "at the gates of the ghetto and later in Pincas Del'Vecchio's alley—only you were taller."

"Boots with built-up soles—surely you have such things among your costume stores here in the theater."

I sat back. Anger was rapidly conquering my other emotions, and I felt unwholesomely warm under my dressing gown. I was certain my cheeks were turning red. "Why did you follow us? Didn't you believe I was going where I said?"

"Tito," Messer Grande leaned forward and responded with a quirk of his eyebrow. "Our friendship had barely begun. Your errand in the ghetto gave me an opportunity to verify your intentions and also to check up on Aram Pardo. I found it deeply interesting that he entered the widow Grazziano's household soon after you and your Hebrew wife."

What was he saying? Did he believe Liya's old life in the ghetto made her somehow partial to Aram and Reyna? I felt compelled to set him straight at once. "My wife has nothing but contempt for Aram Pardo. He has always been a wrongheaded, untrustworthy—"

Messer Grande held up his hand. "I don't doubt it. I only mean that it was quite a coincidence—an eddy of coincidence actually. Zulietta's sister Reyna is married to an unprincipled thief who has a shop on the canal that rings the ghetto. They both stand to gain from Zulietta's will. And it happens that this thief was engaged to marry your wife when she was still Liya Del'Vecchio."

My eyebrows must have jumped up to my hairline. Was there anything this man didn't know?

"Sometimes coincidence is just that," I replied. "Even when it comes in threes or fours." My voice sounded harsh even to my ears.

"Settle yourself, my friend. You do me scant justice if you believe I would leap to rash conclusions. I had several of Aram's lackeys arrested. That was easy enough—they are the type that amuse themselves with untying gondolas moored at private houses or breaking into churches to ring the fire bell. I know because I spent an uncomfortable night in a cell with them. Their chatter made up for the fleabites. On the night of Zulietta's murder, the gang robbed several houses near San Rocco while their owners were here at the theater for *Armida*'s opening night. Aram was among them, whispering orders, directing every step of the enterprise."

"Then Aram had nothing to do with Zulietta's death."

"Correct. He is guilty of robbery, but not murder." Messer Grande gathered his heavy robe around him, seeming to consider. "At least not of Zulietta's murder. Whoever else he might have killed wouldn't surprise me. But I must hand it to the little scoundrel—he's made my murder case go more smoothly."

"But I understood the Council ordered you to suspend investigation once Alessio escaped."

"So they did. As an appointed official I bowed my head and received my marching orders from the secretary to the Ten. I did as I was bade, but no order—no matter how highly placed—can bind my thoughts. I've continued to work on the problem in my own way, and when necessary, I've put my disguises to good use."

"That has you doing double duty."

He shrugged. "My official work is often tiresome. Most thieves and rogues are utterly predictable. Sometimes I think they are all following the same script, written by some playwright who fancies himself a master criminal. But when something different comes along, I don't mind burning the midnight oil. Besides, turning yourself into someone else can be…exhilarating. I imagine it's a little like what the rope dancers on the Piazza must feel when they look down at the pavement and realize just how high they really are."

I nodded slowly, recalling several colorful characters who had crossed my path in recent days. "You were the crab-catcher on the bridge near Zulietta's casino. And the Franciscan on the Campo San Barnaba who refused to let me pass without a donation."

"The crab-catcher, yes. But impersonating a man of God? No, some things are sacred."

"If you've been watching the casino, then you must know…" I let my words trail off, suddenly conscious of the promise I'd made to Alessio.

"You can speak frankly—the young glass prince's hiding place is no secret to me."

"Why haven't you had him arrested again?"

"Keeping watch over Alessio's movements offers more possibilities than holding him in a cell. That accomplished nothing. Unlike our usual run of inmates, Alessio kept his lips shut tight as a clam. He's stubborn, that one."

"Perhaps loyal is a better word."

Messer Grande leaned back on an elbow propped against my dressing table. "Alessio has impressed you, I see."

"Perhaps I do find something admirable in his character."

"You're not alone in that. His men from the factory were willing to risk everything to deliver him from my guardhouse"— Messer Grande gave me an outright grin—"Yes, I know all about the proposed flight to Charles Town, and a man doesn't have to look far to see what was going to fund the trip. La Samsona doesn't realize how close she came to founding a glassworks halfway across the world." He finished on a chuckle.

"What are you going to do?" I asked over a lump in my throat, sick at the thought of Zenobio and his fellow workmen coming under arrest for sedition.

"I have no intention of calling the glassmakers to the attention of the Ten, if that's what you mean. Men are meant to be free, my friend, not fettered to an island, slaves to a glass furnace. If Cesare Pino refuses to admit his workers to the rank they've earned, they should be allowed to take their skills elsewhere. Those men made a brave gesture in freeing Alessio. How were they to know they were presenting me with a windfall? I had racked my brain to come up with some way I could release the prime suspect without bringing the Ten down on my head, and they did it for me."

"You allowed Alessio to escape?" I asked wonderingly.

"Of course. If breaking out of the guardhouse were truly that easy, I might as well rip the locks off the cell doors and let the prisoners stroll in and out as they please. I expected that Alessio's partisans might try something of the sort once I'd run down the sailing captain Alessio had arranged to meet before the opera."

As Messer Grande went on to recount the questions he'd put to the harbor master about ships lingering in port and, later, to the captain of the vessel who intended to make the crossing to Charles Town, I hung my head and rubbed my eyes. I was suddenly feeling every step I'd taken that long day, every tense word engendered by Maestro Torani's new opera, every note I'd sung in competition with young Majorano. Fatigue took possession of my limbs, and a swelling sense of disillusionment invaded my heart. For what little I'd accomplished in searching for Zulietta's killer, Messer Grande was ten steps ahead. Why had I even bothered to involve myself in the investigation?

Heavy thoughts filled my head. I saw myself as ridiculous as those sweet-voiced ladies who've had a few singing lessons and declare they're ready to take the professional stage by storm. I was an amateur, a dabbler. I had no idea what it takes to catch a truly clever criminal.

"Where does all this leave you?" I asked dully, once Messer Grande fell silent. "Have you come to any conclusion about Zulietta's killer?"

"Well," he stood and stretched his arms above his head, causing his wide sleeves to puddle about his shoulders, "now that Aram is out of the question and light has been shed on Alessio's mysterious errand, I can turn my attention to other things—"

"The key," I cut in before I could stop myself.

He brought a key out of his waistcoat pocket. Holding it upright between long fingers, he gave it a concentrated stare. "Odds are the little piece of metal that matches this one is at the bottom of a canal or down a well by now. If by some miracle it's not, I would very much like to find it." With a sudden motion, he flipped the key in the air, then made a neat catch and tucked it away once more. "The other tantalizing item is the note that summoned Cesare to the theater. The killer wanted him on the scene, probably to serve as a very well-recognized and obvious suspect."

"Do you have the note?"

He shook his head. "Cesare burned it. That leaves my hands empty of tangible proofs. From now on, I will simply be following my nose, asking questions. If Signor Albergati would give me admittance to his palazzo, I would start with his hotheaded son Umberto."

"You still haven't questioned him? You were waiting for a writ."

"When the Council of Ten decreed the case closed, the magistrate dismissed my request. The Albergati doors have remained tight shut. Hoping to catch the old gentleman unawares, I approached him as he dozed over his gazettes at a coffeehouse one day—a pair of bravos instantly put themselves in my path."

"But I've been meaning to tell you, I managed to talk to Maria." I felt absurdly heartened that I could provide some small piece of assistance.

Messer Grande sat down again. He listened to every word of my conversation with Alessio's young *fiancée*. "Excellent! Well done, Tito. That gives me somewhere to start." He cocked his head. "Did you perhaps discover anything of similar importance as you and that splendid wife of yours roamed around Venice today?"

I told him about Liya's suspicions regarding La Samsona and how Pamarino had shot them down.

"Oh, no. No. La Samsona had nothing to do with the murder—except perhaps in the very indirect way of being party to the wager." He crossed his arms and shook his head decisively. "I was speaking of your visit to Zulietta's casino."

I considered a moment. Alessio had extracted a promise of silence regarding his whereabouts, which Messer Grande already knew. The proposed trip to Murano had not been included in the promise of secrecy, so I felt justified in relating my plan to question Alessio's gondolier.

"Ah, going to Murano, are you?" Messer Grande crossed to the sofa. He sat beside me and flung his arm around my shoulders. "Perhaps someone there can tell us something about the delivery of Cesare's note. How would you manage that, do you think?"

"I have no idea."

"Well…" he replied judiciously. "I have faith in you. I expect you'll come up with something."

No cunning plans sprang to mind, but despite my empty head, Messer Grande's manner radiated such confidence that I began to feel quite useful again.

Chapter Fourteen

I dreamed there was a toad on my chest. A giant toad who knocked the breath from my lungs every time he hopped up and down, croaking, "Bwark, bwark." I twisted under the beast, seeking to reclaim my peaceful rest on the soft mattress of goose feathers. But then there was an insistent hand stroking my cheek—not a dream, but real. My eyelids flew open.

"Wake up, Papa. The morning is half over. I had my breakfast ages ago." Titolino bounced on my chest again. His knees dug into my ribs like sharp stones.

I groaned and rolled him off onto his mother's vacant side of the bed. Still muzzy from sleep, I pushed up on one hand and massaged my brow with the other. The room was very dim. Instead of sunshine, a gray half-light seeped through the shutters' open slats. As so often happens, the rain had moved out to sea, but the sun lagged behind.

"Shouldn't you be at your lessons?" I asked in a hoarse voice. Titolino was learning his letters and sums at a school run by the parish priest. Benito conducted him there every day at ten o'clock.

"Mama said I could wake you before I go." Still bouncing, he launched himself at my chest again. I collapsed under his wiggling weight. Oh, for just one more hour of blissful sleep.

"I said wake your Papa, not smother him." Liya edged through the door of our bedchamber, bearing a tray of pastry and fruit. She deposited the tray on the table and came to sit on the edge of the bed. Ruffling Titolino's black curls, she took a firm tone. "It's time to go. Benito is waiting for you in the downstairs hall."

"Just one more minute. Enough time for our song. Please—" He vaulted to the floor and pulled his chin into his neck. Making his voice as deep as old King Toad's, he sang, "Firefly, Firefly, golden bright, bridle the filly under your light."

I cleared my throat and answered in a lilting soprano: "Oh, Toad King, Toad King, ready to ride, I'll light your way as you fly by my side."

Our song contained many verses, but Liya only let us get through a few before she hustled Titolino downstairs. When she returned, I was making a meal of grapes and buttery, horn-shaped rolls. Mimicking the boy, I asked in a gruff, deep voice, "Do you have any chocolate for a toad king, my good lady?"

"Todi is warming the milk in the kitchen. Benito will fetch it when he returns." Liya plucked a grape from the bunch and nibbled at it thoughtfully. "Titolino is still begging to visit the menagerie."

I tapped my head with two fingers. "Of course he is. With all our detecting and the upheaval at the theater, I'd forgotten. I will take him, I promise."

"Today?" She arched an eyebrow.

"Not today," I answered with a sigh. "Tomorrow, I promise. As soon as he returns from lessons."

"Why not today?"

"Today I visit Murano. Messer Grande was in perfect harmony with Alessio's suggestion that I should question his gondolier. Our circle of suspects is getting smaller—I may be able to narrow it still further by asking certain questions around the glass factory."

"Messer Grande has ruled someone out?"

I teased her with a mysterious smile but wasn't allowed to keep silent for long. My wife plopped herself on my lap and took my chin in her hand. "Out with it, Tito."

Liya's mouth flew open as I recounted the story of Aram's robberies, then she demanded to hear every detail two and three times over. "I'm not surprised," she finally said. "Aram's arrogance knows no bounds. He has always been convinced that he could get away with anything. He takes it almost as a personal religion." Switching topics briskly, she pressed her palm to the amulet bag that lay beneath my shirt. "You will be careful, won't you?"

"Of course, I just wish you could elaborate on this danger I'm trying to avoid."

She pushed off my lap. As she crossed the room to the mantel, her dark, smoldering eyes never left mine. I watched as she took something from her carved ivory box. Settling once again in my lap, she covered my lips with her own. After I'd returned her kiss, she showed me a card that pictured a man tied to a stake, his half-naked body pierced with ten swords.

"You found a new deck of *tarocchi*," I said slowly. It felt as though a cold, clammy wind had blown into the room, but the balcony doors were locked and shuttered.

She nodded. "Fresh cards, but they convey the same warning."

"A dire warning by the look of it." Now I saw that the man was staked on a desolate plain. The sky above was black, without stars or moon. I repressed a shudder. "Is this the card of violent death?"

"Not necessarily...Though if you were a soldier, it would spell defeat in battle."

"It is rather like a battle. I feel our enemy, but I can't see him. Somehow, he manages to stay one step ahead while spreading his evil all around."

"He?"

"Or she." Last night, Messer Grande had discounted La Samsona, but he had not told me why. My suspicions remained, Pamarino's denial of a fragrance surrounding his attacker notwithstanding. She was a clever woman, this muscular courtesan; it may well have occurred to her to dispense with her attar of roses for the evening.

Liya touched the red flannel bag again. "Just keep this with you. It's all I ask."

"I will," I promised crisply. "And while I'm making the crossing, what will you be doing? You look as if you're going out." At some point, I'd awakened sufficiently to recognize Liya's best day dress decorated with new French ribbon and a freshly pleated fichu. Her clothing generally tended toward the practical rather than the modish, but she had dressed with special care that morning.

She rose and replaced the disquieting card in its box with the others. "I thought I might take Papa a treat. When I lived at home, I used to make a special bread that he loved—a braided loaf with raisins, cinnamon, and other spices. I have some in the oven now."

"I hope you save some for us."

"Never fear. If you delay your errand, you can eat your fill while it's still warm, otherwise it will be waiting when you return. I just hope I have the proportions right—the ingredients I could never forget."

I thought as I chewed on what now seemed like a very undistinguished piece of pastry. Liya didn't usually dress up for her father or Fortunata, and my wife seemed to be worrying over something besides my safety. Perhaps it was time to address the thorny subject that we'd all been ignoring. Swallowing the last of my breakfast, I asked, "Do you expect to see your mother while you're at the shop?"

Liya dipped her chin. She clutched the mantelpiece with one hand. "Papa has given me to hope that I might. He says Mama has actually expressed an interest in how Titolino has grown up so far. Perhaps she has given up her old retributions and will want to meet him someday."

"Hmm. Do Sara or Mara have children? I don't think you've mentioned."

"Daughters. Two apiece. Our family is over blessed with girls, just like Zulietta's. But Mama rarely sees them since they've moved to the mainland."

"And what of Fortunata? She'll be of marriageable age before you know it."

"Fortunata seems quite happy working in the shop, and Papa would be desolated if she left. I wouldn't be surprised if Fortunata stayed home and cared for Mama and Papa as they get older."

So... Titolino was Signora Del'Vecchio's only grandson—and the only grandchild near at hand. His slender shoulders might well support the bridge that would carry Liya back to her mother. Signora Del'Vecchio was a formidable woman, easily angered and sharp-tongued, but she *was* Liya's mother. She and her daughter should at least be on speaking terms. My own mother had died when I was six; her memory was so dim I could barely picture her face, much less anything of her personality. Still, if my mother lived but a few squares away, I couldn't imagine any lingering argument that would keep me from attempting reconciliation.

I joined Liya at the fireplace and took her by the shoulders. "What is the worst that can happen? Relations couldn't possibly deteriorate from what they are at this moment. So, deliver your wonderful bread to the ghetto, and I'll be thinking of you all the while I'm on Murano. I may come back before I go to rehearsal. When do you expect to return?"

"One o'clock at the latest. A relation of Todi's is coming to inquire about the maid's job."

"Do you think you'll hire her?"

"I have to meet her before I decide. She's very young, so perhaps not. After Angelina, I'd rather have a woman who has a bit of life behind her."

"You haven't made any promises?"

"No. Why?"

I shrugged. "I was just thinking. Now that her mistress is dead, perhaps Sary would rather stay in Venice than go to America—that's assuming Alessio would be able to arrange passage after all that's happened."

"Hire Sary to replace Angelina?"

I nodded.

"I have no objection, but I promised Todi I would interview the girl. If I don't give her cousin a chance, Todi will take it as a personal insult and we'll have to put up with overdone chops and burnt risotto." Liya shrugged absently, her anxious smile revealing that the ghetto was more on her mind than house-keeping staff. My wife could benefit from a complete change of subject.

"Now," I grumbled in the toad king's voice, "what has become of my chocolate?"

The gondoliers of Venice are a race apart. Local legend has it that a true gondolier is born, not trained. The sure sign is webbed feet to help them glide over the water. I've never asked Luigi to remove his boots, so I can't be certain about his anatomy. I do know that he inherited his instinctive knowledge of the city's waterways and the surrounding lagoon from his father. Lithe in body, often vexingly arrogant in attitude, Luigi claimed membership in a brotherhood founded centuries ago, when the ancient patricians first developed a sleek, graceful boat for private transport between the low-lying islands that became Venice. Besides carrying people to and fro, often singing or whistling as they rowed, gondoliers had also come to function as messen-gers, local guides, and news carriers. Together they wove a wide, complex web of acquaintance, which I didn't hesitate to exploit. By agreeing to give me an introduction to the man who rowed for Alessio Pino, Luigi made up for leaving me in the lurch on several occasions. Now our accounts were settled.

The mouth of the Canale Serenella appeared soft and dreamy in the moisture-laden air. Drooping willows gathered mist in leafy armfuls while thin spikes of poplars disappeared into noth-ingness. Though the workday was well along, little traffic plied the canal. Luigi's oar broke the water in muffled plops, and all was at peace until a gull caught by a sudden updraft cried with the agony of a burning martyr. For no reason at all, I found myself touching the bump made by the amulet bag under my clothing.

Luigi tied up at a small boatyard. Under a lean-to attached to a long wooden shed, we found a number of gondolas in various stages of restoration set up on wooden racks. Most lay on their sides. Arced bows that usually towered above the water swept outward to form dangerous barriers; their six-pronged steel combs that represented the six districts of Venice were sharp enough to cut a boat, or a man, in half. Picking our way through this maze, we found Alessio's gondolier polishing the lacquered frame of his boat that had apparently undergone minor repair. I hung back while Luigi explained and joined the two men only when summoned by a brisk gesture.

"This is Guido," instructed Luigi. "He prefers to keep his family name to himself, but he's agreed to answer your questions if they will help his master." With a nod of his jutting chin, Luigi disappeared around a stack of lumber and entered the shed. Before the door slammed shut, I heard a burst of masculine greetings rife with friendly swearing.

Guido and I were alone in the stealthy quiet formed by the enveloping mist. The gondolier had the look of a young man who hadn't slept well for many nights. Blue-black stubble covered gaunt, pockmarked cheeks, and shadowed eyes peered at me from beneath a single bristling eyebrow. I had rehearsed my questions during the row to the island, but the gondolier's hunched shoulders and the defensive set to his jaw drove them from my head.

I said quietly, "It's not your fault, you know."

He scowled. "What do you know about it?"

"I know your master describes you as a loyal rower, a man who never let him down until the night of the opera house murder."

Guido bent his head and rubbed his polishing rag back and forth along the gondola's jet black surface. The mellow smell of beeswax and linseed oil met my nostrils. I couldn't see his expression, but I could hear the disgust in his voice. "Who else's fault would it be? Seven years I've been Signor Alessio's boatman, ever since Signor Cesare allowed him off the island by himself. I've carried him back and forth to Venice a thousand times without harm coming to one hair on his head. And now he stands accused of a crime he doesn't have it in him to commit. If I'd gotten my master to the opera house in good time, this would never have happened.

"How can the law believe Signor Alessio killed that woman?" Guido continued, stiffening his back and meeting my gaze. "For all that he's the glass master's son, Signor Alessio is unspoiled in every way—not a wild, arrogant sprig like other rich men's sons. He was always a good boy, now grown into a fine man. While Signor Cesare barely knows my name, Signor Alessio never fails to ask how I'm doing, how my old Mama and Papa are getting on—and he actually waits for an answer. If I have troubles, he sees them righted. Last winter, he had our cottage repaired when a storm blew the chimney down, and the year before that, when Mama took a congestion in her chest, he sent over broth for her and macaroni to feed the rest of us." Guido's expression was cloaked in guilt and regret. "And look how I've repaid him. I should fill my pockets with stones and walk out into the lagoon until the waters take me."

I shuffled my feet, uneasy with such naked emotion. "That would hardly be of help to your young master. Signor Alessio believes someone tricked you that night—that is where the fault lies. I need to understand what happened."

"I was a fool, that's what happened."

"You'll be more of a fool if you don't start at the beginning and spare no detail."

He sighed as he replaced his rag in the wax pot and snapped the lid shut. Propping his elbows on the overturned gondola, he spoke as he stared into the thick mist beyond the boatyard.

"I've rowed Signor Alessio over to the opera house many a time. It makes for a long night. We don't get back until the small hours, and I can tell you it's a cold, lonely crossing. For several years, I made it a habit to stop at La Volta Celeste on the way to the boat dock to collect Signor Alessio."

"A tavern?"

He nodded. "This time of year, I always have a cup of warmed wine—just one cup mulled with cinnamon and cloves—to fortify myself for the crossing, you know."

"Your master said he found you staggering drunk," I observed mildly, unsure how far to push this sorrowful man.

He whirled to face me head-on and stepped close, so close his forceful reply sprayed my cheeks with spittle. "It wasn't the wine. It was something that woman slipped in my cup—some powder or potion that spun my head dizzy and turned my legs into boiled spaghetti."

"Who was this woman? Someone from Murano?" I mopped my face with my handkerchief.

He shook his head violently. "I was born here—I know everyone there is to know. This woman was a stranger, and if I'd used the sense our Lord gave me, I would never have let her near me in the first place."

I nodded sympathetically. "Pretty, was she?"

"Prettier than any woman that's ever looked at me twice."

"Did she have a name?"

"'Caterina,' she told me." He twisted his lips in a sneer. "That's the name of the church at the top of the lane—Santa Caterina della Rosa. You see how much of a fool I was? I took the bait without one thought."

"Isn't it unusual for a woman from off the island to drink in a tavern alone?"

"*Caterina* had a story to explain it. Said she was a lady's maid. Her mistress had come over on the *traghetto* to meet her lover. She didn't want to make the crossing alone, but once they'd arrived, Caterina was in the way. The lady stashed her at the Volta until she was ready to leave."

"Describe Caterina's appearance. Did she dress like a lady's maid?"

"Bit flashy for her station. But you know how the ladies will give their cast-off gowns to a maid, so I thought little of it. Her hair was brown, tucked up under a white cap. Bright, black eyes, too knowing by half. Nose upturned like a pig snout—I overlooked that, her being so bold in her speech and free with her caresses. That's how she must've slipped her evil potion in my wine—one hand down my breeches and the other playing about our cups. When it was time for me to set off for the boat dock, I was all right—right enough to take her around back and give her what she'd been asking for. When I was done, I chanced to look behind me as I went down the lane. She stood at the tavern door watching me. I could see her in the light of the lamp that burns in the yard. Funny expression she had—like she was mighty amused at something. I guess she laughed when she saw me start to stumble."

"What happened then?"

He shrugged. "Don't ask me. My head was taking a nap while my arms and legs were still awake. I don't remember Signor Alessio finding me in the lane, don't remember nothing 'til I woke in my bed the next morning with a head the size of a watermelon. If I hadn't been so easy to gull, Signor Alessio wouldn't have been forced to row the cockle boat to Venice and none of this would've happened."

"You don't know that. Someone went to great lengths to make sure that you couldn't pilot his gondola. If the object was to stop your master from reaching Venice on time, you both might have suffered more direct harm."

"But why?" Guido beat a fist on the side of his gondola. "Who would want to make trouble for Signor Alessio? A finer man never existed."

"I don't know," I answered in truth, though I had a few ideas.

‹›‹›‹›

Cesare Pino's factory was a half-hour walk from the boatyard. Luigi could have rowed me there in half that time, but I wanted a few minutes to sift through Guido's information before I faced the contentious glass master. Under gray skies, I passed fine dwellings and lovely, vine-draped gardens without really seeing them. Instead, I concentrated on a series of questions I posed to myself.

It was obvious that the killer intentionally delayed Alessio to provide a clear field for mayhem. As part of the plan, Cesare was also summoned. Who could have managed both? Umberto Albergati? Perhaps with the help of the other brother, Claudio?

Money, or the promise of it from one of the patrician class, can arrange almost anything. It could buy a woman to pose as a lustful lady's maid; it could buy a messenger to deliver an anonymous note. It could also bribe the house manager to loan out a key for time enough to have it copied. But the key to the Pino box hadn't hung from a peg in the box office. That key had been in the possession of the family for many years. How could Umberto, or any of the Albergatis, have laid hands on it? I wondered if they had ever visited their future brother-in-law in his opera box. I'd heard of using warm candle wax to make an impression from which a clever ironsmith could fashion a replica, but asking for a man's box key defies both logic and good manners. I suppose it could work if Alessio was in the habit of leaving his key lying about instead of slipping it in a waistcoat pocket as most men do. I would have to raise that possibility with the young glassmaker.

I trudged on, still deep in thought. It was more likely that La Samsona had arranged to copy the key. What had Alessio said when describing La Samsona's efforts to attract his notice and win the wager? *She couldn't keep those huge hands off me.* The courtesan had once entranced carnival crowds with feats of strength. Had she also mastered the techniques of picking pockets? If so, she wouldn't be the first traveling entertainer to add to the till by fleecing the audience as they watched her compatriots. With a key that fit box D-17 in her possession, she could have sent one of her fellow courtesans to delay Alessio. By then, La Samsona would have realized that tempting the high-minded Alessio would have been a fool's errand, so she set her friend on his gondolier instead. Summoning Cesare by anonymous note would have been child's play.

I halted suddenly, startling a yellow cat from its nap on a stone wall. Hadn't it been La Samsona who first drew my attention to Cesare's presence at the theater? Yes, of course. The wily courtesan had wanted to make sure I knew that someone else who had good reason to kill Zulietta was lurking nearby. I walked on, more slowly now because I was nearing my destination.

Messer Grande refused to consider La Samsona, but I thought he was merely falling in line with the prevailing chivalry. From maidservant to mistress, the much-admired women of Venice were demure, coaxing beauties. They achieved their goals with charming smiles and gay conversation. Not by force and violence. There had been the odd poisoning or two over the years, but overall, it was difficult to conceive of a typical Venetian woman stabbing a rival and hurling her to her death. But La Samsona was far from typical. Why couldn't Messer Grande see what I did?

As I arrived at the pylons that guarded the path to the Pino glassworks, I put that question aside for the moment. The time had come to beard the old lion in his den, and I wasn't expecting a warm reception. I had searched my brain for a clever stratagem that would push Cesare Pino into a frank discussion. Finding none, I reluctantly decided to approach Alessio's formidable father as I would my own, if Isidore Amato were still alive.

I followed the path to the graveled yard and up to the door of weathered oak. There was no bell cord, so I banged politely with outstretched palm. I was admitted by a boy carrying a heavy basket. He made no inquiries about my business and none of the workers involved in various tasks stopped me as I crossed the spacious workroom.

In the bright glow from the conical furnace, Cesare sat on a low bench that supported a long pipe. A second man, squatting on the floor, blew into the pipe that he rolled continuously back and forth between his palms. Tweezers and shears flashed through Cesare's hands as the master shaped the molten glass at the end of the pipe. His well-timed, graceful motions reminded me of an intricate ballet: press, snip...snip, press, snip...then a scoop of pigment that instantly melted into a vivid slash of purple. There was a third worker I recognized as Zenobio, the inventor of the petal-scope. His job was to gather additional blobs of molten glass on a solid rod and attach them to the main piece so Cesare could work them into the shape he had in mind. The three men worked together so seamlessly, they had no need for speech.

Once the elaborate vase had been transferred to the cooling oven—how odd to think of an oven as a place to lower temperature—Cesare stood and stretched his bowed back with a groan. His scarred, pink cheek glowed slick with sweat, and the lines around his mouth and eyes seemed more deeply etched than I remembered. He acknowledged me with a curt nod.

I executed a low bow. "I must speak with you, Signore."

"About what?" he asked harshly.

"About your son." This was met with a questioning frown. Seconds slipped away, but I refused to elaborate. I held his gaze, only vaguely aware of the heightened attention displayed by Zenobio and the other glassmakers.

"Come on," Cesare said after an uncomfortable interval and led me to a private chamber that served as both study and studio. The glass master sat on a backless stool behind a sloping desk covered with sketches of goblets and other drinking vessels. He motioned me to a similar seat. There was not one comfortable armchair in the room. Cesare would probably consider such an item an abominable concession to laziness.

He said, "Are you here on your own or under Messer Grande's auspices?"

"Both."

"Well? What news do you bring? Has my boy been found?"

"I haven't come to Murano as a messenger." I shook my head. "Alessio is still at large. I came to talk about the note you received the night of the murder."

Cesare threw his chin back and slammed his hands on his sketching table. Several translucent sheets of paper went flying. "At my factory, we have better things to do than retread old ground. I've already answered your lawman friend's questions about that damned note."

"My questions will be different."

He plowed on, unhearing. "I should complain to the Ten—I really should. Wasting a good citizen's time. What—"

I shut his mouth by leaving my stool and bracing my hands on the top edge of his desk. Refusing to let his pugnacious scowl intimidate me, I said, "I have a story to tell you—about a father and his son. A father who saw himself as the star of the show that was his life. And the son he treated like a puppet character he could manipulate for his own gain."

Out came the story of Isidore Amato's enslavement to cards and dice, his growing debts at the state-run Ridotto and private gaming holes, and the terrible bargain he made to pay those debts. By the time I had reached the part where my father was facing imminent death, begging my forgiveness for his sins against me and my sister, Cesare had slumped down with his chin on his chest.

"You have talked to Alessio," he said softly.

"Perhaps," I answered carefully.

The glass master's silver head bobbed up. "I know my son has been unhappy, restless. He disagrees with my decision about not promoting our workmen to master level. But"—he spread his hands, exposing leathery palms—"why should others share in what I've spent my sweat and strength to create? All I've ever wanted was a respected glassworks to entrust to my son in good time. And a son who was worthy of that treasure—a son I could be proud of."

"Zulietta aside, aren't you proud of Alessio?"

He grimaced like a man who has just stepped in something soft and smelly. "To run a furnace, a man needs tender hands to shape the glass and a hard heart to make the business pay. My son has always had it the other way around. He's clumsy with the pipe and shears—I have to toss out half of what he makes—but just let the workers come with their whispered complaints and he's all ears."

"I tell you, Signore, I admire your son. Alessio may not have the talents you respect, but he is steady of mind and stalwart of character. If we had met in other circumstances, I would be proud to call him my friend."

"Humph." Cesare crossed his arms. "Even if Alessio manages to get out of this mess he's made, he'll never be a master glassmaker. He sees the work as obligation and drudgery."

"Perhaps he's not meant to be a master. Have you ever asked Alessio what he wants to do?"

"The boy hasn't experienced enough of life to know what he wants. He talks a noble philosophy, but what does he really understand? Nothing! Look at the woman he took up with. I can't even imagine a more irresponsible escapade. When I ordered him to give her up, he defied me outright."

"Alessio loved Zulietta," I replied simply. "For a man of unbridled principle, he was placed in a terrible position. Filial obedience versus the promises he'd made to the pride of his heart. It hurt him to rebel against you, but he felt he must."

Cesare winced. But in his good eye, I saw a glint of hope. "Does Alessio judge me as harshly as you judge your father?"

"I don't know. Only he can say."

"Tell me," the glass master said with a longing look that made his face appear almost gentle. "Did you forgive your father?"

"He died before I was given the opportunity."

"But…would you have?"

I heard my own voice as if it came from a great distance. The words were as cold as iron: "Once I thought I would have given my forgiveness, but now that I have a son to call my own—I who thought I would never be a father—no. Not in a thousand years."

Cesare glanced in the direction of the furnace workroom and sighed. "What do you want of me, then? How can more questions about this note help Alessio?"

"I believe a woman sent it. I want you to think back. Was it written in a feminine hand? Were the pages perhaps perfumed?"

Instead of answering, the glass master swung around on his stool. A cabinet containing numerous small drawers, much like an apothecary's, stood against the wall. Cesare opened a drawer on the bottom row and plucked out a folded paper. When he handed it across to me, I saw that the wax seal had been broken.

I quickly unfolded the message and scanned its contents. Written in an unschooled but firm hand, the note told me what

I already knew: Everyone attending the opening of *Armida* would soon know that Zulietta Giardino and Alessio Pino were lovers.

I looked up. "Messer Grande told me you'd burned this."

"That's what I told him."

"Why?"

Cesare shrugged. "Let's just say I don't like the way he marches in my factory acting as if that red robe makes him the master of all he surveys. The message was delivered to me. That makes it my property to do with as I please."

"Who delivered it to the island?"

He shook his head. "A man in a gondola. It was handed from messenger to messenger until the details were lost in the telling."

In the end, the details didn't matter. When I held the creamy paper to my nose and took a deep breath, the odor of attar of roses was faint but unmistakable.

Chapter Fifteen

Once I'd reached Venice, my first stop was the Procuratie, the long office building on the Piazza where Messer Grande kept his headquarters. A black-clad clerk raised his head from his ledger long enough to tell me that the chief constable was out. No, he had no idea when he would return.

I wasn't daunted. I could complete my mission on my own. With a swell of pride, I imagined returning to Messer Grande's office and presenting him with the solution to the case on a silver platter.

A few questions in the right ears, ears well known to any gondolier, directed me to La Samsona's casino. The same footman who attended her at the theater answered the jangle of the bell cord. His haughty features were unmistakable, even through the grated rectangle of the peephole. He recognized me, as well.

"Ah, Signor Amato. Do you think I'm deaf? Everyone in the building must have heard your ring."

"I need to see your mistress, Lelio."

"She is dressing. You can come back later, or better yet, see her tonight at the opera."

Dressing was a process that could take several hours, involving as it did a visit from the hairdresser with its invariable exchange of gossip; lengthy application of cosmetics and fixing of patches; then donning layers of hoops, petticoats, and gown. My visit wouldn't wait, and I still had a rehearsal and a performance to get through.

"I must see her now."

"How desolating for you." The little door behind the grate slammed shut.

I pumped the bell cord up and down. The noise reverberated through the wall: loud, rude, clanging, insistent. Yowls of protest came from neighboring apartments.

The main door swung open. I produced my card, but Lelio waved it away. In a manner so cold that frost could have dusted his shoulders, the footman took my cloak and hat. "You have uncommon luck, Signor Amato. My mistress is quite capable of letting a man ring for hours, the neighbors be damned. But when she heard it was you..." With a world-weary sigh, he passed me to a bouncy maid with apple cheeks and pointed chin.

Her manner was as warm as Lelio's was chilly. She didn't speak, but communicated volumes with her appraising glances and saucy shrugs. When we reached an unheated antechamber, she motioned for me to sit and disappeared into her mistress' bedchamber. I had barely settled myself on one of the slick, striped-satin chairs when the door opened again. The maid summoned me with a curled finger.

La Samsona's most intimate chamber was a pink and white confection, daintily pretty in the early afternoon sun that had finally chased the fog eastward. Drapes the color of ripe cherries hung at the windows and the wide four-poster bed, while the wallcovering featured garlands of pink roses supported by gamboling cherubs. A nest of matching sofa and chairs surrounded a table laid with a French porcelain coffee service. All was reflected two and three times over in the procession of mirrors that marched around the walls.

From the doorway, I looked toward the dressing table that was also draped in cherry-colored silk, expecting to find La Samsona in robe and chemise being fussed over by her hairdresser. But, no.

The maid led the way to a raised alcove set at right angles to the main chamber.

I stopped the minute I turned the corner. It was much warmer here, thanks to a crackling fire under a marble mantel. A good thing, I thought, since La Samsona was in her bath, as naked as the day she was born. Her gold-tinted chestnut hair was pinned up loosely; a few tendrils snaked over her damp shoulders that shimmered above the soapy water.

Ignoring me completely, she leaned back in the tin tub and stretched her arms above her head. Rivulets of water coursed over her rounded muscles and formed a confluence between her breasts. "More oil, Marietta," she ordered in a husky voice. "And hot water, too."

It was only after the maid had fetched a steaming pitcher that sat before the fire, poured its contents in the tub, and topped it off with a stream of fragrant oil that La Samsona sent me a smile of smug contentment. "You were very anxious to be admitted, Signor Amato. Did you think of something I could do for you?"

"No, Signora." I approached the tub so I could look down into her flushed face. "I thought of another question."

She heaved a dramatic sigh, then tapped a finger against her chin. "How boring you capons are. It makes me wonder how you stand yourselves. Well then, ask your question so I can get on to more important things."

"Why did you feel it necessary to summon Cesare Pino to the opera house?"

Her mouth opened, lips stretching in a tight circle. "Marietta," she called toward the maid who was freshening bouquets of roses that brightened the chamber. "Leave us."

Once we'd heard the muffled thud of the door closing, La Samsona continued, "I don't know what you mean."

"You do. I've just come from Murano. Cesare Pino kept your note. You might have expected him to dispose of it, but he didn't. And it reeks of your scent. You knew that Zulietta was going to join Alessio in his box that night, that her triumph was secure, and you wanted Cesare on the scene. Why?"

"If you know so much, you should be able to tell me."

"Oh, I can tell you, but I'd rather hear you admit it."

She clamped her lips in a tight line.

"All right, if you insist. You summoned Cesare as a sacrificial lamb. Like all murderers, you wanted to have your cake and eat it, too. You wanted your rival dead, but the consequences if you were caught—facing the gallows—terrifying. What to do? The ill-tempered glass master had made no secret of his desire to see Alessio married to one of Venice's oldest families, and his feckless son was about to ruin everything by displaying Zulietta from his box. Not many would be shocked that he would resort to murder—especially since Zulietta was a Jew and he'd never hid his hatred of that race."

"Really, Signor Amato. I have no time for this nonsense—"

"You don't consider your jewels nonsense."

"My jewels were safe in the Banco Giro."

"You signed a contract to relinquish them if Zulietta won the wager—Zulietta and Alessio could take you before the magistrate—what an embarrassment. If there were even one tiny mouse who hadn't heard of your galling loss, it would once the gazettes competed to publish every detail. Instead of being acknowledged as Venice's leading courtesan, you would be our biggest joke."

"Ridiculous!" La Samsona braced her muscular arms on the edge of the tub and created a miniature flood of bathwater and soap bubbles as she pushed herself up. I saw a goddess rising from the waves. Her flesh was smooth and firm, but this woman was no demurely smiling Venus. Images of Diana preparing to skin a deer or some bloodthirsty pagan goddess of war sprang to mind.

"Hand me a towel," she commanded, fury flaring in her eyes and tone, fury barely controlled.

I did as I was told, refusing to avert my eyes as she rubbed herself dry before the fire. It was not because I wished to view her nakedness, but to prove that none of her weapons could turn me timid.

Once she had donned a dressing gown of green silk, she paced the larger chamber. Her reflection jumped from mirror to mirror, sometimes full on, sometimes at an angle that made her appear grotesquely misshapen. She finally paused. Whirling to face me, she shouted without a hint of Venetian graciousness, "Your accusation is absurd. Mad. You understand nothing."

"Do you deny summoning Cesare Pino?"

"No, I admit sending the note. I also admit I didn't want to lose the wager." She gave a mammoth shrug. "Who likes to lose? Not you. Your battle of vocal cords with Emiliano is crushingly obvious to everyone who follows the opera. Haven't you ever wished your rival would drop dead in the middle of his cadenza? Be honest."

I took a deep breath. Just last week Emilio's claque had booed me unmercifully. My rival had rolled his eyes and laughed behind his hand, spurring the audience to further humiliations. Be honest, the courtesan had said. "Well," I muttered, "wishes don't kill."

"Neither do I. I hoped that Cesare would arrive at the theater in time to talk some sense into his son. Or at least threaten him with something dire enough to stop the culmination of the wager."

"You never give up, do you? I suppose you don't realize that I've uncovered the other half of your plan. Cesare could hardly talk to Alessio since you sent a woman to make sure his gondolier was in no condition to row across to Venice."

"What are you talking about?" Her tone turned raspy.

"Alessio's gondolier had a cup of wine with a woman who slipped something in his drink. With Alessio out of the picture, all you had to do was dispense with little Pamarino and overpower your petite friend. Did Zulietta ever realize it was you, I wonder."

A shadow crossed La Samsona's face. She appeared genuinely mystified.

Another thought struck me. "You sent your maid, didn't you? Your Marietta is certainly saucy enough to interest a lonely gondolier."

The courtesan pulled her chin back and crossed her arms. "Did this saucy woman converse with the gondolier?"

"Of course. Her golden tongue seduced the simple man with lies and promises."

"Well, aren't you smart. Quite the expert at detection. Nothing gets by you."

I shrugged modestly.

La Samsona surprised me with a horse laugh that must have started at her toes. Her entire body jiggled with the hilarity of it. Still gasping, she said, "I wonder, then, how you failed to notice that Marietta is mute."

Mute? I shook my head, momentarily bewildered. I had to admit the maid had shown me into the room without voicing a sound.

"But…but," I stammered. "So the woman in the tavern wasn't Marietta. You could have hired anyone who needed money— a courtesan down on her luck—there must be many in your acquaintance."

La Samsona had stopped laughing. Her expression was perplexed and she chewed on a thumbnail. She said, more to herself than to me, "I suppose I'll have to tell you, though he won't be happy. If I don't explain, you'll spread your outrageous story all over town." She drew herself up. "It's like this, Signor Amato. I couldn't have murdered my friend Zulietta because I was in Messer Grande's box when she tumbled into the pit."

I quickly reviewed that night in my head. As I had scanned the boxes, I noticed Messer Grande sitting alone in the second tier. His box had been one of the few with empty chairs. Also one of the few with curtains a quarter drawn.

"You're lying," I snapped. "I had reason to observe the house closely. I remember Messer Grande watching the opera on his own. I didn't see you in his box while I was singing."

"Oh, you wouldn't have seen me." She sent me a wide smile. "I was on my hands and knees at the time, well covered by his robe."

‹›‹›‹›

Luigi was waiting for me among the gondolas bobbing at the painted posts of the nearest landing. Floating along the canals hardly suited my mood. I needed to move my legs, so I told Luigi his services wouldn't be required until after that night's performance. Skirting puddles and avoiding awnings still dripping from the recent rain, I wandered aimlessly. Or so I thought. My feet knew where they were going; they were carrying me toward the Piazza, toward Messer Grande's office, away from the opera house where I would soon be expected to rehearse a scene from *The Labors of Hercules*.

Why hadn't Messer Grande told me La Samsona had been in his box when Zulietta was murdered? He certainly expected me to report on my conversations with everyone from Maria Albergati to Cesare Pino. His silence wasn't based on overdeveloped moral rectitude—that hardly existed in our society. It would be highly unusual to find a man of his status who didn't have a mistress stashed somewhere. This friendly man had asked me to use his Christian name—Andrea—and had treated me as an equal in the murder investigation, yet he'd kept me in the dark about a central feature of the case.

Brooding darkly, I turned down an alley that would take me to the Mercerie and thence under the great clock that stands on the north side of the Piazza. A weak sun had made its appearance, but its milky rays didn't penetrate this thin shaft. In the dimness, footsteps approached from behind, running lightly though there was no reason for haste. The alley was so narrow, one man couldn't pass another unless they both flattened themselves along the brick walls.

I spun around. My heart had become a tiny hammer; I felt its blows as my fingers went to the bulge of my amulet bag. My follower drew up abruptly. It was a man in the loose yellow shirt and worn loden cloak of a gypsy. His skin was nut brown and an embroidered scarf was tied around his head. He kept his chin on his chest, refusing to meet my eyes.

I didn't know whether to be relieved or disgusted. "Andrea," I said. "You must have better things to do than follow me in your silly disguise. Your mistress is fresh from her bath and would welcome a visit, I'm certain."

As the man raised his chin, the whites of his eyes flashed through the gloom. "*Che diavolo?*" His hand flew to his sash and curled around a silver hilt. His accent was strange, his tone unfriendly. "What is this nonsense you say?"

I was staring into the exotic face of a wary, puzzled gypsy. No amount of cosmetics could transform Messer Grande's features into these. "*Scusi,*" I muttered, nodding a small bow. "I thought you were someone I knew."

With that I turned and strode quickly to the opening at the far end of the alley. My back tingled with each step, anticipating the slash of cold steel. On the Mercerie, the shops had just reopened after the midday siesta, and a swelling tide of humanity filled the street. I dove to my right and exhaled deeply when the corner of my eye caught my gypsy turning left. After pausing for a moment to watch his bright head scarf weave in and out of the crowd, I directed my steps toward the theater. Pushing my way through unyielding shoulders, gawking tourists, and hooded maskers, I reminded myself what I believed about loyalty and justice and wondered if anything in Venice was truly as it seemed.

❯ ❯ ❯

"Master, where have you been?" Benito met me at the stage door, a frown on his thin face. "I thought you would be here long before now."

"Has Maestro Torani been calling for me?"

My manservant flapped a flustered gesture toward the stage. "Not yet. He's been drilling Romeo all afternoon. It's Signora Liya. She never returned from the ghetto."

"What?" The false starts and repeated phrases of a rehearsal in progress met my ears as I dug my watch from its pocket. I clicked the timepiece open. "A quarter after three. Liya was supposed to interview Todi's cousin at one o'clock."

"The girl waited an hour and I got an earful." My manservant shook his head ruefully. "As if I could produce Signora Liya from thin air. I lingered at home as long as I could, hoping she'd come in the door with some good reason for being delayed. Finally I came on to the theater."

I thought back to the scene in our bedchamber that morning. So much had occurred since then to push the details aside. I struck my forehead. Maddening!

"Signora Liya went off with several loaves of bread, warm from the oven," Benito coached like a prompter feeding me forgotten lines.

Yes! Liya had been planning to deliver some of her special bread to Pincas. And something else. She had been worried over a possible encounter with her mother. I shivered as if cold water had been poured down my back. "I must go. Tell Maestro—"

"Tell Maestro what?" Torani was suddenly at my elbow. Romeo's mellow tones no longer filled the theater.

"I must go. Liya is missing."

"Missing?" Torani scratched his head, which was for once covered with a neat tie-wig.

"She went to visit her family in the ghetto," I explained. "She should have been back hours ago."

"I'd hardly call that missing," Torani replied. "She's probably caught up in her visit, forgotten the time. You know how women are when they get to talking."

I pictured Liya's mother, stern and taciturn with all her daughters. "It's not like that. She may be in danger."

"But it's the middle of the afternoon, and Liya's family lives only a few squares away from your house. What kind of threat could there be? You're exaggerating, don't you think? Besides, I'm ready for you." He tried to press a sheaf of music on me.

I shook my head, backing toward the stage door, eager to be off.

"Tito, don't put me in this position." His voice was gruff. "You're scheduled to rehearse and I need you on the stage."

"I'm sorry, Maestro."

"This has something to do with your sleuthing, doesn't it?"

"It might. I don't know." With every breath, a sense of dread squeezed my lungs.

My old maestro stepped forward and reached up, as if to clap a hand on my shoulder. He let his arm drop without touching me. "I'm going to give you some advice, Tito, and I hope you heed it. A singer of your caliber can manage only one pursuit. Your life is your voice, and the stage allows no time for distractions. Let Messer Grande do his job while you do yours. Now send Benito to the ghetto if you must, but you come with me. We need to start knocking Hyllus' aria into shape."

"Hyllus is a thankless role and you know it."

"Nevertheless, it needs to be rehearsed. I demand the best from all my players, even the silent youths who merely hand you a message or carry your train." The look on the director's face made it clear he wasn't going to back down.

"I must go, Maestro. Give the role of Hyllus to Majorano. I'm sure he's hanging around somewhere on the lookout for whatever crumbs might fall his way. I'll take Benito with me, and if I can't get back in time to sing *Armida* tonight, he'll inform you."

The musical scores trembled in Torani's blue-veined hands. He shook his head in disbelief. *Lunatic,* I heard him whisper as I bolted through the stage door.

Cursing myself for giving Luigi his liberty, I trotted toward the nearest public gondola landing with Benito on my heels. Luck was with us. We found a boat for hire and were soon on the Grand Canal. On both sides, stately palaces rose from jade green water; farther on, the marble arch of the Rialto Bridge curved above us. Though the boatman plied his oar with vigor, the ride seemed to last forever. Benito tried to calm me by making conversation; I shushed him, somehow believing that small talk would hinder our progress. When the gondola finally turned into the canal that led to the Cannaregio, I felt like giving a cheer. We disembarked at the Ponte della Guglie and hurried down the pavement and through the gates of the Hebrew enclave.

Pincas' shop had acquired a bewildering inventory of clothing over the years. We found shelves laden with shirts, waistcoats, and breeches; shoes and boots piled on their own counters; and gowns and coats suspended from wires that crisscrossed between joists. My father-in-law could usually be found lounging in the doorway watching the world, or his little corner of it, pass by. If Fortunata wasn't helping a customer, she would be in a sagging elbow chair by the window, depending on its light to mend a never-ending series of ripped seams.

But today neither father nor daughter tended the shop. Somehow I sensed the commotion upstairs before I heard raised voices.

"Someone's upset," Benito remarked dryly.

"Come on," I replied, making for the back of the shop. Behind a tattered curtain, the low, slanted ceiling of the staircase forced me to remove my tricorne and duck my head as I climbed to the Del'Vecchio living quarters.

A cramped chamber served the family as both salon and dining area, but no one was sitting or eating. Three women stood in a cluster beside a scrubbed pine table that held the remains of two loaves of bread and a carving knife. Liya and Reyna Pardo were staring at each other like she-cats with ruffled haunches and flattened ears, while a gray-haired woman who possessed Liya's firmly chiseled nose and determined chin kept up a forceful diatribe. I recognized Signora Del'Vecchio. Liya's mother had aged since I'd last seen her, but her tongue was as sharp as ever. Across the room, at the double casement window, Pincas wore a miserable expression. Fortunata made a small shadow at his side, the youngest daughter, always there to comfort her father.

I cleared my throat—loudly—and the three women spun around. The first person to speak was Signora Del'Vecchio. "Ah," she declared. "Just what the situation requires—performing capons."

Liya and I exchanged lightning glances. She seemed to be all right. No blood. No broken bones. "Tito!" she cried. "What are you doing here?"

I took a few steps forward, motioning for Benito to stay by the doorway. "You didn't return home for your appointment. I couldn't think what had delayed you."

My wife flew across the room and tucked her arm under mine. "Mama wasn't here when I arrived, but Fortunata said she wanted very much to see me. I waited and waited and finally Mama showed up with…her." This last was said through gritted teeth and accompanied by a slit-eyed look toward Reyna.

Zulietta's sister approached us in slow, deliberate steps, gathering her black shawl to her bony chest as she came. As before, her black hair was scraped into a tight bun held in place with silver pins. Her eyes were bloodshot, more from anger than crying I thought, but her voice was steady.

"So here is your famous husband, such as he is. At least you still have him. If you hadn't poked your nose in where it didn't belong and asked questions all over the ghetto, I would still have mine."

"Reyna—" Liya began, but the black-clad woman went on in a strained voice.

"Aram would be at home with his family instead of sharing a cell with Venice's rabble. Do you have any idea how a Jew is treated in the Doge's prisons? My husband will be fortunate if he even lives to stand trial."

I watched Liya's face as she gulped and blinked back tears. I hoped she wasn't crying over Aram Pardo. "Your husband got no more than he deserved," I said to Reyna. "Thievery is a crime and demands punishment."

The angry Jewess tossed her head.

Liya found her voice again. "And don't pretend you didn't know what Aram was up to, Reyna. You probably helped him plan the whole string of robberies. You're just lucky Messer Grande didn't arrest you, too."

"How dare you criticize this good woman? The daughter of our dear friend!" Signora Del'Vecchio entered the fray with her characteristic venom. "At least Reyna respected her parents' wishes enough to marry a man of the ghetto."

"A thorough villain!" I cried.

"A family man," Signora Del'Vecchio tossed right back, "an intrepid businessman trying to survive under your country's stifling regulations. You see the red hats and kerchiefs we are forced to wear outside these walls, but do you see the rules that bind us like chains and set prosperity forever out of reach? Pincas' family has lived in Venice for four generations, but are we citizens of your jealous Republic? Can we claim the rights of the filthiest, laziest Christian lout on the Piazza? Bah!" Ending on a rattle of phlegm, she pursed her lips and spat on her own spotless floorboards.

A gentle voice spoke up. "My dear, you're not being fair." Pincas was wringing his hands. Fortunata looked on with a flush climbing her white neck. Liya's father continued, "Tito is not responsible for the terms of the *condotte* that bind us. He's a *virtuoso*, an artist far removed from the workings of government."

"A singer. A prancing peacock." Signora Del'Vecchio's tone was scathing. "This is what my eldest daughter has turned her back on us for."

Reyna's jaws bulged as she ground her teeth. "At least Aram was providing for his family as best he could. Now we're all likely to starve."

"Hardly," I replied. "Your late sister's bequests should put meat on your table for years to come."

Reyna chose to ignore me, instead asking Liya, "What does Signor Capon provide for you, except a shameful living? He can't even give you children."

My mouth flew open, but Liya pressed my hand tightly between her palms. She said, "There is no shame in our house. Tito is a respected star of the opera, and he has claimed my son as his own."

"Your bastard brat, you mean." That was Signora Del'Vecchio. "The boy that this eunuch can't even legally adopt because you're not married in the eyes of our god or his."

Liya gasped, obviously taken aback by the attack on Titolino. "Mama..." she faltered. "That's your grandson you're talking about..." Confronted by Signora Del'Vecchio's implacable stare, Liya's voice broke and faded to nothing. I squeezed her arm, but she seemed not to notice.

"Please—" Pincas began, extending an open palm to his wife.

"Hold your tongue, old fool. The child with the Christian name is no grandson of mine." With rapid steps that belied her age, Liya's mother took the knife from the bread board and waved it in our faces. "Because this is no daughter of mine. She thinks she can worm her way back into the family with pretty speeches and fresh-baked bread? You may play along, Pincas, but not me." She wielded the knife as Maestro Torani did when he beat time with his baton. Her hard black eyes flashed a warning. "You're not welcome here, girl. You made your choice years ago. Since that day, you've been dead to me and forever will be."

Pincas gave a loud moan and Liya a smaller one. A flicker of pain raced across my wife's face, and she swayed on her feet. Together Benito and I half-carried her down the dark, tight staircase, through the shop, and into the alley.

"Home. I want to go home," she murmured.

"Yes, right away—" I stopped with a jerk, feeling a tap on my shoulder. It was Fortunata with Liya's cloak bundled in her arms.

"Tito, Liya. I didn't know Mama was fetching Reyna. You must believe me. If I'd known she planned to carry on that way, I never would have urged you to stay."

Liya roused herself and stood very straight. Stroking her young sister's cheek, she said, "I know, little one. It's not your fault, but don't expect to see me for a while. For Titolino's sake, I may never enter the ghetto again."

Fortunata's face fell.

I covered Liya's shoulders with the cloak. "Don't say that, my love. Time will pass and..." I fell silent, dismayed.

Liya was glaring at me as if I were the one who had just disowned her. For a moment she said nothing. Then I heard her make a very faint sound: "You..."

"My love?"

"You encouraged me to come to Papa, to ask questions about Zulietta's murder even though I had my doubts." She raised her chin with a gesture that recalled her raging mother. "I shouldn't have listened to you. I should have returned in my own good time—when the cards would have foretold a warm welcome."

I looked around for support, but Fortunata had retreated back upstairs. Benito merely shrugged helplessly. I grasped my wife by the elbows. "Liya, how can you blame me? I'm your husband, remember, the one who's on your side. I'll take you home now. We'll talk this out—"

"No." She broke my hold and stepped away. Holding my gaze for a moment, she said, "I can't talk about it now. I must think. I'll see you tonight. After the opera."

Before I could come up with an argument to dissuade her, Liya gathered her cloak and skirts and darted down the alley like a caged animal suddenly set free.

"Should I go after her, Master?" Benito shifted his weight, ready to race away at my command.

"I don't know," I answered, all at once befuddled and forlorn. Events were happening so fast. Too fast. "Should you?"

He gave me another wordless shrug and spread his hands. Benito struck speechless—an ill omen, indeed.

Chapter Sixteen

I sang poorly that night, but it was of little importance. *Armida* had been running for so many performances, it was no longer fashionable to listen to the music.

My arias competed with an atrocious din. A few songs inspired the pit dwellers to raise a unified voice and sing along, but afterward, they quickly reverted to their muddled shouts, laughter, and invective. In the lowest tier of the crimson and gold boxes, the minor courtesans and faro dealers enjoyed a busy trade, paying no attention to the stage whatsoever. The wealthy box holders above played chess or cards, took refreshment, or had their curtains closed altogether.

I was especially interested in Messer Grande's box. Each time I glanced his way, the chief constable was slouching on the rail in mask and robe while surrounded by a gaggle of excited ladies in their middle years. They kept up a marathon of talk and gossip and also trained their glasses on persons of interest and pointed with closed fans—a breach of fan etiquette that would have embarrassed any true lady. Did I only imagine that Messer Grande stared at La Samsona's darkened box with longing?

After the opera I was anxious to leave the theater behind, as much because of Maestro Torani's very obviously displayed cold shoulder as the inattentive audience. Benito and I had completed my change to street clothing and were strolling along the water landing toward Luigi's boat when I saw Messer Grande handing his twittering, screeching party into a large, two-oared gondola.

If a flock of chickens could don human form and spend a night at the opera, that is exactly how they would conduct themselves, without a mite of decorum. Turning my head away, I walked a little faster, hoping to reach Luigi before the constable caught sight of me.

I wasn't fast enough. I heard my name called and turned with a sigh.

"I was hoping to run into you." Messer Grande had pocketed his mask. His naked face regarded me forlornly, and he gestured toward a sleek boat with the Lion of San Marco emblazoned on the *felze*. "My party is taken care of and I have my own gondola waiting. Please join me."

"I must get home. My wife is…unwell."

"I'll see you back to the Cannaregio…after we've talked." His manner was stiff and uneasy.

Benito questioned me with a raised eyebrow. "Go on," I told him. "Tell Liya I'll be with her soon."

Luigi and Benito headed north. I watched their gondola recede until its lantern became just one floating firefly among a multitude of others. Then I ducked under the canopy of Messer Grande's boat and settled back on the velvet cushion. Facing me across the shadowy space, the chief constable was merely an uncertain silhouette. I suppose I must have seemed the same. A tense silence was the third passenger in the boat. It lasted as the gondolier picked his way through the canals and guided us into the choppier waters of the basin.

"Where are we going?" I finally asked.

"The Cannaregio, as I promised. But the long way round."

"Oh." Looking left, toward the Piazza, I saw scattered torches glimmering at docks and the dark outline of the Campanile against a blue-black sky filled with stars. The soaring tower seemed to shudder as a cascade of bells tolled the hour. Midnight.

The boat had navigated the eastern tip of the island and was coming up on San Pietro before Messer Grande spoke again. "You're angry." He shifted uneasily. "I don't blame you. You think I've been hoarding information."

"You must have spoken to La Samsona."

In the gloom, I sensed his nod.

"But your mistress wasn't at the performance tonight…unless you had her under your robe again, hidden from your party of females."

He slid forward on the slick cushion until I could see his face. His expression was as close to chagrin as I had ever seen. "That was my wife, her favorite aunt, and a sampling of cousins. My box would never accommodate the total number. Let's just say that I keep La Samsona as far away from my wife and her numerous relatives as possible—she told me about your visit when I stopped by her casino before the opera. You must understand that I'd already let you in on the important part of the story. I assured you that La Samsona couldn't have murdered Zulietta and that was perfectly true—you should have left it at that."

I grunted. "I would have if Cesare Pino hadn't produced the scented note. Or did your mistress leave that part out?"

"No, she admitted summoning Cesare."

"And?"

"And…what?"

"No apology for impeding an official investigation? Doesn't that transgress some statute of the public code?"

He hesitated, staring at me steadily, nostrils flaring with each breath. The sour smell of wine filled the space between us. Finally he said, "Let it be, Tito. It doesn't matter, anyway."

"Why?"

"Because we're at an impasse. We'll never know who delayed Alessio's gondolier or find the duplicate box key that's probably been tossed away. You've done me a great favor, letting me parade my suspects before you and asking questions that would never be answered if I'd asked them. But we still haven't caught our fish. Nor are we likely to."

My thoughts wandered as the gondola slowed to navigate the canals of the Cannaregio. At one time or another the patterns of my internal petal-scope had pictured the killer as Cesare Pino,

Aram Pardo, La Samsona, or even Alessio Pino himself. Now, none of them made sense. But…

"Wait," I cried. "What about Maria Albergati's brothers?"

"They're out of it." Messer Grande shook his head. "If you had been a fly on the wall of the Albergati kitchen this morning, you would have seen me peeling a basket of potatoes by the fire. My efforts earned me a seat at the servant's table where I fell into conversation with the footmen. When Zulietta was killed, Umberto was gambling and Claudio was paying his respects to the family of a wealthy, marriageable young lady."

My curiosity was instantly aflame. "What disguise did you use?"

He answered with a sketchy smile. "Veteran mercenary wounded at the Battle of Fontenoy—peg leg and all—now reduced to begging scraps at kitchen doors. Young men can't resist trading stories with a soldier who's seen battle action, especially one with a few medals on his jacket…" His words grew soft and seemed to meld with the night breeze. Smiling no more, he bowed his head as if the weight of the hour had suddenly overcome him.

"This is the end, Tito. Zulietta's killer remains hidden behind his mask, and there's not a damned thing either of us can do about it. Even now the populace is near to forgetting—new scandals pop up with such regularity. By this time next month, no one outside of Zulietta's family and friends will remember her name."

My lips parted, but what was there to say? Hearty words of false hope? Concern over the depths to which Venetian justice had fallen? I was spared from having to frame a reply by an insistent voice hailing us from the pavement. It was Benito. Our gondola had reached the Rio della Misericordia, and my man-servant was running along the pavement, waving his tricorne.

"Master! Master! I've been waiting for you. Urgent news."

"What on earth?" My voice was a trembling whisper. My stomach tensed. Had something happened to Liya?

At the same moment, Messer Grande poked his head out of the *felze* and shouted to Benito. "Who's that with you?"

Then I saw my manservant's companion—a boy of ten, or twelve at most, in the ragged trousers and jacket of a street urchin—a complete stranger to me. I pushed Messer Grande aside. "Liya?" I called. "Is she all right?"

"Safe at home," came Benito's reply.

Messer Grande's boatman steered his craft alongside the *fondamenta*. Benito fell to his knees, heedless of silk stockings and silver shoe buckles. I stretched up. We were eye to eye.

"What is it, then?" I asked in a more normal tone of voice.

"The boy brings news of Sary. She requires your presence."

"But why?" I asked the boy for the third time. "What does Sary want of me?"

As before, he merely shook his head and shrank farther into the corner of the *felze*. He eyed me with a mixture of curiosity and dread and tried not to look at Messer Grande at all. His thin cheeks could have used a good scrubbing, but he seemed intelligent enough. His name was Paolo, and he laid the fires and fetched water for the apartments in Zulietta's building. Sary had dispatched him to my home with an urgent plea to come at once.

"Think, Paolo. What else did she say?" My impatient tone only deepened Paolo's muteness.

Messer Grande's voice rumbled from the dimness. "Take your time, boy. We just want the truth. There's no right or wrong answer."

Paolo gnawed at his lower lip, eyes darting toward the passing buildings and bridges. He finally whispered in a very small voice. "I think..."

"Yes?" I breathed.

"I think Sary has something to show you."

"What?"

"I don't know. While she was describing where I would find you, she kept one hand balled up in her apron pocket like she had a gold doubloon and wasn't about to let anybody see it."

Messer Grande and I shared a quick look.

That was all we could get out of the boy. Paolo rested his chin on his chest, giving a wonderful impression of a bone-weary youth, but when we'd tied up at the mooring near Zulietta's casino, he shot out of the boat like a bullet.

"Hold him," Messer Grande shouted.

The gondolier snagged Paolo by locking elbows, then taking a firm grasp on his collar. Once we'd disembarked, the chief constable took charge. "Not so fast, my good lad. I may need your help. We'll all take a look at Signorina Sary's gold doubloon together."

But when the three of us reached the first landing, the door was off the latch. It swung open at the first application of Messer Grande's open palm.

"Is this usual?" he asked, cocking his head toward Paolo.

The boy shook his head.

In contrast to the torch-lit stairwell, the gloom of the entry hall was almost impenetrable. Unease filled my belly and raced toward my throat. My feet wanted to shuffle back to the landing, but I forced them to move forward.

"I know where Sary keeps the tinderbox," Paolo announced in a hushed voice, but he didn't move. Suddenly he seemed glued to Messer Grande's side.

"In a moment," Messer Grande replied. "Tell me, where are the nearest candles located?"

"By that mirror above the table. There." Paolo pointed. "Take three steps forward and put out your left hand."

My eyes were adjusting. A pale wedge of gray spilled through the right-hand doorway, compliments of the dying fire in the sitting room. I saw Messer Grande's wide sleeve unfurl like a flag, a shade lighter than the surrounding shadows.

"Interesting," he said, as he fingered the tapers in the girandole. "This wax is still soft. Someone was here quite recently. Now you may fetch the tinderbox, boy, and light our way."

Candles and lamps winked on as Paolo flew around the apartment. Neither Messer Grande nor I bothered to call Sary's name. Though there was no smell or other obvious sign of death, we both knew the maid wouldn't be able to answer.

We found her body on the floor in front of the sofa. She lay on her side with arms drawn tightly to her chest and hands clawing at the rope encircling her neck, cutting into her black flesh. Despite her being strangled with a common garrote, the maid's bright yellow skirt, white apron, and red kerchief were barely disarranged.

"Bring a light, Paolo. We must take a good look here." Messer Grande went down on one knee. The boy approached with a three-armed candelabra. When he saw Sary, he clapped his free hand over his mouth and whimpered behind it.

"Are you going to be all right?" I asked. The little fellow was practically a child, just a few years older than Titolino, too young to be exposed to violent death.

Messer Grande answered for him. "Paolo will be fine. He's a brave one." And with a heartening nod toward the water boy, he continued, "Aren't you, son?"

Paolo stopped mewling then and held his light with a rock-solid arm.

Though I knew it would haunt my nightmares, I forced myself to the floor to study Sary's face. Her amiable, rounded features were distorted in a horrible mask of agony. Her eyes were black pools rimmed in red, and her lips had receded from teeth slightly parted to show a gray sliver of tongue. Or was it?

"Andrea, there's something in her mouth." Grimacing, I touched my forefinger to the gray sliver. Metal!

"What is it?"

"I'm not sure. A coin?" I tugged, but Sary's strong, square teeth were clenched in a death rictus. "Help me loosen her jaws."

After a few gruesome minutes, we had retrieved our prize. A small, cast iron key graced my palm.

"Could it be?" I whispered. The key carried no markings, but the short shaft and arrangement of teeth looked decidedly familiar. "Do you still carry—"

"Of course." Messer Grande was already rummaging in his waistcoat pocket. He drew forth the key he had removed from Zulietta's corpse and held it up to Paolo's light. This official key was highly polished and impressed with D-17, the Pino box number.

I brought the key from Sary's mouth up beside his. The metal was dull and contained a few nicks and dings, but side by side, the teeth made a perfect match.

"Paolo," asked Messer Grande. "Do you know the man who has been staying here?"

The candles wavered. Paolo peered at them as if they were in someone else's control. "I'm not supposed to say his name."

Messer Grande stood. He towered over the boy but looked down on him with a kindly expression. "Do you understand who I am?"

"Y...yes."

"Do you understand that I'm investigating the murder of the woman who used to live here and that now I have another murder on my hands?"

Paolo nodded.

"A killer is loose somewhere in the city. Innocent people may be in danger. I mean to catch this devil, but I can't do it alone. I need help. Tito—this man here—he is one of my best helpers. I need your help, too."

Paolo's voice and hand steadied. "I can be your helper."

"Good, good." Messer Grande nodded. "I'm asking you about Alessio Pino. When did you last see him?"

"Earlier today, when I brought the first bucket from the well. Sary scolded me for being late. The ten o'clock bells had just rung. But…"

"But what, lad?"

"I think Alessio was still here when Sary sent me out after him." He pointed at me with a grubby finger. "Alessio hardly ever leaves the apartment, and as I was making for the door, she went over to the bedchamber and said a few words."

"What were they?" Messer Grande raised his eyebrows into his long forehead.

"She said, 'Not long now.' And 'Don't worry. Signor Amato will advise us.' If he answered I didn't hear it."

I asked, "Did Sary seem upset? Was she afraid or angry or nervous?"

Messer Grande showed me his palm. "Too many questions at one time, Tito." And to Paolo: "Just describe how Sary seemed to you."

He shrugged. "About like always. She wasn't laughing or anything, but she wasn't afraid. She just told me how important it was to go straight to your house and bring you here. I wasn't supposed to loiter around."

"And you didn't," Messer Grande observed. "You followed instructions to the letter."

Paolo nodded fiercely.

"I'll have more instructions for you. But a question or two first. Did anyone from outside visit the apartment today?"

"Not that I saw, but the well is on the square around the corner. I made a lot of trips."

"Of course. Did Sary go out, do you think?"

He shook his head.

"Now, look around, Paolo. Is anything different or out of place?"

Furrowing his forehead, the boy made a grave circuit of the entire casino. As Messer Grande and I dogged his steps, I made my own survey. In the days since Liya and I had visited, Sary had boxed up most of Zulietta's clothing and personal items. Wooden crates made a pile by the door in the foyer. It was a wonder we hadn't tripped over them in the dark.

"Well?" Messer Grande asked once Paolo had halted by the entry door with hands on his hips.

The boy shook his head. "I don't see anything different."

I wasn't so sure. Something besides the crates seemed out of place—something where it shouldn't be or something missing. The thought irritated like a gnat buzzing in my ear, but I brushed it aside. From long experience, I knew the memory was more likely to return if I didn't concentrate on it.

"All right, Paolo." Messer Grande laid a hand on the boy's head. "You've done your best and I appreciate it. Now I have another errand for you. Do you know the guardhouse near the Rialto Bridge?"

"Absolutely." Paolo was already hopping from foot to foot, anxious to be off.

"Go there and tell the night sergeant to send three of his best men to attend Messer Grande here. Understand?"

"As you command, Excellency." At last the boy remembered to use Messer Grande's honorary address.

Paolo scampered away. As we heard his boots clunking down the stairs, Messer Grande hung his head and massaged his brow. "Have I been blind, Tito? Have I been wrong about Alessio Pino all along?"

"If you have, we both have." I shook my head, glancing toward the humped, lifeless figure by the sofa. Sary had obviously been talking with someone she knew when she was attacked. My skin warmed as I imagined her blazing moment of surprise and sudden dread. "No matter how this looks, I can't imagine Alessio twisting that garrote around Sary's neck. Or plunging a dagger into Zulietta."

Messer Grande jiggled the pair of keys he still held in his palm, then examined them with a gimlet gaze. "There's something else to consider. Why would Alessio go to the trouble of making a duplicate of his own key?" He tapped the shiny San Marco key. "According to Sary he gave this key to Zulietta several days before the opera's opening night. He wouldn't need another key to enter his box. After he'd met with the ship's captain and gone on to the theater, Zulietta would admit him as a matter of course." The wrinkles around his eyes deepened. "It doesn't make sense. Nothing does. Why would Alessio kill Zulietta in the first place?"

"The dwarf believes Alessio and Zulietta argued."

"From what we've learned about both of those young people— their histories, their dreams—does that strike you as credible?"

I sighed. "Love can turn quickly to hate—it happens in the operas I sing all the time."

Messer Grande gave a barking laugh. "That's it! Put real life aside and base your conclusions on stage dramatics—a fine way to make sense of things."

"You're right, of course. I'm being ridiculous. What are you going to do now?"

"The same as I did after Zulietta's murder. First—send for the charnel house wagon. Second—find Alessio Pino."

"How can I help you?"

"You can't." He sent me one of his crooked smiles. "I'll put the force of the law in motion while you return to your beautiful wife…who isn't feeling too well."

‹›‹›‹›

"Poor Sary. She wanted to tell you where she'd found the key and was killed for her trouble."

"So it would seem." I adjusted my head on the pillow. I couldn't see Liya in the blackness of our bedchamber, but I felt the mattress give as she turned on her side toward me. When I had returned home, she met me with a contrite apology for running away. I could tell that the scene in the ghetto was causing hurtful pangs, but she refused to discuss the matter, instead insisting that I tell my tale as we readied ourselves for bed.

Now, her soft hand found my temple and stroked my hair away from my brow. After a moment, I grasped her hand and pressed her fingers to my lips. I was rewarded with the smell of lavender and bergamot.

She spoke again. "The key must have been somewhere in Zulietta's apartment, don't you think? Where else would she have come by it?"

"Sary may have gone out into the city for a time. Paolo couldn't have known where she was all day—hauling water is an endless job."

Liya reclaimed her hand and pushed up from the waist. "Tito, if we hadn't visited the casino and discussed the importance of the second box key, Sary would still be alive." Her tone carried a heavy helping of regret.

I also sat up in the darkness. "It's unfortunate, my love. But how were we to know?"

She returned a heavy sigh. "We couldn't have, but we can't just go to sleep like nothing has happened."

"But there's nothing we can do. At least not for now. Messer Grande is onto Alessio's scent. He may have him in custody by the morning."

"You can't really believe that fine young man is a murderer?" I didn't require a lamp to read her expression—it would be at once dubious and prodding.

"No," I answered softly. "But it must be after two in the morning. What do you propose I do?"

Liya swung her legs around, causing a small avalanche of bedclothes. "You can light the candles so I can see my cards."

When roused by injustice or curiosity, my wife can be as single-minded as I can. She merely pursues a different course. By the time I'd fumbled with the tinderbox and had our room ablaze with light, she had fetched her cards, seated herself at the mahogany table, and shuffled the deck the requisite seven times. I watched over her shoulder as she laid the cards in a cross one by one.

The first depicted a youth dressed in motley. He shouldered a staff with a bag hanging from the end and raised an innocent face to the sun. Unfortunately, he was about to step off a rocky crag. "Who is that careless fellow?" I asked.

"We call him the Fool. He has no idea where he's going."

"Must be me, then," I answered grumpily.

"He represents all of us, Tito. The important thing is that he is prepared to take the plunge."

"To crack his noggin? Then he's a fool, for certain."

"He's on a quest for the truth. He understands there is risk in every discovery." She reached up and patted my hand that lay on her shoulder. "Now be quiet and let me work."

I did as I was told, but my heart skipped a beat when Liya turned over the now-familiar card showing the man pierced with swords. She merely shook her head and went quickly on, completing the Greek cross and laying cards in a circle around it.

She seemed most interested in the card that crowned the circle: a juggler entertaining a crowd from a makeshift platform, only he wasn't juggling balls or clubs, but large golden coins.

"This is the final card to guide us on our way." Liya tapped the juggler with a decisive forefinger.

"What does it mean?"

She took a few deep breaths. On a prolonged exhale, she tipped her head back against me and closed her eyes. Seen from that angle, her clear brow surrounded by a cloud of jet-black tresses, her finely molded nose and lips as perfect as those of a marble goddess, she seemed beautiful beyond words. How lucky I am, I thought, and then she gave a slight jerk. Afraid she would slide to the floor, I steadied her with both hands.

Liya's eyelids fluttered and she spoke in a voice so hollow and otherworldly that a chill ran up my spine. "A player on a stage—the crowd roars and applauds—a mask gains your trust—but you won't be fooled for long."

She ended on a little moan. From long experience, I knew she would say no more. I carried her to bed, then extinguished the candles. Liya fell asleep at once. I pressed close, adjusting my curves to hers, but I didn't close my eyes. I stared into the darkness, wondering at the power that allowed my wife to see beyond the present moment and bring hidden secrets to light.

Was the old magic to be believed? A player on a stage, Liya said. Someone I'd come to trust. Had Zulietta's killer been right under my nose, one of the company that sang *Armida*? While I was alone on the stage, commanding the attention of a rapt audience, had one of my fellow singers crept through the pass door and completed a murderous errand on the fourth tier of the auditorium? And later killed Sary because the maid had discovered the all-important key?

Colorful new patterns exploded in the darkness. Click, click. Had Emilio known Zulietta? Click. Had Vittoria? Click. I remembered standing at the curtain peephole with Maestro Torani on opening night. How nervous he'd seemed, twisting his wig in his hands. Over the years, I'd known him to frequent a courtesan or two. What if Torani had been one of Zulietta's discarded patrons, overtaken with jealousy so profound he was driven to murder?

Sick at heart, I pondered the dizzying possibilities until dawn's gray light crept around the edges of the shutters.

Chapter Seventeen

I must have managed to get several hours' sleep, because I awoke to my wife and son flanking the bed. Liya shook me from one side, Tito from the other. Both loudly insisted that I'd promised to take the boy to see the rhinoceros.

"Today?" I asked, stretching stiff arms and legs.

"Today," Liya and Titolino answered in tandem.

Leaning over from the foot of the bed, Benito seemed as excited as Titolino. "They say the beast nearly escaped her pen yesterday. She kicked over the gate, and if her keeper hadn't beaten her back with his whip, she could have charged around the Piazza, trampling everyone in her path."

I sat up tall, hands on my knees. "A rampaging beast? That sounds like an excellent reason to stay well away from the menagerie."

"No!" Titolino cried.

I cocked an eyebrow at Liya.

She tapped her chin thoughtfully. "The animal is called Clara, and from what I've heard, she's as sweet and meek as her name. I'll bet the rumor about her escape was started by her owner in an effort to increase the till. People who've actually seen Clara describe her major occupations as eating hay and dropping dung."

Tito clutched my hand and regarded me with big brown eyes. "Papa, please. I want to see Clara."

I was clearly outmaneuvered. "All right," I said, running a hand through my loose, tangled hair.

Tito hugged himself in a thrill of rapture, Liya chuckled, and Benito hurried to my wardrobe to find an ensemble suitable for rhinoceros viewing.

The day was perfect for our undertaking. Above the Piazza, the sky was an inverted bowl of cerulean blue. The recent rains had scrubbed it to a high shine, and puffy white clouds crossed its arc in an orderly procession. The air was cool—it was November, now—but the sun warmed our backs and the wind blew only hard enough to flutter the colorful pennants hanging from poles and balconies. Benito, Titolino, and I stood in a line at Clara's enclosure on the waterfront for over an hour. There were other animals on view, but the rhinoceros was clearly the most popular attraction. Later I would have a rehearsal at the theater, but I pushed that thought aside for now. There would be plenty of time to address my harrowing suspicions of the night before. For now, I gave Titolino my full attention.

When we reached the entrance, an African man almost as black as poor Sary took my coins, even though a broadsheet pasted to the wall behind him informed us that the great and noble rhino had been captured in Bengal. I supposed a lackey of Indian hue couldn't be found on short notice. Once inside, another attendant ushered the three of us to a raised bench several rows back from the large display pen. The first row had been partitioned off by a rope of crimson velvet, set aside for those of patrician rank. As the seats around us slowly filled, I stared at the hairless mountain of brown-gray hide that had occasioned such wonder.

Clara had plenty of room to pace in a circle and exercise her stumpy legs, but as Liya had warned, her preferred activity seemed to be munching mouthful after mouthful of the hay that was available in abundant quantities. When she tired of the hay, she emitted a few hoarse snorts and immediately went to work on a loaf of bread supplied by her keeper. Above all, she put me in mind of very large, very pampered, armored dog.

"Papa," Titolino whispered in awe. "Where is her horn?"

The boy was observant. All the broadsheets showed Clara with a pointed horn springing from her snout, but instead of that amazing appendage, her nose was topped by a round patch of darkened skin.

Benito quickly spoke up. "I heard what happened. When the beast was in France she reduced an oak tree to splinters, right under the eyes of King Louis and his court. Unfortunately, her horn splintered too."

"You don't know what you're talking about," an onlooker behind us scoffed. "Everyone knows that Clara dispensed with the horn herself. While in Rome, she took to rubbing it against the boards and it fell off. Look there, the keeper has it in his hand."

Titolino's eyes grew even larger as we stared down at the pen. The man who'd fed Clara her five loaves of bread was passing the shiny, wicked-looking horn to the favored spectators on the first row. A woman who'd shed her *moretta* as completely as Clara had her horn drew back with a delicate sneer, refusing to touch it. Her companion, a man in an expressionless *bauta*, grasped the horn readily, then didn't want to give it back. As the keeper remonstrated with the stubborn aristocrat, Clara turned tail and deposited a mound of steaming dung in front of the group.

I wrinkled my nose. "I think I've seen enough. What about you?" I asked Titolino.

He responded with a brisk nod. Even an exotic animal can only hold a seven-year-old boy's attention for so long. Once we had left the enclosure, Titolino wouldn't hear of returning home. He pulled me away from the gondola mooring where we'd left Luigi, and Benito and I navigated the shifting crowds of the Piazza hand-in-hand with the boy in the middle.

Everything delighted Titolino. Under the arcades surrounding the great square, he sniffed at the door of cook shops roasting cheap meats, drooled over the pastries set out before the bakers' stalls, and gazed at the café tables swarming with people from far-flung places. He cocked his head at the sound of so many foreign voices and was heartily impressed by the multitude of masks and costumes. It was easy to forget that the boy had spent most of his young life in the one corner of the city not drenched in carnival celebration. Eventually he tugged us onto the main part of the Piazza where the entertainers held sway. We stopped at a trestle stage where an acrobatic troupe was just starting a performance.

I bent to whisper in Titolino's ear. "We can watch for a while, but then I'll have to send you home with Benito."

"Why, Papa?"

"I have to go to work. Maestro Torani expects me for rehearsal."

A fleeting scowl crossed Titolino's smooth features, but given the lightning changes of childish moods, he was soon laughing at a quartet of clowns bounding around the stage and bumping into each other. The performers ran the gamut in size. The tallest was at least my height, the shortest a dwarf. After their initial antics had drawn a good-sized crowd, they launched into a series of somersaults that ended with a game of leap frog. The dwarf was the last to jump, but instead of following the program, he pushed them all over into a heap. Then he ran in circles, bandy legs kicking out to the side with each step.

Benito cleared his throat. "Master…Master…" he said insistently.

I tore my gaze from Titolino's joyous expression. "What is it?"

"Look at that little one. Isn't that…"

I followed Benito's questioning stare. The other clowns had disentangled themselves and laid hands on the dwarf. The little man's wide-open mouth was ringed with white grease paint, and his nose was decorated by a red splotch, but I recognized the face. It was our friend Pamarino, Zulietta's former companion. Instead of his dignified soldier's jacket with the silver epaulets, he wore a one-piece suit of orange and yellow plaid and an undersized hat that resembled a squashed lemon tart.

"You're right," I said to Benito. "That's Pamarino. He managed to find work after all—his luck must have changed."

Benito's rolling shrug told me what he thought of Pamarino's new position, but I fancied the dwarf must be happy with it. How else could he expect to earn his bread?

We watched as Pamarino was soundly cuffed for his mischievous trick. Finally, to the amusement of the crowd, the other clowns hoisted his little body over their heads and carried him behind the curtains at the back of the platform. One by one the clowns returned. Each performed a solo act to show off his special talents. The tall one was a master juggler, the next a contortionist who could squeeze himself into small barrels and trunks, and the third balanced a tower of crystal wine glasses on his upturned nose. Good solid tricks, but I'd seen better.

Shifting from foot to foot, I glanced at Titolino. Of course, the boy was hanging on every move. I hated to take him away, but it was time for me to go. One more routine. I'd see what Pamarino would present for his star turn, then we really must set off.

The central slit in the back curtain parted to reveal the stocky dwarf, still clad in his suit of orange and yellow. He seemed to float in space considerably above his natural height. He must be standing on something I couldn't make out because of the people crowding between me and the platform. I stretched up and craned my neck around a man with a wide-brimmed hat. What was Pamarino up to?

With a cheery wave to his audience, the dwarf lurched forward with clumsy gait. I saw what lifted him. Strapped to the outside of each leg was a five-foot pole with a wooden block that fit under each instep. Stilts! Pamarino was stilt-walking and doing a damn fine job of it. Once he found his stride, he strode, swaggered, danced, and hopped with practiced ease.

Surrounded by the applause and appreciative shouts of the crowd, I felt as if my brain were trapped in the tube of the petalscope. Slowly, painfully, my thoughts were being twisted, and a new pattern was forming before my eyes. I watched Pamarino pivot on one stilt without so much as a wobble and catch a red ball tossed by the tallest clown. Even as I marveled at his dexterity, a terrible recognition clicked into place. Zulietta's killer had moved with that same jerking walk. I'd only had a glimpse, it was true, but that walk was like no other man's.

Pamarino pivoted again and tossed the ball into the crowd. Someone threw it back. My mouth took on a dry, unpleasant taste. Blood pounded against my eardrums. I had never suspected Pamarino. Not for one moment. He was a little man—the top of his head barely reached my chest—and the killer had been a tall brute. But the proof of my eyes was showing me how a dwarf could grow three feet by merely strapping on two pieces of wood. Could Pamarino have murdered the mistress he had served so loyally?

As the ball went back and forth, a red blur above my head, I pushed toward the platform. I was deaf to the crude complaints of people I elbowed aside, deaf to Titolino and Benito's calls. The frolicking dwarf swam in my oily gaze. I had to have a closer look.

Without quite realizing how I'd got there, I found myself gripping the splintery edge of the platform. Pamarino saw me. He froze with the ball over his head in mid-throw. His mud-brown eyes searched my face, then took on a malevolent glitter. My cheeks grew hot, just as they had when Zulietta's masked killer had glared at me across the theater auditorium. The final pattern had clicked into view. I didn't know why, but I knew how.

Pamarino had strapped on stilts, covered his identity with cloak and *bauta*, and stabbed Zulietta. Then he'd locked the door to the box and arranged the scene in the cloakroom so he would also appear to be a victim. I'd finally tumbled to the truth. And Pamarino knew it.

This time I broke the scorching stare. Titolino and Benito, both greatly puzzled by my behavior, had pushed in beside me. The boy was whining and pulling on my sleeve.

I shook him off and grasped my manservant by the arm, digging my long fingers right down to the bone. I hate to think what my expression must have looked like. "Take Titolino home at once."

Benito actually cringed. "Master?"

"Go." I flung my other arm out in the general direction of the jetty. "Find Luigi and take the boy home. I'm going to the theater."

Diving through the crowd, I left Benito staring, open-mouthed, with his hands on the boy's shoulders. Titolino looked as if he might burst into tears. There was no help for it. Explanations would come later. Right now I had several tasks to accomplish. Knowing who had stabbed Zulietta wasn't enough. I would have to prove it to Messer Grande.

Sometimes I fancied the opera house must be honeycombed with spy holes and secret passages. A person could do nothing without everyone else knowing his business within minutes. I was searching the cloakroom off the fourth-tier corridor when Maestro Torani limped through the door.

"Tito, have you taken leave of your senses? I need you on the stage."

I answered by kicking a pile of discarded clothing, uncovering nothing but a cloud of dust. My nose exploded in a disgusted sneeze. The items I sought were nowhere in sight.

"Tito!" Torani's tone was more exasperated than reassuring, but I knew the old man meant well. I thought back to all those times when he had coaxed magic from my throat, when he had believed in me when no one else did. How could I have ever thought him capable of killing Zulietta? Liya's mystifying *tarocchi* should take the blame for my misguided suspicions. A stage, they had indicated. Well, what was I supposed to think? The stage that ruled my life was here at the Teatro San Marco. Why would I have thought of a trestle stage in the middle of the Piazza?

"I'm looking for evidence," I replied more calmly than I felt.

"You're still playing bloodhound," he accused.

"I'm not playing, Maestro, though everyone else seems to be. The simple, unvarnished truth doesn't exist anymore. Reality has sailed away from our island, and make-believe reigns. An evil little man hid behind Venice's most popular disguise to murder an innocent woman right here in your theater. You should be helping me, not worrying over a fantasy spectacle that will only be heard a few times."

He sagged wearily against the door frame. "If solving the crime is so important to you, my son, then it is also important to me."

I nodded slowly, feeling a warm glow radiating from my heart. This was the Rinaldo Torani I'd loved and trusted for so many years. I gave him a brief explanation, ending by pointing out the wicker hamper Pamarino had mounted to hide under the long cloak while the opera patrons retrieved their outdoor clothing. "When he judged it was time to call attention to himself, he kicked it aside and began yelling and drumming his heels on the wall."

Torani fingered his lower lip. "I see, but you say the dwarf discarded a pair of sticks?"

"Stilts." I looked around the small room. "I'm sure I saw them here—at the time, I had no idea what they represented."

"I know nothing of this, but we'll find someone who does."

A word from Torani to a passing lackey summoned Biagio Zipoli, the broom sweeper I'd questioned on the morning after the murder. The lanky old fellow eyed us warily, certain he was the object of some complaint.

I said, "There's nothing to fear, Biagio. Maestro Torani and I are searching for two pieces of wood that I saw here in this cloakroom. About so high"—I indicated with a flat hand—"polished wood with smaller blocks attached. They may have had straps on them."

Biagio nudged back a lock of white hair that flopped over his eyes. He stared into space. Finally he said, "Are you talking about that pair of sticks I took to Aldo? I thought they belonged backstage, but he fussed at me for littering the wings with worthless trash."

Torani and I were down the stairs and behind the stage within two minutes. I hadn't realized the old man could move so fast. Majorano spotted us and approached with a score in hand. "Maestro, I've learned Hyllus' aria—would you—"

"Later." Torani waved him away.

"But Maestro—"

"He said 'later,'" I yelled with the full force of my lungs.

Sucking in a startled breath, the handsome castrato backed away as if I'd just escaped from the madhouse. Stage carpenters dropped their tools, and the ballet master who was filling the rosin boxes gave a frightened squeak.

"Aldo? Where's Aldo?" Maestro Torani shouted.

The stage manager emerged from his cubby hole beside the pass door, hitched up his breeches, and advanced with a pugnacious set to his shoulders. Aldo Bossi had become quite plump over the past few years; his round, alpine face displayed greasy remnants of his midday meal, and the gray eyes behind his wire-rimmed spectacles were wary. Every aspect of his person suggested he was ready to leap to his own defense. Like Biagio, Aldo apparently believed a bellowing summons from Torani could only mean trouble.

His manner became a bit friendlier after Torani explained what we were after. "That pair of sticks the idiot from the front of the house brought in?" Aldo asked incredulously. "What use do you have for those things? Looking to build a fire?"

"You didn't burn them, did you?" Alarmed, I laid a hand on Aldo's arm, then jerked it away at his black look. Aldo had never approved of castrati.

"No. I'm sure I didn't." He made an ambiguous gesture. "I put them…somewhere…behind something…over there perhaps?"

The stage manager was gazing toward a pile of carpenters' scraps. The wood was raw, none of it finished and polished as the stilts had been. Santa Maria! Would I lose the trail just as I had come to the truth?

Aldo scratched his head. "Wait. I remember now. Madame Dumas carried them off. Sneaky old crone. She thought she was getting away with something, stealing those sticks right from under my nose." He gave an unsettling laugh. "I was only letting her get rid of the rubbish."

My stomach gave a sudden lurch. An episode from days ago sprang to mind. "Madame Dumas' workroom," I whispered. "The brown velvet she was so proud of—I unrolled it onto the table..."

"Tito?" Torani gaped at me. Worry creased his forehead. "What are you mumbling?"

"Maestro, I had one of the stilts in my hands—God save me—if only I'd realized." I took off at a run for the costume shop. Torani followed, this time at a slower pace.

To Madame Dumas' credit, she did nothing to restrain me while I manhandled her bolts of costume fabric. After I'd flung several aside and located the right ones, I unrolled yards of butter yellow silk, then followed it with finely spun wool of periwinkle blue. I was left with two matching poles that could serve equally well for storing cloth or boosting a dwarf to the height of a tall man.

Madame surveyed the knee-high blue and yellow tangle. Her expression was pained, but her manner was collected. The seamstress had never been one to let her emotions hold sway. She said, "I'm certain you have a very good reason for this, Signor Amato."

Nodding, I handed the stilts to a panting Torani, who'd arrived in time to see the last bit of fabric slither off the bolt. "I must ask you to trust me, Madame. Those pieces of wood are the ones you removed from backstage. True?"

"I admit it. I took them without permission." She took a hard gulp. Her sharp cheekbones seemed ready to break through her papery skin. "Aldo must set great store by his sticks."

"Not Aldo, old friend. Me. To me, they couldn't be more precious if they were dipped in gold."

Her bloodless lips curved in a hesitant smile. "I don't understand."

"You don't have to." I kissed her on both cheeks—twice. "But thank you a hundred times over."

I turned to Maestro Torani. "Keep these safe—under lock and key at all times. I believe the dwarf came back for them the day after the murder—I happened upon him roaming the corridors. Grief stricken, I thought." I shook my head. "He was more likely trying to work out why his precious stilts weren't where he left them."

"You know you can count on me," Torani replied. "But where are you going?"

"To find Messer Grande," I called, already with one foot out the door.

I blew through the auditorium and foyer and left the theater by the front entrance, intent on getting to Messer Grande's office. Sunlight slanted from the west, throwing the crowded, narrow alleys between the theater's *campo* and the Piazza into murky twilight. In the shadows, walls and bridges became fuzzy and indistinct. The pavement beneath my feet seemed uneven, causing me to stumble several times. People going about their everyday business, even mothers with babes in arms, appeared as outlandish as the masked merrymakers that passed in rowdy groups of threes and fours. I peered at everyone as if they were absurd characters of a dream—until one face rounded a corner and popped out of the gloom with perfect clarity.

Benito fell on my neck and pulled me into a recessed doorway. His eyes were glassy and feverish.

"Benito, what's wrong? Are you ill? How did you get back from the house so quickly?"

He shook his head wildly. "I haven't been home. I've been looking for the boy."

"What?" I stared blankly, unable to make sense of his words for one shocked moment.

"Titolino begged to stay on the Piazza for a few minutes. I saw no harm. He was bored with the acrobats, so I let him watch a dumb show for a while—the men were pretending to duel with swords—and then he spied some marionettes a few booths along." Benito's face contorted in anguish. "I don't know how he got away from me. One minute he was laughing at Punchinello, and the next minute, he just wasn't there."

With my heart hammering against my ribs, I whirled and shot out into the stream of passersby. Benito dragged me back. "Master, we must go the other way."

I staggered, almost falling to my knees, amazed at my frail manservant's strength.

"I've searched the entire Piazza...asked everyone if they've seen him." His words tumbled one over the other. "Luigi is looking still. My one hope is that Titolino had the idea of visiting you at the theater."

"How could he know his way there?"

Benito shrugged helplessly. "He's a bright boy—he could ask directions."

A bright boy. Yes, he was. But also a very small boy loose among the filthiest dregs of Venice's overflowing bucket of vice. Swindlers, thieves, cutpurses, whoremongers, and worse. The blood drummed in my ears like thunder. Liya was at home, cheerfully going about her duties, thinking we were on a pleasant expedition to see the rhinoceros. How could I possibly return with the news that we'd lost her son?

Chapter Eighteen

The window of Messer Grande's office in the Procuratie allowed an expansive view of the Piazza. The glittering spires and bulging domes of the Basilica lay at the extreme left, the towering Campanile across the square. Covering every inch of pavement was a gaudy maze of booths and tents and trestle stages where Venice's visitors sought gratification and delight. Somewhere in their midst, Benito was leading a contingent of constables on a frantic search for Titolino.

Messer Grande stared down at the carnival concourse as if he could make the boy appear by sheer force of will. To me, the sight might as well have been a barrel of writhing worms. Tito wasn't down there—I felt his absence in my bones.

The chief constable tore his gaze away from the window and moved to sit behind the desktop that was supported by a pair of carved griffons with folded wings. With an open palm, he invited me to take the wing chair that sat across the shining expanse of mahogany. "It has to be more than coincidence, Tito. Pamarino glared at you with every indication that he realized his stilt-walking display had nudged you toward the truth. A few minutes later, the boy disappears."

"Surely Titolino just wandered away. It must happen all the time." I gestured toward the window with an impatient hand. "Look at all the delights that could catch a boy's attention. He could have gone back to see the rhinoceros. Or perhaps he was swept up the Mercerie by the crowd and didn't know how to get back to the square."

Messer Grande's face wrinkled into a mask of concern. "Those lost children are quickly found, Tito. They realize they can't see their Mama and start to cry. People want to help. Neighbor asks neighbor, 'Where does this little one belong?' Mama and child find each other once more."

"If this is more than a lost child, why are we still searching the Piazza?"

Messer Grande gave an uncomfortable shrug. "What else can we do? Now if we were to receive some word from Pamarino..."

I rubbed my forehead with both hands. "I just can't believe Titolino would go off with Pamarino. He doesn't know him— he's never even seen him before today."

"Children are trusting creatures, especially when lured by someone of their own size. Pamarino could have convinced the boy to go with him as part of a game or told him he was taking him somewhere to surprise you. Who knows? He could have even tempted him with the promise of a toy or a puppy."

"If he does have Titolino, what do you suppose he means to do with him?"

"I believe the dwarf took the boy because he wants something from you. Exactly what we should soon see. Have you sent word to your wife?"

"Luigi rowed home, both to see if Titolino somehow showed up there and to bring Liya to me. He had orders to keep silent and allow me to tell her what's happened, but if I know my wife, she'll have it out of him in five minutes."

Our heads turned at the sound of the door opening. An apologetic clerk stumbled over his feet as he burst into the room. "Excellency, you must forgive my intrusion. This woman—"

"I demand to be admitted. You—" a feminine voice cried and was cut off.

"It's all right, Brunetti," said Messer Grande, rising from his chair. The clerk didn't hear. Intent on his perceived duty, he put a shoulder to the door. A determined foot in a dainty boot slipped through the crack. After a brief contest of strength, Liya pushed into the chamber.

My wife's cloak was askew, and she'd forgotten or lost her *zendale*. Her mass of black hair had escaped its pins and fallen down her back. I met her halfway across the floor, and we embraced for a long moment. When she pulled away, I saw that her eyes and nose were red. She'd obviously been crying but had managed to compose her features. She stared at Messer Grande as she blurted out, "What are you doing to find my son?"

The chief constable explained that his men were fanning out from where Benito had last seen Titolino, searching every chest or barrel large enough to hold a seven-year-old boy.

"You must stop them," said Liya.

"Signora?" Messer Grande questioned, surprise in his face.

She produced a folded note from her drawstring bag. "A gondolier brought this to the door a few minutes before Luigi arrived. Apparently he went to the theater first. Since you'd already gone, Aldo sent him to our home."

I snatched the paper that bore my name, cocked it toward the light from the window, and read, "For the boy's sake, come to the Mascoli Chapel at four o'clock. Come alone. If even one constable follows you into the Basilica, the boy will pay." I jerked my chin up, dividing my frantic gaze between Liya and Messer Grande. "It's not signed."

"It doesn't need to be." Messer Grande strode to the door, beckoned a waiting constable, and began giving orders.

"Tito, it will soon be four." Liya's voice faltered. Tears formed in her eyes and spilled down her cheeks.

I gathered her into my arms. I yearned to hold her forever—to make this sudden nightmare recede with a brief, ecstatic caress. Impossible. The truth must be faced. "I'll get going right away. I'll make the dwarf tell me what he's done with Titolino."

"Be careful." Her whispered words plunged into my ear with the strength of a steel blade. "There's danger all around—I saw black clouds forming over both of you."

Clouds? Ah, yes, my wife's endless attempts to peer over the edge of tomorrow. I kissed her wet cheeks and forced my tone to be calm. "You must stay with Andrea—Messer Grande—and do as he says. Be strong and believe that all will be well."

The chief constable turned his attention back to us. "It's arranged. None of my men will enter the precincts of the Basilica, but they'll continue to comb the Piazza and surrounding buildings. Once you've heard the dwarf out, I'll be waiting for you at the front, at the base of the middle flagpole."

"And then?" Liya stiffened in my arms.

I stepped away, every muscle straining to be off. "It all depends on the dwarf." Messer Grande agreed with a solemn nod.

The immense Basilica was as deserted as the Piazza was crowded. Passing through its bronze portals, I might have stepped into a series of enchanted caves with walls ornamented in precious metals and gemstones. When the Doge presided over a service, arriving in a canopied sedan chair from the depths of the corridor that connected his palace to the Basilica, there would be brilliant light licking the golden facets of the mosaics, a trumpet fanfare followed by a swelling choir, and robed Senators and councilors filling the nave. Today I found only a vast, silent space pervaded with the lingering scent of incense.

At the high altar, a priest in a severe black soutane genuflected before a bank of candles before hurrying away and disappearing through the sacristy door. A few other figures, foreign travelers by the look of them, were admiring the pillar that had once commemorated St. Mark's relics. Moving away from that domed island of light, I darted between rows of marble columns and pushed deep into the silent, murky space where pleasure-mad tourists rarely found anything of interest.

My footfalls echoed softly and my sense of unreality deepened as I approached the tiny chapel dedicated to Our Lady. Her votive candles had been extinguished, throwing the sculpted reliefs that depicted the scenes of her life into shadowed folds.

But I could see someone waiting for me: a squat, hunched figure leaning against one of the pair of prayer railings that faced each other in front of the altar table.

Pamarino let me come within a few steps before he straightened and nodded with an air of cool malevolence. He had changed from his clown costume to his usual blue coat. He withdrew a pistol from a deep pocket, cocked the hammer, and pointed it at my stomach. "Good afternoon, Tito. I wasn't sure you'd make it."

"Did you really think I could ignore your summons?" In this chapel sequestered by the Basilica's convoluted floor plan, our voices would be indistinguishable to any casual visitors, but I still felt compelled to whisper.

Pamarino apparently felt the same. "I knew you'd come if you received my message, but there are so many ways a note can go astray." He spoke as he used his free hand to pat my pockets and waistband. Finding my dagger, he tucked it away with a toothy smile.

"Must you?" I asked. "It was a gift from my brother."

The dwarf shrugged. "He'll have to buy you another." He motioned the pistol's long barrel toward the nearest railing and forced me to sink down on the knee board while he remained standing. Thus positioned, I was looking up at him for once. "Now we talk," he said.

"Where is Titolino?"

"You do come right to the point, don't you?" The dwarf rolled his eyes.

He was enjoying the moment, this evil tin soldier. So be it. The more he talked, the more time Messer Grande's men would have to search. And if I managed to be very clever, I might just be able to trick him into dropping a hint concerning Titolino's whereabouts. "You can at least tell me if he's all right."

"Not one hair of his head has been harmed—yet."

"Why do you need Titolino? If you have business with me, we can simply talk it out as men should."

He gave a nasty laugh. "And have you run straight to your friend in the constabulary? Not likely. I fooled you both for a good while, but when I saw you watching my stilt act, I knew you'd guessed that I was the man in Zulietta's box. I needed to strike a bargain with you—a quick bargain, too. Unfortunately, I found my pockets empty of anything you might find tempting. I could have danced a jig when I saw you put the boy in the charge of that witless poof. You handed me the engine of your own destruction."

"How did you get Titolino away from Benito?"

"That's of no consequence. It is enough that I have him in my power."

"Where? Where have you stashed him?" My hands tightened on the railing. Hearing my voice grow raspy, I took a hard gulp. I must remain calm if I was going to get Titolino out of the dwarf's clutches.

"The boy is under the guard of…an associate. In a place that you would never discover in fifty years." He snorted as if he'd made a good joke. "Should you live so long."

"What do you want?"

"I have a simple bargain to offer. You will tell no one of your suspicions until I've had time to travel out of Venetian territory. In three days, I should be well away. If you can keep your tongue from wagging during that time, the boy will be released on the Piazza unharmed."

"And if I don't agree?"

"If I am arrested, my confederate will slit his throat and consign his body to the lagoon." The little man spoke without anguish or remorse, as easily as he might speak of setting out poison to kill a rat. I had faced murderers before, but never one so thoroughly unrepentant.

Though sweat broke out under my clothes, I shivered in the church's cold air. My boy's life was in this creature's hands, and I didn't trust the dwarf as far as I could walk on his stilts. For all I knew, Titolino might already be dead. But what could I do? I couldn't overpower Pamarino and strangle the truth out of him. His pistol was trained on my heart.

I drew a deep breath. "I agree—I'll say nothing."

Pamarino nodded. "Very wise. I would expect no less, even though you do have a reputation for aiding the law."

"But," I said wildly, casting around for a question that would keep Pamarino talking, "how can you be certain your confederate will follow the plan you've laid out?"

The dwarf's mouth opened to reply but abruptly snapped shut.

From out of the air came a great throbbing sound. A giant's wail.

Pamarino twisted toward the chapel entrance. "What in Hell's name—"

"It's the organ," I whispered. "Only the pipe organ in the choir loft. The organist must be practicing for the next service."

Indeed, the first tentative chords settled into a recognizable tune. Somber and slow moving, it filled the Basilica with aching melancholy. Pamarino turned back toward me. It had grown darker. He was little more than a blurred shape between me and the doorway.

"Your confederate?" I prodded.

"You have nothing to fear—as loyal as the day is long."

Did I dare push him? Would I weep for the rash words I was about to speak?

"It would be very easy to dispose of a small child," I said, shifting my weight from one knee to the other. "Much easier than keeping him under wraps for three days and releasing him without a fuss."

The dwarf's eyes glittered in the dimness. His voice was taut. "I'm not as cruel as you might think. If I get clean away, the boy will live. I don't kill without reason."

"Meaning you had reason to kill Zulietta and the maid, Sary?"

The dwarf clamped his jaws shut. He showed no surprise that I was aware of Sary's death. Neither did he contradict my accusation. Had I gone too far? I felt a sudden, cold foreboding in my chest.

Finally Pamarino spoke. His words were wracked with pain. His agony, accompanied by the deep strains of the organ, lent him a dignity I could never have imagined. "Zulietta—yes, I can call her that now—in death there is no mistress and servant—she was going to throw me away like a piece of trash. Or a stained handkerchief. For years I served her, and for most of them, I loved her. In this world that was never meant for my kind, I lived only for her smile, a kind word, the touch of her hand. My love was never returned, but still, it gave me reason to face each new day. Without her..." His voice trailed off until only the sorrowful music remained.

"Do you mean that Zulietta wasn't planning to take you to the New World, after all?"

"No, I only pretended that I wasn't sailing to America because I feared crossing the sea. In truth, I would have followed Zulietta anywhere—to the northern ice caps, to the deserts of Arabia, to the pit of Hell itself." He took a sharp breath. "In private, I begged her to take me along. I could have persuaded her, too... if it hadn't been for Alessio Pino. For some reason, he thought it was a fine idea to take Sary. But me? No. I would only remind him of Zulietta's old life as a courtesan. There would be no passage for me, no place at the new glassworks in Charles Town."

"So Zulietta offered you a pension instead."

"A slap in the face! After all I'd endured to ensure her success! Can you imagine what it felt like to know she gave her body to those who were my inferior in every way except height?" In a flash, his manner had changed from agonized to angry. "I swore a holy oath to myself—if I couldn't make the voyage to America, neither would Zulietta. Neither would any of them. But I had to fashion a plan that would leave me free to enjoy my triumph. I glued a silly smile on my face and bided my time, nursing the pretense that I applauded Zulietta's selfish schemes. When La Samsona's jewels were about to be snatched, I knew I had to act. My plan to destroy Zulietta and her sentimental suitor took final shape when I learned that Alessio would be late for the opera due to his meeting with the sea captain."

I recalled the tale Alessio had told—something didn't fit. "I thought no one besides the people involved knew anything about that meeting."

He shook his head. "People see me, yet they don't—little Pamarino, always underfoot. Put yourself in my place. What would you do to gain information?" He went on without waiting for an answer. "I fit my smallness into small places and kept my ears open. I was actually under Zulietta's bed when Alessio gave her his box key and explained that he would join her at the theater once he'd arranged the passage to America.

"Perfect, I thought—Zulietta alone in the box on opening night. The entire audience would have eyes and ears for nothing except the performance. I could leave her on some pretext and hurry to the cloakroom to don my disguise and stilts that I would stash there earlier in the day—if any servants happened to see me re-enter the box, they would describe a tall man in a *bauta*, not Zulietta's four-foot companion. In my mask, I could take her by complete surprise and plunge my dagger home before she even uttered a scream. On my way out, I would lock the box using the key Alessio had supplied."

I was beginning to fathom the depth of the dwarf's hatred for Alessio. From the little man's point of view, his plan made inexorable sense. Attempting to quell my disgust at his triumphant tone, I continued with his train of thought, "You must have originally intended to stage your capture as soon as you returned to the cloakroom. As you hung from the hook, you were going to make a racket loud enough for every footman on the fourth tier to come running. Once freed, you would report that Alessio Pino clonked you on the head. Desperate with worry over your mistress, you would lead the witnesses to the Pino box, which would of course be locked. Receiving no answer to your knocking, you would insist that the door be broken down. In the curtained box, they would find one murdered courtesan. The obvious suspect—Alessio Pino. You had even arranged for him to be delayed so he wouldn't show up and ruin your plans."

A look of confusion passed over the dwarf's face at my last observation, but then he nodded with a thin smile. "You do love to tease out secrets, don't you?"

I went on, "But something you weren't expecting happened. Zulietta fought like a tigress, pulling the box curtain down and finally tumbling over the railing. Now the entire theater was on the alert, and Alessio's key was in Zulietta's pocket on the floor of the pit. That's when our eyes met across the auditorium—that fateful moment that led Messer Grande to draw me into his investigation." I leaned forward, forearms on the railing. "I confess I'm puzzled—how did you come to have a duplicate key? And why did you use it?"

"You've put your finger on my mistake," Pamarino replied. "It was easy to borrow the key once it was in Zulietta's hands—too easy. Every time I saw it laying on her dressing table, I got to thinking an extra key might come in handy, so one day, I took it to the ironsmith. In the end, the duplicate just caused problems. Standing there in that box, my crime exposed to the world, I must have gone mad for a moment. You say our eyes met—not really—I wasn't aware of you at all. The only thing in my mind was escape. I hardly remember leaving the box—I suppose I locked it because I'd rehearsed the movements in my head so many times. I barely made it to the cloakroom before people began pouring out into the corridor. I thought it better to wait to make my presence known until the tumult died—"

Pamarino fell silent and swayed slightly. The organ had stopped playing. Its final chord echoed off the walls and lingered under the soaring curves of the Basilica's five domes. He raised the pistol which had sunk to his side while he'd been talking. "Get up. Time to go."

"Wait," I cried, still striving for delay. Though I knew the answer perfectly well, I asked, "What about poor Sary? Why did you need to kill her?"

"She had something that belonged to me, and very unwisely refused to give up its hiding place. She paid with her life."

"The duplicate key, perhaps? I noticed that something was different in Zulietta's foyer. It finally dawned on me that your trunk had been removed. Perhaps Sary had become suspicious enough to search the contents before you came for it. But if that's the case, why on earth would you leave an incriminating item in your baggage?"

Pamarino screwed up his face. Was it undiluted resentment? Or regret over his own blunder? He motioned for me to stand. "No more questions—I've already said enough. We're going to walk toward the front—slowly, calmly. Once you're through the main entrance, you won't see me again. I know another way out." He underscored his words by nudging my back with the pistol, then tucked it under his jacket.

We walked. Out of the chapel. Down a row of columns; right turn at the north aisle. A few more people had entered the Basilica to gawk at its treasures. At least one had come to pray. An elderly woman, bent over her beads, was kneeling at the end of a bench under the Pentecost Dome. With my senses heightened by fear for Titolino, I noted the extraneous details of her humped back and the wiry gray hair escaping from under her lace *zendale*.

Just as we reached the vestibule that passed between a pair of staircases leading up to the galleries, a man's voice hailed me.

"Hey, there! It's Tito Amato, isn't it?" A spry old gentleman clattered down the last few steps. "I haven't seen you in ages."

As Pamarino drew a sharp breath, I recognized a musician friend of my father's from years back. He must have been the organist who'd been playing the dirge-like piece in the loft. "Signor Angelini!" I raised my hands to ward him off, but he trotted forward, wrinkled face filled with good cheer.

From the corner of my eye, I saw Pamarino's pistol fly up. "You've deceived me. I warned you—no tricks—no lawmen."

"No, no," I cried. "It's not a trick. This man is a friend."

"You may be a fool, but I'm not." Pamarino took aim at the harmless organist who'd finally halted in his tracks. Angelini's mouth formed a perfect oval of terror.

How could things go wrong so suddenly and completely? Swiftly, I kicked my foot upwards with as much force as I could muster. I connected with the dwarf's wrist. He grunted and the pistol went sailing into space. But not before he'd pulled back on the hammer.

An orange flash exploded near my head, and a shot rang out. Across the aisle, the bullet chewed a chunk of marble out of a fluted column. Surprised shrieks, male and female, echoed off the walls. As I reeled back, I saw Signor Angelini fall flat to the floor, alive and waving all four extremities. Thank the merciful Lord! But Pamarino was fleeing toward the back of the Basilica.

I had to stop him. He was the only one who could lead me to Titolino.

I lost a few precious seconds in the struggle to regain my balance. Once I had my feet pointed the right way, swiftly skimming the floor tiles, a strange sight met my eyes. Beneath the golden mosaics of the central dome, the hunchbacked woman was in full pursuit of the murderous dwarf. Her knees pumped under her brown skirts, and her lace shawl streaked behind her. The priest coming back through the sacristy door froze in shock at the scene.

"Halt," the woman shouted in deep, resonating tones. "In the name of the Doge."

That was no woman. I recognized the voice. It was Messer Grande, and now I saw his right hand waving a pistol.

Pamarino did stop for a brief moment. In the light shed by the candles on the high altar, he whirled this way and that, a goblin possessed by pain and hatred. Our eyes met—no mistake this time—and he glared at me with all the fury that must have been building since the day he was first taunted for his misshapen little body.

Messer Grande had almost reached him. I lengthened my strides, lungs bursting.

The dwarf refused to be taken so easily. The glint of metal flashed in his hand—my dagger—the one he had taken from me in the chapel. He sprinted the few steps to the startled priest.

Jerking the man's arm behind him, Pamarino held the blade to his flank. Forcing the priest backward, the dwarf retreated toward the sacristy door.

Oh, no! He meant to make a hostage of this man of God. But the priest either found a scrap of courage or collapsed entirely. He folded suddenly forward, pulling Pamarino off his feet. For a moment they struggled as a single, writhing creature.

Then the dwarf broke free. Rocking back on his knees, he threw up an arm, dagger in hand. Messer Grande raised his pistol.

"No—oo!" I screamed on a desperate breath.

The powder flashed, the shot was away. My heart contracted as the dwarf's body stiffened upright, then toppled heavily onto the moaning, black-robed priest.

I was upon them in an instant. Messer Grande had pulled off his gray wig and was shrugging out of the vest that created his humped backbone. He regarded his smoking pistol, then me. He said numbly, "Tito, I had to fire. I couldn't let him kill again."

Dropping to my knees, I shook the dwarf by the shoulders, yelled in his ears, slapped his cheeks. All to no avail.

Pamarino's stare remained fixed and unblinking.

Chapter Nineteen

"You might as well say it—it's written all over your face. You think I made an unforgivable mistake." Messer Grande had traded his disguise for his official scarlet robe. We again stood at his office window, looking down at the Piazza. Night had fallen, and the great square was marked with the fires of braziers and torches. The merry tootling of a brass band came through the glass.

"You couldn't allow Pamarino to stab the priest," I replied, keeping my gaze on the dark window. The reflection of my unhappy, drooping features was superimposed on the dancing flames down below. "You acted rightly."

"Then…you understand?"

I sighed, nodding. I understood that Messer Grande had only been doing his duty, but I doubted that Liya did. She sat in an armchair across the room, face buried in her hands, silently rocking forward and back.

Messer Grande placed his hands on my shoulders. "I believe the boy's still alive, Tito. The dwarf's death is known only to a few, mostly priests and constables. They'll keep quiet as ordered, at least for a while. So will the organist. Poor old Angelini was so shocked, he can barely speak anyway. He hardly expected to face a pistol as he left his afternoon practice in the choir loft."

I nodded. "We don't have much time. We must find Titolino before Pamarino's waiting confederate realizes something has gone wrong."

The chief constable squeezed my shoulders with both hands. "We will, Tito. By the blood of St. Mark, I'll pull down every brick in Venice if I have to."

For my friend's sake I raised a halfhearted smile. Inside, I felt cold and hollow. Venice was a compact cluster of islands, a mere speck on Alessandro's maritime maps. But when you're searching for one little boy, Venice might as well have encompassed a thousand square miles. "Where do we start? We can't go barging all over the city without a plan."

"I've sent a man to fetch someone who may be able to provide some guidance." Messer Grande dropped his grasp and massaged his fleshy jawline as if he had a toothache.

I questioned him with my eyes.

"Alessio Pino. We arrested him early this morning as he returned from Murano."

"Why was he on Murano?"

Messer Grande shrugged. "As usual, the young man keeps his own counsel—for the best, in this case. If he's arranged passage for the glassworkers, I don't want to know about it. I was forced to lock him up, but with the dwarf's admission that he killed both Zulietta and Sary, Alessio is now cleared of all suspicion."

"He should be relieved. How can he help us, I wonder? And would he even bother? We've both caused him a good bit of trouble."

"Here he is. Ask him yourself." Messer Grande nodded toward the young man who was entering the office with a wrinkled jacket over his arm.

Alessio's second stay in the guardhouse had only deepened his brooding good looks. His brown hair curled wildly about his cheeks and his eyes held a haunted expression. Despite his travails, he was willing to try to recall any mention of Pamarino's activities or associates that he might have overheard during his romance with Zulietta.

Alessio's arrival roused Liya out of her lassitude. As Messer Grande called for coffee and food to revive our flagging strengths, the four of us gathered around his huge desk to tackle the question of where Pamarino's confederate might be hiding Titolino.

"I don't recall the dwarf ever calling any man his friend," said Alessio. "As per custom, he earned one afternoon and one evening off for each week of service. Zulietta would not have kept him from his leisure, but he generally refused to go abroad in the city without her. The only person outside of Zulietta's small circle that he ever talked about was a sister, but I don't recall her name. Elisabetta, perhaps."

Liya clicked her fingernails on the desktop. "Yes, the sister. Sary mentioned her the day Tito and I visited Zulietta's rooms. The maid didn't seem to think much of her—" Liya snatched a breath and brandished a pointed finger. "Estrella! That's her name, and according to Sary, she works as a common prostitute."

Alessio nodded excitedly. "You're right. I caught a glimpse of Estrella once—she'd brought the dwarf a basket of figs for his name day. Now that I recall, she asked for Giacomo. I was astounded to learn that the little demon had a real name, just like any normal person."

A servant eased in the door bearing tiny cups of black coffee and horn-shaped rolls layered with ham and cheese. His tray had barely touched the desk before Alessio and I tore into both. As I attended to my hunger and thirst, I also tried to piece together information I'd gathered from a host of people during the past several weeks.

Sary had told us Estrella's brothel was located near the Arsenale, and I'd shared a cup of wine with Pamarino at a tavern near that vast shipyard. So far, so good. He'd been bedding down in a closet at a brothel—the best Estrella could arrange. How had he described her? *My older sister who carried me on her hip as she went about her chores.* What else might she have done for her brother?

I quickly swallowed a mouthful of ham, recalling another memory. "Alessio, what did Estrella look like?"

"About what you would expect. Dark coloring, not particularly tall or well formed. Her face might have been pretty once—now she relies on paint to keep the years at bay."

"Did any one feature stand out?"

Alessio wrinkled his brow. "Now that you ask, she did have one of those pushed-up noses—"

I clapped my palms together. "Your gondolier told me the woman who slipped him the sleeping powder had a nose like a little pig's snout."

"You've talked to Guido?"

Liya broke in as I nodded. "Tito, do you think Estrella is Pamarino's confederate?"

"Who else could it be? All of the acquaintances he had through Zulietta have disappeared, and he must barely know the clowns he started performing with. Just several days ago he was so desperate for work he asked me if I could give him a recommendation. Who would he trust more completely than the sister who practically raised him?" I turned to Alessio. "He sent Estrella to delay your gondolier, and I'd bet my last *soldo* he's entrusted her with Titolino."

"And she has orders to kill him if her brother isn't allowed to escape Venice!" Liya jumped out of her chair and ran around the desk to Messer Grande. Standing over him, she fired a barrage of agitated questions. "Where is this whores' lair? How fast can you muster a contingent of men? We have to get—"

Messer Grande rose and took my wife's hands in his. His tone, even and resolute, seemed to calm her even as he delivered bad news. "The quarter surrounding the Arsenale is a veritable labyrinth—secret courtyards, canals that lead in circles, blind alleys. It's infested with brothels and taverns that hire rooms by the hour. I haven't heard one scrap of information to tell me which one of those infernal establishments houses Estrella."

Alessio and I exchanged dark looks. His also held a tinge of pity. "I have no idea," he said.

I thought furiously, trying not to surrender to the paralyzing fear that radiated from my stomach. What if we couldn't find Estrella's brothel before she realized Pamarino wasn't coming back? Did she also possess a dagger? Or would she use a garrote as her brother had on Sary? I buried my face in my hands. Stop, I ordered myself. Think.

"Tito?" asked Messer Grande. "Anything?" The wily lawman had no plan to offer. Nothing.

My fingers slid slowly down my cheeks. Liya abandoned Messer Grande, gripped one of my arms, and pulled it away. Feeling that my heart must surely break, I looked into her burning eyes and shook my head. "I suppose I could find the tavern Pamarino frequented."

"It's a place to start," my wife said in a determined tone, nodding first at me, then Messer Grande. "We can search house to house, fanning out from there."

Messer Grande pursed his lips, then sighed. "My dear, once my men enter that quarter, news of our presence will spread like a wind-whipped fire. Unless we are fortunate in the extreme, Estrella will get word of what we're about and kill the boy straightaway."

"No, no. This is unbearable." Liya fell against me, drooping like a withered blossom. "We must think of something else. Can't we shout Titolino's name throughout the *calli*? He may hear and call out—"

I clutched her tightly. Another thought had struck me. A mere possibility, but it offered more hope than any of our other options. "We can't call his name—that would give us away as quickly as a concentrated search. I have a better idea."

A silver wedge of moon rose above the crenellated towers of the Arsenale; its rays illuminated the mist blanketing the waterway that led to the closed gates. Standing in the prow of Luigi's boat, my cloak unfurling lightly on the breeze, I peered at the neglected buildings that flanked our small flotilla. A century ago, Venice had possessed the greatest shipyard in Europe. Thousands of men had been employed in constructing and maintaining a mighty fleet. Now the Arsenale had dwindled to a skeleton, and the district around it had sunk into squalor, venery, and wretchedness.

"Turn right before you reach the main gates," called Messer Grande from his gondola that made a close shadow to ours. Instead of his official red, he wore a gray cloak and a tricorne unadorned by lace or cockade. Another boat carrying constables in civilian dress trailed behind. To the casual observer, we could have been...anyone.

As directed, Luigi piloted the gondola around the tight corner, and I knew that my time was fast approaching. This canal was narrower, and the moldering buildings closed in more tightly. Mooring posts rose from the mist in front of well-worn steps that angled up to badly lit entry doors. Here and there, lamplight outlined a low-hanging balcony. Behind the few undraped windows, I caught glimpses of men and women sharing a drink, a capering dance, or a rough caress.

As we slid under a small bridge, I touched Liya's amulet that hung at breastbone level beneath my shirt. She hadn't demanded to join me in the boat as I'd expected, but she had made absolutely certain that I wore her handpicked charms.

"It's Titolino who's in danger—not me," I'd told her before we set off from the gondola basin behind the Piazza.

"Just now, you're safe beside me, praise the goddess Aradia. But never forget, circumstances can change in the space of a heartbeat."

"I could fail, is that what you mean?" I realized I was shaking like a man in a fever.

"No, whatever happens, we won't call it failure. Just be very careful and do your best to bring Titolino back safe and sound." After a glancing brush of her lips, her little hands had rushed me into the boat, and she went to stand on the quay between Alessio and Benito. I was relieved to see my manservant and my wife lock elbows. As our boat floated forward, the lantern in Luigi's prow bathed their profiles in a golden glow and ignited the tears sparkling on both of their cheeks.

Now that we had reached our destination, Messer Grande's whisper mixed with the fetid, salt-drenched mist. "Tito, this is a likely spot."

I squeezed my eyes shut. The carnival mirth on the Piazza was a faint, distant din, no louder than the soft drip of water off the mist-coated balconies and bridges. With a fervent prayer to Our Lady, I opened my eyes and my mouth and commenced to sing. There was always music on the canals—the gondoliers' lilting serenades, the sweet strum of a mandolin, a fiddle playing worn-out ditties or even arias from the latest opera—but no one else had ever sung this song on Venice's waterways. The song that filled the air belonged only to me and Titolino—the song of Firefly and Old King Toad.

That was my plan—the slender reed that held the hope of Titolino's deliverance. Using lung power that could blister paint on the fifth tier at the opera house, I was going to propel Titolino's special song between boards and bricks, through crack and chink, and into every corner of every house in this accursed quarter. If fortune favored, Estrella would be otherwise occupied, allowing the boy to reply to my signal with a yell or a shout. Then Messer Grande and his men would storm the house.

I started with the toad's lines, Titolino's part, but a sudden gust of wind pulled the mist into ropes and all but snatched the words from my mouth. I began again, deftly lowering and raising pitch to suit first the royal toad, then the mischievous firefly. After each refrain, I paused and our boats floated in silence on the black mirror of the shimmering canal. Though I strained my ears to the utmost, I heard no answering call. We traversed the full length of the canal twice without producing so much as a twitch of a curtain or cracking of a shutter.

"Andrea…it's not working." My voice quavered in despair.

Messer Grande spoke across the small space that separated our boats. "Don't falter, my friend. There are plenty more canals to try. Have Luigi take the next left. That one will be more sheltered from the wind."

Our boat shot ahead and made the turn. The other two followed at an increasing interval. In the misty shadows, I gathered my strength and sang a few lines of the firefly's refrain: "Toad

King, Toad King, ready to ride, I'll light your way as you fly by my side."

"Louder, Signor Tito. Fill up the sky." It was Luigi, urging me on from his perch in the stern.

Yes, I was being too tentative, afraid to give myself away as a stage professional. But the stakes would never be higher—I needed to sing as I had never sung in my life. I filled my lungs to their depths, then loosed a new stream of melody. As the notes reverberated off the surrounding stones, I felt the power of the simple folk song well up within me. All the children of Italy who had ever sung the firefly chant as they ran after the bobbing points of light on summer evenings seemed to gaze down from heaven, smiling on my endeavor.

Thus fortified, my song rose higher than the crumbling buildings. Higher than the towers of the Arsenale. As high as the moon, I was convinced, and as wide as the infinite blue-black sky arching above.

At the next turn, Luigi paused. So did I, cocking my head in a wordless blending of hope and dread. I held my breath, listening intently. Was that…? Luigi shook his head; he'd heard nothing. He dipped his oar and pushed forward.

"No…listen." I leaned out over the water, rocking the boat. Faintly, as if from a great distance, I heard a high, thin cry. Had I only imagined it? No, it came again: "Papa! Papa!"

"There, Luigi!" I pointed to a house of stone and cracking plaster halfway back the way we had come. Its lower windows were barred with iron, but a balcony jutted out from the floor above. "You must go back."

I lived in anguish as Luigi completed his turn, not an easy matter in such a narrow canal. By the time we reached the building, the other pair of gondolas had caught up with us. Making certain Messer Grande could see me, I put a finger to my lips. With the other hand I pointed to the balcony. I sang one more refrain.

"Papa! Help me, Papa!" I recognized Titolino's boyish treble in the terrified cry.

Messer Grande's boatman rowed to the foot of a stairway leading to a barred, grilled door. The chief constable disembarked with a leap. As he pounded on the boards with a closed fist, the shutters of the balcony window crashed open. A wailing Titolino pitched onto the narrow, railed perch, struggling in the grasp of a black-haired woman in a flowing scarlet gown. Estrella!

Pamarino's foul sister wasn't going to let Titolino escape without a fight. In helpless frustration, I watched as she laced her hands around his slender neck and bent her strength to choking the life out of him.

Messer Grande also saw what was happening. He bellowed a command to release the boy in the name of the Doge. That absolute authority must have given Estrella pause. She loosened her grasp just long enough for Titolino to twist free and scramble over the railing. There the boy crouched, bare toes fighting to hang onto their grip, one arm curling around the iron railing.

"Jump, Titolino," I shouted. Luigi and others echoed my urging.

He shook his head wildly, pale face a mask of terror.

Behind him, Estrella had regained her courage and was attempting to tear Titolino's arm from the railing.

Panic bubbled up in my throat. Titolino was afraid to jump because he didn't know how to swim. I'd always meant to take him out to the Lido and teach him as Alessandro had taught me, but I'd never made the time. If he didn't jump now, Estrella would soon have him in her power once again.

I tore out of my cloak. Locking my gaze on the boy's, I motioned him toward me with both hands. "Jump, son. Don't be afraid—I won't let you drown. Just let go and I'll get you out of water."

It worked. My brave Titolino pushed away from the balcony. As he hurtled toward the canal, Estrella was left holding the sleeve to his little blue jacket.

A splash sounded on my left hand. I dove toward it, and my fingertips connected with the remaining portion of the jacket. Though the boy screamed and flailed arms and legs, I managed to pull him into my grasp and guide his arms around my neck. Luigi was leaning toward us, tipping the boat, practically laying out over the black water. With a mammoth frog kick, I delivered Titolino to his arms and safety.

But Estrella wasn't done with us. She beat angry fists on the balcony railing, rained curses down upon us. Despite the freezing water, I actually smiled. What could the whore accomplish with her ranting? In a moment, Messer Grande would be breaking down her door and arresting her for kidnapping.

The next moment seemed to unfold at half speed. Still gripping the railing, Estrella jumped up and down in fury. Her loose, shiny gown made scarlet waves around her knees as the balcony's floorboards protested with sharp creaks. Suddenly, the woman seemed off kilter. Her screams changed from anger to fright. She struggled to stay upright, but her feet were sliding out from under her. One end of the derelict balcony was pulling away from the wall!

An instant later, Estrella, boards, and iron railing crashed onto the prow of Luigi's gondola. A long dark shape flew toward me. A sliver of the broken boat? Luigi's oar? It caught me just below my chin.

My head snapped back as my throat exploded in pain. High above, stars that hadn't been there before dipped and danced.

I floundered desperately, gagging and gulping for breath, clawing at my neck. I felt something snap, but a mouthful of icy water swamped my lungs and sent me under. As the dark water closed over my head and the stars went out, all I knew was...oblivion.

Epilogue

"Papa, a woman and a man wearing a funny old suit came to see Mama. They want to see you, too." Titolino hovered in the doorway of my study. When he saw me set my staves and quill aside, he rushed over to the harpsichord, giggling and out of breath.

The boy's ordeal had left him withdrawn and fidgety for several weeks. There had been a few particularly bad nights when he'd awakened in wordless, screaming panic and I'd carried him to our bed to nestle in warm security between Liya and me. As more weeks passed, it seemed that Titolino might forget the incident and return to his carefree days of play. But certain worries continued to nag. I once caught him regarding the canal outside our house with a grave stare that sent chills down my spine. As with other matters, time would tell whether the dwarf's abominable deed would mark the boy as he grew to manhood.

I shook off my gloomy thoughts. Just then, Titolino was a happy, excited seven-year-old. Wintery sunlight streaming through the tall, leaded windows made a checkerboard pattern on the floor, and he was making a game of hopping from one bright square to another. Suddenly recalling his mission, he bounded over and tugged at my sleeve. "Hurry, Papa. We're going to have cake! Mama sent Benito to fetch it from the baker's."

I nodded vigorously. Searching among my scattered papers for the cap to the inkwell, I wondered about the identity of the visitors who merited a special cake. Unfortunately, I was not able to ask Titolino. The injury that had sent me to the bottom of the black canal had played havoc with my throat. With some painful straining, I could manage a hoarse whisper, but I seldom bothered. I had been advised to maintain total silence. At least for a while.

Singing was out of the question, of course. I'd consulted every respected physician in Venice and had been subjected to bleeding, poultices, and plastering in turn. "Pack his neck with ice," one doctor had said. "Wrap it in warm flannel," prescribed another. Nothing seemed to help. I'd banished them all when one ancient physician with snuff crusted on his nose had painted the inside of my throat with a concoction that smelled and tasted of rotten eggs.

Finally, my friend Andrea had suspended his constabulary duties and traveled to Bologna to bring back an esteemed professor of medicine from the university there. After practically climbing down my throat with his mirrors and instruments, this wise scholar had offered the best advice yet: refrain from using my voice entirely and it would return with the warm breezes of spring. Most importantly, Liya, my resident herbalist, concurred. Both declined to predict whether my healed throat would be capable of producing stageworthy singing. I waited in optimistic hope.

My colleagues at the opera house reacted much as I expected. Maestro Torani stopped by several times a week, brimming with fatherly concern. He'd found a libretto that he'd always meant to set to music—the story of an Indian queen whose land was invaded by Alexander the Great—and encouraged me to try my hand at composing. I enjoyed the challenge. I don't know if my efforts showed any real promise, but at least the composing kept me from being restless and bored.

Torani wasn't the only one to offer support. Vittoria loaned me some of her vocal students. Their fees kept the household coffers from going totally dry, and our lessons were only slightly inconvenient, as I had to deliver my directions and criticisms in writing. In my absence from the stage, Emilio had once again secured lead roles at the opera house. He didn't visit, instead sending me a bouquet of roses that I took to express gratitude rather than condolence.

"Papa, can't you hurry?" Titolino's voice squeaked in antici-
pation.

Nodding, I took his proffered hand. Why was I woolgathering
when mysterious guests and cake awaited? I let the boy lead me
downstairs to the salon where I found Pincas Del'Vecchio enjoying a glass of my best Montepulciano and Fortunata admiring
a piece of Liya's needlework.

"My boy." Pincas rose, crossed the floor, and kissed my
cheeks. "Forgive us for not coming sooner."

Before he could step back, Fortunata embraced us both in an
enthusiastic tangle of arms. She whispered in my ear, "*I* wanted
to come last week."

After returning their greetings, I gestured for all to be seated
near the warmth of the fire. Benito arrived bearing a splendid
panforte, a thin wheel of heaven bursting with walnuts, dried fruit,
spices, and honey, dusted with a sugar topping. For a few minutes,
conversation gave way to the clinking of forks on china.

"Your son is a brave boy." Pincas spoke to me, but nodded
toward Titolino, who was wheedling his mother for a second slice of
cake. "Liya told us how Titolino wiggled out of the cords the dwarf
had tied around his wrists and ankles, then broke out of the locked
wardrobe when he heard you singing. To treat a child so cruelly! A
lead ball in the heart was too easy a death for Pamarino."

I nodded in agreement. I would have loved to see the dwarf
face the hangman. Yes, he had been born with a deplorable
condition and had been forced to endure society's ridicule, but
such circumstances don't justify murder. A man is nothing but
a beast if he allows revenge to rule his heart. I could only con-
sole myself with the knowledge that his sister Estrella had been
arrested and would soon face trial.

Hearing his name, Titolino had come over to Pincas. He
looked his grandfather solemnly in the eye and wiped cake
crumbs from his jaw with the back of his hand. "Do you want to
hear our song? It goes like this." Without waiting for a reply, he
launched directly into a rendition that melded both the firefly's
and toad's parts.

Once the boy had finished, Pincas applauded, then ruffled Titolino's hair. "And you weren't going to let that terrible woman stop you from escaping, were you?"

"She tried to stuff me back in the wardrobe, but I rolled under the bed. I found a hatpin under there, and when I saw her bare feet on the other side, I poked the pin in her toes and rolled toward the window and busted right through." Titolino's eyes glittered with more than excitement. His tone had climbed to a shrill pitch.

As I reached out to pat his shoulder, my gaze caught Liya's. She was ahead of me, as usual. She had cut another slice of *panforte*. Calling Titolino over to the sofa, she made a place between herself and Fortunata. The boy happily turned his attention to his extra treat while surrounded by doting mother and fascinated young aunt.

Pincas spoke again, more quietly. "The boy isn't the only brave one. You put yourself in harm's way, both at the Basilica and in the Arsenale district. It makes me think of the young singer who braved a fire to rescue two of my precious daughters." He made a blunt gesture toward the three on the sofa. "Do you realize none of them would be alive if it weren't for you?"

I shrugged, opening my mouth to say I knew not what, but Pincas forestalled me with a hand on my arm. "No. I'm not trying to tempt you to speak. I'm apologizing for the times I should have found more courage. I'm also giving you my word that I will never disappear from Liya's or my grandson's life again." He shook his head gravely. "No matter what anyone says."

I put one hand over his and squeezed. After many years, all was understood between me and my father-in-law, spoken or unspoken.

Benito broke the moment by coming to refill our wine glasses. Pincas wiped something from the corner of his eye, then crossed to warm his backside at the fire. As he summoned Titolino to question him about his lessons, I sank back against the chair cushions and touched my fingers to the small lump of the amulet bag. It had been the miracle that saved me. That terrible night, in my frantic struggle beneath the water, its cord had snapped from my neck, allowing the red bag to float to the surface. It had been the only thing to mark my location. Luigi would never have found me without it.

Liya and I saw her family out together. With a catch of long-ing in her voice, my wife reminded them that our door would always be open for a visit. I seconded her invitation by bowing to Pincas and kissing Fortunata's hand. With my arm around Liya's waist, we stood on the pavement watching them retreat toward the lofty buildings of the ghetto. We stood there even after they'd turned a corner. It was Titolino's voice that called us back inside where I slowly climbed the stairs to my study, playing with a new melody for the Indian queen's aria in my head.

Author's Note

Over the centuries, dwarfs have inspired amazement, fear, fascination, laughter, and ridicule. The eunuch singers that represented the unique musical and cultural phenomenon of the castrati aroused similar emotions. Tito's real-life counterparts were angels to some, monsters to others. Both Tito and Pamarino would have been considered extraordinary characters in eighteenth-century society, and I found the parallels between these two marginalized groups interesting.

Though the operatic castrati were created by a surgeon's blade—*made freaks* in the parlance of traditional sideshows—they shared the life of a vagabond performer with many little people who earned a living by making a spectacle of their own bodies. Just as the entire Tito Amato mystery series puts a human face on the castrati, I hope this particular volume will do the same for historic dwarfs. Those interested in the social history of dwarfs may consult Betty M. Adelson and Julia Rotta's *The Lives of Dwarfs: Their Journey from Public Curiosity toward Social Liberation* (Rutgers University Press, 2005).

A few other matters raised in *Her Deadly Mischief* may be of interest: We would call Zenobio's "petal-scope" a kaleidoscope. Its real inventor was Scotsman David Brewster who named and patented the device in 1816. Though there is no historical precedent, it made sense to me that a creative Murano glassmaker could have developed something similar and never received formal credit.

Also regarding the glass industry, most of the material on Venice's treatment of the rogue glassmakers comes out of my research on the so-called War of the Mirrors, which set Venice against French authorities who attracted a group of Murano artisans to Paris in the seventeenth century. Venice sent clandestine agents to terrorize the workers; several were poisoned to death. Their wives who remained in Venice were threatened or actually imprisoned to force the glass masters' return. It was not an isolated incident.

Clara, the rhinoceros who fascinates Titolino in Chapter Seventeen, was a wildly popular attraction of the era. In her journeys across Europe and Britain, she stopped in Venice in 1751 and became the subject of several famous paintings by Pietro Longhi. To fit the needs of this novel, I've taken the liberty of moving her visit back to 1742. For interested readers, I recommend this charming account of Clara's travels: *Clara's Grand Tour: Travels with a Rhinoceros in Eighteenth-Century Europe* by Glynis Ridley (Atlantic Monthly Press, 2004).

As usual, most of my research was conducted with the assistance of the Louisville Free Public Library. I consulted books from their collection, obtained hard-to-find volumes by interlibrary loan, and delved deep into Internet resources linked to their website. Going some years back, I can also say there would be no Tito Amato if it weren't for the library. My mother introduced me to the Crescent Hill branch at an early age, and I have a very clear memory of checking out my first Agatha Christie mystery at age nine. A list of library books that have provided at least a crumb of inspiration for the Tito Amato mysteries would fill a volume of their own. I extend my heartfelt appreciation to all the staff, especially at the Highlands-Shelby Park branch, who've fielded my questions and requests over the years.

In closing, I wish to express my thanks to everyone who helped bring *Her Deadly Mischief* to completion. My wonderful husband, Lawrence, tops the list. This installment of the Tito Amato mysteries reached the page with more gnashing of teeth than usual; without my husband's kind and patient support, it might never have reached it at all.

I am also grateful to the following: Joanne Dobson and Kit Ehrman for valuable comments on the manuscript, my agent Ashley Grayson for his friendly encouragement, Tara Maginnis for advice on eighteenth-century dress, my editor Barbara Peters for her wise and welcome guidance, and all the members of the Ohio River Valley Chapter of Sisters in Crime for their unflagging enthusiasm and support.

For the use of teachers, librarians, and book clubs, a Readers' Guide is available for each novel in the series. These may be obtained by contacting the author through her website at www.beverlegravesmyers.com.

To receive a free catalog of Poisoned Pen Press titles, please contact us in one of the following ways:

Phone: 1-800-421-3976
Facsimile: 1-480-949-1707
Email: info@poisonedpenpress.com
Website: www.poisonedpenpress.com

Poisoned Pen Press
6962 E. First Ave. Ste. 103
Scottsdale, AZ 85251

CPSIA information can be obtained
at www.ICGtesting.com
Printed in the USA
LVOW08s1626310117
522741LV00005B/971/P